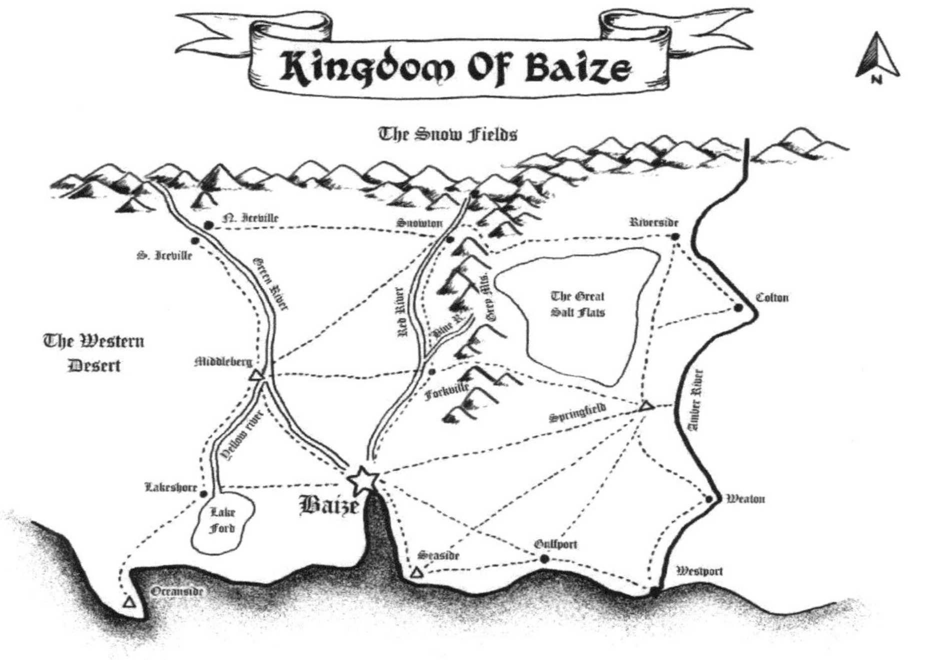
Kingdom Of Baize
The Snow Fields
The Western Desert
N. Iceville
S. Iceville
Snowton
Riverside
Colton
The Great Salt Flats
Deep Mts.
Green River
Red River
Blue R.
Middleberg
Forkville
Springfield
Amber River
Weaton
Lakeshore
Yellow river
Lake Ford
Baize
Seaside
Gulfport
Westport
Oceanside
N

Franconia
Capital
City   > 10,000
Town > 1000 - 10,000
Village < 1000
N
The Snow Fields
Caperian Mts.
Caperian Mts.
Frostberg
Ivory R.
Pearl R.
Three Forks
Riverton
Amber River
Coral Islands
Colton
Farmdale
Emerald River
Crimson River
Haven
Sundock
Hayford
Fairview
Sapphire River
Crystal Lake
Kingdom
of
Baize
Kingston
Jade Swamp
Black Mts.
The Eastern Ocean
Prairieville
Weston
Southville
Westport
Stone Mts.
Southport
Gratton
Eastport
The Low Sea

THE COMPASSION OF ENEMIES

By
ROBERT JONES

CHARACTERS

Wizards

Wizard Edward Francis, *Royal Expeditionary Force (REF)*
Wizard Noland, *Headmaster, Franconian Wizards Academy*
Wizard Faith, *Gatekeeper, Franconian Wizards Academy*
Wizard Toffin, *Serums Instructor, Franconian Wizards Academy*
Wizard Daniel, *History and Enhancements Instructor, Franconian Wizards Academy*
Wizard Mira, *Seemings Instructor, Franconian Wizards Academy*
Wizard Dylan, *Forces Instructor, Franconian Wizards Academy*
Wizard James, *Chief of Army Wizardry, Baizian Army*
Wizard Lake, *Chief of Naval Wizardry, Franconian Navy*
Wizard Cassandra, *Court Wizard of Franconia*
Mage Kathy, *Assistant Court Wizard of Baize*
Mage Elianna, *Headmistress, Middleberg School of Magic, Baize*
Mage Andrew, *Battle Mage, 1st Squadron, 1st Fleet*
Mage Curtis, Battle Mage, *Royal Expeditionary Force*
Sorcerer Terry, *Mentor, Franconian Wizards Academy*
Sorceress Rachel Turner, *Mentor, Franconian Wizards Academy*
Level Three Magician Donovan Francis, *Student, Franconian Wizards Academy*

Soldiers

Field Marshall Guzman, *Commander, Franconian Army*
General Diaz, *Commander, Baizian Army*
Admiral Cross, *Admiral of the Fleets, Franconian Royal Navy*
Admiral Vandall, *Commander, Baizian Navy*
Major Gerald, *Commander, Royal Expeditionary Force*
Commodore Matthews, *Commander, 1ˢᵗ Squadron, 1ˢᵗ Fleet, Franconian Navy*
Senior Specialist Dirk, *Assassin, 1ˢᵗ Company, REF*
Senior Specialist Lance, *Assassin, 2ⁿᵈ Company, REF*
Captain Fletcher, *Commander, 2ⁿᵈ Company, REF*
Captain Smith, *Commander, 1ˢᵗ Company, REF*

Civilians

King Henry XI, *King of Franconia*
King Donald, *King of Baize*
Minister Leonard, *Franconian Minister of Finance*
Minister Williams, *Baizian Minister of Public Works*
James, *Owner, Prestige Arms*
Beverly Perrucci, *Mage Andrew's mother*
Bruce, *recluse who lives near Southport*

Dragons

Ard, *Great Dragon, Gek's grandfather*
Gek, *Great Dragon, Azure's mate*
Cobalt, *Sea Dragon, Gek's Father*
Azure, *Sea Dragon, Gek's mate*
Teal, *Sea Dragon, Chief of the Sea Dragons*
Bliz, Frost, *Snow Dragons*
Jasper, Amber, *Stone Dragons*
Rose, Fern, *Fire Dragons*

TABLE OF CONTENTS

Dedication

For Linda, with love

Acknowledgement

Designers at Author Book Publications (www.authorbookpublications.com) for the cover design and portraits

Rizky Nugraha for the maps and illustration

About the Author

Robert Jones served in the United States Army for 23 years before retiring. He currently works for the Federal Government. This is his third novel in the Honor of Dragons series, and is the sequel to The Valor of Sorcerers. He lives in Northern Virginia with his wife and two children.

Foreword

Azure the Sea Dragon is pregnant! But, is the child human or dragon? Azure and Gek need help. Together, they must seek out Sea Dragon 'Changed Ones' (dragons transformed into humans through magic) who can answer their questions about Azure's child.

Wizard Edward and the Royal Expeditionary Force fought through the Fire Dragon ambush and seized the Baizian city of Springfield, but they didn't find what they expected. Now, Edward must travel to the capital city of Baize and try to convince King Donald not to launch a war against Franconia.

Donovan is advancing rapidly through the course of instruction at the Wizards Academy, and he has also become very attached to his Mentor, Sorceress Rachel. Meanwhile, Donovan's cousin, Sorcerer Andrew, is fighting for his life aboard the HMS VALOR, which is fending off continuous Sea dragon attacks.

Wizard Noland, the Headmaster of the Wizards Academy, is still searching for dragon 'Changed Ones' at large in the kingdom, who are intent on bringing harm to the humans.

This is a deadly game of 'Who's Who' and 'Hide-and-Seek,' with the losers usually ending up dead.

Chapter One:

LEVEL THREE

Donovan laughed as the fireball sped toward him. Assuming that this was just a Seeming, as had happened at the end of his Test to advance to Level Two, Donovan put only a minimal amount of power into his shield to counter the seemingly frightening but otherwise harmless illusion. The resulting blast hurled him to the ground and sent him skidding across the sandy soil of the Forces Training Area. *They never made anything easy here, did they?* He rose, shook his head and reformed his shield for the next fireball, which was already speeding toward him.

His Level Three Testing had been going on for hours, and he was nearly exhausted. It had begun with the Military History Exam. Wizard Daniel had arrived at the Lecture Hall and presented Donovan with a terrain map. The map showed the area around an unidentified town. There were military symbols of an enemy force of battalion strength, arrayed to attack the town. "Donovan, I want you to depict on the map how you would deploy a Franconian Battalion to defend this town from the enemy depicted. Show where you would position our troops, the Battalion Commander, and the

Sorcerer. When you are done with that, here is an identical map, with an enemy force positioned to defend the town. Show me how you would attack it with the same battalion," said Wizard Daniel. "You have one hour."

Donovan got right to work. Defending the town was simple. He arrayed archers on the flanks and positioned two squads of infantry in the center, with symbols indicating that they were to fall back, drawing the enemy into the area between the archers. The bottom of the 'kill box' was the remaining company of infantry, in fortified positions. Once the enemy was in the box, the Battalion's cavalry Troop would sweep around the back, completing the encirclement. The Battalion Commander and the Sorcerer were positioned in the center, behind the infantry, with the Sorcerer acting as the Battalion's reserve force, ready to move to wherever he was needed.

Finished with the first map, Donovan moved to the second map; the enemy was arrayed in a three-up, one-back formation astride the road leading to the town. Three companies of infantry were positioned in a line across the road, with the cavalry company in reserve. There was no magician depicted with the enemy in either scenario. Donovan thought hard, then came up with a creative attack plan. When he was finished, he called Wizard Daniel over to grade his work.

"Your defense is a classic 'moving ambush,'" he said. How will you protect the archers from the enemy cavalry?" "The Sorcerer will use a Dig spell to create trenches in front of the archer's positions," explained Donovan. "Very good. This is a Passing answer."

"Your attack plan looks like a double envelopment, with two companies circling around to strike each enemy flank, but why is the Sorcerer alone in the middle of the road?" asked Daniel. "He is creating a Seeming of the attacking Battalion, sir," said Donovan. "If the enemy is focused on the Seeming—" "Then the real forces will be able to achieve surprise," said Daniel. "It might work, but it could cost the Sorcerer his or her life." "Sir, you told us that in war, some risks must be taken," replied Donovan. "So I did, and so they must," said Daniel. "Pass."

"Let's proceed to the Enhancements Test," said Daniel. "We will start with the Sensing and Concealment spells. Please wait here for ten minutes while I head over to the Enhancements Training Area, then come and find me." Wizard Daniel vanished, and the door to the Lecture Hall opened and closed. Donovan immediately began Sensing where the Wizard was going. It appeared that he had stopped right outside the door of the Lecture Hall. When ten minutes was up, Donovan scooped up a pebble from the floor, walked out the door and tossed the pebble at the concealed Wizard, saying, "Tag, you're it."

"I didn't think that was going to work," said Daniel with a smile. "Very well, now you head over to the Enhancements Training Area and conceal yourself. I will give you ten minutes, then follow. If you can elude me for ten minutes, you will pass this part of the test." Donovan went immediately to the training area and considered where to hide under concealment. He finally decided to sit on the back porch of Wizard Noland's cottage. He didn't think the Headmaster would mind. He sat down, erected his concealment shield and waited for Wizard Daniel.

A few minutes later, Daniel arrived; he roamed about the Enhancements Training area, blowing gusts of sand at various spots, trying to find Donovan. After ten minutes, he said, "All right, Donovan, you can come out now." Donovan dropped his concealment shield and walked further into the training area. Wizard Daniel shook his head at Donovan's audacity. Over the next hour, Wizard Daniel tested Donovan on his mastery of the Smell, Strength, Healing, and Stamina spells. When they were finished, Donovan asked, "How are you going to test my Secrecy spell?" Wizard Daniel smiled. "Terry, I need your assistance for this."

Sorcerer Terry, Donovan's Mentor, appeared at his side, dropping his concealment shield. "Now, Donovan, I want you to tell Terry something, then cast your Secrecy spell. I will ask Terry what you said. If he can give me the correct answer, your spell was ineffective." Donovan thought for a moment, then said, "We are having squid for lunch today." "I doubt it," replied Terry, with a smile. Donovan then said, *"CONFIDO,"* and placed his right index finger against his lips. Donovan felt the power drain, so he knew the spell had been cast.

Daniel asked Terry, "What did Donovan say we are having for lunch today?" Terry replied, "I have no idea." "Pass," said Wizard Daniel, and Terry vanished again.

The next part of the testing was Serums. Donovan returned to the Lecture Hall and had to prepare Serums for Paralysis, Stamina, Truth and Healing (major wounds) and test them all on himself (except the Healing Serum, which was given to a patient in the Academy Infirmary). While the test was difficult, Donovan was able to concoct all of the Serums within the required time limit. Next came the Seemings Exam.

When Donovan arrived in the Seemings Training Area, Wizard Mira, the very attractive Seemings and Changes instructor, said, "Donovan dear, can you please create a Seeming for me of a Royal Cavalryman, riding a white horse around the area?" This was the most difficult Seeming that Donovan had ever attempted. Creating moving Seemings was much more difficult than ones that were stationary. Creating a rider, no, a *soldier*, on horseback, moving, was challenging. Seemings usually took very little power to create because they weren't real, but this one was an exception to that general rule. When Donovan was finished, he called Wizard Mira over to inspect his work. She just smiled and told him to head over to the Forces Training Area for his Martial Arts Test. Donovan groaned.

As he entered the Forces Training Area, Wizard Faith was waiting. "Donovan, you have already passed your Martial Arts Test, but this portion of the Level Three Test is designed to tire you physically, before your Forces Test. So, we can either spar for half an hour, or you can jog around the training area carrying your staff." Donovan said that he had enough practice running and that they might as well spar. "I was hoping you'd say that," said Faith, handing him his staff. "No magic," she said, indicating that this bout would not allow Seemings or other Force spells to be used. After thirty minutes of sparring with Wizard Faith, Donovan was seriously reconsidering his decision about not jogging. When the time ran out, Wizard Faith said,

"That's enough, Donovan; Wizard Dylan is waiting. Good Luck."

Donovan turned and found Wizard Dylan, the Forces instructor, standing behind him. The Forces Exam entailed Donovan performing the Tether, Reduce, Enlarge, Adhesive, and Sleep spells. Once all those were complete, Wizard Dylan said, "Now it's time for me to test your protective shields. Defend yourself!" Wizard Dylan began by blowing things at Donovan's shield: rocks, sand, cauldrons, and anything that wasn't nailed down in the Forces Training Area was hurled at Donovan from the front, back, sides and top. Donovan's shields held until the fireballs, which he assumed were Seemings, since the test for advancement to Level Two had culminated with Seemings of fireballs.

The first fireball had been a shock, the next two less so. Finally, three hard strikes came against his shield that Donovan never saw coming. Wizard Dylan smiled and said, "Congratulations Donovan, you have passed." "How did you cast a fireball?" asked Donovan. "I thought you told us that we could not cast fire, only ignite things at a distance." Wizard Dylan smiled and said, "I conjured a cloud of sawdust, blew it towards you with a Wind spell, and ignited it on the way." "What was that at the end?" asked Donovan, "I didn't see anything." "I cast a concealment spell over several rocks and blew them at you. I have found that a very effective technique against unprepared magicians."

Suddenly, all of Donovan's instructors and his Mentor appeared beside him. Wizard Noland unrolled a scroll and read, formally, "Level Two Donovan Francis, pending completion of your final task, you are hereby promoted to Level Three and will report to the appropriate instruction on Firstday morning. Congratulations." Wizard Nolan left as the other Wizards came forward to congratulate him.

"What do you mean, you think you are pregnant?" asked Gek. "Just what I said. I think I may be pregnant." Why?" asked Gek. Azure said, "I feel different, and something is stirring in here," she explained, rubbing her abdomen. "How could this have happened?" asked Gek, stupidly. "Gek," said Azure, "We have been rather *vigorous* in our mating, both in Dragon and human form."

"Is the baby Dragon or human?" asked Gek. "I do not know," said Azure with concern. "I have never been pregnant before. I do not know if conception occurred as a Dragon or a human or if it even matters." "Who can we consult?" asked Gek. Both Azure and Gek looked at

Bruce, the recluse that they had been staying with. "Don't look at me!" said Bruce. "I don't know nothin' about pregnant Changed Ones. Celeste and I were never blessed with children. It could be because we were different *species*, if you know what I mean. If it's human, you need to talk to a Midwife."

"What is a Midwife?" asked Azure. "A Midwife is someone who helps with the birthing process. She knows what to expect and has salves and potions to ease the pain. That sort of thing." "Well, we clearly cannot ask a human Midwife for advice about a pregnant Dragon," said Gek. "What about other Changed Ones?" mused Azure. "Especially those that have had children. They must know something." "I suppose," said Gek, "Bruce, do you know any Sea Dragon Changed Ones we can ask?"

Bruce thought for a minute, then said, "Well, Celeste used to go down to Grotton every once and a while to visit a friend named Olive. I think I remember her saying that Olive and her husband were both Changed Ones, and they had two human children. She should be able to advise you." "How far away is Grotton?" asked Gek. "Well, it would take about two weeks walking, one day swimming as a Sea dragon, or a couple of hours flying," said Bruce. "It's the next big city along the coast; you can't miss it."

"I wonder if changing form is harmful to the baby," wondered Azure, "we know so little." "How about if we split up?" asked Gek. "I can fly down to Grotton, consult with Olive, and be back in a couple of days. If we both go, it will mean at least two transformations: into Dragons here, then back into humans in Grotton, then maybe back into Dragons to return."

"I do not think we should risk it," said Azure. "I hate splitting up, but it is certainly the safest thing to do." "I agree," said Gek. "So, Bruce, how do I find Olive?"

"So, how are we doing, Timothy?" asked Wizard Edward. "I would say that you're doing better than we could have hoped for," said Timothy, the elderly Baizian Wizard. "The healing clinic has been a huge success, and the people are very appreciative. Your soldiers have also restored law and order, and the merchants have actually started paying their taxes again."

"That's good to hear," said Edward, "because I'm not sure how much longer we can stay." "You're not leaving?" asked Tim, shocked. "Tim, King Henry sent us here to raid the Springfield Treasury, rout any Baizian forces we encountered, then return. He did not envision us occupying the city and setting up a military government. Besides, what do you think is going to happen when King Donald of Baize learns of our presence?"

"He'll probably send the Army," said Tim, "but probably not here." "What?" asked Edward. "If I was the King, I'd send the Army to Westport. Springfield's too far away. Besides, all of our trade goods have to be shipped down the Amber River. It's too far to send them overland—too expensive. The traders would never make a profit. When do you think you'll have to leave?" "I'll talk to Major Gerald about it, but we can probably only stay about another week," said Edward. "I should probably head over and let what's left of the City Council know, so we can start preparing for your departure," said Wizard Timothy.

Edward left the vacant Mayor's office and walked over to the empty Garrison Commander's office that Major Gerald was using. He noted the guard outside the door. "Good morning, Major. How are things today?" "As well as can be expected," said Gerald, the commander of the Franconian Royal Expeditionary Force. "I was just wondering when you thought we'll have to be heading back to Kingston," said Edward. "I've been thinking about that m'self," replied Gerald. "We can't stay too much longer; the King'l be expectin' us back before too long. He's probably already wonderin' what's takin' us so long."

"I had the same thought," said Edward. "It's a shame, really. We just got this town back to some kind of order. However, I'm sure King Donald will be none too happy when he learns we're here." "You got that right!" said Gerald. "This city has some defenses, but we could never stand up against a large force for very long, even with a Wizard and a Battle Mage." "Wizard Timothy thinks that the King will send his forces to Westport, rather than here," said Edward.

"He's probably right. There would be no point in sending the Baizian Army all the way out here. All the trade goods have to come from or be sent to Westport or Weaton along the river, and Weaton is still recoverin' from the dragon attack."

"I wish we could be of more help to these people," said Edward, "but you're right, we don't want to get into a fight with the Baizian Army," mused Edward. "You know, I wonder if that's the dragon's plan: provoke us into fighting each other, then attack when we are both weakened." Gerald whistled. "That's a complicated plan, sir Wizard. Are you sure that a bunch of ignorant beasts could come up with it?" "I'm sure that Victor could, and it sounds just like something he would do. Even though he's dead, they could still be following his plan, and I'm not so sure that dragons are as ignorant as you think they are. That ambush they set up for us was pretty slick."

"You're right about that. I'm just not sure what we can do." "What if Timothy and I went to King Donald and tried to convince him about the need for our two countries not to go to war?" asked Edward. "We would have to divulge what we know about dragons, and he may take some convincing, but I think it's worth the risk." "You may be right," said Major Gerald. "So, what do you recommend?"

"How about this: Wizard Timothy and I head to Baize; you leave 1st Company here, with Mage Curtis, and take 2nd Company back to Kingston and report to the King. It would leave you without any magical support, though." Major Gerald laughed, "Before I met you, we never had any magical support, and we frequently split the companies to perform multiple operations simultaneously. I like it." "I'll talk to Wizard Timothy and brief him about what we know about dragons." "OK," said Gerald, "I'll let 2nd Company know that we'll be leaving in about a week and have them start getting ready."

Edward walked over and found Timothy in the Mayor's office. "I just talked to Major Gerald, and we have a plan," Edward told Timothy about the dragons, how they could understand human speech, conjure magic spells, and transform into humans. He also told him about his idea that the dragon's plan was for Baize and Franconia to fight each other, weakening both kingdoms, before the dragons attacked. Timothy was shocked by the news but said, "You know, I'll bet the former Mayor was one of those 'Changed Ones' you mentioned. He made some damn stupid decisions over the last few years, some that no one could understand."

"You said he left with the last of the soldiers?" asked Edward. "Yes. Mayor Slate took off with the last battalion, probably taking most of the treasury with him. He claimed he was going to the King to ask him to reconsider removing all the forces from Springfield," said Tim. "Wait, the Mayor's last name was 'Slate'?" "That's right, Aldon Slate. Why, is that significant?" asked Tim. "It could be," replied Edward, "All of the Stone dragons we discovered had last names that were types of rock. It could be just a coincidence, though."

"Stone dragons?"

"Yes. There are five kinds of dragons: Great dragons, which are gold in color, Sea dragons that are blue or green, Stone dragons that are gray or black; Snow Dragons, which are light grey or white; and Fire dragons, like the ones we fought in the pass, that are red." "I had no idea. I thought all dragons were red," said Timothy. "According to our cooperating Changed Ones, there should only be Fire and Stone dragons on the west side of the Amber River, although, I expect the Snow dragons don't care much about river boundaries, since they live exclusively in the Snow Fields to the north," said Edward.

"Well, this has been an interesting morning," said Tim, "I'd best go let the council know about the new plan and start getting ready for our journey." Just then, Major Gerald walked in. "Good morning, Wizard Timothy. I guess Wizard Edward has told you our plans?" "Yes, sir, and I appreciate your leaving some troops here along with Mage Curtis. Without me, there would be no one to offer healing to the citizens of Springfield," said Timothy.

"Is there anything else we can do before we leave?" "No, there is one thing I should mention," said Tim. "Several of our, let's just say, more *ruthless* merchants have all suffered fatal accidents in the last two weeks." "Really?" asked Edward, feigning concern. "Have you investigated? "I have. It seems that one fellow fell down a flight of steps and broke his neck, another drowned, two had heart attacks, and one was thrown and trampled by his horse."

"Are there usually so many accidents in Springfield?" asked Edward. "We have our share, but they usually happen to folks in the lower or middle-class. It's seldom that someone of wealth has such an accident," said Tim. "Would you like me to look into it?" asked Edward. "We certainly want Springfield to be safe." "No need, sir Edward, I just thought I'd mention it." Timothy left the office smiling slightly.

"Did we get them all?" Edward asked the seemingly empty corner of the room. Lance and Dirk both lowered the hoods of their concealment cloaks. "I think so, sir," said Lance, "there is one more person we're keeping an eye on. She's the owner of the Fielder's Choice Tavern. We think she is drugging the ales of her customers, then arranging for them to be robbed when they stagger out. We have *interrupted* several such attempts lately."

"Hmm," said Edward. "Here's what I want you to do. Both of you go visit her tonight, with your cloaks on. Once she is alone, drop your concealment and let her know your suspicions and what will happen to her if another customer gets anything *extra* in his or her ale. Then disappear again." Both Senior Specialists laughed, "That we can do, sir! With pleasure." The Specialists departed, and Edward addressed Major Gerald, "How are the troops doing with keeping the peace? I know they're not trained as Enforcers."

"They're good men, and they know right from wrong. Your idea about having some of the troops wear their concealment cloaks was genius. It saved a couple of 'em from bein' jumped. I think all the local crooks have learned not to mess with my troops," said Gerald with a smile. "I wonder…" said Edward. "You have that look," said Gerald, "what now?" "I was just thinking how useful it would be if I had a Specialist along with me when Wizard Timothy and I go to visit King Donald. If I need to sneak into his bed chamber to deliver my message, having Lance or Dirk with me could be very useful."

"If you want, you can take 'em both," said Gerald. "No," said Edward. "I'm already leaving you without any magical support; I'm not taking your Specialist too. You may need him. If Dirk comes with me, then Corporal Knox, his apprentice, can remain here with 1st Company, and Specialist Lance can go with you and 2nd Company. Would that work?" "Certainly, "said Major Gerald. "Let me just go and tell them." "No need," said Edward, speaking to the empty corner, "Corporal, go let Specialist Dirk know that he'll be accompanying Wizard Timothy and me to Baize." Corporal Knox lowered the hood of his concealment cloak, grinned slyly, and headed out of the office.

"Those three are going to be the death of me," said Major Gerald. Edward laughed and said, "Before you go, I have another message for you to deliver to Wizard Noland for me."

"Of course," said Gerald. Edward handed over a piece of parchment that read:

<u>Serum Supplies</u>

Juniper

Anise

Sunflower seeds

Mint Leaves

Ivory

Nightshade

Eggplant

Oregano

Nutmeg

Yarrow

Xiao Mi La Pepper

Rachel

Chapter Two:

BLIND MAN'S BLUFF

Donovan and Terry returned to the Level Two dormitory. As expected, Donovan found that all of his personal belongings had already been removed and that the sheets, pillow and blanket were neatly folded and placed in the center of the bed, just as they had been when he advanced from Level One to Level Two. "I suppose my 'final task' as a Level Two is to remove my name from the door," said Donovan. "Exactly right," said Terry with a smile. Donovan walked confidently to the door and slapped his hand on the wooden plaque with his name on it. Nothing happened.

"They never make anything easy around here, do they?" asked Donovan. Terry's smile widened. "No. Why should they?" Donovan thought for a minute, then decided that the Remove spell was the appropriate spell for this task; as he approached the door and prepared to cast the spell, Terry said, "Please be careful. One overconfident but unlucky student lost his hand at this point in his training." Donovan froze. "Jacob?" he asked. Terry nodded sadly. Donovan concentrated, then said, *"DELERE,"* and 'flicked' his right wrist at the door plaque. His name disappeared instantly.

Donovan turned to Terry and asked, "Could nothing be done for Jacob? After coming this far?" "Unfortunately not," said Terry, "once gone, his hand could not be healed or replaced." "Couldn't he have continued as a one-handed Level Three?" asked Donovan. Terry shook his head, "Seven of the eleven Level Three spells require the use of either the left or both hands. Even so, the Wizards might have shown him mercy, but he went crazy when he realized what he had done. He attacked his Mentor, set fire to the hallway, and then tried to use the Dig spell to escape the Academy. The Wizards cornered him, put him to sleep, and removed his spark. It was a mercy that he was allowed to remain here instead of being sent to the Road Crews. Anyway, let us head down to the dining room for lunch."

When they entered the dining room, the other Level Two students all came over and congratulated Donovan for passing his test. When Phillip approached, Donovan asked, "Did your parents get here all right?" Donovan had lent Phillip a gold in order to bring his family up from their home in Southport for a brief visit. Phillip had not seen them for almost three years, ever since he'd been apprehended by the Southport Regional Mage for counterfeiting coins and brought, unwillingly, to the Academy. "Yes," said Phillip. "They arrived yesterday, as soon as I'm released for Endday activities, I'm going to meet them at the Happy Maid Tavern. You should join us."

"I appreciate the offer," said Donovan, "but this is your time, and you haven't seen them in ages. I suspect I have new Level Three spells to learn this afternoon, anyway. Have a good time with your parents. I'm sure I'll see you in the Level Three classes soon." Lunch was broiled steak with fried potatoes, and it was delicious. Terry joined the Level Twos for the meal, devouring the steak but passing on the vegetables. "I guess they knew you'd be joining us for lunch," said Donovan with a smile. Terry wiped steak juice off his chin and said, "There is very little that goes on around here that the staff does not know about. In fact, here comes Jacob."

Jacob was the kitchen helper that Donovan paid to wake him up each morning in order to avoid an ice-cold bucket of water from his Mentor if he overslept. Jacob was also Phillip's older brother. "Here's your pay for the last week," said Donovan, handing over a copper. "I really appreciated your help, Jacob. Can you recommend someone on the Level Three staff who could help me the same way?" Jacob thought for a second, then said, "I would recommend Leonard." "And how will I recognize him?" asked Donovan. "Leonard is very fat," said Jacob. "The other kitchen workers tease him about his weight. It would be a kindness he would very much appreciate." "That's very thoughtful of you, Jacob. I'll certainly ask Leonard for his help as a Level Three," said Donovan. Jacob smiled and returned to his duties in the kitchen. When the meal was over, Terry escorted Donovan over to his new room in the Level Three dormitory.

The Level Three dormitory was laid out exactly like the other student dormitories, only it was three stories high. The kitchen and dining room were in the center of the building on the first floor, with corridors leading left and right. There were common rooms on the second and third floors over the kitchen and dining room area. As usual, the men's rooms were to the left, and the women's rooms were on the right side of the building. As Donovan entered his third-floor room, he noticed that it was a suite, with a private toilet and shower and a study, complete with a desk, bookshelves and a sturdy but comfortable chair. The bedroom was carpeted and had a queen size bed and a wardrobe with a full-length mirror.

"So, no more group showers?" asked Donovan. "Correct," said Terry. "Also, now that you are a Level Three, you are permitted to have female company in your room. Only Level Threes or Mentors, please. Try not to get a reputation as a lady's man. Remember, a jilted lover, who is a magician is not like a tavern maid that you had a one-night stand with." Unsure of how to respond to that message, Donovan merely nodded.

"And this is where I leave you," said Terry. "Your new Mentor will be Rachel, and she should be waiting for us in the second-floor common room." "What?" said Donovan, clearly not expecting a new Mentor. "Donovan, I have four other Level Twos to Mentor, did you really expect me to remain as your Mentor as you advanced?" "No, I guess not," said Donovan. "It's just so sudden." Terry smiled, "Everything about you is sudden, Donovan. In case you do not know it, you have advanced to Level Three faster than any student in the history of the Wizards Academy. Normally, I would have been your Mentor for two or three years, but you have advanced so fast, it has been just over one year. I will still be around if you have *Dragon* questions, but right now, let us go down and meet Rachel."

They descended the stairs to find an attractive brunette wearing a brilliant orange shirt with a short pale green skirt. As they approached, she said, "You must be the famous Donovan Francis I've heard so much about!" Donovan felt the blood rush to his cheeks as he stammered, "H—Hello, Sorceress Rachel, I'm honored to meet you." Terry laughed heartily, clapped Donovan on the back and said, "Goodbye for now, Donovan. I will see you around." Terry left quickly down the stairs, humming, *Strangers in the Night.*

"What was all that about?" asked Donovan, confused. "Oh, that's just Terry being Terry. He's kind of a loner. You know, for a while, we were beginning to think he didn't *like* girls. Then we found out he was a dragon 'Changed One.' Some of the girls were repulsed, but others think he's *exotic,*" said Rachel. "I had a lot of reservations when Wizard Nolan assigned him as my Mentor, but I learned a lot from him. I never really thought about what it must be like being a Changed One in a school full of magicians," said Donovan.

"Well, enough about Terry," said Rachel, "Here's your new class schedule."

<u>Level Three Class Schedule</u>

First Period– Serums (Firstday & Midweek)

Martial Arts – (Twoday & Foursday)

Second Period– Forces

Luncheon

Third Period– Enhancements (Firstday & Midweek)

History (Twoday & Foursday)

Fourth Period – Changes (Firstday & Midweek)

Martial Arts (Twoday & Foursday)

Mentor Testing– Endday mornings

"Now, let's head over to the Enhancements Training Area, where I need to teach you your first Level Three spell," said Rachel. As they left the dormitory, Donovan asked, "So, how many spells do I need to master at this level?" "There are five Level Three Enhancement spells," said Rachel, "Seeing, which is a rare ability, Silence, Healing for near-mortal wounds, Detecting Magic, and the Change spell. Your Force spells are Blast, Paralyze, Replicate, Compulsion, Binding and Kill. Your Serums are Love, Healing, and Death. Instead of Seemings, you have to learn to Change something into something else."

They proceeded to the Enhancements Training Area, where Rachel said, "Now, your first Level Three Enhancement spell is Silence. Using it, you can make yourself virtually silent." "What do you mean *'virtually'?*" asked Donovan. "Any sound you make should be silent; however, if you step on dry leaves, the leaves will make the sound of being stepped on," explained Rachel. "Oh, I get it! It's like my crossbow," said Donovan. "Excuse me?" asked Rachel.

"When we were on our way to fight the dragon north of Farmdale, my father discovered a weapon called a crossbow. It fires iron arrows with incredible power, enough to penetrate a dragon's scales. He replicated one for me and put a Silence spell on it, so it would be silent when fired, but he cautioned me that if I dropped it on the floor, the floor would make the sound of a crossbow hitting it," explained Donovan. "Yes. That's exactly right! So, while *you* may be silent, the things around you will make noise if you touch or step on them," said Rachel.

"I understand," said Donovan. "The incantation is *"SILENTIUM,"* and the gesture is putting your left index finger in front of your lips, like so," said Rachel, demonstrating the gesture. "Now, I want you to invoke the spell and say something to me," said Rachel. Donovan thought a minute, then said, *"SILENTIUM,"* while performing the gesture. He felt the energy drain, so he was confident that the spell had worked. He looked at Rachel and said, "I like your shirt."

"Thank you," said Rachel, "It's my favorite." Donovan looked around, confused, and asked, "Didn't the spell work?" Rachel said, "What? Release the spell." *"CODA,"* said Donovan. "I said, 'Didn't the spell work?'" "It worked perfectly," said Rachel with an impish grin. "Then I don't understand how you knew what I said about your shirt," said Donovan. "Easy," said Rachel, "I read your lips."

"How is that possible?" asked Donovan. "I learned to read lips as a child," explained Rachel, "You see, my father is deaf, so lip-reading and sign language were the only ways we had to communicate." "Your father lost his hearing?" asked Donovan. "No," said Rachel. "He was born deaf." "Couldn't he be healed?" asked Donovan. "No," said Rachel sadly. "Since he was born that way, there was no injury to 'heal.' He has adapted, though, and has a good life. He runs a tailor shop in town. I'll take you by to meet him sometime."

"You said there was a 'sign language' that you use to communicate with deaf people?" asked Donovan. "Yes, it's a system of gestures that is used by deaf people to communicate with each other and with people with normal hearing," said Rachel. "I don't understand," said Donovan. "Well, people who are born deaf, don't learn to speak like we do," she explained. "Since they can't hear what the words sound like, it's very difficult for them. If you lost your hearing in an accident or because of old age, at least you'd know how to speak because you learned it before you lost your hearing."

"I understand," said Donovan. "Can you teach me this sign language?" "You really are special," said Rachel. "I've been at the Academy for almost ten years now, and no one has ever asked me to teach them sign language. Why do you want to learn it?" "A few reasons, actually. First, because it might come in handy sometimes if I need to communicate with someone who is deaf; second, it would be helpful in a military operation when you need to communicate silently; and last, how am I going to talk to your father if I don't learn some?" Rachel laughed. "All right, here is your first lesson; put your right hand, fingers together on your chin, then move your hand away." "Like so?" asked Donovan, repeating the gesture. "Exactly right," said Rachel. "So, what does that mean?" asked Donovan. "Thank you," said Rachel.

"Now that you know the Silence spell, it's time to play Blind Man's Bluff," said Rachel. "How do we play?" asked Donovan. "You put on this blindfold," said Rachel, handing him a black silk bandana, "Then I move away from you and cast a Silence spell on myself. Then I walk towards you and try to touch you before you detect my approach. If you hear me coming, you toss a pebble at where you think I might be and say, 'Tag, you're it.' But you only get one toss, so use it wisely."

"I don't think this is going to work," said Donovan. "Why not?" asked Rachel. "Because I can sense where people are without any incantation or gesture. You won't be able to sneak up on me, no matter how silent you are," said Donovan. "I pretty much spoiled Level Two hide-and-seek for my partners because I always knew where they were, despite their Concealment shields." "Amazing!" said Rachel. "Do you know how rare that ability is?" "My father also has it, so maybe it's hereditary. Anyway, I just thought you should know."

"Then we'll start the game outside, where it's much harder because of all the other noises around. Playing inside, it's easier to sneak up on someone, as long as the floor doesn't creak," said Rachel. "I'm going to walk over to the Magnolia tree. You stay here, and when I wave, you put on the blindfold, and we'll see how this works."

Rachel walked between the stables and Wizard Noland's cottage, towards the giant Magnolia tree in the center of the Wizards Academy courtyard. When she reached the tree, she waved, and Donovan put on the blindfold. As expected, Donovan was able to track Rachel as she circled around the stables and approached him from the right. While she was still thirty feet away, Donovan used a Wind spell to scoop up a small pebble and toss it at her. When it bounced off her shoulder, he said, "Tag, you're it."

"If you sensed me from that far away, you're right; a Silence spell won't work on you. Let's see how you do with the 'sneaking up on someone' part. I'll stay here, you go to the tree, and we'll try this again." Donovan headed over to the Magnolia tree and waved; he waited until Rachel had the blindfold on, then cast the Silence spell. Instead of taking a circuitous route, as Rachel had done, Donovan walked directly towards her, stepping carefully on the sandy soil of the courtyard, then the grass in the Enhancements Training Area.

When he got to within two feet of her, he conjured a small gust of wind that blew the gravel near her right foot along the ground. Rachel smiled broadly, tossed her pebble at the gravel, and said, "Tag, you're it," just as Donovan touched her left shoulder. Rachel jumped in surprise.

"I would've had you, except for that gust of wind," she groused. "Not really," said Donovan, "you see, *I* conjured the wind." Rachel looked stunned. "You shouldn't be able to hold two spells at once!" she said. "I was holding the Silence spell," explained Donovan, "a small gust of wind was no problem. I didn't *hold* it; I just cast it. The energy drain was minimal." "Humph," said Rachel, "It's going to be hard to teach you anything!" "What do you mean," said Donovan, "you've already taught me the Silence spell and how to say 'Thank you' in sign language." Rachel smiled.

Stephen left Middleberg just past noon. He selected a black stallion that seemed eager to get out of the stable and get some exercise. Packing his few possessions into his saddlebags, he was as ready for this trip as he would ever be. Inside a hidden pocket in his jacket was the message that Mage Elianna, the Director of the

Middleberg School of Magic, had prepared for Mage Kathy, the Assistant Court Wizard. The message said:

Kathy,

Court Wizard Louis paid us a visit this week. After he departed, I discovered that the beef stew we had prepared for our dinner was poisoned with Nightshade. A promising young magician died as a result of the poisoning before I was able to detect it. I was able to stop the other students from consuming any stew, and they are unharmed but distressed. Wizard Louis was the only visitor we had that day, and I personally gave him a tour of the school (including the kitchen where dinner was being prepared). I have no proof that Louis poisoned the stew, <u>but I have no other suspects</u>.

Additionally, that night, three brigands broke into the school and attempted to steal over a hundred vials of Healing Serum that I and my students had prepared for the people of Middleberg. I anticipated the break-in, and we captured the criminals. Two were lackeys with no knowledge of who hired them (I terminated them), but the third confessed to being sent by Wizard Louis, who I had informed of our efforts to produce a sizeable quantity of Healing Serum for the city.

Unfortunately, while the ringleader was being transported to the Garrison Dungeon, he suddenly dropped dead of unknown causes. I suspect another magician was involved, but I have been unable to determine who was responsible.

I need to get this information to someone reliable, and you were the first person I thought of. I cannot leave Middleberg at this critical time. The dragons may attack at any moment, and I cannot, in good conscience, abandon my eleven remaining students and leave the city with only two Sorcerers. I do not know what you can do with this information, but I needed someone to know what has happened to us, and I do not trust Messenger Hawks. This message is being delivered to you by Stephen, my most advanced student. He has brown hair and a scar on his left wrist. He is the only one I trust to deliver it to you safely.

Mage Elianna

Mage Elianna had used a Reduce spell on the message after rolling it up and sealing it. It now appeared to be a small stone. She had also given him a gold, three silvers, and several coppers. "Replicate whatever money you need for the journey from these," Elianna instructed. Stephen rode casually through the city, not wanting to arouse suspicion. When he reached the city limits, he cast a Concealment spell on himself and his mount as he headed down the road to Baize.

Unfortunately, Stephen's departure did not go unnoticed. A wrinkled old woman with grey hair saw him leave the school and she followed him through the city, always keeping to the back alleys and the shadows cast by the buildings. She was watching as Stephen left the city, and observed his casting of the Concealment shield. Guessing his destination (this road only went to Baize), the woman hurried back to her Apothecary shop and prepared a Messenger Hawk for Wizard Louis. The message was short and to the point:

Louis,

Mage Elianna survived the attempt. I eliminated the co-conspirators, but they may have told the Mage more than she should know. A young man with brown hair and a black steed has been dispatched to Baize by Elianna.

A Friend

Once the hawk was away, the old woman resumed her post at the shop, selling herbs and potions to the citizens of Middleberg.

Gek landed in a cornfield just west of Grotton a couple of hours before dawn. Quickly changing into human form, he headed into town to try and locate Olive or any of the other Sea Dragon Changed Ones who could advise him about Azure's pregnancy. According to Bruce, Olive and her husband lived on the outskirts of the town, on the beach. Grotton was a bustling city, with all sorts of trade and commerce coming in and out of the port. Everyone was talking about the Sea Dragon attacks and how the Royal Navy was attempting to protect shipping, which was the lifeblood of Grotton. The people were also concerned about the report of a recent attack on the east coast port city of Sundock.

Gek smiled at hearing the panic in some of their voices but was concerned that he never once heard anyone mention the Kingdom of Baize as being responsible for the attacks on the Franconian ships. So, while the people were worried, the plan to get the humans to fight each other did not seem to be working. As he headed out of the city on the coast road, Gek came upon a large commercial cannery with a bright blue sign that read "Olive's Tuna." A deepwater pier stretched out into the sea for several hundred yards, and there were several medium-sized fishing trawlers tied up alongside the pier, with workers preparing the ships for the next day's fishing.

Gek entered the cannery's office and was greeted by an old man in gray, tattered overalls. He wore a greasy brown bucket hat over his thinning hair, and heavy rubber boots completed his ensemble. "What can I help you with, young fella?" asked the old man, as he edged his way along the counter gingerly. "You lookin' fer work? We can always use more help around here, 'especially since them darn dragons started scarin' all the sailors and fishermen off."

"Sir," began Gek, "I am looking for Olive. Is she here?" "Not in a long while," said the old man, sadly. "My wife died almost two years ago. Why would you be looking for her?" he asked, sniffing the air and blowing his nose into a dirty gray handkerchief. "A friend of mine named Bruce mentioned that she lived in Grotton and said I should look her up if I ever made it this far east," said Gek cautiously. "Bruce! Now, that is a name I have not heard in a long, long time. How is old Bruce?" asked the old man. "Bruce was fine when I left him," said Gek. "And what about his wife? What was her name—Clarice?" "Celeste," said Gek. "Sadly, she passed away some time ago."

"So, what were you looking for Olive for?" asked the old man. Gek hesitated, then said, "My wife is pregnant, and we need some advice about how to handle...*things.*" "Hmm, Olive was no midwife, if that is what you are lookin' for. You would do better lookin' in town for somethin' like that," said the man. "Well, I just thought I would ask," said Gek, disappointedly. He turned to leave when the old man asked, "Before you go, do you have change for a one?" Gek stopped in his tracks, then replied, "No, but my wife might." "Come back tonight, after all the workers have gone. My sons will be home by then and maybe we can answer some of your questions. I am sure they are Great ones," said the old man with a knowing grin.

Chapter Three:

ANSWERS

"I am reassigning the VALOR to First Fleet," said Admiral Cross. "You'll take command of what's left of the First Squadron and patrol the sea around the Coral Islands. That means you are hereby promoted to Commodore, Captain Matthews, and you will be the Squadron Mage, Sorcerer Andrew." Captain Matthews and Andrew stood there, stunned. Just like that, no preamble, no 'good afternoon,' just; 'you're promoted and reassigned.'

"Sir, if I might ask," said Captain (now Commodore) Matthews, "What brought this on?" The Admiral of the Navy looked at the map on his wall for a moment, then replied, "The dragons attacked our fleet while they were at anchor in Sundock. We lost four ships and had two more badly damaged. Several merchant ships were also sunk or heavily damaged. It's the worst disaster ever to befall the Franconian Navy."

"I understand, Sir," said Commodore Matthews, "What are our orders?" "You are to take the VALOR east at all possible speed and rendezvous with the VICEROY, the VICTORY, and the COMFORT. I know our squadrons normally have five ships, but this is all I can muster right now. The VICEROY and the

VICTORY were escorting a small convoy of merchants and were not in port during the attack. The COMFORT was in Sundock and has damage, but I don't know how bad. The crew is attempting to repair her, but I don't know if they'll be finished by the time you arrive. You are to repair the COMFORT, then patrol the ocean around the Coral Islands; Second Squadron, consisting of the ABLE, the SEASPARROW, the SEAHAWK, and the SEAGULL will patrol between Sundock and Frostberg, and the Third Squadron, composed of the SENTINEL, the WATCHDOG, the GUARDIAN, and the SENTRY will patrol the area between Sundock and Eastport. Vice Admiral Jordan is the First fleet commander, and his flagship is the HMS SENTRY."

"Sir," said Andrew, "are you sure I'm the best magician to assign as Squadron Mage? I'm very junior—" "I know," interrupted the Admiral, "but the First Squadron's Mage was killed in the attack, and the other two Sorcerers appear to be less capable than you. For whatever reason, the VALOR has had more success against these damn dragons than any ship in the fleet. I hope you're at least partially responsible for that." "I understand, Sir. I'll try not to let you down," said Andrew humbly.

"Now, to the hard part of this mission," said the Admiral." We have reason to believe that the Sea dragons have a base in the Coral Islands, so you're headed into dangerous waters. I've pulled the records, and there have apparently been sightings of 'sea serpents' around those islands for years, but for some reason, the reports were buried, or discounted as hallucinations."

"Sir," said Andrew hesitantly, "am I correct in assuming that you've been informed about how dragons can understand human speech, perform magic, and take on human form?" "WHAT?" raged the Admiral. "NO, I DAMN WELL HAVEN'T BEEN TOLD THAT! WHEN DID WE DISCOVER THIS?" "We learned about it just before I left the Wizards Academy, Sir. I'm sorry, I know the King wanted it kept 'close-hold,' but I assumed that they informed the military and all of the magicians in Franconia, so you would know what to watch for," said Andrew.

"TYPICAL! I can't believe we weren't told! So, do you know how to smoke out these imposters?" asked the Admiral, still seething. "Yes, Sir," Andrew explained how to detect a Changed One and the steps the Wizards at the Academy had taken with the ones they discovered. The Admiral was very unhappy. "Sir, I don't know why you weren't informed. I do know that the King was concerned about a general panic if the citizens of Franconia suddenly found out that there were dragon Changed Ones among us. There would be riots and lynchings; neighbor might turn against neighbor, each accusing the other of being a dragon in disguise. Onboard a ship; it could be chaos," said Andrew, trying to calm the angry Admiral.

"I get it," said the Admiral, "but I want my Headquarters and my ships swept off these vermin! Wizard Lake, you gather all the magicians here at Headquarters and use Mage Andrew. I want every Sailor and Marine examined. Don't tell them why; just get it done! Andrew, how long will it take?" "At least two days, Sir," said Andrew. "We need to move deliberately but disguise what we're doing; otherwise, any Changed Ones may transform and attack or flee before we can apprehend them." "How do you suggest we conduct this dragon hunt?" asked Wizard Lake, the Chief of Naval Wizardry.

Andrew thought for a moment, then said, "Sir, I would recommend that we gather all of the magicians together this afternoon and check them first. Then tomorrow, Admiral, you order a general muster; gather everyone in ranks on the parade ground; then we—well, the Army would call it 'trooping the line,' we go down each row, and you ask each Sailor the same question— 'How old are you?'" "I don't understand," said Admiral Cross. "Sir, if I asked you that question, how would you respond?" asked Andrew. "I'd say, 'I'm 57," answered the Admiral. "EXACTLY!" said Andrew, excitedly.

"You see, Sir, a Changed One would say "I am 57, not *I'm 57.*"

The Admiral smiled, catching on. He nodded approvingly at Commodore Matthews, "I can see why you've had success against the dragons; this one's sneaky. What do we do once we have our answers?" "Then we take note of everyone who didn't say 'I'm,' and bring them in separately for questioning, without letting the others know what we're doing," said Andrew. "I can't believe there are many Changed Ones at Headquarters, but even one is too many." "Make it so," said Admiral Cross.

"So, what do you think?" asked Edward. "I like it," said Timothy. "I really appreciate your keeping a Healer and Mage Curtis here to see to the sick and injured in Springfield. Without me, there'd be nobody to tend to them." "Do you think that King Donald will listen to reason?" asked Major Gerald. "It depends," replied Timothy, "his majesty's been under a lot of pressure lately, and there are times that I'm not sure he's getting the best advice from his Ministers." "Hmm," said Edward, "I understand. In Franconia, the Court Wizard was a Changed One. Wizard Victor had the King's ear, and he gave the King a lot of bad advice over the years." After thinking about it for a while, Timothy said that he wasn't shocked by the news and that he had suspected something was amiss for quite some time. He just hadn't considered dragons pretending to be humans.

"Just so you know, Tim," said Edward, "We've searched Springfield for any Changed Ones and found nothing. If there were any here, they probably left with the Army." "It wouldn't surprise me a bit if Mayor Slate was one. He was always trying to stir up trouble between us and Franconia lately," said Timothy. "Anyway, can you be ready to leave tomorrow morning? I don't think we should tarry; I'm not sure how much more time we have," said Edward.

"I'll inform what's left of the City Council about our plan and make sure they know not to make any trouble for those soldiers staying behind. I doubt there'll be any ruckus; the people appreciate what you all have done for us. Well, I'd best be off to talk to the Council and pack for our journey. Until tomorrow, then." "I'll meet you in the town square one-hour past dawn," said Edward. Timothy left smiling.

It was after dark when Gek returned to the Cannery, and the lamps inside were lit, providing a warm glow that illuminated the inside of the building. When Gek knocked, the old man answered immediately and escorted Gek to what appeared to be a break area, where workers rested and ate lunch during the workday. There were several other people in the room, waiting. "So, Great one, I understand that your mate is pregnant and you have questions. Where is she?" asked the old man. "Azure is staying with Bruce for the time being," answered Gek. "We were unsure if changing into Dragon form, then back into a human when we arrived here, could bring harm to the baby." Those assembled murmured their approval.

"First," said the old man, "let me introduce everyone. I am Beau, a Sea Dragon Changed One; Olive was my wife. These others are Maya, Cerulean, Columbia, Cyan, and Cornflower. We are all Sea Dragons who have changed and prefer to live as humans. I have two human sons, Antwan and Dell, who will join us shortly. So, how can we help you?"

Gek said, "I am Gek, son of Liza, a Great Dragon, and Cobalt, a Sea Dragon; my mate is Azure, daughter of Teal, Chief of the Sea Dragon Clan. We were searching for other Changed Ones among the humans, when, two days ago, Azure told me that she thinks she may be pregnant. We are unsure if the baby is human or

Dragon and if changing forms could bring harm to our unborn child. We are both rather young."

"It is well that you found us," said Beau. "We have all been where you are now. First, do you know what form you were in when the child was conceived?" "No," said Gek. "We have changed form many times lately as we search the countryside for Changed Ones." "Hmm," said Beau, "well, the child started out as either human or Dragon, depending on the form you were in when the pregnancy occurred. Now, changing forms does not harm the unborn. Each time she changes form, the child changes from human embryo to Dragon egg and back. She will notice that each change becomes harder and requires more energy from her. This is natural, since she is changing for two. You understand?" Gek nodded, relieved.

"In Dragon form, the baby is contained in an egg. After about eight months, the egg will come out. It must be kept warm and protected and will hatch in about four weeks. Human babies remain in the mother for about nine months and are born live," said Maya. "So changing form does not injure the child?" asked Gek. The Changed Ones looked at each other, and then Cornflower said, "Indigo" quietly. "Who is Indigo?" asked Gek. "She was a member of our community, and she wanted her child to be human, but during the birthing process, the pain was too much for her, and she took a chance and tried to change back into Dragon form. When the change was complete, both mother and child were dead. The energy drain was too much," said Maya sadly.

"Pain?" asked Gek. "Yes," said Beau, "Birthing Dragon eggs is generally painless, but human births can be very painful. That is why humans usually request the assistance of someone called a Midwife. A Midwife is experienced in human childbirth and has potions and herbs to ease the pain and comfort the mother. Wealthy humans may even hire a magic-user to aid in the birth of a child, but Changed Ones could never employ a magic-user; the risk of being discovered would be too great."

"What else should we know?" asked Gek. "Human babies suckle from their mothers, much the same as Dragon infants do, but changing forms after giving birth will confuse and frighten the child. Also, during the pregnancy, Azure may experience strange food cravings and morning sickness. She will also require more food than usual, since she is eating for two now. She may also become irritable for seemingly no reason," said Cyan, earning him a slap on the back of his head from Cornflower, his wife.

"I understand," said Gek. "Thank you all for meeting with me." "Why are you searching for Changed

Ones?" asked Beau. Gek thought quickly. "We are looking for any other Great Dragons," he said finally. "My grandfather Ard and I may be the last of our Clan." The other Changed Ones accepted this explanation and headed for the door. "Goodbye, Gek, I hope all goes well with Azure. I am sorry to disappoint you, but there are no Great Dragon Changed Ones in Grotton," said Beau. "Best you return to your mate quickly, before you are discovered by the magic-users in town."

Gek left the building, disrobed and transformed back into a dragon, then flew off into the night.

Stephen was only about an hour outside of Middleberg when he spied the vultures circling in the air above a section of the road. Knowing that it usually meant a dead body, animal or human, Stephen kept a close lookout and soon found the carcass of the horse Wizard Louis had borrowed. The poor beast looked to have been attacked by wolves or some other large predator. Stephen dismounted to examine the body. It was badly mauled and mostly eaten, with only some scraps of meat left on the bones. Curiously, there were no wolf tracks around the body, and the tracks that were there were unfamiliar to Stephen, who had grown up in the forests north of Middleberg.

It was certainly a large beast, with sizeable teeth and claws, and some of the bones were snapped in two, so whatever it was, it had a ferocious bite. With nothing left to learn, Stephen mounted his horse and accelerated to a canter, eager to put some distance between himself and whatever killed and ate the Wizard's horse. The black mount seemed to agree with Stephen's assessment of the situation and tried to gallop off as fast as he could, causing Stephen to have to rein in the charging horse. Stephen knew that it was a five-day journey to Baize and that he could not gallop all the way without killing his mount.

Stephen wondered whether Wizard Louis had survived the attack on his horse; he was a Wizard, after all, and perfectly capable of defending himself from wild animals. *But if he'd killed or driven off the aggressors, where were the bodies?* There was also a chance that he might be injured. Stephen knew that it was about a three-week walk to Baize from Middleberg, and if he had run into a similar situation, he would've walked back to Middleberg to get a new mount. Since Stephen had not passed Louis on the road, he concluded that the Wizard was proceeding to Baize on foot. Since there were no towns or even villages between Middleberg and Baize, it was going to be a long walk for Wizard Louis. Stephen decided that he would need to slow his pace so as not to meet the Wizard on the road. It wouldn't do to overtake the murderous Wizard by accident. Once clear of the carcass, Stephen slowed his horse to a walk. Getting to Baize undetected was going to take a lot longer than Mage Elianna thought.

Donovan's staff flew out of his hands, barely missing Stam's head; a second later, a strong jolt knocked him out of the saddle and onto the sandy ground. As Donovan got up, Stam nosed him to make sure he was not injured. "It's OK, boy," said Donovan, feeding his horse a sugar cube from his pocket. "I'll try to do better next time." Sparring with staffs while mounted was proving to be more challenging than expected.

"You need to anticipate better," said Rachel from atop her chestnut mount, "You keep expecting me to use my staff instead of my shield. A shield can be projected out farther and won't endanger your horse." "I understand," said Donovan, "I've just never tried projecting a shield out that far." This was the first time Donovan had sparred against Rachel on horseback, and he had underestimated his Mentor's prowess. As a

Level Two magician, Donovan had been unmatched by his peers, and sparring on foot, he was almost untouchable.

"Are you worried about hitting a girl?" asked Rachel mischievously. "No," said Donovan, "I've hit Wizard Faith plenty of times. I guess I was just overconfident." "Yes," said Rachel, "I heard all about how you terrorized the Level Ones and Twos with your staff work, but you're in the big leagues now." Donovan massaged his shoulder, brushing off the sand, "I'm still not sure when I'd ever have to fight on horseback."

"Well," said Rachel, "there have been several cases of new Sorcerers being attacked on the road, enroute to their first assignments." "Really?" asked Donovan. "That seems like a stupid thing to try." "The brigands didn't know they were trying to rob magicians," explained Rachel. "They thought they were just unwary travelers, on the road alone and an easy mark." "I'll bet they learned their lesson," said Donovan. "Most of the time, but not always, and there's nothing more embarrassing to a newly promoted Sorcerer than having to walk back to the Wizards Academy and report that you were robbed on the road."

Donovan remounted and said, "Let's try that again." For the rest of the Martial Arts lesson, Donovan was able to remain in the saddle, but he never scored a touch on Rachel. Suitably humbled, he led Stam back to the stables, took off the saddle and added some oats to the feed trough. Rachel watched from across the stable. "The stable boys will take care of that, you know," she said. "I know, but Stam has been with me a long time, and I like to make sure he's well cared for."

As they left the stables and headed for the Forces Training Area for his next lesson, Rachel asked if there were any Level Three classes that he was struggling with. "Not struggling, exactly," said Donovan, "but I don't understand why we need to learn to make Love Serum. It seems dishonest, somehow." Rachel laughed. "It's mainly used by the Regional Mages at the request of the Courts after a domestic violence arrest." "I don't understand," said Donovan. Rachel explained, "Let's say someone is arrested for beating their wife or children. Sadly, it's not uncommon. We could put them in prison or on a Road Crew, but that would hurt the family as well, since they would suddenly have no income. So, instead, we administer a Love Serum to the abuser. It usually solves the problem, at least temporarily." "Why only 'temporarily'?" asked Donovan. "Because over time, Love Serum wears off. It usually lasts about a year."

"So, what happens if the violence keeps recurring?" asked Donovan. "I think that after three doses of Love Serum, more drastic measures are taken. The abuser is warned when the last Serum is administered, that if they're charged again, it's the Road Crew or Women's prison for them," said Rachel. "Women's prison?" asked Donovan. "Sure, sometimes it's the wife that's the abuser."

Chapter Four:

FEMALE PROBLEMS

There were no Changed Ones at Naval Headquarters. At least none that Andrew and Wizard Lake could find. However, Wizard Lake's assistant, Sorceress Green, was missing. The afternoon after briefing the Admiral, Wizard Lake had called all of the magicians in Grotton to a meeting, including the ones in the Regional Mage's Office. All were in attendance, except Sorceress Green, who couldn't be located anywhere. After testing and smelling the magicians present, Wizard Lake explained the situation to them. The magicians were astonished and a little worried. After spelling them to Secrecy, the magicians were instructed to resume their duties but to keep a lookout for anyone they suspected of being a Changed One.

A further search of Sorceress Green's office turned up a note, under her desk pad that read:

Wizard Lake,

I will be gone by the time you read this. I overheard your conversation with the Admiral this afternoon and felt it best that I depart before I am discovered. I was born a Sea Dragon. In my youth, I learned the spell of Change, and once, on a dare, I transformed myself and

came into Grotton to have a look around. The Regional Mage found me within an hour of my arrival and immediately had me escorted to the Wizards Academy. Seven years later, I was assigned here as your assistant and I have done my best to be a good human. I bear humans no ill will, and I am personally unhappy and confused by the recent Dragon attacks on Franconian ships. I am returning to the Sea Dragon Clan to try and discover why they have suddenly become hostile. I may or may not return, depending on what my inquiries reveal.

Sorceress Evelynn Green

"Well, what do you know about that," said the Admiral after reading the note. "A dragon. Right under our noses. At least we know that there aren't any left in Headquarters. Lieutenant! Give Commodore Matthews my compliments and tell him he's free to depart for Sundock at his earliest convenience." The Admiral's aide closed his notebook and left the office quickly, headed for the dock.

"Your Majesty, I have disturbing news about the Royal Expeditionary Force," said Jasmine, the Franconian Minister of Internal Security. "My information indicates that they were ambushed outside Springfield and suffered heavy casualties." "What?" exclaimed the King. "How could that happen? They had Wizard Edward and an additional Sorcerer with them! They should never have been foolish enough to ride into an ambush! How is this possible? Could you be mistaken?"

"It is true that my agents are not always perfectly reliable; I mean, they are not the most *reputable* people in the land. However, I have heard from several sources that the Expeditionary Force was taking the most direct route to Springfield, which led through a pass between the city and the Amber River. Apparently, they were ambushed by a combination of dragons and Baizian soldiers, working together. I understand that those who did not flee were either killed or captured," said Jasmine.

The King sat on his throne, speechless. Nothing like this had ever happened to the Royal Expeditionary Force before. They were his best troops, and Wizard Edward was one of his most capable magicians. "What about Major Gerald?" he asked finally.

"He may be with the survivors, Sire," said Jasmine smoothly. "I understand that some five or ten soldiers escaped and are headed back this way, but I do not know if he is among them." "What can we do to help them?"

asked the King. "Sire, they may be beyond our help. I understand that both soldiers and dragons are pursuing the remnants of the Expeditionary Force. They may already be dead. My information is almost two days old."

"Marshall Guzman, do you have anything to report?" The Field Marshall stepped forward and said, "Sire, my last report from the Royal Expeditionary Force was when they departed Prarrieville, almost five weeks ago. They reported that they were taking a smuggler's trail through the forest in order to get to the ford across the Amber River as quickly as they could. Taking either of the main roads would have added several days to their travel time, and they knew you wanted their mission completed expeditiously. I have had no word from them since they crossed the river into Baize."

"Could they have been ambushed?" asked the King. "Your Majesty, any force can be surprised. Major Gerald is an excellent commander, but against a force with multiple dragons, Baizian soldiers, and perhaps even Baizian magicians, it is certainly possible. Especially since we know so little about the terrain on the west side of the Amber River." "How can we know for sure?" asked the King.

Marshall Guzman stood, thinking, then said, "As I recall, when the Royal Expeditionary Force went in search of the first dragon, north of Farmdale, Mage Edward cast a Seeing spell to find the murdered farmers and burned farms. Perhaps another magician could use the same spell to search for the Expeditionary Force?" "An excellent suggestion, Marshall! Wizard Cassandra," said the King, speaking to the relatively new Court Wizard, "can you cast such a spell?"

Cassandra looked down and shook her head, "That is an exceedingly rare ability, Your Majesty. To my knowledge, besides Wizard Edward, there are only two other magicians in Franconia who can cast that spell, Sorcerer Curtis, who accompanied the Royal Expeditionary Force, and Mage Roark, the Regional Mage in Three Forks." "Are you telling me, that two of the only three magicians in all of Franconia who can cast this Seeing spell went out together and got themselves ambushed? HOW IS THAT POSSIBLE?" shouted the King.

"Sire, enemy magicians have the ability to conceal their forces, even from a Seeing spell. If we are indeed fighting both dragons and magicians, this is a new kind of war," said Marshall Guzman solemnly. The King sat back, now more worried than angry.

"Jasmine, what do you recommend?" he asked. Jasmine pretended to think over what to say, then said, "Sire, I think you need to mobilize the Reserve Forces in the Kingdom. Call every man who has ever served in the Franconian military back into service and begin a rapid training program. All active forces should be deployed to the border except those necessary to defend the Capitol. We may even need to begin calling up all able-bodied men in the Kingdom and pressing them into service."

"Marshall, what are your thoughts?" "Sire, first, I would like to send out scouts from the forces in Prarrieville to determine what actually happened to the Expeditionary Force; calling up the reserves is complicated and will impact the economy of the Kingdom, as veterans are forced to leave their jobs and re-enter active service. We may be able to recall those most recently discharged, but a full recall would take months. Additionally, pulling troops from our eastern frontiers and sending them to the border with Baize will be exorbitantly expensive and will undoubtedly provoke a corresponding action from Baize."

The King sat, pondering. He had no desire to waste gold moving forces around in haste, but he could not sit idly by while the neighboring kingdom slaughtered his soldiers. Finally, he said, "Marshall Guzman, please recall the veterans from the cities of Westport, Weaton,

Prarrieville, and Colton and return them to active duty, move what's left of the Second Regiment to Prarrieville, and see if you can increase recruiting here in Kingston to beef up my Personal Guard. Wizard Cassandra, please contact the Wizards Academy and see if they can spare any magicians to support the Army. Jasmine, I need better and more timely information about what is going on in Baize; use whatever resources you need. Dismissed."

"Hello, Loren," said Donovan. "Come to gloat, have you?" asked a despondent Loren. "No. I just wanted to talk." "You want to know *why*, right?" "I guess I do. On our way back to Kingston, Healer Bone said the 'why' didn't matter, only the 'who;' that once we figured out who was working against us, we could figure out the 'why,' but I just don't understand. Was your life as a human so bad? Was your anger that great?"

"My life as a human has been loveless and lonely. Can you understand that? The Great Betrayal killed all of my family, right down to my most distant cousins. All gone in a single night! Can you imagine? Wandering the snow fields, alone, helpless and hungry," said Loren.

"Is that why you transformed into a human? Hunger?"

"Hardly. I survived as a Snow Dragon for almost two hundred years. After The Great Betrayal, there were so few Dragons left, that there was plenty of prey for all. No, I learned the spell of Change out of curiosity," said Loren.

"A thirst for knowledge?"

"Call it what you will. I guess, after two hundred years, I was just *bored* of being a Dragon. Transforming was interesting. A new adventure! Then I ran into the only Sorcerer in Frostberg! What a stroke of ill-fortune! Before I knew it, I was here, trapped in a wizard's prison. I spent ten years as a student here. Mastering spells is more difficult for Changed Ones than it is for normal humans. After several years as a Mentor, I decided that I would devote myself to helping other captured Changed Ones survive and escape this place without having their spark removed. I excelled in History. Being two hundred years old helped. Eventually, I prevailed upon the Headmaster to let me stay, even though I never took the tests to become a Wizard or even a Mage."

"Incredible," said Donovan.

"Yes. I suppose so. In the beginning, my title was "Honorary Wizard" Loren, but over time, people just forgot about the 'Honorary' part. As students rotated through the Academy, the new Level Ones just called me Wizard Loren."

"If you were so lonely, why did you stay here?" asked Donovan. "The job opportunities for Wizards in Franconia are very limited. Other than the Academy, the only other Wizard positions are in the military," said Loren. "You could have just retired." "I thought about it many times, but then another Changed One would be brought in, and I felt the need to stay."

"But when the other Changed Ones would not join you and Stuart, you were prepared to kill them." "Old habits are hard to break, and Dragons killing Dragons is not really that unusual," said Loren.

"So how does this end?" asked Donovan quietly. "Excuse me?" asked Loren.

"You once told me that the dragons only wanted food, only wanted to survive. *So how does it end?* Can we ever have peace between our species?" "Are you suggesting another Treaty?" asked Loren, incredulously. "I know, it's been tried before. Does that make endless war the only other alternative?"

"More likely a series of wars, broken by brief years of peace, while one side or the other regroups and rebuilds," said Loren. "There must be a better way," said Donovan

"Perhaps, but it would require sacrifices on both sides," said Loren. "My father thinks that you would make a good Ambassador to the dragons when and if the time comes, that you could help bridge the gap between our two species," said Donovan.

"Why would you trust me?" she asked, a glimmer of hope coming to her face. "Because you have walked in both worlds, and you know the history between our races. You could help us avoid the mistakes of the past. When that time comes, I hope you are here to help us find our way through. I believe that you still have something to contribute, Wizard Loren," said Donovan.

Mage Kathy was unsure what to do about Charolette's attempted assassination. She was fairly sure that Wizard Louis was behind it, but without proof, she could hardly accuse the Court Wizard of hiring (or ordering) Admiral Vandall's secretary to try and push her out of her tower bedroom window. She decided that the best course of action was probably to do nothing and see what the reaction was to Charolette's disappearance.

After Kathy had dispatched Charolette, she used the Remove spell to dispose off the body and all the evidence of the attack. She imagined that Wizard Louis was going to be quite surprised when she showed up for work in the morning and Charolette was nowhere to be found. Just to be safe, Kathy erected several magical wards on her rooms to alert her if anyone tried to enter or tamper with any of her belongings.

If Wizard Louis was behind the attack, as she suspected, she was going to have to do something about him soon. She could not stay on the defensive indefinitely; sooner or later, she would have to take the fight to Louis.

At the appointed hour, Kathy arrived at her office and began going over the ledgers of the Kingdom, looking for evidence of fraud, waste or abuse in the various accounts, much as she did every day. Around mid-morning, Wizard Louis stopped by and nonchalantly asked her how the accounts were looking. Kathy smiled sweetly and said that, so far, everything looked to be in order. Louis nodded curtly and strode off down the corridor as if he were late for an appointment.

Kathy set the ledger she was working on aside and moved to the window. From her office, she could see Wizard Louis walking quickly towards the Admiralty building. She imagined his surprise when he discovered that Charolette had not come in to work today, and no one had seen or heard from her. *That should give him pause,* thought Kathy, as she flicked her new fan open and closed absent-mindedly. The fan had a hidden blade concealed in the handle which activated at the push of the decorative inlay. It had been invaluable in dispatching the treacherous Charolette. Kathy resolved to carry the fan with her everywhere.

Gek landed behind Bruce's ramshackle hut and quickly transformed back into human form. As he entered the hut, he found Azure in dragon form, eating a large bowl of eels. "I thought you hated eels," said Gek. "I did," replied Azure, "I just got a craving for them. They are not as bad as I remembered. Do you want some?" "Pass," said Gek, "Where is Bruce?"

"He is out looking for more driftwood. I think that is all he has to do to pass the time. So, did you find Olive? What did she say?"

"Unfortunately, Olive died of old age two years ago. I was able to talk to several Sea Dragon Changed Ones who have given birth, though. They said that the baby changes form each time you do. So, right now, it is a Dragon egg, but when you change back into a human, the baby also changes into a human fetus," explained Gek.

"Will it hurt the child when I transform?" "No, but they said that it will take a lot more energy from you each time you change because you are transforming for two. It usually takes about eight months for a Dragon egg to be ready to come out, and then we have to keep it warm for about a month before it hatches. A human baby normally takes nine months to be born. They said that giving birth to a human baby is very painful, but a Dragon egg, much less so. Once the birthing begins, you cannot change forms. It would kill both you and the baby," concluded Gek.

"Which means that in about five months, I need to be in Dragon form and not change again until after I lay the egg," said Azure. "Maybe sooner, just to be on the safe side," said Gek. "We also need to find a safe place for you to give birth, probably back on Acropo."

"But who will guard the human, Andrew?" asked Azure. "Hopefully, Cobalt or another Sea Dragon can take over for a while. You will be occupied for at least a month, before the egg hatches, then taking care of the baby after it is born. It could be a while," said Gek. "Speaking of Andrew, I saw his ship in the port of Grotton. They looked like they were getting ready to return here."

"We should fly there today and guard the ship on its way back. I would not want anything to happen to him.

I know we have told the Sea Dragons in this area, but there may still be some who did not get the warning. We can leave as soon as I am done eating," said Azure. "No," said Gek. "It looks to be a bright sunny day with no clouds; we need to wait until nightfall. Besides, I just got back. Do you need anything?"

"Yes, I would like some kelp to go with these eels," said Azure. "KELP?" asked Gek, confused. "Just for a little flavoring, PLEASE?" said Azure. Gek headed down towards the beach to gather some kelp. He wondered what other weird things he would be sent out for in the next few months.

The boulder exploded. Spectacularly. "Excellent!" said Wizard Dylan, as Donovan collapsed to the ground. "Too much power, again, though. You don't need to pulverize the boulder; just break it. Are you all right?" Donovan got to his knees and took a long pull from his water bottle. "I'll be OK in a minute," he rasped. "I'm sorry. I guess I just thought that rock was tougher."

Rachel, his Mentor, kneeled down next to him and put her hand on his shoulder. "It takes practice. Start with less power. You can always Blast it again if your first spell isn't strong enough. The rock isn't going anywhere." Donovan staggered to his feet; the last thing he wanted was sympathy or comfort from his Level Three classmates. For some reason, Wizard Noland had not only assigned him a female Mentor but also put him in a group with four girls: Laura, Joyce, Hope, and Mary, and they all seemed to want to be Mrs. Donovan Francis. They all wanted to sit next to him at meals or play Blind Man's Bluff with him. Fortunately, during Blind Man's Bluff, Donovan could sense them before they got within arms-length distance, so he didn't have to contend with any inappropriate touching. He also made sure that he only touched his classmates on the arm, shoulder or back. Donovan liked girls, but the constant attention was beginning to get irritating.

Mary, who was 19, had a reputation for sleeping around, and Donovan decided that that was definitely *not* what he was looking for in a partner. Laura was 22, and she was looking for *a commitment*. Pass. That left Hope and Joyce, both 19. They were nice, and he enjoyed their company, but he remembered Terry's advice and had not gotten too close to either of them (yet). He found that he was most attracted to Rachel, but since she was his Mentor, he had concerns about pursuing any kind of romantic relationship with her. They'd spent a good deal of time together as she taught him sign language. One problem with learning to sign was that some of the hand motions were very similar to the gestures used to invoke spells, and it got confusing sometimes.

He also wasn't sure how it worked if two magicians got *involved* at the Academy. Would they be assigned together upon graduation? Kept here as Mentors? Donovan knew that assignments to the military were normally solo jobs, but he supposed that you could be assigned to different Battalions in the same Regiment, or to a Regional Mage's Office in the same town or city as the military unit. He wondered who he could ask about it. Certainly not Wizard Noland. Probably Wizard Daniel. This was not a conversation he wanted to have with Wizards Mira or Faith. That was a problem for another day.

"Let's try it again, Donovan," said Wizard Dylan. "Please Blast that rock," he said, pointing to a large granite boulder. *"CONCUSIO,"* murmured Donovan, making a throwing motion with his right hand. The boulder was pushed about five feet but remained intact. "A bit more power. Try it again," said Dylan. *"CONCUSIO,"* repeated Donovan. This time the rock cracked in half, and his classmates applauded his success. "Excellent!" said Wizard Dylan. "You see the difference?" "Yes, I think so. Wizard Dylan, I know that all rocks are not the same. How can I tell the hard ones from the softer ones?"

"An excellent question," said Dylan. "The hardest rock is granite, but there are several types of granite, even different colors. It's really hard to tell the difference, especially from a distance, and normally, it's not worth the effort. Just start with a medium-power Blast, then adjust as needed. All right, class, that's enough for today. There's the bell for lunch."

The students headed off towards the dormitory for lunch, with several of the girls approaching Donovan to ask if he was OK and if he needed any healing that they could provide. Donovan politely declined their kind offers and told them he was fine, if just a bit hungry. When they entered the dining room, Leonard waddled over and asked what they wanted to drink. Donovan asked for lemonade, and unsurprisingly, all the girls asked for the same. Donovan smiled; he wondered if he asked for muddy swamp water to drink, everyone at his table would ask for it, too. Leonard returned with the drinks.

"How are you today, Leonard?" asked Donovan. "I'm fine, sir—Donovan. How was Forces training?" "Strenuous," replied Donovan. "I didn't realize that Blasting rocks was so tiring." "Hmm," said Leonard, "have you tried casting a Stamina spell on yourself first? I seem to remember that working for some of the other students." "What a great idea! Thank you." Leonard smiled, then headed back to the kitchen.

"Is that why you're always so nice to the staff here? Because they give you tips like that?" asked Laura. "No. I really feel sorry for them," said Donovan. "But I do appreciate some of their insights. They've been very helpful over the years."

"I think Leonard has actually lost some weight lately," observed Hope. "I've been encouraging him," said Donovan, "besides, he has to walk up and down three flights of stairs every morning to wake me up." The girls giggled. "So, what are we going to be learning today in Enhancements class?" "I think I overheard Wizard Daniel say we were going to start learning the Change spell today," said Hope. "That's great!" said Donovan. "I've been wanting to learn that one."

As they departed the dining room, Donovan looked at Leonard and said, "Looking good, Leo." Leonard smiled.

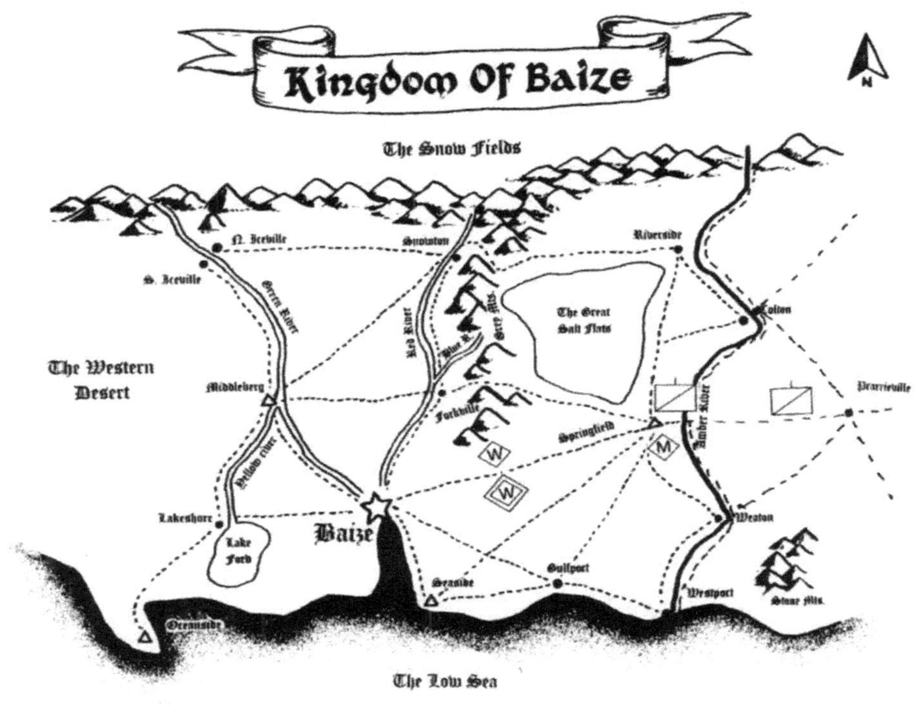

Kingdom Of Baize
The Snow Fields
The Western Desert
The Low Sea
The Great Salt Flats
N. Iceville
S. Iceville
Swinton
Riverside
Colton
Prairieville
Green River
Red River
Silver R.
Sire Mts.
Middleberg
Yellow River
Forkville
Springfield
Lakeshore
Lake Ford
Baize
Seaside
Gulfport
Weston
Westport
Stone Mts.
Oceanside
Amber River
W
W
M
N

Chapter Five:

WIZARD TROUBLE

"**A**re you certain?" asked Wizard Noland. "I'm certain that is what Minister Jasmine reported to the King," said Wizard Cassandra. "The King was most distraught by the news. He asked me to perform a Seeing spell to locate the remnants of the Royal Expeditionary Force, but, other than Edward and Curtis, the only other magician I know who can perform that spell is Mage Roark, and he's in Three Forks. Is there anyone here at the Academy who can conjure it?"

"Perhaps, but I hesitate to use him. It's Edward's son, Donovan. He can Sense people, at least here on the Academy grounds. We've never asked him to try using the Seeing spell with a map. That would be a terrible way to learn about his father's death," said Noland. "You're right, but he's going to hear rumors of it as soon as he goes into town. The news is all over the city. The King has called up the Reserve forces in Westport, Weaton, Prarrieville and Colton, and has ordered Marshall Guzman to increase recruiting for the King's Personal Guard," said Cassandra. Noland sighed, "Then I guess there's no harm in asking Donovan to attempt a Seeing spell. Jerry! Go and find Level Three Donovan and bring him back here. I don't care which class he's in." Jerry ran for the door.

A few minutes later, Jerry arrived, with Donovan following close behind. "Come in, Donovan, and have a seat. Oh, this is Wizard Cassandra, the new Court Wizard," said Noland. "I'm pleased to meet you, Wizard Cassandra," said Donovan. "And I, you," replied Cassandra. "Now, Donovan, I'm going to give you some information that is troubling, then ask you to try a spell that you've never attempted before to help determine the truth of the matter."

Donovan took a long, steadying breath, "It's about my father, isn't it?" he asked. "Yes," said Noland, "The Franconian Minister of Internal Security reported to the King that the Royal Expeditionary Force was ambushed on its way to Baize and that there were many casualties. We have no confirmation of this report, and I, for one, refuse to believe that Edward would allow the force to be ambushed." "My father told me that he had suspicions about Minister Jasmine before he left," said Donovan softly. "He told me the same thing," said Noland, "that's why I have my doubts about this report. It could be that the force was attacked, and the initial report was hasty and erroneous, as is often the case with battle reports. The first report is seldom accurate or complete. Nevertheless, we'd like you to use your sensing ability to try and locate the Royal Expeditionary Force and your father if you can."

"I'll do my best, sir," said Donovan, worriedly. Noland offered a smile and a comforting hand on Donovan's shoulder. "Donovan, this may be the fourth time that your father has been reported dead prematurely. If this report is also untrue, he has just set the record for resurrections. Let me get you a map." Wizard Noland left the office and returned quickly with a large map that contained both Franconia and the Kingdom of Baize.

"Now, the Royal Expeditionary Force was ordered to conduct a punitive assault on the Baizian city of Springfield, here," said Noland, pointing at the map. "Our information is that the Force took this small trail after leaving Prarrieville and headed towards this ford here," he said, pointing again. "The ambush is reported to have occurred here, in the pass between these two hills. Now, the map may not be accurate for the areas west of the Amber River. We don't have very accurate maps of the Kingdom of Baize beyond the coastal cities and the towns along the river, so don't be alarmed if the spell shows the Expeditionary Force in the middle of a lake."

"I understand, Sir," said Donovan. "How do I make the spell work?" Noland and Cassandra looked at each other questioningly. "Well," said Cassandra hesitantly, "when Mage Edward conjured the spell to locate the burned farms and dead farmers around Farmdale, he held his truncheon over the map and concentrated. Then symbols appeared on the map, flame symbols for burned farms, small skulls for dead people, then a golden dragon."

"I don't have a truncheon," said Donovan. "That's OK, you may use mine," said Wizard Noland, handing over an ornately carved three-foot wooden club. "So, what do I do?" asked Donovan. "Hold the truncheon over the map and think of the Royal Expeditionary Force; the soldiers that you know, and your father. You could also search for any dragons that you can locate," said Wizard Noland.

Donovan sat down on the couch with the map spread out on the table before him. He held the truncheon over the map and concentrated, looking for his father and Major Gerald. The truncheon began to emit a bluish-green glow, and the military symbol for a Wizard appeared on the map; halfway between Springfield and the city of Baize, the symbol for a company of cavalry and a mage, appeared in the city of Springfield, and a second symbol for a cavalry company appeared just outside of Prarrieville. Donovan maintained the spell, his hand shaking, and shockingly, the symbol for an enemy Wizard appeared next to the one between

Springfield and Baize. Finally, seven red dragon symbols appeared, two on each hill astride the road to Springfield, one in the middle of the road inside the pass, and two on the road before the pass. The red dragon symbols faded as Donovan held the spell.

"I think we've seen enough," said Wizard Noland happily. "It seems that the Royal Expeditionary Force was indeed ambushed by no less than seven Fire dragons on the road to Springfield, but they somehow prevailed. Major Gerald has split his Force, leaving one company in Springfield with Sorcerer Curtis, while the other company is returning to Kingston, and Edward is traveling to the Capitol city of Baize, either in the company of, or being followed by, a Baizian Wizard. Well done, Donovan!" As Noland turned to congratulate the young magician, he noticed that Donovan was passed out on the sofa, still clutching the truncheon.

Gek and Azure informed Bruce about what Gek had learned from the Changed Ones in Grotton and that Celeste's friend, Olive, had sadly passed away. They told him that they were heading to Grotton, now that they knew it was safe for Azure to transform without causing harm to the baby. "Once we let all of the Sea Dragons around Grotton know how to identify Navy ships, we may come back or continue on along the coast towards Eastport," said Azure. "Thank you for your help and hospitality, Bruce." "Come back anytime," said Bruce, "I'm not going anywhere."

They walked behind Bruce's hut and disrobed, preparing to transform into dragons, when Gek observed, "We are going to have to get you some new clothes soon; those are getting a little tight." Azure rapidly made the change, and while Gek was still in human form, she slapped him with her tail, sending him flying into the tall sage grass. Gek sat up and rubbed his jaw, "That was a little harsh," he said. "I guess I am just a little touchy about my figure lately," said Azure. Gek transformed quickly and silently.

"Ready?" he asked, noting the lack of an apology from Azure. "Yes. Just give me a moment. The Changed Ones were right; the Change spell has left me a little light-headed." "Whenever you are ready," said Gek diplomatically. About ten minutes later, Azure said that she was feeling better and was ready to head out. Gek suggested that they fly along the coast, out over the water, in case Andrew's ship had already left Grotton, heading back to Southport. Azure agreed, and they took flight. If Gek noticed that Azure was not flying as fast as she usually did, he kept it to himself.

They reached the bustling port city of Grotton just after midnight without passing any ship convoys heading towards Southport. They landed behind Olive's Cannery, confident that the VALOR was still in port. They transformed back into Human form and entered the Cannery. Beau was still there, working late. Gek introduced Azure and asked if there was someplace they could stay for the rest of the night, before Gek went into the city the next morning to meet someone. Beau said that by going into the city, Gek was risking discovery by the Regional Mage, but that it was his decision. Gek assured him that he would only be gone a short while and would head into town just before dawn and be back before anyone was really up and about.

"Just watch out for anyone walking with a group of Enforcers. That will be the Regional Mage or one of his Sorcerers," said Beau. "What are Enforcers?" asked Gek. "They are usually big, serious men with no sense of humor. They wear dark red capes and carry short wooden clubs. They are what passes for lawmen in Franconia. They usually have a magician with them. The Enforcers are looking for criminals; the magicians are looking for people with the spark of magic." "Thank you for the warning. I will be sure to steer clear of them," said Gek.

Just before dawn, Gek left the Cannery and headed back towards the pier where he had last seen the

VALOR. The docks were nearly empty at this hour, and Gek only saw a few sleepy merchant's guards. When he got to the pier where the VALOR had been moored, he was shocked to find the ship gone, the berth empty. *Where could it have gone?* Gek wondered. They had certainly not passed it on their way from Southport. They would have to search for it from the air tonight. As he turned to head back to the Cannery, a voice behind him said, "HEY! YOU! HOLD IT RIGHT THERE!"

Gek suddenly found himself surrounded by three hulking Enforcers who pinned his arms behind his back. Then a black-caped magic-user strode up and said, "Well, what have we here? A rogue magician! It's no use denying it; I sensed the spark in you from two blocks away! What's your name?" "Um, Jed," said Gek, thinking quickly, "and you must be mistaken, Sir. I do not have the spark. I am just a poor fisherman, headed back to the Cannery to start my shift."

"The Cannery, eh," said the magic-user, "I've had my eye on that place for a while now. There's something fishy going on there." The Enforcers laughed at the pun. "No matter, I'll investigate that place another day. In the meantime, *sir*," he said sarcastically, "let's find you some transportation to Kingston and the Wizards Academy."

Ard sat alone on his usual bench overlooking the docks in Southport. At this point, he wasn't really sure that he was accomplishing very much. He saw Beverly on those days that she came down and sat with him in the evenings, waiting for her husband Joe to finish his work shift, loading and unloading cargo on the various ships that frequented the port. Her visits had been fewer of late. Her health was declining, and Joe's wasn't much better. They were both old (for humans), and the inevitable march of time was taking its toll.

"How are you this evening, Alan?" Beverly asked. "As well as can be expected, I guess," replied Ard. "How are you?" "My arthritis is acting up again. Frankly, I don't think I can keep making the trek down here. It's so far from the house, you see," said Beverly. "I am sure that Joe appreciates your walking him home in the evenings," Ard temporized, realizing that if Beverly stopped her visits, he would have to find another spot to keep watch over her, which would undoubtedly arouse suspicion.

"I know he does, but he doesn't want me to fall again and hurt myself," she said. "He's not in much better shape than I am. He gave his notice, and at the end of the month, he'll have his pension, and he can retire. He's been working for the same company for 40 years, so we'll get a small stipend each month; not much, but enough to live on."

A fit of coughing gripped her momentarily. "Are you all right," asked Ard. "Yes, it's just the ague. It comes from living here all these years." She shivered, as if cold, even though the evening was warm. She wrapped her shawl around her slender frame more tightly. "I hope Joe gets here soon," she said, her teeth chattering. A few minutes later, Joe started up the hill towards them. "I asked you not to come down here," said Joe. "You're not up to it anymore."

"I know, but I just had to tell Alan why he won't be seeing me anymore. And I wanted a last look at the port at sunset," said Beverly. "You'll have plenty of opportunity after you get your strength back," said Joe reassuringly. "It's just for a little while." Ard rose as the two embraced and said, "Well, I am sure I will see you around town. Take care of yourself. Goodnight." "Goodnight, Alan," they said as they turned and walked up the hill, back to their home. Ard waited a few minutes, then followed them discretely. He had to know where they lived if he had any hope of continuing his protection mission.

Ard followed them at a distance for about half a mile until they entered a small cottage next to an imposing building that had a sign on the front door that said 'SOUTHPORT REGIONAL MAGE.' Ard quickly backtracked, putting some distance between himself and the magic-user's office. *Now what?*

While Louis was pondering what to make of Charolette's disappearance, a message arrived for him. He unrolled the sealed parchment scroll, quickly scanned the contents, then burned the message, scattering the ashes around his office. *One more thing for the maids to clean up,* he thought. Louis considered the message. *So, the poison had not worked as he intended, or at least Mage Elianna had survived, and she had dispatched that boy, Stephen, to relay her suspicions to the king. That would never do.*

He would need to post a watch outside the city. Even a boy could make the trip in about a week, Louis decided. If Stephen simply vanished without a trace, it would take a while for Mage Elianna to even become concerned about him. Louis decided that once he eliminated the boy, he probably had at least a month before he would have to take more drastic measures against Elianna. *Plenty of time.* By then, he might even arrange a dragon attack on Middleberg, with special emphasis on the schoolhouse.

He also decided that he needed to begin intercepting all of the Messenger Hawks that came into the city, just in case. Fortunately, he had an accomplice in the Courier Office who was reliable, if not too bright. *Well, what could you expect from a Stone Dragon Changed One?*

After the 2nd Company had departed Springfield, heading home, Edward and Timothy bid their goodbyes to Mage Curtis and the rest of the 1st Company, who were remaining in Springfield until Edward returned. Edward and Timothy rode along the dusty road in silence for the first hour, Dirk riding ahead under his concealment cloak, acting as a forward scout, although Wizard Timothy said that it was unnecessary, since they were unlikely to encounter anyone heading towards Springfield. Finally, Edward said, "So, what can you tell me about the Kingdom of Baize?" Well," said Timothy, "we used to be a more prosperous nation. Then, the Great Salt Flats started expanding to the south and east, wiping out farms and ranches. You can't grow crops in salt, and the grazing land for the livestock started to shrink until most of the ranchers just moved to the area between the Red and Green Rivers. The land there is mostly pasture, good for farming and such."

"What caused the Salt Flats to expand?" asked Edward. "Too much rain," said Timothy. "Every time it rained, the water had nowhere to go, so it just flowed outwards, carrying the salt with it. Once the rain stopped, the water evaporated, and suddenly, the Salt Flats were bigger than they were before." "Couldn't you build some sort of barrier to contain the water?" asked Edward. "We tried for a while," said Tim, "but the water just flowed around the sides or under the walls. Building a barrier all the way around the Salt Flats would have required more resources than the King was willing to commit to it. It's all we can do to keep the water from flowing into the Amber River and the salt killing everything in it." Edward nodded his understanding.

"So, what are your main industries?" asked Edward. "With what little farming we have, we rely on our sea trade. We ship out iron from the Grey Mountains and timber from the forests west of the capital. We've also got a pretty good ship-building industry going." "What's on the west side of the Green River?" "Mostly the Western Desert. Just sand and more sand. A few scattered watering holes that may or may not be, where any map says they are. There are a few nomads that live out there, but how they eke out a living is beyond me," said Tim. "How far does the desert extend?" asked Edward. "I'm not really sure. Supposedly, there's an extensive mountain range that marks the edge of the Kingdom, but to my knowledge, no one's been out there in decades," replied Tim.

Edward was about to ask how long it was going to take to get to Baize when Dirk rode up and said, "Sir Wizard, there's a rider approaching. He's wearing a red sash across his chest and has two spare mounts with him." "That's a courier," said Tim. "I wonder what he's doing out here all alone." "I don't know, sir, but he looks like he's about twelve years old," said Dirk. "Dirk, let's you and I slip off to the side here and get under concealment. I'd like Tim to talk to the courier without him knowing we're here."

Tim halted his horse and waited for the courier, while Edward and Dirk slipped quietly off to the left side of the road. A few minutes later, a dusty and very young courier approached. "Wizard Timothy?" asked the boy, shyly. "I am Wizard Timothy," replied the Wizard. "How can I help you?" "I have a message for you from the King," said the courier, quickly opening his courier pouch and handing over a parchment scroll. "I see," said Timothy, "and the King sent you all this way by yourself?" The courier blushed.

"You see, sir, I'm the smallest and the lightest of the Royal Couriers. The King decided that I could get to you the fastest. There are two senior couriers on the road behind me, but I imagine that I'm at least a day ahead of them." "Very well," said Timothy. "Just wait here for a moment while I read the King's message." Tim unrolled the scroll and read:

Wizard Timothy,

I have been reliably informed that you surrendered the City of Springfield to elements of the Franconian Army without resistance. You are ordered to report to me immediately and account for your deplorable dereliction of duty.

Donald, King of Baize

Chapter Six:

THE THINGS WE DO

FOR LOVE

Donovan regained consciousness slowly. He opened his eyes and immediately knew that something was wrong. This was not his room; there were others nearby, some of them moaning or thrashing in their sleep. He had to get out of here. Panicked, he sat up too quickly, and a wave of dizziness engulfed him, forcing him to lie back down. His movements woke someone sitting next to him, and a cool, soothing hand caressed his forehead. "It's alright, Donovan," said Rachel, "you just overdid it when you cast your Seeing spell. You're going to be fine."

"Where am I?" he asked, his voice harsh and raspy. "You're in the infirmary. You've been here for three days now," answered Rachel. "Thirsty," said Donovan. Rachel put her arm around his shoulders and helped him to sit up. She handed him a large mug of water, which she cooled before placing it in his hands. She put her hands over his to steady him. Donovan drank deeply. When he was finished, he handed the mug back to Rachel. "Thanks."

Rachel smiled and said, "I'm just glad you finally came around. We were getting worried. You have to get better at managing your power exertions," she said, taking his hand in hers. "I didn't realize I was using so much," said Donovan. "One minute, I was looking at a map, and the next thing I know, I wake up here with a pretty girl by my side." Rachel blushed.

"So, what were you looking for that took so much power?" she asked. "My father and the Royal Expeditionary Force," said Donovan. "Minister Jasmine said that they'd been ambushed and that many of them had been killed or injured." Rachel looked worried. "And what did you discover?" "That Jasmine is a liar," said Donovan angrily. "I located my father on a road half-way between Springfield and the Baizian capital, one company of the Expeditionary Force is in Springfield, and the other company is on the outskirts of Prarrieville." "Where's Springfield?" Rachel asked, confused. "It's a major Baizian city on the west side of the Amber River," said Donovan, stifling a yawn.

"You Sensed your father from that far away? That's incredible! No wonder it took so much power! Wizard Noland should have warned you!" said Rachel, releasing his hand and becoming angry. "About what?" asked Donovan. "That Sensing someone from so far away drains power from the conjurer far more than most of them realize," said Wizard Daniel, walking up behind

Rachel. "Awake at last, are we?" asked Daniel, putting his hand on Donovan's forehead. "No fever, that's good. How do you feel?"

"Like I was run over by a carriage," said Donovan, as he started to drift back to sleep. "NO!" shouted Daniel, clapping his hands together loudly. Donovan woke back up with a start. "Sorry, Donovan, but I can't have you falling back into unconsciousness just yet. It might be days before you awaken again. You need to stay awake for at least a glass. Then you can go back to sleep." Donovan thought as quickly as he could, then said, "Rachel, could you get me my blue nightshirt out of the closet in my room? This gown is itchy."

Rachel frowned, but Donovan said, "Please?" "All right," she said, "I'll be right back, Wizard Daniel. Will you watch him for me while I get his shirt?" "Certainly," said Daniel. As Rachel hurried out of the infirmary and down the stairs, Daniel gave Donovan a knowing look and said, "OK, she's gone. What did you want to ask me, that you didn't want your Mentor to hear?"

"Sir, um, ah, are there any Academy rules about a student dating his Mentor?" said Donovan shyly. Wizard Daniel laughed. "No. At least not in your case. You see, if there's a chance that a student won't be able to advance to the next level, and if he or she is romantically involved with their Mentor, there's a conflict of interest. You understand?" Donovan got the picture immediately. "In your case, I don't think we need to worry about that happening, but you do need Wizard Noland's permission." "I understand," said Donovan, dreading *that* conversation. Wizard Daniel seemed to read his mind, "Would you like me to ask him for you?"

"I appreciate the thought, Sir, but I think this is something I should do myself," said Donovan. "If you had given any other answer, I would have said that you were not serious enough or determined enough. I'm sure Wizard Noland will approve. Now, I expect Rachel back any second. Is there anything else you want to know about dating another magician?" "I think we have a few more minutes, sir. You see, my nightshirt is actually green; Rachel is going to have a hard time finding a blue one in my closet." Daniel laughed again, "You seem to have inherited your father's deviousness. What else can I answer for you?"

"What happens when two magicians are *involved* when they graduate? Do they get assigned together or split up? I know the military—" "First, you're getting way, way ahead of yourself. Second, Wizard Noland tries to ensure that *involved* magicians are assigned together, usually in the same Regional Mage's Office or the same city if one is posted to the Army. Assignments to the Royal Navy are more complicated." "Thank you, sir. I didn't know who else to ask." Just then, Rachel came tromping loudly up the stairs, carrying a blue nightshirt.

"Where could he be?" asked Azure, as she paced around the Cannery. "He has been gone way too long!" "Maybe he had to take a long way around to avoid the Enforcers or the Regional Mage," said Beau, "Or maybe the ship has been moved, and he had to look around some to find it. Give him some more time before you think the worst." "Maybe you are right," said Azure, "I have been a little grouchy lately." Gek was late, really late. He had departed before dawn, and it was almost midday now. Beau didn't want to worry Azure, but she was right; something must have gone terribly wrong this morning.

"I am going to send my sons out to look for Jed," he said, finally. "They are both human, and neither has the spark, so they are in no danger from the Regional Mage. I will have them check the docks and see if they can pick up any news of a disturbance this morning." Azure nodded gratefully, still concerned. Two hours later, when they returned, they did not have good news. First, the HMS VALOR was not in the port of Grotton; it must have sailed with the evening tide yesterday. Second, and more troubling, Beau's eldest son, Antwan, heard from a warehouse guard that a young man had been picked up by the Regional Mage and three Enforcers near the docks that morning and was probably already on his way to Kingston and the Wizards Academy.

"I am going after him," said Azure. "Which way is it to Kingston?" "Hold on just a second," said Beau, "It is a long trip to Kingston by coach, so you have plenty of time to catch them before they get there. You need to let them get a way out of the city first anyway." "Why?" asked Azure. "Because if you are seen by anyone in the city, the whole countryside will be out hunting for Dragons before nightfall. You need to be smart about this."

Azure was in the throes of a psychotic break. *How could Gek have been taken? How was she going to get him free? What would happen if they put him in the Wizards Academy? She needed to be doing something.* Fortunately, Beau had a much clearer head. "First, you need to calm your mind and stop thinking about the worst thing that can happen. Let us look at the facts: Gek was grabbed by the Regional Mage this morning; they are going to put him in a carriage and give him an escort to Kingston and the Wizards Academy; they are *not* going to hurt him; it is going to take a couple of days for them to get him to Kingston; and, lastly, you could fly to Kingston in about two hours, so we have plenty of time to devise a plan to get him free."

Over the next hour, they strategized. There was only one road from Grotton to Kingston, so no problem there. The carriage probably only had one driver and a single magic-user inside guarding Gek. Azure could knock the driver off the coach with a jet of water, then stop the carriage and deal with the magic-user. It was probably a good thing that Azure could not breathe fire, as that would not help at all.

She would need to get the magic-user with a jet of water before he or she could attack either of them. If she could free Gek, he could help with the magic-user. The coach was most likely made of wood, so talons or teeth could tear it open, but without knowing where Gek was inside, that was risky. They finally decided that Azure should wait on the edge of the Jade swamp for the carriage, since the road passed within sight of the swamp. Azure did not have fond memories of the swamp, but she decided that if another alligator tried to eat her, she would make a bag out of it to put her human clothes in. Beau said he was sorry that he could not come along to help but that he and the other Changed Ones were too old and they would just slow her down.

Once night fell, with a half moon to light her way, Azure transformed and headed north, towards the swamp. She had a carriage to catch.

Gek was truly miserable. After being frog-marched back to the Grotton Regional Mage's Office by the three Enforcers, with no opportunity to escape or even transform back into a dragon, he had been questioned for hours by the mage. *Where was he from? Did he have any family that should be notified? Did he have any practical use of his magic?* On and on. Gek kept insisting that he did not have the spark, had no family in Grotton, and had never done any magic, but the Mage was unconvinced.

"Once you get to the Wizards Academy, they'll bring out your spark. I think you'll find that being a magician is a much better life than working in a Cannery for a living," said Mage Charles. "In the meantime, the carriage should arrive any minute, and we'll get you on your way. It's a three-day, two-night ride to Kingston, so you'll have some time to reflect on your choices. We're really not such a bad lot after all. Ah, here's your escort," Mage Charles said, addressing the golden-haired young woman who entered the office, "Sorceress

Celeste, here's your first escort job as a member of the Grotton Regional Mage's Office; we found this young fellow here, wandering the docks this morning. He says his name is Jed. As I'm sure you can sense, he has the spark and we're sending him to the Academy. You will accompany him in the carriage. Don't harm him, but don't let him escape either. The carriage should be here soon. I'll give you two a moment to get acquainted while I check on your transportation."

The young magician took the chair next to Gek and said, "Hello, Jed. I know this is very sudden and unexpected. No one is going to hurt you, but we need to get you to the Wizards Academy, where you can be properly trained in how to use your magical abilities. I just left there a short time ago, and I can tell you that it's a wonderful place where you'll meet new friends, many of them, who arrive just like you will. It takes a while to adjust, but you'll be fine." Gek sat silently, not meeting the young magician's eyes. He wanted to protest that he did not have the spark, but that issue seemed to have been decided; he wanted to explain that he had a pregnant wife at home, but that would only draw attention to Azure. He just wanted to scream.

A few minutes later, a two-bench wooden carriage pulled up in front of the office. Mage Charles said, "In you go! I'll remove the manacles, so you'll be more comfortable, but we can't have you conjuring any magic, so Celeste, would you please cast a Paralysis spell as soon as I have them off, just so he can't cause you any problems?" Celeste nodded and prepared her spell. Gek anticipated Mage Charles coming closer to release the bindings holding his hands behind his back, so he readied himself to lunge forward, clap his hands, and transform. Charles said, *"DELERE,"* and flicked his hand at Gek. The manacles magically disappeared, but before Gek could move a muscle, Celeste said, *"LIGARE,"* making a fist with her left hand. Gek was instantly paralyzed from his neck to his toes. He sat on the bench, stunned by the speed of the spells. Charles saw the surprise on Gek's face. "Perhaps you thought we'd be slower, like we'd never done this before? Well, someday, you'll be able to do the same. Now, relax and enjoy the trip."

Celeste climbed into the carriage, taking the bench with her back to the driver, facing Gek. Mage Charles leaned in and said quietly, "Watch this one carefully. If I'm any judge of character, he's going to try and make a break for it before you reach Kingston. Keep him immobile all the way. Tether his arms when he has to relieve himself." Celeste nodded in understanding. "Once you deliver him to the Academy, spend a day in Kingston to rest the horses, then return. The driver knows where the relay stations are along the way, you'll change drivers every six hours, and there is food and drink for you at each stop. Feed him by hand. DO NOT RELEASE HIM FOR ANY REASON," emphasized the Mage. "I understand," said Celeste.

"We do this all the time," said Charles, "this is just your first trip of many to come. Goodbye, Jed. I hope to see you again someday under more pleasant circumstances." Gek could only glare at the Mage. Charles shut the carriage door and nodded to the driver, and they were on their way to the wizard's prison.

"Here's your stupid, blue, non-itchy nightshirt," said Rachel, throwing the shirt at Donovan. "Well, it seems that I'm no longer needed here," said Wizard Daniel. "Donovan, if you survive the night, I'll see you tomorrow in History class." Daniel hurried down the stairs, leaving an angry Rachel staring down at Donovan. "Now, what was all that about?" asked Rachel. "I needed to ask Wizard Daniel something in private," said Donovan, defensively. "I'm your Mentor! What could you possibly need to ask Wizard Daniel that you couldn't ask me?" Rachel raged. "I needed to ask Daniel," said Donovan, speaking slowly, suddenly unsure of himself, "whether Level Three magicians were allowed to date their Mentors." Rachel just stood there, completely but happily, surprised. *Will you have dinner with me tomorrow?* Donovan signed. *I would love to,* Rachel responded.

Wizard Timothy

Chapter Seven:
ROAD HAZARDS

"It seems that I am ordered to report to King Donald immediately and explain why I surrendered Springfield without a fight," said Wizard Timothy aloud. Wizard Edward, under his Concealment shield next to Specialist Dirk, cast a Silence spell and said to Dirk, "I'm going to drop my Concealment shield. Keep your cloak on; I don't want to expose both of us. I don't think this young man is much of a threat, but I don't want to take any chances. Stay concealed until I call for you." Dirk nodded his understanding as Edward murmured *"CODA"* and appeared next to Wizard Timothy.

The young courier started and quickly turned his mounts around, preparing to bolt. "I wouldn't if I were you," said Timothy. "We're on our way to see the King, so you might as well ride along with us. It's safer for you that way." The courier thought it over, then gave in to the situation. "Thank you," said Edward. "You wouldn't have gotten very far, but I'd hate to start our acquaintance by dumping you on the road, then having to heal your bruises. I am Wizard Edward, and I assure you, I mean you no harm."

The courier drew himself up to his full five-foot height and said, "I am Courier third-class Reginald Bronson, sir, and in the name of the King, I am placing you under arrest for the unlawful invasion of the Kingdom of Baize." Edward laughed loudly, and the young courier blushed red. "I understand your position, and rest assured, I shall inform King Donald of your courageous attempt to arrest me when we meet in a few days. When was the last time you watered your mounts?"

The question confused the courier, but he stammered, "It's been almost a day, Sir. The old watering hole just west of here has dried up. Their pretty thirsty." "Easily fixed," said Edward, dismounting. He proceeded to dig a shallow trench in the road, then added some water from his water bottle, then replicated it, filling the trough with water. The courier's horses drank eagerly, followed by Edward and Timothy's mounts. Edward refilled the trench with water and said, "We'll just leave this here for the next rider that comes along. It won't last too long, but someone else might appreciate it," said Edward, looking toward where Dirk was concealed. "Courier Reginald, if you guide us to the last dried-up watering hole, I might be able to do something about refilling it."

They headed back down the road, the courier completely intimidated, but glad to still be alive. "So,

Reggie," said Edward, "How long do you figure it will be until we meet the other couriers headed in our direction?" The courier thought for a moment, then replied, "I believe that I was two days ahead of them, so we should reach them by nightfall tomorrow." "And are they reasonable men?" asked Edward. "I'm not sure what you mean by 'reasonable,'" said Reggie. "I mean," said Edward, "are they going to hear us out, or are we going to have to restrain or kill them?"

The courier looked worried but considered the question. Finally, he said, "I have always found Senior Courier Keith to be most reasonable, sir, and Courier Paul, much less so." "Thank you for your candor, Reggie. I hope not to have to restrain or harm either of your companions; but our mission to your King is vital to both our Kingdoms and will brook no delay. You will find me a reasonable Wizard, but I do not suffer fools gladly, and I punish deceit harshly," said Edward.

The three rode west for the remainder of the day. Late in the afternoon, they came upon the dry watering hole the courier had mentioned. The still-moist patch of sand indicated that there was still a spring beneath the ground but that, over time, the ever-encroaching sand had covered the spring. Edward dismounted, used a Wind spell to blow much of the sand away from the top of the spring, then used a narrow Dig spell to reach the water below. Immediately, the water bubbled up, restoring the watering hole. After they had watered their mounts, Wizard Timothy said, "You know that the sand is just going to cover the spring again in a few weeks, a month at most." Edward considered Timothy's words. He walked to the edge of the spring and, combining the sand with an Adhesive spell, created a two-foot-high wall around the spring. "That should hold back the sand for a while," said Edward. "As long as travelers keep the sand from piling up and over-topping the barrier."

Wizard Timothy stared at the watering hole, impressed. "You have just helped the Kingdom more in a day, than the Royal Engineers have done in a decade." Edward nodded and said, "We'll do the same for any other watering holes we come across during our journey. How many are there?" he asked the courier. "There are nine more, each about a day's ride apart," said the courier. "Most are in better condition than this one." "I hope so; otherwise, I'm going to present the King with a bill for magical engineering support," said Edward. Timothy laughed.

"Is there a good place to camp for the night nearby, or should we just stay here?" asked Edward. They both looked at the courier for an answer. "Sirs, I wouldn't know," he said with a yawn. "I have ridden for the past two days without stopping." "We camp here then," said Edward, "If you two gather some firewood, I'll construct a permanent fire pit. This place might make a good Travelers Rest stop." Timothy and Reginald moved off to gather some firewood from the surrounding area while Edward built a small fire pit using the same technique he used to build the wall around the spring. Before long, they had a fire going, and the evening meal was bubbling in the cooking pot. The courier sat quietly, unsure what to make of the 'enemy magician' that was being so helpful. After they had eaten, Edward took the pot with the remaining food out to 'clean it' and left it on a flat rock nearby for Dirk. When he returned, the courier was already asleep, curled up by the fire.

"So, what do you think, Tim?" asked Edward. Timothy pondered a moment, then said, "I think the King wants answers quickly, and he deduced that a very young courier was less likely to be killed by myself or the Franconian troops. I suspect that the other two couriers are actually scouts, with orders to see what we do with the courier. I'll bet they're not nearly as far away as he thinks they are." "So, we'll see them tomorrow morning?" "Early tomorrow morning, would be my guess," said Timothy. "Should we meet them on the road or wait for them here?" "The road, I think. We should at least appear to be complying with my orders. I assume you're not going to just walk into the audience chamber with me to meet the King." "You're right about that. I haven't exactly figured out my plan yet, but it doesn't involve getting arrested or any other such nonsense," grinned Edward.

Edward told Timothy that he would take the first watch and awaken him at the first glass after midnight. As Timothy settled into a comfortable place by the fire, Edward walked out to speak with Dirk. "Timothy thinks that we'll meet the two trailing couriers early tomorrow morning. I intend to break camp at dawn and meet them on the road. Courier Reginald says that one of them is reasonable, and the other less so." "Do you want me to take care of the less reasonable one?" asked Dirk. "No," said Edward, "If I can't handle one unreasonable armsman, I need a new job. I suspect that we're going to run into much bigger problems once we get closer to Baize. I want to keep you as an ace up my sleeve. Just stay with us and listen as you can, but don't reveal yourself until I give you the word." "And if one of them tries to stick a knife in your back?" asked Dirk. "Then they'd better be able to get through my shields on the first stroke because they'll be dead before I turn around," said Wizard Edward.

The carriage bumped along the uneven road, jostling Gek. Being paralyzed, he was unable to brace himself when the carriage lurched from side to side or even stay seated when the wheels hit a rock in the road. To make matters worse, the annoying magician, Celeste, would not *shut up*. She kept droning on and on about how great the Wizards Academy was and how much Jed was going to enjoy his time there. It was enough to drive a Dragon mad. Gek was also very concerned about what was happening at the Cannery. By now, Azure and the others must have realized that something had gone wrong when he had not returned. *Would they go into town to look for him?* Gek hoped not. The Regional Mage seemed very adept at finding those with the spark. He also worried that the Mage would visit the Cannery and discover the other Changed Ones. *What a mess!*

When they stopped at the first way-station to change drivers and horses, Celeste released the Paralysis spell, tethered Gek's arms to his sides, and helped him climb down from the carriage. She led him a short distance into the woods and, to his great embarrassment, made the adjustments to his trousers so that he could relieve himself. How humiliating. After a short break, they were back in the carriage. Celeste fed him some cooked chicken pieces and gave him a drink from a water bottle. The carriage rumbled on through the night, and Gek drifted off into a restless sleep.

As the sun broke the eastern sky, Gek roused. Celeste was nodding, still half asleep, but her Paralysis spell was still as strong as ever. Gek struggled against his bonds, but nothing worked. "You'll only weaken yourself by struggling like that," said Celeste. "The Paralysis spell, once cast, requires no energy from me and is unbreakable except by the most powerful Wizards. Are you hungry?" "No," said Gek. "How much further?" "Well, we're approaching the southern edge of the Jade Swamp, so we're almost halfway there. We should be in Kingston by noon tomorrow."

Suddenly, there was a cry from the driver as he was flung from his seat and went sailing into the trees alongside the road. The horses bolted in terror at the sight of the dragon in their path. They careened down the road, weaving from one side to the other as the frightened horses each tried to escape in the opposite direction. The carriage tilted, first to one side, then the other, balancing on two wheels, then slamming down hard as the horses changed course again.

Above the chaos, Azure cursed. She got the driver as planned, but the damn horses would not stop. No matter what she tried, they just sped on, going faster and more recklessly as they tried to escape the dragon. She was afraid that the carriage was going to overturn and injure Gek if she did not do something fast. Out of other ideas, Azure used the Dig spell to create a ditch in front of the horses. She figured that that would surely stop them. She was right. The pair of horses hit the ditch, breaking their front legs and sending the carriage airborne over them until it slammed into the ground upside down.

"Haul that line, you laggards!" bellowed the Captain of the HMS COMFORT, "Get that mast in place! We don't have all day!" Repairs to the COMFORT were underway but a long way from complete. The damage had been much worse than the Admiral had known. When Commodore Matthews and the HMS VALOR and the other two ships had arrived in the port city of Sundock, the COMFORT was still taking on water, all three of her masts were broken, and lines and rigging crisscrossed the deck, making footing treacherous. Without a magician to help with repairs, it was all the exhausted crew could do to work the manually operated bilge pumps to keep the ship from sinking.

A day later, the ship was sitting high in the water and was no longer in danger of sinking. Newly promoted Mage Andrew and the two Sorcerers from the VICEROY and the VICTORY had completed repairs to the hull and rudder of the ship and removed some of the tangled rigging. All that remained was to get the masts back in place and re-rig the sails. The crew was attempting to hoist the main mast up and into the hole in the deck, where it would slide down through the lower decks and be secured. As the crew maneuvered the hoist over the opening for the mast, the straps slipped, and the mast began sliding towards the deck and the sailors below.

Thinking quickly, Andrew ran towards the mast, murmuring *'FORTIS'* and flexing his right arm. When the bottom of the mast reached him, he grabbed hold of it, slowing its descent. As he guided it into the opening, he yelled for the other Sorcerers to conjure Strength Enhancements and help him. The three magicians together managed to align the mast with the opening, and slide the mast into position (if a little faster than recommended). The sailors raised a rousing cheer for the magicians and quickly secured the mast in place.

Commodore Matthews had a few choice words for the crew manning the hoist, then quickly made his way over to Andrew. "Are you all right?" "Yes, Captain, just a few scrapes and splinters," said Andrew, displaying his raw and bleeding hands and forearms. "I'm sure that one of these fine Sorcerers will be able to heal my injuries in no time." "That's the damnedest thing I've ever seen," said the Commodore quietly, "I thought that mast was going to punch a hole right through the keel. That was quick thinking and boneheaded at the same time. Did you know that you could lift something that heavy?"

"I didn't *lift* it, sir; I just slowed and directed its fall. That mast is much too heavy for me to lift, even with a Strength Enhancement spell. It was fortunate that the other two Sorcerers were here to help me." The Commodore grunted his agreement. "And what if you hadn't been able to get the end into the opening?" he asked. "I was planning to toss it over the side," said Andrew reasonably. "I assume it would float, and we'd just have to try again." Commodore Matthews just shook his head in amazement. "You're something else, Andrew. You keep doing stuff like that, and the crew will think you can do anything. Go get yourself healed; we still have work to do."

As the Commodore moved aft to supervise the installation of the next mast, Andrew sank down onto a pile of rope. He took a long pull from his water bottle and asked Sorcerer Marvin to please heal his injuries. A few minutes later, he was good as new but as tired as he had ever been. Andrew had been using a Wind spell for the past few days to get the VALOR to Sundock as quickly as possible. The other Sorcerers had similarly used their skills to increase the speed of the VICEROY and the VICTORY to keep up. They had arrived in Sundock last night and immediately begun assisting in the repairs to the COMFORT.

As Andrew sat resting and recovering his strength, a young sailor approached carrying a large burlap sack, "Sorcerer Andrew?" he asked, clearly awed by what he had just witnessed. "Mage Andrew, actually," replied Andrew. "What can I do for you?" "Sir, this parcel was just delivered by coach. It is addressed to Sorcerer Andrew Perrucci, HMS VALOR. Is that you, sir?" "It is indeed. I wonder who would be sending me parcels," said Andrew wearily. He took the bulky sack from the sailor and tried to open it. The draw string wouldn't budge. Confused, Andrew tried again, using more force; nothing. It must be sealed with magic, he decided, *'DELERE,'* he mumbled, flicking his right hand at the top of the bag. With the top of the bag cleanly removed, Andrew was able to extract a crossbow from the sack. With it was a note from Wizard Noland.

Andrew, Congratulations on your promotion to Battle Mage. I hereby confirm the actions of Admiral Cross. Enclosed, find a crossbow. Replicate as many as you can for the sailors assigned to the HMS VALOR, and the other members of the Squadron. They may come in handy.

Noland,
Headmaster
Franconian Wizards Academy

P.S. It might interest you to know that Donovan has passed his test for advancement to Level Three and is currently dating his Mentor, Rachel.

M.N.

Andrew read the last part again and smiled. Commodore Matthews walked up and asked, "What's that?" pointing to the crossbow. "It's a crossbow, sir. Wizard Noland sent it to me from the Wizards Academy, although how he knew I'd be in Sundock is beyond me." "So, what's a crossbow?" "It's a new weapon that allows non-magicians to kill dragons, sir. It fires these heavy iron arrows with incredible force, enough to penetrate a dragon's scales. It's what the Royal Expeditionary Force used to kill that dragon that was terrorizing the farmers north of Farmdale," explained Andrew.

"Helpful, but I doubt that just one is going to make much of a difference," said the Commodore. "Sir, I—I mean we," said Andrew, looking at the other two Sorcerers, "are going to replicate a crossbow for every man in the squadron."

What could be keeping that boy? wondered Wizard Louis. It had been over two weeks now, and no one fitting Stephen's description had been seen on the road from Middleberg to Baize. *Did he suffer some kind of accident, or just get lost? How could he get lost? There was only one road between the two cities! Brigands?* Louis supposed it was possible; the roads were not as safe as they had once been. Louis decided that he would wait one more day, then send out a search party. *That boy had to be somewhere!*

Stephen was actually still a week away from Baize. At least going at the pace he had been maintaining for the past two weeks. *This was ridiculous! If Wizard Louis was walking, Stephen should have overtaken him by now.* Tomorrow, he would pick up the pace. Mage Elianna couldn't wait forever to get this message through. The closer he got to Baize, the more worried Stephen became. *How was he going to sneak into the city without Wizard Louis knowing? What if he went cross-country and reached Baize by river transport? The Green River was close now. That might be smarter. But what about the horse?* Stephen eventually decided that he would trade the horse for river transport. He was close enough now, so that it would be a favorable trade for any boatmen on the river.

Stephen decided that he could always buy another horse for the return trip to Middleberg or go back by boat, for that matter. Maybe Wizard Louis had also cut across and entered Baize by boat. Stephen kicked himself for not thinking of that possibility sooner.

As the 2nd Company of the Royal Expeditionary Force entered Prarrieville, Major Gerald breathed a sigh of relief. He'd been more worried than he'd let on about heading home with no magical support. *How had it ever come to this?* He wondered. Before Mage Edward accompanied them in search of the dragon, the Royal Expeditionary Force had *never* had magical support. Now, he couldn't think of starting a campaign without it. *Times change*, he thought.

Captain Brock, the commander of the 11th Battalion, rode out to meet Major Gerald. "Welcome back, sir! Did you have any luck?" "If you call being ambushed in a narrow pass by seven Fire dragons lucky, then yes, we had lots of luck," said Major Gerald wearily. Captain Brock sat back on his mount, shocked. "How bad were your losses?" he asked, scanning the lone company of the Royal Expeditionary Force.

"We lost two men; the other company remained in Springfield with Mage Curtis. I'll explain later; right now, I need to get the men some hot chow and see to our horses. Not necessarily in that order. Then we need some rest; it's been quite an expedition."

Captain Brock sent a messenger to the kitchen, ordering them to prepare an early dinner for the returning soldiers, then led the company to the garrison stables where they could feed and groom their mounts while dinner was being prepared. After they had cared for their horses and eaten a hot meal, the soldiers of the Expeditionary Force headed into the garrison for a good night's sleep. It was the first time they had not had to post a watch in several weeks, and the men were grateful for the respite.

Over the next two days, the Royal Expeditionary Force rested in Prarrieville. They replaced worn or lost horseshoes, mended torn clothing, sharpened dulled swords and spears, and repaired damaged armor. Major Gerald described what had happened to the Force since their departure from Prarrieville to the Regimental Commander and assembled Battalion and Company commanders. He assured them that there were no Baizian soldiers in Springfield, ready to attack Franconia. After the assembled officers left to attend to their duties, Major Gerald took the 1st Regimental commander aside and explained Wizard Edward's conclusion that the dragons were trying to get the humans to fight each other, so they could attack when the humans were weakened from the struggle.

The Regimental commander agreed that it was a complex plan, but also feasible. He understood why Wizard Edward was going to Baize to try and convince King Donald not to order an invasion of Franconia. As he was leaving the commander's office, Major Gerald asked if he could recruit two men from the 1st Regiment to replace his losses. The commander agreed and told Gerald to select any two soldiers in the Regiment. Gerald informed him that there were very specific requirements to be in the Royal Expeditionary Force: a soldier had to have been in the guard for at least five years, be able to read and swim and be able to ride well. The commander said that there were only a few men in the cavalry squadron that met all of those qualifications and that he would send them to Major Gerald for him to pick from. Major Gerald expressed his thanks and headed out to check on his men.

Later that afternoon, three soldiers approached Major Gerald, having been sent by the Regimental Commander for possible assignment to the Royal Expeditionary Force. After interviewing them, Major Gerald selected Sergeant Cooper and Corporal Sleet. The Major had no idea that Corporal Sleet was a Snow Dragon Changed One.

Sorceress Celeste

Chapter Eight:
HEALING

"No! No! No!" Azure screamed as she landed next to the upside-down carriage. Using her talons, she gently ripped the door off its hinges and threw it into the woods. Gek lay on the ceiling on the far side of the carriage, his body contorted unnaturally and blood dripping from a gash on his head; the unconscious body of Sorceress Celeste was draped across Gek's legs. Unable to get into the battered carriage in Dragon form, Azure quickly transformed into a human and crawled inside. With Celeste unconscious, the Paralysis spell was broken, and Azure was able to pull Gek outside, onto the grass by the roadside.

"Gek! Gek! Can you hear me?" she shouted frantically, trying to rouse him from his stupor. Gek stirred slowly, then screamed in pain. Azure tried to keep him from thrashing around, afraid that he would cause further injury to himself. "What can I do?" cried Azure. "Gek, I am so sorry! I just wanted to stop the horses! I had no idea it would cause the carriage to overturn! How can I help you?"

Gek grimaced through the pain. "I think my shoulder is broken, maybe some of my ribs too. Something in here," he said, pointing to his chest, "feels wrong, and my head is spinning." A fit of coughing racked his body, and he sprayed blood and mucous on the grass. He was growing pale and weak. Azure was frantic, unsure of what to do to help him.

"Help me out of this coach, and I'll try to heal him," rasped Sorceress Celeste. Azure looked up, seeing the young magician crawling forward through the shattered carriage towards them. Not knowing what else to do, Azure scrambled over and dragged her out of the carriage. As Celeste knelt by Gek's side she murmured, '*SALVARE,*' while placing both of her hands on Gek's chest. Gek's breathing immediately eased, and his color returned. Celeste slumped to the ground next to Gek. As she lay there, she whispered, "In my handbag, there is a vial of Healing Serum. Have him drink it slowly. Don't let him eat anything; it will only make him sick up."

Azure scrambled back inside the ruined carriage, searching desperately for whatever a 'handbag' was. Eventually, she located a brightly colored satchel that contained some feminine personal items, a hair brush, and a small vial of liquid in a padded case. Azure quickly returned to Gek's side and raised his head so he could sip the liquid from the vial. Miraculously, the gash on his head closed, and the bleeding stopped, and his shoulder resumed its natural (for a human) shape.

Azure sobbed with relief, as she turned to thank the young Sorceress, the carriage driver came rushing up. "Did you see it?" he asked, looking around frantically. "I swear it was a dragon! It came out of nowhere and knocked me off my seat with a blast of water! I'm lucky I landed in a bog, or I might have broken something! Wait, why aren't you wearing any clothes?" the still-dazed driver asked Azure. *'INCOGITA,'* said Azure, moving her left hand from left to right with her palm down. The driver slumped into a deep sleep. Gek smiled, "I never thought we would get any use out of that spell."

"You're Changed Ones, aren't you?" asked Celeste, groggily.

Stephen moved cautiously along the narrow trail. It was really no more than a footpath, worn down by fishermen who traped up and down the riverbank, looking for the best spot to catch fish. Stephen was leading his horse because the trail was narrow and muddy. The last thing he wanted to do was have the horse slip and fall into the river.

Eventually, he came to a spot with a wide embankment, where a barge could put into shore and load cargo and passengers. Stephen settled down to wait by the slow-flowing river. It wasn't long before a half-empty flat-bottomed barge came around the bend upriver. Stephen waved excitedly at the boatmen on the barge, but they just waved back.

Before the barge passed him, Stephen conjured a Tether spell, grabbing the barge. The current moved the ship to the riverbank, despite the urgent efforts of the boatmen to stay in the river channel. Once the boat was grounded on the riverbank, Stephen approached and said, "Good morning, gentlemen. My name is Stuart, and I'm heading for Baize. Do you suppose that I could purchase passage on your fine vessel? I understand it isn't far."

The eldest man said, "We don't usually take passengers. Especially with mounts, but I guess for three silvers, we could give you a lift to Baize." "Three silvers," temporized Stephen, "That's a bit more than I have. How about a trade? I will give you this fine horse in exchange for a ride to Baize." The man looked at Stephen suspiciously. The horse was worth almost a gold, far more than the cost of a short ride downriver. "He isn't injured or stolen, is he?"

"No, Sir," said Stephen, "but once I get to Baize, the cost of feeding and stabling him will be more than I can afford. I'd rather get something of value for him before

I have to sell him for less than the three silvers you are offering." The man considered the offer, then said, "Climb aboard! Has the horse ever been on a barge before?"

"I really couldn't say, Sir," replied Stephen. "You see, I won him in a card game in Middleberg, so I haven't had him very long." "You came from Middleberg? Why didn't you take a boat all the way?" "I thought riding would be fun. Instead, I find that my thighs are chapped and my bottom bruised. I would much rather drift down the river without all the bouncing." The boatman laughed and said, "Come aboard then. Just lead him off the bank and onto the barge."

Once the horse was secured, the boatmen used long poles to push the barge back into the mainstream (after Stephen released the Tether spell). "How long to Baize?" Stephen asked. "About four hours," said the boatman. "We'll have you on the dock in Baize in no time."

Ard sat on the bench overlooking the port and did not know what to do. *Beverley lived next to the Regional Mage's Office.* That meant that there would be magic-users coming and going at all hours of the day and night. Staking out her apartment was out of the question. The risk of being discovered was just too great. *If she stays at home, she is probably safe,* he thought. *No dragon in their right mind would attack someone that close to a magic-user's office.* Maybe he should just go back to the quarry and await the next meeting of the Dragon Council. *Still, what if a Changed One harmed her, even accidentally?* He sat and pondered his dilemma all night. As the sun rose in the east, he heard the slow plodding steps of Joe, heading down to the pier to start his day. He seemed slower today, as if some great weight was burdening him.

Ard rose and greeted him tiredly, "Good morning, Joe. How are you today?" "I'm a broken man, Alan," said Joe sadly. "Beverley died in her sleep last night. I knew she was ailing, but I didn't know how bad it was. The Regional Mage had been helping her with healing, but eventually, old age catches up with all of us. I'm just really sad that this happened so close to my retirement. We never got to just sit here together and watch the boats. She loved that."

Ard was both sad and relieved at Beverley's passing. On the one hand, there was no need for his presence here any longer and no threat to the Dragon Council from his Binding spell, at least not where she was concerned. On the other hand, he felt empathy for Joe. Ard knew what it was like to lose someone you loved. Finally, he rose and said, "I am sorry, Joe. Beverley was a good woman. I will miss her company."

"Would you sit with me for a while?" asked Joe. "I just don't want to be alone right now." "Of course," replied Ard. And so, they sat there, the old man and the ancient dragon, watching the sunrise.

"I do not know what you mean," said Azure, seizing the driver's cloak to cover herself. "I think you do," replied Celeste. "I thought 'Jed' here smelled funny, but I wrote it off to his working in a Cannery. I mean, I've never smelled a dragon before." *"INCOGITO?"* said Gek, hopefully, performing the gesture.

"Stop that!" said Celeste, "I just saved your life. That's not very appreciative." Gek looked at Azure and shrugged. "It was worth a try," she said. "So, it's true, you are magic-using dragons, transformed to look like humans," said Celeste, "I'm not hallucinating or anything."

"The question is: What do we do with you now?" said Gek. "Well, if there's any of that Serum left, I could use a drop or two. My leg is broken, and it's very painful," said Celeste, hopefully. Azure handed over the not-quite-empty vial of Healing Serum, and Celeste drank down the last few drops, grimacing as she did. "Ugh, it tastes as bad as I remembered. I had hoped not to need any of that ever again."

"You have had it before?" asked Azure, conversationally. "Yes," replied Celeste, "at the Wizards Academy, we have to test our Serums on ourselves, to see if they work. It's an effective teaching method, but Healing Serum still tastes bad. I guess it's worth it, though, because, as you can see, my leg is healed. So, I take it that you're not like the Changed Ones we found at the Academy, who prefer to remain as humans."

"Definitely not," said Gek and Azure together. "I see," said Celeste, sadly. "So where does that leave us?" Gek thought for a moment, "Well, you did save my life, so killing you would be *ungrateful*, to say the least. Still, you are a human magic-user and our sworn enemy." "Why is that?" asked Celeste, "Why do we have to be enemies?"

"A magic-user killed my mother! Your ancestors slaughtered most of our race through treachery two centuries ago!" shouted Gek. "Is there no hope of reconciliation, then?" asked Celeste. "I am sorry for what happened to your ancestors, but *I* am only 22 winters old. I had nothing to do with the poisoning of the cattle!" said Celeste forcefully. Softening her tone, she continued, "And I believe that you're mistaken; Sir Edward did *not* kill your mother. It was a member of the Royal Expeditionary Force."

Though still angry, Gek paused to consider her words. Finally, he said, "I am not sure there can ever be peace between humans and Dragons, but for saving my life, I name you a Dragon-friend. When the war comes, we will try to spare you harm. Now, we must depart."

"I wouldn't recommend changing form so soon after healing," advised Celeste. "While your injuries are mending, complete healing takes several days, maybe even more for a dragon." "What about him?" said Azure, pointing to the carriage driver. "He saw me." "I'll place a Secrecy spell on him, so that he can't tell anyone what he saw," said Celeste. "I'll say that brigands dug a trench across the road to waylay passing coaches. We were injured in the crash, and when we awoke, you were gone," she said, pointing at Gek.

"The need for such secrecy has passed. You may tell everyone that, or the truth, that a Sea Dragon attacked and rescued her mate, a Great Dragon Changed One. The choice is yours," said Gek. "In any event, we should be going before someone comes." "Wait!" said Celeste, "Before you go, may I have your names, please?" Azure looked at Gek and nodded. Gek said, "I am Gek, and I am a Great Dragon; this is Azure, and she is a Sea Dragon." "It is nice to meet you both," said Celeste.

Azure quickly changed into Dragon form, and Gek gingerly climbed aboard her back, just above her wings. Celeste stood, awestruck at the sight. "Goodbye, Celeste. If there are more magic-users like you, there may be hope for a reconciliation someday. But it is not today." As Azure flew off into the afternoon sun, with Jed/Gek clinging to her back, Celeste waved goodbye, cast her Secrecy spell on the driver, and then fainted again.

Andrew finished replicating the last crossbow and set it aside. The ship's Quartermaster would pick up the last few shortly, and then everyone in the crew would have one. He hoped that they would make a difference in the coming fight. As he sat in his cabin thinking, an idea occurred to him. *What if I made them bigger?* A larger crossbow, firing larger bolts with even greater force, might be useful. The ones he had in mind would be too big and cumbersome for the Army but could easily fit on the deck of a ship. Should he ask the

Commodore or wait until he made one, just in case it didn't work.

No. He would have to try this up on deck. A crossbow as big as the one he was imagining would not fit through his narrow cabin door, and if he started working on this on deck, the crew would gather around to see what he was doing, and before long, the Commodore would be there. *Might as well ask him first.* Andrew headed up on deck, carrying his just-replicated crossbow; he found the Commodore supervising the loading of foodstuffs into the hold. He turned as Andrew approached.

"Good morning, Mage. How are you today? Ready to get underway?" Andrew reconsidered the wisdom of what he was doing, then said, "Sir, I know that Admiral Cross wanted us patrolling the Coral Islands yesterday, but could we delay our departure for a couple of days? I have an idea that might help us against the dragons." "This idea of yours better be a game-changer if I'm to delay for that long. What do you have in mind?"

"Well, sir, I was thinking, 'What if these crossbows were bigger?' Say four or five times the size of a standard crossbow, and they fired harpoon-sized bolts? I mean, we know that standard crossbow bolts will penetrate a dragon's scales, but bigger bolts, fired with even more power, might be even more effective."

"Hmm," the Commodore thought, "Where would we put 'em?" "I could mount them on the deck amidship, maybe one on each side. It'll probably take a crew of three or four men to use it, though." "Why?" "Sir, these bolts are going to be heavy, and I'm going to have to work out some type of crank system, like we use on the hoists, to pull back the drawstring. I'll mount the bow on some kind of swiveling platform so it can traverse from side to side and elevate up and down, depending on whether the dragon is flying or swimming. I figure it'll take one man to load the bolt, one strong man or a magician with a Strength Enhancement to draw the string, one man to aim, and someone, probably an officer, to give the order to fire," said Andrew. "Why an officer?" "Sir, these bolts are going to be a real pain to make, and we aren't going to have many, at least not initially, and once fired, hit or miss, that bolt is gone forever."

"How long is this going to take?" "Enlarging this crossbow will take minutes," said Andrew. "Working out the swiveling platform and the crank system may take a while. I could use some help from the ship's carpenter and an engineer, plus the other Sorcerers." "And you can't do this underway?" "Sir, I'm not sure I can do this *at all*, much less bobbing around on the high seas," said Andrew reasonably.

The Commodore thought it over, then said, "Three days. If it works, fine; if not, we work on it enroute." "Thank you, Commodore. I'll gather the help I need. I'd appreciate it if you could keep the rest of the crew from interrupting us while we work. I know they're going to be curious about what we're doing." The Commodore smiled and said, "That, I can handle. By the way, what are you going to call these contraptions? They're not really crossbows." "How about Seabows?" asked Andrew. "I like it," said Commodore Matthews.

For the rest of the day and into the night, Andrew, the Sorcerers from the VICEROY, and the VICTORY, along with the four ship's carpenters, all worked quickly to fashion what Andrew had in mind. First came a circular platform, that sat on an enormous dowel and a ring of greased ball bearings. The platform was constructed to swivel 180 degrees from left to right. In the center of the platform was a pedestal with a fork at the top with a steel rod through the middle. There was a hole in the Seabow beam that the rod fit through, allowing the Seabow to elevate and depress. The bow itself was eight feet long, four times the size of a standard crossbow.

The biggest challenge was figuring out a way to draw and hold the bowstring. The steel bow was incredibly stiff, and Andrew had to experiment with several different types of steel to get one that would flex and then spring back into shape without just bending under tremendous pressure. Once they had that problem solved, they found that it took two men to man the crank and draw the Seabow. They also had to devise a way to lock the Seabow into place while they were drawing the bow.

At a glass past midnight, Andrew ordered the others to bed, with instructions not to return until after they had had a hot breakfast in the morning. Andrew stayed up a few minutes longer, tinkering with the gear mechanism, but soon retired to his cabin. He was concerned about how they were going to test the weapon without wasting too many bolts, which he assumed were going to be difficult to replicate. When he awoke the next morning, he had a possible solution. He rushed on deck, found the Bos'n and asked him to bring up a 100-foot long coil of thin rope. Once the rope arrived, he fastened one end to the back of the steel bolt.

By now, several of the crew were gathered around and the carpenters and Sorcerers had returned. Andrew had them practice several dry-runs, stringing, swiveling, and firing the Seabow without the bolt loaded. Once they had the process down and the rough edges of the device smoothed out, Andrew called the Commodore over to witness their first test.

"What do you plan to use for a target?" asked Commodore Matthews. "I thought we might throw an empty barrel over the side and use it for target practice," said Andrew. "Sounds good to me," said the Commodore. A few minutes later, an empty flour barrel was heaved over the side, but it simply bobbed up and down a few feet away from the hull of the VALOR. Eventually, they had to launch a longboat to grab the barrel and tow it farther out, away from the ship. Once the longboat and crew were back on board, they were ready for the test.

Andrew locked the Seabow in place and a bulky crewman wound the crank handle, drawing the bowstring. Once it was locked in place, another crewman hefted the iron bolt into position in the groove on top of the Seabow. Andrew made sure that everyone was clear of the coil of rope on the deck beside the weapon, then took aim at the barrel, allowing for the bolt to drop in flight. The incoming waves were making it difficult to stay on the target, as the barrel bobbed up and down with each new wave. Finally, Andrew took his best guess and pulled the lever, releasing the bowstring.

The bolt shot from the Seabow with blinding speed, overshooting the floating barrel by at least ten feet. The bolt landed in the water twenty feet beyond the barrel and immediately sank out of sight. The rope attached to the bolt played out rapidly, and Andrew realized that he had failed to secure the other end of the rope to the ship before firing. He quickly cast an Adhesive spell, gluing the rope to the deck. Once the rope was all played out, Andrew asked a sailor to haul the bolt back onto the deck so they could try again. It took four tries to hit the barrel. Andrew had to compensate not only for the bobbing of the target but also for the movement of the ship. At sea, this was going to be even more difficult.

The Commodore walked over to Andrew and said, "You certainly obliterated that barrel once you finally hit it. But it took you long enough." "Yes, sir," said Andrew, "but part of that was the delay in retrieving the arrow, and the crew is still getting used to how the Seabow works. With a bit of practice, I think it will work." "What will you do with the time you have left?" "Now that we have a working prototype, the other Sorcerers can replicate this Seabow. Once we get one on each ship, we can make more while we're underway," said Andrew.

"And just how in blazes do you think you're going to get something that big and heavy to the other ships once you replicate it," asked the Commodore. Andrew smiled. "Sir, once we get them replicated, I can use a Reduce spell to shrink them down to pocket size if I need to. Getting them to the other ships won't be a problem. With enough time for replication, we could make one for every ship in the fleet. Then, their Sorcerers could Enlarge them and Replicate their own. We might need to send someone to the other ships to train them on how to use them.

"How long will it take to replicate one?" "It takes about an hour to replicate a normal crossbow," said Andrew. "This is much bigger and more complicated, say about five hours for each replica. If we make four, one for each of the other ships in the squadron, then leave one here with the Regional Mage. He can start replicating them and give them to the other ships in the fleet when they make port. We should also give him a regular crossbow to replicate for the other crews." "You know, Andrew, you may just have saved the entire Fleet with these," said the Commodore gratefully.

"Sir, just remember to send a message to the Admiral and the Chief of Naval Wizardry. They should probably start equipping the Second Fleet with these also," said Andrew. "Are you still worried about not telling Admiral Cross about the dragons?" asked Commodore Matthews. Andrew nodded. "Stop worrying about it. There was nothing he could have done about it if he'd known, and your idea about the ensigns has probably saved a lot of Franconian ships. This idea with the Seabows will probably get you promoted to Wizard." Andrew smiled.

Chapter Nine:
SIGNS

"**K**iss me," said Donovan. Rachel gave him a passionate kiss, then said, "Fail. A Compulsion spell should be used to make someone do something they don't want to do, not something I've wanted to do all morning." It was Endday morning, and Donovan was undergoing his Mentor testing to determine if he had mastered the spells and enhancements he had received instruction on during the week. This week, he had learned the Compulsion spell. The incantation was *'NECESSITAS,'* and the motion was crossing your fingers on your left hand. The spell was intended to compel someone to do something they were either neutral about or opposed to doing.

"I understand," said Donovan, with a smile, "but I haven't cast my spell yet. "I just wanted a kiss. *'NECESSITAS,'* he murmured, crossing his fingers, "don't slap me." Rachel glared and said, "I ought to slap you, but I choose to be flattered instead." "Then my spell worked," said Donovan. "What spell?" asked Rachel. "My Compulsion spell, for you not to slap me." "Well, in that case, Pass," said Rachel, smiling.

Donovan and Rachel had been dating for a couple of weeks now, and it was wonderful. Donovan had forgotten how much he enjoyed female companionship in the almost two years he'd been at the Wizards Academy. Dating Rachel, his Mentor, had also curtailed all of the attention Donovan had been receiving from the other Level Three girls. Rachel made it clear to them that Donovan was 'hers' and to keep their hands off. They got the message almost immediately, and while they remained cordial, there were no more requests to play Blind-Man's-Bluff from any of them.

Donovan had not even thought about pursuing a romantic relationship with anyone since he'd arrived at the Academy. At first, he'd been too focused on learning magic in order to kill dragons, but his hatred of them had softened of late. *Maybe they just wanted to survive, like we do.* He decided. But he had more time now; while the Level Three spells and Serums were much more deadly than any others he had learned, there were fewer of them. He only had four Enhancements, six Force spells to learn, and three Serums (Love, Healing-Mortal wounds, and Death).

The Serums were complicated, and a mixture of ingredients and incantations and getting them just right was difficult. All except the Death Serum, that is. That was just Belladonna juice, with a Concealment spell to make the liquid clear, a Smell spell to make it odorless, and a Stamina Spell to make it last. Death Serums were difficult to test (for lack of volunteers). They were only used on injured or infirm horses in the stable or on prisoners scheduled for execution. In those cases, the Serum was mixed in with their last meal, either in their food or drink.

At least it was more merciful than being hanged or beheaded. It was also safer for the executioners, since prisoners condemned to death often became violent when being led to the gallows or the block. At least, it was easier when the Serum worked. There were rumors of some Serums that had failed, either just putting the convict to sleep or, in one case, making him extremely violent. In that case, the Serums instructor had used a Death spell and ended the rampage.

"So, now that you have passed your Endday testing, what would you like to do this afternoon?" asked Rachel, taking his hand in hers. "Believe it or not, I thought we could go visit your father this afternoon," said Donovan tentatively. Rachel beamed. "Do you know how different you are from the other students here?" she asked. Donovan shook his head, confused, "No, what are you talking about?" "Most students that are *dating* slip off on Enddays to anyplace with some privacy and a flat surface," she teased. "I've never heard of a boy asking to meet his girlfriend's parents."

"First," said Donovan, "I wasn't planning on spending the whole afternoon with them, and second, I have a house in town, and my father is a thousand miles away," said Donovan with a lecherous grin. "Maybe you are like the other boys after all," said Rachel with a willing smile. "Let's go."

They left the gatehouse and walked through the city hand-in-hand, until they came to a tailor shop on Queen Street, near the Kingston military garrison. As they entered the shop, Donovan noticed that the lantern on the stand near the door dimmed, then brightened again as the door closed and the draft from outside subsided. *Clever*, thought Donovan. The lantern allowed the owner to know when a customer entered, even though he could not hear the door open and close.

A middle-aged man in a blue apron entered from the back room. He smiled when he spied Rachel and signed, *Rachel! How wonderful to see you! Who is this fine young man?* Rachel said, slowly, "Father, this is my boyfriend, Donovan. Donovan, this is my father, Brian Turner." *It is very nice to meet you, sir,* signed Donovan. *Rachel has told me so much about you. This is a fine shop you have.* Mr. Turner beamed at Donovan's signing skills.

How long have you been teaching him? he signed to Rachel. *Only a few months. He is a fast learner.* Mr.

Turner waved them into the back room, where he had a work table and a few mannequin forms for assembling various types of clothing. He had racks with bolts of cloth in every texture and color, spools of threat, and rolls of paper. "What is the paper for?" asked Donovan, curious.

"My father uses it to cut out forms and pieces for clothing, then he cuts the fabric to match the paper, then sews the pieces together," explained Rachel. Donovan walked around, examining the material and the sewing equipment, while Rachel and her father signed more rapidly than he could follow. He assumed they were talking about him, and he chose not to interrupt their conversation. After a few minutes, Donovan said, "I'm thirsty. Is there any tea around here?" Rachel asked her father, who indicated that there was a kettle on the fire upstairs in the living quarters. He volunteered to go make the tea, but Rachel forestalled him and said she would be right back with tea for all of them.

As soon as Rachel headed up the stairs, Donovan signed to Mr. Turner that he wanted to commission a nice set of dress clothes, for his dates with Rachel, just in case he wanted to take her someplace really special. Mr. Turner frowned, then signed that such an outfit would be costly, and he knew that Academy students were rarely wealthy enough to afford such luxury. Donovan smiled and signed that he was one of those rare students that came from a prosperous home and that he could afford whatever the cost would be for three sets of formal wear and a dress cape that would go with any of the outfits.

Mr. Turner sat back, shocked, *I don't think you understand,* he signed, *such an order would cost almost five golds!* Donovan reached into his money pouch and extracted six golds. He handed them over quickly and signed: *Use the extra to make something nice for Rachel.*

When Rachel returned with the tea, Donovan was standing on the fitting platform, and Brian was taking his measurements. "What's going on?" she asked. "I've asked your father to make me some nicer clothes," said Donovan. "All that I have is several years old and a bit travel-worn. It would be nice to have something a little more presentable when I'm out on the town with you."

"Can you afford it?" she asked. "My father does quality work, but he charges accordingly." "Rachel," said Donovan seriously, then began signing, *I have money. Unless your father wants fifty golds for a shirt, I think I can afford some new clocks.* Rachel and her father began to laugh. "What?" asked Donovan. "You signed that you wanted some new *clocks*," said Rachel. I think you meant 'clothes.' Donovan blushed.

After his measurements were taken and meticulously recorded, they drank tea while Rachel and her father talked in sign. After about an hour, Rachel's mother returned from the market, where she had been doing the family's Endday shopping. Introductions were made, and the two women headed upstairs to unpack and put away the groceries, leaving Donovan and Mr. Turner alone.

What color clothes did you have in mind? Mr. Turner signed. Donovan said, slowly, "With my blonde hair and light complexion, I tend to favor greens and yellows, but my best outfit now is maroon." *Solid colors or prints?* asked Mr. Turner. "Definitely solids," said Donovan. *Are you sure you can afford this?* he asked. *More than sure,* signed Donovan. *Can you recommend a good cobbler?* Donovan asked, not knowing the sign for 'cobbler' and having to spell out the letters individually.

Mr. Turner tried to sign his recommendation for a cobbler, but Donovan's brain had reached overload, and he just couldn't follow the words. "Rachel, help!" he cried. Rachel raced down the stairs, thinking something was wrong. "What's the matter?' she asked worriedly. "I asked your father to recommend a good cobbler, but he is signing words I don't know, and my brain is fried." "Is that all? The way you yelled, I thought the shop was on fire!" She turned to her father and translated the explanation. "My father says that the best cobbler is a *blueberry cobbler*, but if you want *shoes*, the shop next to the Academy Gatehouse is the best in town. He was trying to make a joke." "That explains it," said Donovan, "I don't know the sign for blueberry."

They left the shop a few minutes later, with Rachel's father promising to get right to work on Donovan's order, with Donovan telling him to take his time, that he would take the outfits one at a time. As they walked through the late afternoon sun, Rachel was in high spirits. "My parents really liked you," she said. "Your dad is amazing, but I barely spoke to your mother," said Donovan. "You went out of your way to learn sign language," she said, "just so you could talk to my father. That impressed her more than anything."

"I didn't learn sign language just so I could talk to your father," said Donovan. "I am learning it so that I can spend more time with you."

As expected, Wizards Timothy and Edward, along with Courier Reginald and the concealed Specialist Dirk, met up with the two approaching couriers shortly after dawn as they headed west on the road to Baize. Also, as predicted, Courier Paul was not very reasonable. "Why is this man not in manacles?" he demanded. "Perhaps because I refuse to wear them, soldier," said Edward calmly. "I arrest you in the name of the King for—" said Paul. "The unlawful invasion of the Kingdom of Baize," finished Edward. "Yes. Courier Reginald has already arrested me, and I will tell you what I told him; I am on my way to see King Donald. You may accompany us if you wish, but I have no intention of being handcuffed or any other such nonsense."

Courier Paul reached for his sword. "If that sword leaves its scabbard, I will remove your right hand," said Edward coldly. Paul froze, then, ever so slowly, slid the sword back into its sheath. "A wise decision, I assure you," said Edward. "When was the last time your horses were watered?" "A day's ride back," said Senior Courier Keith. "They're a bit thirsty." "Then, as a show of goodwill, allow me to help them." Edward dismounted and dug another trench in the road and filled it with water for the horses. Both Couriers dismounted to allow their mounts to drink. While Edward's back was turned, Paul drew his dagger and lunged. The dagger shattered against Edward's shield, and then Paul clutched his chest and fell to the ground dead.

Without missing a step, Edward said, "I did try to warn him." The two Baizian Couriers looked shocked, unsure of what to do. "Please finish watering your horses so we can be on our way," said Edward. Edward remounted his horse, then asked, "Would you like me to bury Courier Paul or just leave his body in the road?" "Um, we're so far from any town," said Keith, "I suppose we should bury him." Edward turned and, using a Dig spell, dug a six-foot hole in the ground, then, using a Wind spell, blew the dead Courier's body into it and covered it with sand. The whole process took under a minute.

"Now, if you two Couriers will ride in front of us, I promise to stay on the road within a hundred yards of you," said Edward. The Couriers hastily agreed and moved off at a brisk pace, eager to get some distance from the polite but deadly Wizard.

"I have good news, Your Majesty!" said Jasmine, rushing into the throne room. "It appears that at least one company of the Royal Expeditionary Force escaped the ambush. They are just outside Prarrieville and headed this way. They should be in Kingston within two weeks." The King sighed his relief at this news. It was about time he had a positive report about something. The attacks on Franconian shipping were increasing, and he had just learned about the Sea dragon attack on the port city of Sundock.

"Is Major Gerald with the Force?" he asked. "I believe that he is, Sire. Although, as you know, my sources are not always reliable," said Jasmine. "Obviously," replied the King testily. "Why was your first report so inaccurate?" "Inaccurate, Sire?" asked Jasmine, feigning surprise, "I believe that I reported that the Force had been ambushed and scattered and that the survivor's whereabouts were unknown. That was certainly true." "No," said the King. "You told me that my Royal Expeditionary Force had been ambushed, that there were many casualties, and that the survivors were being pursued by Baizian forces and perhaps even dragons. If they are in Prarrieville, that is certainly not the case."

"Sire, if an entire company of your best troops has been lost, I would call that 'many casualties,'" said Jasmine, reasonably. "I have warned you before that many of my sources are rather unsavory characters. What can you expect from people who are betraying their king for money?" The King calmed somewhat, then said, "Well, we'll find out what happened soon enough. What else can you tell me?"

"I am certain that Marshall Guzman has told you that the recall of veterans in Weaton, Colton, Westport, and

Prarrieville is going well and that several hundred men are being retrained and re-equipped as we speak. The news from the Royal Navy is less good. So far, we have lost five Navy ships, with four more damaged, and at least a dozen commercial ships have been sunk. The Merchant's Council is very concerned and is preparing some sort of document to be delivered to you next week, demanding that you take action to protect their trade."

"Demanding! That's outrageous! I'm doing all I can to protect their precious ships! The Navy is doing practically nothing else but escorting their convoys! What do they expect?" raged the King. "I am not sure of their exact demands, Sire, but I believe they will advocate for a raid on the Baizian port cities of Gulfport and Seaside and demand reparations for their losses from the Kingdom of Baize, of course," said Jasmine. "Is that all they want?" "I believe that is all of their current demands, Sire. I do have an agent on the Merchant Council. Is there some message you would like me to convey?"

The King thought for a moment, if it became known that he had agents trying to influence the Merchant Council, it could create a bigger problem than he already had. Finally, he said, "No. Nothing specific, just let them know that I am doing the best that I can." "Of course, Sire."

Mage Kathy was getting exceedingly tired of this. Over the last two weeks, she had encountered poison in her food, poison in her water pitcher, and even a snake under her bed. During each occurrence, Wizard Louis had been elsewhere, in a meeting with Wizard James, conferring with the King, or asleep in his quarters with a dozen witnesses.

At least, she thought she was going to get a respite for a few days. Wizard Louis had announced the day before that he had received information about a dragon's nest a day's ride west of Baize. He had enlisted an entire company of archers and three Sorcerers to go investigate, promising not to return until they had found and slain the beasts. As they rode out of town, Kathy breathed a sigh of relief, thinking that she was at least safe for a little while.

Wizard Louis was not really looking for dragons; he was searching for Stephen. The Court Wizard had grown tired of waiting and had decided to take a more proactive approach. The soldiers searched the road, while the Sorcerers used Sight, Hearing, and Smell Enhancements to try and locate a supposed nest of dragons. After two days of fruitless searching, the soldiers encountered an old man driving a broken-down cart, headed for Baize. The man told Wizard Louis that he had come from Middleberg to sell his bolts of cloth in the Baize city square on Endday. When questioned, the man said that he had left Middleberg almost three weeks ago and had not encountered anyone else on the road.

Louis moved off into the underbrush on the left hand side of the road, transformed into a dragon, and proceeded to kill two of the Sorcerers and half of the soldiers, sending the survivors fleeing back down the road toward Baize. He then changed back into human form, took off, and set fire to his Wizard's robes, then put them back on and went limping down the road, pretending to have barely escaped the dragon's wrath.

He hadn't found Stephen, but at least he had eliminated two Sorcerers from the Baizian defenses. Eventually, he stumbled back into Baize, ranting about being abandoned by the worthless soldiers and the surviving Sorcerer. While his cover was intact, he was still no closer to finding the elusive Stephen.

Azure landed outside the old coal mine northeast of Smithville. It looked the same as it did the last time they stayed there: dark, dusty, and cold. Gek slid off her shoulders and onto the rocky ground, stumbling as he leaned on her for support. He was still pale and shaky from his injury. He entered the mine cautiously, making sure that nothing else had moved in while they were away. Azure waited outside in the darkness.

"It looks OK," said Gek. "Come on in." "I cannot, said Azure, "the entry is too narrow. I will not fit." "Then just change into human form," said Gek wearily. "I do not have any clothes," said Azure shyly. "Since when has that ever stopped you before?" asked Gek, rapidly growing tired of this conversation. "My human form looks hideous," she said. "My belly is getting fat, my feet are swollen, and my chest is expanding for some reason!"

"You are carrying a child, for goodness sake!" said an exasperated Gek. "I am sure that it is perfectly normal for a pregnant human female. Now transform and get in here before someone sees you." "Hand me your shirt first." Gek sighed, realizing that he was not going to win this argument. He painfully stripped off his bloody shirt and tossed it outside. "Turn around," said Azure. Gek complied grudgingly.

Azure completed the transformation and put on Gek's shirt. It would not close in front, so she held it closed with her hands, cursing as she walked into the mine. "Now what?" she asked crossly. "Now, we rest," said Gek. "I do not know about you, but I am tired, sore, hungry, and thirsty." "This shirt does not fit," groused Azure, "we should have kept the coach driver's cloak." "And how would Celeste explain that?" asked Gek. "It is going to be hard enough for her to explain the wrecked carriage and the missing human. That Regional Mage is no fool."

"I suppose," said Azure. "Come here and sit with me. We will be all right. Thank you for rescuing me," said Gek, yawning. Azure slipped down next to him on the cold stone floor. She shivered, and Gek put his arm around her shoulders. She began sobbing into his neck. "I was so worried," she cried. "I did not know what to do. Fortunately, Beau came up with a plan for me to reach you. I just wish I could have stopped those stupid horses."

They sat there for a while; then Azure began to examine Gek's injuries. He had big scars across his right shoulder, extending down his side, a scar on the right side of his head, and a large purple bruise on his left cheek and jaw. "How did you get this bruise?" she asked. Gek fingered the bruise gingerly, "That is from when you slapped me with your tail while I was in human form." "Sorry about that," said Azure.

They slept fitfully in the mine. Gek was uncomfortable because of his injuries, and Azure was just uncomfortable: she was cold; she had no pants; it hurt to lay on her back; it hurt to lay on her right side; it hurt to lay on her left side; she could not sleep on her stomach; and she wanted a sea urchin sandwich.

As the day finally faded into dusk, they moved back outside the mine entrance. Gek retrieved his shirt, and Azure transformed back into a pregnant Sea Dragon. She was still not happy. She complained that she could not see her feet when in human form. It did not help when Gek pointed out that she never could see her back feet as a Dragon. Hesitantly, Gek asked if she could spray some water on his shirt in order to get the blood off it. Azure responded with a high-pressure jet that tore a hole clean through both sides of the shirt and blew it across the ground. Now, the shirt was bloody, muddy, covered with coal dust, and had holes in it.

"I hate to ask, but I need water. Could you just spit some into that bucket over there," said Gek, pointing to a dented, rusty bucket that the miners had left behind. Azure worked her jaw, then spit a small amount of water into the bucket. Gek took a tentative drink, then his thirst overcame his caution, and he guzzled the rest of the water in the bucket.

They decided to head for the coast where Azure would be able to find some fish to eat and maybe even a sea urchin (although now she wanted a sea *cucumber* sandwich). When Gek was healed enough to transform, they were going to head back to the island of Acropo, where they could stay with the Sea Dragon Clan. As Gek climbed onto Azure's back, she asked him if the water she gave him was OK. "It tasted like Dragon spit," said Gek, grinning. "I would slap you again, but in your weakened condition, it would probably kill you," said Azure.

They moved out a glass after dawn and headed down the road towards Kingston. They rode past the training ground where the recently recalled veterans were being issued their equipment and assigned to auxiliary companies in the Second Regiment, which had recently arrived in Prarrieville. The men recalled to active duty did not look either happy or fit. Many were old, fifty winters at least; some were grossly overweight, and others were clearly nursing old injuries. It was not an impressive force.

"We're certainly scraping the bottom of the barrel with that lot," said Major Gerald to Specialist Lance.

"Sir, as I understand it, those men are the *best* of the recalls. The others were even worse and were assigned to strictly administrative or logistical duties." "It's curious why the King felt the need to mobilize them," said Gerald. "We never even saw a Baizian soldier, and while I'm sure Wizard Timothy is a competent magician, he's no spring chicken either."

As they were speaking, Corporal Sleet rode up. "Corporal! Good ta see ya," said Major Gerald. "How are you finding things in First Squad?" "Very busy, sir," said Corporal Sleet. "Is it true that you fought a Dragon in Baize, sir?" "Actually, it was seven Fire dragons that tried to ambush us in a narrow pass. We were most fortunate that Wizard Edward discovered their trap and helped us avoid it. We could have all been killed," said Gerald.

"Seven!" exclaimed Corporal Sleet, "How ever did you manage it?" "Well, the Wizard made us all Concealment cloaks like the one Specialist Lance has. With them on, we're practically invisible. It gives us an advantage no force has ever had before." Corporal Sleet was stunned by this news. If the Royal Expeditionary Force had cloaks that made them invisible, the conflict could go badly for the Dragons. If this capability spread to the rest of the Franconian Army, the Dragons were doomed. He needed to get this information to the Dragon Council at their next meeting, almost a month hence. Before then, he would just have to see what sort of mischief he could cause without giving himself away.

154

Mage Elianna

Chapter Ten:

THE ROAD TO BAIZE

As they rode towards Baize, they stopped at each watering hole, and Edward cleared the sand away, built a retaining wall around the water, and deepened the channel to the water source. Courier Reginald told Keith that the Wizard had done such to every rest stop along the road and that it would be very helpful in the future. "If it lasts," said Courier Keith skeptically. "It will last until the water runs out or changes course underground," said Edward. "I don't understand," said Keith. "There is a vast underground river, or lake, called an aquifer; the water bubbles up in places where the aquifer is closest to the surface. Over time, the underground river changes course, and wells and springs dry up," explained Edward. "How often does that happen?" asked Keith. "Oh, every thousand years or so. It is the same with rivers aboveground."

"If it only happens every thousand years, why worry about it?" asked Reginald. "I won't live a thousand years." "Because we don't know how long it's been since the last change," said Edward. "It could have been a hundred years ago or a thousand; the water may not change course in your lifetime, or it could change tomorrow."

They continued their journey, past the generally empty countryside. Edward commented on the lack of people in this otherwise fertile area. "This would seem to be ideal farmland," he said to Wizard Timothy. "Why has no one settled here?" "There used to be a few farmers, but brigands raided the farms so often, they simply moved closer to Baize. There were never enough of them to provide for their own security, and they lost the appetite to grow crops only to have them stolen on the way to the market." "The King did nothing?" "There were not enough people to warrant a military post, and the amount of goods stolen was inconsequential to the crown."

"How much further?" Edward asked. "It has been many years since I traveled this road, but I believe that we should be in Baize in another day or two," replied Timothy. "Then tomorrow, we should close the distance between ourselves and our Courier escorts. I don't want one of them making a break for it and arriving in Baize before us. We are likely in for a cold reception as it is, and I don't want to be greeted by a squad of soldiers." "More likely a full company," said Timothy.

That night, after the watering hole had been upgraded and the evening meal consumed, Edward asked Keith when he thought they would reach the city. "If we pick up the pace, we could be there by tomorrow night. I for one, would like to sleep in a bed tomorrow.

I have been on this damn road for twice as long as you."
"I can appreciate that," said Edward. "However, I don't think we should intrude upon the King and his Counselors during the night. How about if we start later tomorrow, then plan on arriving mid-morning on the day after tomorrow?"

"I suppose one more night on the road won't kill me," said Keith grumpily. "I will see you in the morning." Keith headed off to the far side of the fire, where he laid out his bedroll and prepared for sleep. Edward noted that Keith had chosen a position close to the horses and suspected that he was planning to slip off during the night. As was his custom, Edward took the remnants of the evening meal away from the campsite to supposedly dispose of the leftovers and clean the cauldron away from their sleeping area. He was actually taking dinner to the still-concealed Specialist Dirk.

When he decided that he had gone far enough, he waved Dirk to him and cast a Silence spell around the two of them. "How are you doing, Dirk?" he asked. "I am well, thank you for asking. How much further, do you think?" asked Dirk. "The Senior Courier says that we could be in the city by tomorrow night if we speed up our pace. I informed him that, rather than arrive in the evening, we will sleep late tomorrow and spend one more night on the road, then make our appearance in the city at mid-morning the day after tomorrow," explained

Edward. "That sounds reasonable." "I'm not sure Keith agrees," said Edward. "I think he's planning on sneaking out of camp tonight and trying to warn the King of our approach." "I take it that you want me to prevent that," said Dirk.

"Yes. I don't want to give advanced notice of our arrival. How long do your tranquilizer darts last?" "You mean if no one wakes him?" "Yes," said Edward. "He will sleep for about six hours after I hit him with a dart," said Dirk. "Hmm," said Edward. "Then this is what we'll do, I'll stay up until just after midnight. You get some sleep until then. I'll come out and wake you. I expect Keith will pretend to be asleep, probably snoring loudly to convince me. Once he sees that I'm asleep, I expect him to saddle his horse and try to depart quietly. Tranquilize him before he leaves the camp."

"Why don't you just spell him to sleep?" asked Dirk. "Because the spell might wear off too soon. Sleep spells are designed to *put* someone to sleep, not *keep* them asleep for a specific period of time," said Edward quietly. "In any event, I don't want him leaving tonight, or tomorrow night for that matter. I may have to use stronger methods as we get closer to the city."

"I tell you, Captain, that wagon wheel was fine when we left Prarrieville. I checked it myself," said Corporal Brown. "Well, it's broken now; get to work fixing it," said Captain Fletcher, the 2nd Company commander. "I'll go let the Major know." Major Gerald was not happy. This was the third incident since they'd left Prarrieville. The first day out, the water barrel had sprung a leak, and all the water had run out, so they had to return to Prarrieville for a new barrel and more water; then it was an enormous tree down across the road, in a spot that was too narrow for the wagon to get around. Without a magician, it had taken most of the day to chop up the tree and clear the roadway; now this.

"Someone find me, Specialist Lance," said the Major. "I'm right here, sir," said Lance. The Major moved away from the soldiers who were working quickly to repair the broken wagon wheel. "I want you to keep an eye on the two new recruits," said Gerald. "I'm not so sure that all these incidents are just accidents." "Sir, do you really think one of them is responsible? These all look like simple accidents," said Lance. "I know, but I'm suspicious. It seems strange that three 'accidents' all happened just two days out of Prarrieville. It reminds me of our trip to Farmdale," said the Major, referring to the Expeditionary Force's mission to the northern village of Farmdale, where they encountered a dragon. There were several attempts to delay the force on the road, all thwarted by Battle Mage Edward. Now, without any magical support, the Royal Expeditionary Force had had three accidents in four days.

"Just keep an eye on them. They're both in the First Squad, so it shouldn't be too difficult," said Gerald. "You got it, Major. Do they both have the new cloaks?" "No. Those cloaks were burned up by the dragon, and I forgot to have Wizard Edward or Mage Curtis make us replacements while we were in Springfield," said Gerald. "That should make it easier," said Lance, "unless they borrow one from someone else. Maybe we should gather all the cloaks up and only issue them for special missions." "That's a good idea, but it'll have to wait until we reach Kingston to get replacement clothing," said Gerald. "I can't take the men's cloaks now; it looks like rain."

Mage Kathy was seated at her desk when she was startled by a knock on her door. No one ever knocked; they just barged in. She cautiously opened the door to find a young man who looked extremely relieved to see her. "Mage Kathy?" he asked. "I'm Mage Kathy. What can I do for you?" "My name is Stephen, and I'm a student at the Middleberg School of Magic. I have a message for you from Mage Elianna," said Stephen, entering and closing the door behind him. "Would you be so kind as to cast a Silence spell around us? Mage Elianna has not taught us that one yet."

Kathy quickly cast a Silence spell and asked Stephen, "So, what's so important that you came all the way here?" Stephen ripped open the secret pocket in his jacket and handed the message to Kathy. "Mage Elianna used a Reduction spell to shrink the message in case I was intercepted on my journey here. She did not trust this missive to Messenger Hawks."

Kathy examined the compressed bundle of parchment, then used an Enlarge spell to return the message to its original size. It said:

Kathy,

Court Wizard Louis paid us a visit this week. After he departed, I discovered that the beef stew we had prepared for our dinner was poisoned with Nightshade. A promising young magician died as a result of the poisoning before I was able to detect it. I was able to stop the other students from consuming any stew, and they are unharmed but distressed. Wizard Louis was the only visitor we had that day, and I personally gave him a tour of the school (including the kitchen where dinner was being prepared). I have no proof that Louis poisoned the stew, <u>but I have no other suspects</u>.

Additionally, that night, three brigands broke into the school and attempted to steal over a hundred vials of Healing Serum that I and my students had prepared for the people of Middleberg. I anticipated the break-in, and we captured the criminals. Two were lackeys with no knowledge of who hired them (I terminated them), but the third confessed to being sent by Wizard Louis, who I had informed of our efforts to produce a sizeable quantity of Healing Serum for the city.

Unfortunately, while the ringleader was being transported to the Garrison Dungeon, he suddenly dropped dead of unknown causes. I suspect another magician was involved, but I have been unable to determine who was responsible.

I need to get this information to someone reliable, and you were the first person I thought of. I cannot leave Middleberg at this critical time. The dragons may attack at any moment, and I cannot, in good conscience, abandon my eleven remaining students and leave the city with only two Sorcerers. I do not know what you can do with this information, but I needed someone to know what has happened to us, and I do not trust Messenger Hawks. This message is being delivered to you by Stephen, my most advanced student. He has brown hair and a scar on his left wrist. He is the only one I trust to deliver it to you safely.

Mage Elianna

Kathy read the message twice, then said, "Stephen, please show me your left wrist." Stephen rolled up his sleeve and displayed a three-inch scar. "Thank you. I just had to be sure," said Kathy. "Do you know what this message says?"

"I can guess," said Stephen, "probably something about Wizard Louis poisoning our dinner after visiting the Middleberg School of Magic, then three thugs trying to break in and steal our Healing Serum." "Exactly right," said Kathy. "Did you have any trouble on your way here?" "No, not 'trouble,' exactly, but I did find the horse that Wizard Louis was riding when he left us, about an hour outside of Middleberg. It had been killed and eaten by some large predators that I have never encountered before. Not wanting to run into Wizard Louis on the road, I slowed my pace to a walk. Otherwise, I would have been here two weeks ago."

"Did you see him?" asked Kathy. "No. I think he must have cut across to the Green River and come to Baize by boat."

"Hmm, Wizard Louis has been in Baize for the last three weeks." "That's impossible!' said Stephen. "How did he get here, fly?" Kathy smiled, "You ask good questions. Unfortunately, I have no idea how Wizard Louis got here from Middleberg so fast. Did anyone see you coming to my office?" Stephen thought, "Just a maid, I think," said Stephen, "I was trying to avoid Wizard Louis." "A wise decision," said Kathy. "What are your plans now?"

"Mage Elianna told me to return to Middleberg as soon as I had delivered the message. It's kind of late in the day, though," replied Stephen. "Indeed," said Kathy. Just then, there was a commotion out in the courtyard.

Wizard Louis and the soldiers had returned, but much the worse for wear. Wizard Louis was cursing loudly, "Never seen such cowardice! You should all be reduced in rank! How could you let a single Dragon kill two Sorcerers and half a company of men?"

In the midst of Louis's rant, a servant approached him, whispering something to him. "Stephen, come here," said Kathy, "Is that the servant you saw in the corridor?" Stephen peered out the window, careful not to be seen. "I think so. Why?" "That's Marissa," said Kathy. "She is a cook's assistant. She may have simply been bringing dinner to one of the Ministers. Still…"

"You will stay in my room tonight and leave once I figure out what to do about your message." Stephen beamed, hopefully. Kathy noticed the familiar look and said sternly, "I said in my *room,* not in my *bed!* I am much too old for you and not looking for that kind of company." Stephen's countenance fell.

"Anyway, please cast a Concealment spell on yourself and follow me." Stephen cast the spell and followed Kathy upstairs into her room in the tower. "I expect you're tired, so why don't you get some sleep on the sofa over there? I will take the first watch," said Kathy. "Watch?" asked Stephen, confused. "Yes. Someone is trying to kill me. I suspect Wizard Louis.

You are in danger as well. Tonight, one of us will be awake at all times."

Gek and Azure spent several days on the beach while Gek's wounds fully healed. They saw four ships go by, heading north, but had no idea of their destination, or if there were any magic-users aboard them. Azure wanted to go out and attack them, but Gek put his foot down. "Absolutely not. There are four of them, and they may all have magic-users. If I was healthy, it might be different, but the two of us, taking on four ships is foolhardy. Besides, you are pregnant," said Gek forcefully. "What does that have to do with anything?" asked Azure.

"I do not want to risk harm to our child," said Gek reasonably. "Gek, it has only been about three months! Are you saying that I cannot fight the humans for five more months?" "All I am saying," said Gek, "is that I do not want you to take any unnecessary risks. Attacking four ships, by ourselves, is an unnecessary risk." "Fine," said Azure, in a tone that meant it was definitely not 'fine.'"

"When do you think you will be able to transform?" asked Azure. "I will try tomorrow. My ribs are still sore, and I am not sure what will happen when I change back. Celeste is not around to help us again," replied Gek. "She was not what I expected," said Azure softly. "She was afraid, but still she healed you, before she tended to her own wounds. I wonder if there are other such humans." "Probably not many," said Gek. "Did you notice how quickly she identified me as a Changed One?" "Yes, she must have encountered some other Changed Ones at the wizards' school, ones that did not wish to change back into Dragons. Maybe she expected me to feel the same way." "Whatever she thought, she saved your life, and I am glad that we did not have to kill her," said Azure.

The next morning, Azure woke early and roused Gek. "Time for you to make the change," she said. "What is the rush?" asked Gek sleepily. "I just want to get out of here," said Azure. "I suddenly have a bad feeling about those ships we saw the other day. They could be headed to our islands." "All right, I am up. I should probably eat something before I attempt the change, though." "Fine," said Azure, "I will be right back." "No sea urchins!" shouted Gek as Azure dove beneath the surf.

An hour later, Azure returned carrying a large, purple, multi-armed sea creature in her mouth. "What is that thing?" asked Gek. "It is an octopus," said Azure, "a great delicacy for a Sea Dragon." "Well, I am certainly not eating that thing!" said Gek, "It looks disgusting." "Suit yourself," said Azure, swallowing the creature whole. "So, what am I supposed to eat?" "Do not be such a baby," Azure admonished, "Here is a flounder I scooped up off the seabed on my way back. Eat that."

Gek grimaced. Flounder was one of his least favorite fish, but he settled down to eat without complaint. As he swallowed his last bite, Azure was already up, ready for him to cast the Change spell. Gek braced himself, then said, '*MORPHIUS,*' while clapping his hands. This time, the transformation happened much more slowly than usual. First his tail appeared, then his torso and legs, followed by his wings, and lastly, his head. It only took a minute, but it seemed to take forever, compared to the instantaneous changes of the past. Once transformed, Gek screamed in pain.

The scales along his right side were torn and bleeding, with several barely attached to his skin. His right wing seemed to be out of its socket, and he was making it worse by thrashing around. "Gek, stop! You are making it worse! How can I help?" cried Azure. "Help me into the water," gasped Gek, his spasms abating. "Then I will need you to push my right wing back into position." Azure draped Gek's good wing over her back and slowly waded into the surf. The seawater stung his open wounds, and he winced, reconsidering the wisdom of getting into the water. Once he was wing-deep in the water, he asked Azure to *gently* grab the top of his wing and move the bone back into its socket. He warned her that he might scream and maybe even breathe fire, but she needed to get it done on the first try and be quick about it. "I may pass out from the pain," he said. "Please do not let me drown."

Azure moved in beside him and hooked her talon under his wing and the bone that connected it to his torso. "Ready?" she asked. Gek nodded, gritting his teeth. Azure pulled up and forward. She could feel the bone dragging across the bones of Gek's shoulder; then, as she aligned the top of his right wing with his left, the bone sank in with a satisfying 'POP.' She turned to tell Gek that she was finished, only to find his head underwater and a great cloud of bubbles coming out of his mouth. She quickly released her hold on his wing and raised his head above the water. "I am all right," sputtered Gek, spitting water. "And Ard was right; I cannot breathe fire underwater." Azure helped him out of the water and up onto the beach.

"We need to get back under cover," said Gek, "before someone sees us. I hate to disappoint you, but I do not think I am going to be able to fly for at least another week." "I am sorry I rushed you to make the change," said Azure. "We should have waited a while longer." "I am not sure it would have mattered much," replied Gek. "It could just be that human bones and Dragon bones are so different that they do not heal the same way or at the same speed."

"We will wait here as long as you need," said Azure.

As expected, Courier Keith tried to slip away shortly after Edward fell asleep. He had saddled his horse and was in the process of leading him away, when the tranquilizer dart from Dirk's blowgun dropped him in his tracks. Dirk roused Edward, and they unsaddled the confused horse and re-tethered it to the hitching line. Then they removed the dart, and Edward healed the wound in the Courier's neck. They placed him back on his bedroll and covered him with his blanket. Then, they both went back to sleep.

When Courier Keith awoke, it was mid-morning, and the others were in the process of breaking camp and saddling their mounts. "About time, sleepy-head!" said Wizard Timothy cheerfully, unaware of what had transpired during the night. "Where am I?" asked Keith. "Right where we camped last night," said Edward. "Where else would you be?" Keith shook his head groggily and began packing up his gear and saddling his horse. Once mounted, Edward looked at the Senior

Courier and said, "Senior Courier Keith, we will all arrive at the court of King Donald together. Do you understand?" Keith nodded sullenly.

"We ride together the rest of the way," said Edward loudly. Wizard Timothy looked at him questioningly. "The Courier tried to slip out of camp last night, no doubt intending to warn the King of our arrival. I anticipated his actions and prevented it. He is probably a bit confused this morning. If I were you, I would speak to him today and convince him to stay with us. Otherwise, I will Compel him to do so."

They rode quietly for the rest of the day, with Senior Courier Keith frequently looking back over his shoulder to see where Edward was. Wizard Timothy had a *spirited* conversation with the Courier, after which, Timothy rode back to Edward. "It's no good. Keith is convinced that it's his duty to give advanced warning of our arrival to the King. He's going to attempt to escape us, probably in the morning. We'll still be several hours away from the palace."

"I applaud his dedication to duty," said Edward. "How are your concealment skills?" Edward explained his plan: First, a bit of sleeping Serum in the couriers' evening meals, to ensure they did not try to escape during the night, then a Seeming of the two Wizards being left far behind when the two Couriers raced ahead to warn the King. Edward and Timothy would follow the Couriers closely under Concealment and Silence spells. Once they reached the audience chamber, they would drop the concealments and address the King. "I like it," said Timothy, "This way, no blame falls on the Couriers." "In the morning, I'll cast a Stamina spell on each of our horses, so they will have no problem keeping up with the Couriers," whispered Edward.

Edward walked out of camp that night and explained the plan to Dirk, reminding him not to reveal himself unless Edward called for him. Dirk said that he had misgivings about this plan but that he'd be there if and when the Wizard needed him.

The next morning, as expected, as soon as they were on the road, the two Couriers raced off as fast as their mounts would carry them. Edward cast his Seeming, followed by his Concealment and Silence spells, and the chase was on. The Couriers had excellent mounts, and without the Stamina spells, the two Wizards would have been left far behind. As it was, both Edward and Timothy were right behind the two Couriers when they entered the audience chamber as soon as the palace guards opened the doors for the morning session.

Keith pushed to the front of the assembled crowd and said, "Your Majesty, Senior Courier Keith, reporting. Four weeks ago, you sent me to arrest Wizard

Timothy of Springfield for failing to resist the invasion of Franconian forces. I arrested Timothy as ordered, but he is in the company of a Franconian Wizard, named Edward, who refused to be arrested. Courier Reginald and I escorted the two Wizards to the outskirts of the city, arriving last night. This morning, we raced ahead of them to warn you of their impending arrival." The King sat back, shocked. "A Franconian Wizard, here? When will they arrive?"

Before Keith could answer, both Wizards dropped their Concealment and Silence spells and appeared before the King. "I am here now, Your Majesty," said Edward, bowing low, "and I assure you, I mean you no harm."

Wizard Louis

Chapter Eleven:

THE COURT OF KING DONALD

The King sat back on his throne, stunned by the abrupt appearance of Wizards Edward and Timothy. A military officer strode forward and said officially, "I hereby arrest you in the name of the King for—" "the unlawful invasion of the Kingdom of Baize," finished Edward. "Is that all your military officers know how to say, Your Majesty?" Wizard Timothy laughed, and even Courier Reginald smiled. The King suppressed a grin as the officer stepped forward, placing his hand on his sword. Edward looked him in the eye and said, "I will tell you what I told Senior Courier Keith over there. If that sword leaves its scabbard, I will remove your right hand at the wrist."

The officer froze, unsure of what to do. The King said, "You have a very intimidating manner about you, Wizard. What is it that you would say to us?" "Your Highness," began Edward, "I am here to try and convince you not to declare war on Franconia, despite recent events. I have important news to share with you that will be of great benefit to both our Kingdoms. However, I would ask for a more private setting with only your key Ministers present. My information is not for everyone's ears."

"And why should we entertain such an audacious request from an invading Wizard?" asked a robed man standing to the King's right. "You would have to be the Court Wizard," said Edward confidently. "As a show of good faith, I would be willing to submit to a Binding spell to do no harm to the King for the duration of our discussion. I would also agree to be questioned under the use of Truth Serum." There were murmurs of approval from the assembled Ministers and Counselors.

"Wizard Louis, advise me on this Binding spell he speaks of," said the King. "Sire, a Binding spell holds a magician to a promise made. It can either be for a specific period of time or forever, depending on the promise," said Wizard Louis. "And what happens if the magician breaks his promise?" asked the King. "He dies, Sire, immediately."

"Hmm," said the King. "A most useful spell. And can a magician overcome Truth Serum with some sort of magic?" "Not one of *my* Truth Serums, Sire," said Wizard Louis arrogantly. "Very well, I accept your terms, Wizard Edward of Franconia. I will allow General Diaz, Minister Conklin, Minister Stevens, Admiral Vandall, and Wizard Louis to attend this conference. Along with Wizard Timothy and Senior

Courier Keith," said the King. "The rest of you are dismissed; we will inform you of any decisions made after our discussion."

As the rest of the people in the audience chamber filed out, Wizard Timothy whispered, "Are you sure about this, Edward?" "Yes," Edward replied. The King said, "Let us retire to my private conference room where we'll be more comfortable, but first, your promise, Edward." Edward drew himself up to his full height and stated formally, "I, Wizard Edward Francis of Franconia, do solemnly swear that I will not harm, or seek to harm, King Donald of the Kingdom of Baize, for the next glass of time, commencing at this moment." As he spoke the words of the vow, Wizard Louis murmured '*PROMISA*' and drew the index finger of his right hand along the floor. A shower of sparks descended from above, surrounding and enfolding Edward.

The Binding spell was complete; the participants left the throne room through a back door and entered the King's private conference room. It was strikingly similar to King Henry's conference room, only with green draperies instead of red. The King seated himself at the head of the table and said, "Now, Wizard Edward, what would you tell us?" "One moment, Sire, I believe that we should administer the Truth Serum before we begin," said Wizard Louis. "Of course," said the King.

Wizard Louis produced a vial from a pocket of his robes and presented it to Edward. Edward examined it closely, uncorked the vial, and handed it back to Louis, "You first."

The Court Wizard recoiled from the proffered vial, "How dare you insult the Court Wizard of Baize!" he shouted, "This conference is over!" *"NECESSITAS,"* said Edward, crossing his fingers, "Drink a few drops of the Serum, Louis." The Wizard's hand shook violently, but slowly, inexorably, the vial came to his mouth, and a few drops touched his lips. He immediately began convulsing, and within seconds, Wizard Louis lay dead. One of the Ministers drew a hidden dagger from his coat and drew back his hand to throw, *"INCOGITA,"* said Edward, making a gesture. The Minister collapsed in his chair. The others screamed their protests. Edward said calmly, "The Minister is only asleep; I could have killed him but did not. The vial Wizard Louis offered me was Death Serum, not Truth Serum. I never agreed to drink Death Serum, so I compelled him to sample it first. If it had been Truth Serum, Wizard Louis would still be alive. This meeting is not off to a very good start, Your Majesty."

The King sat back in his chair and smiled. "You are a cunning and ruthless man, Wizard Edward. How do you propose we proceed?" "I would suggest you revive your unconscious Minister, then I would offer you the same conditions I stated before: have another of your magicians bring in a vial of Truth Serum; I will ask him or her to sample it, then ask them to confirm that it is, in fact, Truth Serum. Once it is confirmed, I will drink the rest of the Serum and answer your questions truthfully." The King agreed, the Minister was awakened, and the King summoned the Assistant Court Wizard, Mage Kathy, and sent her to secure a vial of Truth Serum. As they were waiting for Kathy to return with the Truth Serum, Edward spoke to the King, "Your Majesty, I have an unusual request. I would like to remove Wizard Louis's head. I will use a Remove spell, so there will be no blood shed." The King was shocked by this highly unusual request, "Why would you do such a thing?" he asked curiously. "Sire, the final lesson we teach our students at the Wizards Academy in Franconia, is to never believe that an enemy is dead unless their head is removed from their body. I personally have killed two assailants who mistakenly believed that they had killed me. I do not want to make the same mistake as they did."

"Very well," said the King, "You may proceed." Wizard Louis's head was cleanly and efficiently removed from his body by the time Kathy returned with the Truth Serum. Edward requested that she sample the Serum, which she did without hesitation; he then asked, "Is this really Truth Serum?" "Yes, it is," replied Kathy.

Edward immediately took and drank the remaining liquid from the vial, then turned to the King and said, "Your Majesty, dragons can understand human speech and perform magic spells, including the Change spell, enabling them to walk among us in human form. I believe that the dragon's intent is for Franconia and Baize to fight each other in order to weaken both our Kingdoms before they eventually attack."

Mage Charles entered Olive's Tuna with three enforcers behind him. They corralled Beau and the other five Changed Ones in the breakroom. "Six citizens with the spark, all in one establishment, and all much too old for the Wizards Academy!" said Mage Charles. "I would never have believed it. Anyway, since you are all no doubt wondering, the Academy does not accept students over twenty winters old. Since you have all managed to keep your magic under control for this long, this is what's going to happen. I'm going to ask each of you to promise never to harm anyone with magic and never to use magic to counterfeit coins. I will use a Binding spell to ensure that you keep that promise. If you *ever*, and I do mean *ever*, use magic to harm another or use magic to replicate coins, you will die, instantly. If, however, you keep your magic under control, as you have obviously done for many years, you'll never see me again. Are there any questions?"

The assembled Changed Ones were too stunned to speak, amazed at their good fortune. One by one, they all made their promise and were placed under the Binding spell by the Mage. When he was finished, he said, "By the way, in case you were wondering how we identified this place, I apprehended a young man with the spark named Jed a few days ago down on the docks. He told me that he worked here, so I came to investigate. Jed should be at the Wizards Academy by now. In ten or twelve years, if you live that long, you may see him again."

Andrew slumped in his chair, completely exhausted. Over the past 36 hours, he had replicated nine Seabows, then Reduced them to travel-size. There was now one Seabow for every ship in the First Fleet and one that was being crated and shipped to Admiral Cross and Wizard Lake in Grotton for replication and installation on the fifteen ships in the Second Fleet. In addition to making Seabows, Andrew and the other Sorcerers assigned to the First Fleet had made standard-size crossbows for every member of the crew for all four ships in the First

Squadron. The Seabows and crossbows were relatively easy, the iron bolts were hard.

Despite his fatigue, Andrew walked down the passageway to the Commodore's cabin and knocked. "Come!" said the Commodore's voice from behind the door. Andrew opened the door and entered wearily. "Ah, Andrew, my boy, all done making Seabows and bolts?" Andrew nodded tiredly, "Yes, sir. At least for now. I'm sure that I and the rest of the magicians in the Royal Navy will be making bolts constantly until the war ends." "We set sail at dawn," said the Commodore. "Is there anything else we need to do tonight?" "Have we received a replacement Sorcerer for the HMS COMFORT, Sir? I'd hate to leave without one." "Yes. *She* came aboard about two hours ago. I told the Admiralty that women are not allowed on Navy ships, but they said, 'She's not a woman, she's a Sorceress.' Her name is Anne. Do you know her?"

Andrew thought, then said, "There was a Mentor at the Academy whose name was Anne, but I thought Wizard Noland assigned her to the Sundock Regional Mage's Office." "He did, and now the Regional Mage has pawned her off on me!" raged the Commodore. "Sir, the Sundock Regional Mage is also a woman, and she's the only magician in the office. I guess it was a choice of either her or Sorceress Anne, and the Regional Mage is not going to leave her office in the hands of a newly appointed Sorceress," said Andrew reasonably. "I suppose I can understand that," said the Commodore. "Since you know her, I want you to go over to the COMFORT and get her settled and let her know where things stand. She may be a Sorceress, but she's also the only woman on a Royal Navy ship. You get my drift?" Andrew did, indeed, see the potential for problems. Once the Commodore dismissed him, Andrew hurried over to the COMFORT.

As he boarded the ship, the Bos'n piped him aboard, "BATTLE MAGE ON DECK!" the crew stopped their work and saluted. "As you were men," said Andrew, still getting used to his new rank and position, "Anyone know where I can find the ship's magician?" "She's amidship, Sir, looking over the new Seabow!" Andrew nodded his thanks and headed aft, towards the port-side Seabow. He found Anne there, inspecting the mechanism of the Seabow. "Anne!" said Andrew. "Andrew! I mean, Mage Andrew. It's good to see you again. However, did you manage to make Mage so soon? Why, it's been less than a year, hasn't it?"

Andrew lowered his voice, "Yes, and I'm only the Battle Mage because the former Squadron Mage was assigned to the COMFORT. He was killed when the dragons attacked, and the Admiral sent Captain, now Commodore, Matthews, and the HMS VALOR over here from Second Fleet and made him the Squadron commander. So, what do you think of my little invention?" he said, pointing to the Seabow.

Anne looked at the Seabow with a critical eye, "The gearing could be smoother, and it would be better if the pedestal were made of steel instead of wood, but the design is solid." Andrew laughed, "Where were you when the carpenters and I were building this darn thing? I know there's room for improvement, but we sail at dawn, and I don't think I would've had the strength to make and replicate all of these in steel instead of wood. We can make modifications and improvements after our sea trials. By the way, how's your sister, Celeste?"

"She was re-assigned from the Grotton Regional Mage's Office," said Anne, angrily. "Why?" asked Andrew. "She was on her first escort mission, taking a young man with the spark to the Wizards Academy, when brigands attacked the coach. She and the driver were knocked unconscious, and when she awoke, the young man was gone—either killed or carried off by the brigands. Regional Mage Charles was furious and sent her back to the Academy in disgrace," said Anne. "Wizard Noland made her the Mentor's supervisor."

"I'm sorry. That sounds terrible, but Wizard Noland will take care of her," said Andrew. "So, have you settled in yet?"

"Yes. At least my meager possessions are in that tiny room you call an officer's cabin." "Don't complain, my cabin is the same size, and I'm the Squadron Battle Mage. Let's go below. I need a word before we cast off." They headed below decks to Anne's cabin, as expected; it was the same size as Andrew's. Andrew settled into the chair while Anne sat on the bed. "You know that you're the only woman in the Royal Navy, right?" asked Andrew. Anne nodded. "And you know what that means?" "What?" "It means that you can't ask for any special treatment because you're a woman, no special food, no shirking a deck watch, nothing. You're expected to perform all your duties like any other sailor."

"I understand," said Anne. "Now, we're headed into a war zone. The Admiralty thinks that the Sea dragons have made their home on the Coral Islands, one, two, or all three of them. That means we're going to be fighting, and there are going to be casualties. How are your healing skills?" "Excellent," said Anne. "Good," said Andrew. "The Spells you'll need most are Wind, to help maneuver the ship; Blast, to attack dragons; Enlarge and Adhesive, to repair damage to the ship; Strength and Stamina; and the Sight Enhancement for searching the sea for dragons or ships in trouble. Lastly, there is no fraternization allowed between officers and crew. It's never been an issue on a Navy ship before, but these are desperate times. The ship's officers are the Captain, the First Mate, the Quartermaster, the Ship's Carpenter, the Boatswain or Bos'n, and the ship's Magician."

"We sail at dawn and should be near the Coral Islands within three days if the wind holds. If you get seasick, apples and crackers help. Navy regulations prohibit magicians from consuming alcohol at sea; the crew is allowed, we are not. Fight hard, Anne. Be creative with your spells, and help the crew. Many of them are terrified and still in shock from the last dragon attack that killed their Mage and their Captain. Give them confidence that they can survive and conquer, and you may not be the last woman to serve on a Royal Navy ship."

"Dragons can disguise themselves as humans?" asked the King, incredulously. "Yes, Your Majesty. I know it's incredible, but it's true. We unmasked fourteen of them at the Wizards Academy in Franconia. Twelve students and two instructors. I knew both instructors for over a decade, and I never suspected a thing." "What did you do to them?" asked the King. "We removed the hands of the two Wizards, so that they couldn't transform back into dragons or harm anyone with lethal spells, and we spelled two of the Changed Ones to sleep and removed their spark of magic." "What about the other ten?" asked the King. "Believe it or not, they preferred to remain as humans, so we placed Binding spells on them. They promised to never injure a human and to never transform back into a dragon. They are still at the Academy."

"Why would a dragon prefer to live as a human?" "According to the Changed Ones, life as a dragon is not easy. They are always hungry, constantly hunting for prey, and hiding from humans. When prey is scarce, it's not uncommon for dragon parents to eat their children to survive. It is supposedly not a very happy life. Most Changed Ones prefer to live as humans, seldom hungry, and not afraid. Some of them have even married humans."

"So, why are the dragons suddenly hostile?" "That's a question I can't answer, Sire, because I just don't know. I know that several Fire dragons attacked your city of Riverside and that three Stone dragons attacked the Franconian city of Weaton. There have also been attacks on both our nation's ships by Sea dragons. That's why I believe that the dragons are trying to provoke a fight between our two countries, so that we bloody each other so they can attack us when we're both weakened."

"Why did you attack Springfield?" "Your Majesty, at the insistence of Minister Jasmine, the Franconian Minister of Internal Security, who I now believe to be a dragon Changed One, King Henry ordered the Royal Expeditionary Force to conduct a punitive expedition against Springfield in retaliation for the attack on Weaton. Our orders were to engage any Baizian forces we encountered and raid the Springfield Treasury. We were ordered not to cause any unnecessary civilian casualties and not to destroy any civilian infrastructure, unless it had military value."

"Please describe your attack on Springfield," commanded the King. "We crossed the Amber River at the ford near Springfield but were ambushed in the pass leading to the town." "Ambushed, by whom?" "Seven Fire dragons; three on each side of the pass, and one blocking the road." "How did you survive the ambush?" "I can Sense people from a distance, Your Majesty, it's a rare gift in a magician, but I can project forces and people onto a map. Before crossing the river, I discovered the dragon ambush. Where I was expecting Baizian soldiers, I found only dragons. We circled around behind the dragons during the night, then created a Seeming to distract them the next morning. The dragons were so focused on the Seeming, we were able to creep up behind them and attack. None of the dragons survived."

"What happened next?" "We proceeded down the road towards Springfield, where we met Wizard Timothy." "Yes. Wizard Timothy, why did you surrender the city without a fight?" asked the King. "What were we to fight with, Sire? Over the last year, you've ordered all of the troops out of Springfield. The last battalion left for Westport three months ago. The Mayor left with them. I was alone, and as I informed Wizard Edward, I am no match for a force that can defeat seven dragons,"

"What do you mean, I ordered the troops out of Springfield? There should still be two Battalions stationed there!" said the King angrily, glaring at General Diaz. "Sire, I saw the orders myself. They were properly sealed and witnessed by the Court Wizard!" "I am betrayed," said the King. "Why would Wizard Louis act so?" "I believe that he was also a dragon Changed One, Your Majesty, which is why he tried to kill me before I could tell you about the dragons."

"How can you identify a Changed One?" asked the King. "We have discovered two ways: first, dragons do not use contractions the way humans do. They can't say 'can't,' 'won't,' 'I'm,' or any other contraction." "You're telling me that dragons can't say 'can't'?" "Just so, Your Majesty, that's how I know that you're not a dragon," said Edward, smiling. "It's incredibly simple but incredibly complicated at the same time. Dragons also smell different than humans do," said Edward. "They smell different? How?" "They have a reptilian scent, Sire. I believe that if you have General Diaz here, smell the Court Wizard's body; he can confirm what I'm saying." The King nodded, and the General reluctantly got down on his knees and sniffed the corpse. He nodded, "It's just as the Wizard says, Sire. It's faint, but definitely there, and certainly not human." Edward nodded his thanks and continued, "Dragon Changed Ones have learned to mask their scent with cologne or perfume, so it's often difficult to detect them just by their smell. I believe that's how Minister Jasmine, the Franconian Minister of Internal Security, eluded me. She always wears a heavy vanilla scent. It's also unseemly and disconcerting for a Wizard to go around smelling everyone." The King and his ministers laughed.

"You mentioned different kinds of dragons. How many types are there?" asked the King. "There are five types of dragons, Your Majesty: Fire dragons, which are red in color; Stone dragons, which are black or gray; Sea dragons, are blue or green; Snow dragons, are white or light grey; and Great dragons, are gold in color. According to the Changed Ones at the Academy, there should only be Fire and Stone dragons living on the west side of the Amber River. The Snow dragons live in the

Snow Fields of the north, and the Sea dragons inhabit the oceans."

"I have one final question for you, Wizard Edward," said the King, "How many of my citizens have you personally killed?" Edward thought for a moment, then said, "When I walked in here, I would have said 'one,' but I now believe the answer is 'zero,' Your Majesty.'" "I don't understand," said the King. "Your Majesty, after Senior Courier Keith and Courier Paul arrested me on the road, and I refused to be restrained. I provided water for their horses, which were dehydrated and panting. While my back was turned, Courier Paul attempted to stab me in the back with his dagger. My shields shattered the dagger, and I killed Courier Paul, but I now believe that he was a dragon Changed One, not a citizen. As to your Court Wizard, he was also a dragon, so I don't think I've personally killed any Baizian citizens."

"Senior Courier Keith, is this true?" asked the King. "Yes, Sire. I would also like to add that on our journey here, Wizard Edward repaired and enhanced each water station along the road. A more generous act than any I have ever seen from a magician, *any* magician." "Wizard Timothy, what is the current situation in Springfield?" asked the King

"Sire, at my invitation, one company of the Franconian Royal Expeditionary Force, along with their Battle Mage, is currently in Springfield. They are maintaining law and order that broke down when the last of the Baizian soldiers departed, and the City Enforcers all abandoned their posts and took employment with the remaining merchants who could afford to pay them. Mage Curtis and a Franconian Healer are operating a medical clinic for the citizens of Springfield in my absence. Additionally, the local merchants have again begun paying their taxes, which had lapsed in the absence of any enforcement mechanism," said Timothy in his most neutral, non-accusatory voice.

"I see," said the King, "And what of the Springfield Treasury that was to be plundered?" "Sire, when the Franconian forces saw the sad state of the city and its people, the commander of the Royal Expeditionary Force, Major Gerald, declined to take any of the hundred silvers remaining in the Treasury. Instead, he requested three wagons, to replace the ones that were destroyed in the fight with the dragons. I eagerly agreed to provide the wagons."

"And where is the rest of the Expeditionary Force?" asked the King. "They returned to Franconia, Sire, to report to King Henry. As I explained to Wizard Timothy, our mission was not to occupy and set up a military government but to raid the Treasury in retaliation for the attack on Weaton, then return. King Henry is probably wondering why they have not returned yet," said Edward

"And you came all the way here to warn me about the dragons?" the King asked Edward skeptically. "Sire, a year ago, I was nearly killed by a Great dragon outside the village of Farmdale; the beast broke my back and several of my ribs. I have no love for hostile dragons. However, having spoken to friendly Changed Ones, I have gained new insight into their way of thinking. I believe they are highly intelligent creatures and that some of them might be reasoned with. Others like Louis will try to destroy the human race. We cannot afford to fight each other. Once I return to Franconia and eliminate Minister Jasmine, I believe King Henry will heed my counsel. He already thinks highly of me because his own Court Wizard, Victor, was also a dragon Changed One who murdered his parents." "What happened to Wizard Victor?" asked the King. "I cut him down without mercy and removed his head, of course," said Edward.

Chapter Twelve:
FOOTPRINTS

"**I** am beginning to see that you would be a formidable enemy, Wizard Edward," said the King. "I would much prefer to be your friend. I have just one more question to ask; I know you said that the Royal Expeditionary Force snuck up behind the dragons and killed them, but how? From my reports, swords and spears, even arrows, are next to useless against dragon scales." Edward hesitated; while he wanted to secure King Donald's cooperation, he was not eager to disclose the existence of crossbows to a foreign leader.

"I see you're hesitant to answer," said the King, "what if I told you that we already know about these wonderful crossbows that the Franconian Army is using?" "Your Majesty, the crossbow technology was supposed to be a carefully guarded secret in Franconia. I'm astonished that you've heard about them." The King smiled. "News of your fight with the dragon near Farmdale has traveled far and wide, and the marvelous weapon that was so effective against the dragon has been the subject of much speculation here in Baize. I hope you won't be too shocked to learn, that for a mere two golds, one of my agents was able to purchase a crossbow from a soldier in Westport."

"I'm disappointed in our soldier, but I didn't expect the secret to last for long; so, in answer to your question, yes, every soldier in the Expeditionary Force was issued a crossbow and used them to great effect against the dragons that were positioned to ambush us," confessed Edward. "Your discretion is honorable, Sir Wizard, but if we are to fight these dragons together, we need the means to be successful. What can you tell us about these crossbows?"

Edward decided that full disclosure was his best option and said, "Sire, the crossbow is not a long-range weapon, and it is slow to reload, but the penetrating power of the iron bolt it fires is impressive. I've seen the weapon pierce plate armor at 100 yards. It's the only weapon I know of, short of a magician's Blast spell, that can penetrate a dragon's scales." "Then why the great secrecy?" asked General Diaz. "Sir, how are military officers selected in Baize?" "Why, they're normally recruited from the nobility, traditionally the second sons, who are unlikely to inherit, or the sons of wealthy merchants and traders in the Kingdom. Why does that matter?" asked the General. "It is much the same in Franconia, General. Now let me ask you this: if it became known that a common foot soldier with a crossbow could fell a mounted officer in plate armor, how would the nobles of the Kingdom react?"

The General looked troubled and replied, "Not well. I take your point. The nobles would be very unhappy to know that their sons were at risk. Although, it might improve the quality of our officer corps," he said with a sly grin. Edward laughed. "King Henry has much the same concern. I'm afraid that crossbows are going to change the nature of warfare." "How so?" asked the King. "Sire, the crossbow is going to make our current armor obsolete, which means that speed and concealment are going to be increasingly important, and we're going to have to develop new, lighter but tougher armor to counter the crossbow's power." Edward stopped himself, realizing that he'd probably said too much. "There is also the concern with brigands."

"Brigands?" asked one of the Ministers. "Imagine a band of criminals armed with crossbows and the damage they could do. That's one reason that the armorers making crossbows in Franconia are prohibited from selling them to anyone but the crown for the next three years." "You make very good points, Sir Wizard, and we will consider them carefully," said the King. "You must be tired from your long journey. I will have quarters prepared for you here in the palace, and would speak with you again once you're rested. I will not detain you in Baize for long, as I'm sure that you need to return and report to King Henry. I appreciate your candor in this matter, Wizard Edward." "I have been as truthful as I can, Your Majesty, and I hope you note that the glass of safety promised by the Binding spell has long passed, and the Truth Serum I drank wore off some time ago."

The squadron sailed at dawn, headed for the Coral Islands. The HMS VICTORY led the way, followed by the HMS VALOR, then the HMS VICEROY, with the HMS COMFORT trailing. The wind was strong out of the south, for which Andrew was grateful. He was fatigued from the effort required to replicate Seabow bolts. He wanted as many as he could make before they engaged the dragons and ordered the other ships' Sorcerers to do the same. It felt strange, giving orders to magicians who were older or the same age as he was, but Commodore Matthews told him that that was the nature of command and that he'd get used to it before long.

Once he had twenty bolts for each Seabow, he rested. He would need his strength for the coming battle. The ocean was empty before them, with nothing but blue water and cloudless skies above. Occasionally,

Andrew thought he saw a flash of something in the water off the starboard bow, but it could have been a school of fish or a trick of the sunlight on the waves.

At dawn on the third day, Andrew climbed up to the Crow's Nest, a wicker basket lashed to the uppermost section of the tallest mast. From there, he could see for miles, especially with a Sight Enhancement. While the view was spectacular, the motion of the ship was nauseating. Being up that high, every rise and fall of the bow was like riding a bucking horse, and Andrew had to hang on to the basket to keep from being thrown into the sea. About midday, he spotted the southernmost of the Coral Islands. "LAND HO!" he cried, as he began the treacherous descent back to the deck.

The Commodore met him at the base of the mast, "I might have known it was you, Andrew," he said. "No one else can see that far. RAISE THE BATTLE STANDARD! ALL HANDS ON DECK! MAN YOUR BATTLE STATIONS!" he bellowed. The triangular red flag was raised to the top of the mast, signaling 'BATTLE STATIONS' to the other ships in the squadron. In short order, all four ships were flying the battle flag, indicating that they had seen the order and were prepared for battle. "DIAMOND FORMATION! VICTORY IN FRONT, VICEROY TO PORT, VALOR TO STARBOARD, COMFORT AFT!" More flags went up, signaling the Commodore's orders. The ships assumed a diamond formation, intending to pass by the islands off the east side, every sailor scanning the sea and sky for dragons.

They sailed around the Coral Islands. Twice. And found nothing. Nothing in the water, nothing in the air, nothing on the islands. Andrew approached the Commodore. "Sir, are we just going to keep circling these islands? I don't see anything—even with Sight, Hearing, and Smell Enhancements, I don't detect anything on any of these islands." "I know. I don't see anything either," said the Commodore, lowering his telescope. "I think we'll anchor in the cove on the east side of the northern island for the night, then send a party ashore tomorrow to have a look around."

"Is there a water source on any of these islands?" asked Andrew. The Commodore consulted his map, "No, the map says that these islands are 'dry,' which means no freshwater." "That's odd," said Andrew. "Why do you say that?" "Well, Sir, unless dragons can drink saltwater, these islands would make a pretty poor base for them. Also, did you see all the trees and vegetation on the islands?" "Of course. What about it?" "Sir, trees don't grow without water, and I don't think that all that vegetation could stay that green just from the rain," said Andrew. "Then tomorrow, you go ashore with the Bos'n and three men and take a good look around. If there is a freshwater spring on the island, we might just establish a forward base here."

"The humans have come," said Cobalt. "I know," said Teal, "I received reports of their progress from their city of Sundock." "What are we going to do about it?" "Right now, they have four ships anchored in the cove off Acropo," said Teal. "I think they may be looking for us. They have never sent so many ships to our islands at once. It also appears that these are Navy ships with magic-users aboard. I think we should just hide in our caves and wait for them to leave." "You mean for us to hide?"

"Yes," said Teal. "If they find no trace of us, they will soon tire of searching and depart. If we attack them, they will send more ships, maybe too many for us to defeat." "I do not like it," said Cobalt. "If the humans attempt to build a permanent structure on one of our islands, we may have to do something more drastic. At least we know that the human, Andrew, is not with them. His ship was last reported escorting ships between the human cities of Grotton and Southport. Have two dragons stand guard on each island, under concealment, in case the humans discover us. For now, the ships are on the east side of Acropo; tell the Clan to go out tonight and gather enough food for three days. The humans will surely depart by then," said Teal. "Very well," said Cobalt. "I hope you are right." "As do I," said Teal.

The next morning, Andrew boarded the longboat, along with the Bos'n and three heavily-armed crew members. They rowed to the shore and began a careful survey of the island. Andrew noted that the beach was swept clean by the tide, and there were no indications that anyone or *anything* had been walking along the beach recently. They proceeded inland, looking for the freshwater spring that Andrew was convinced must be on the island. They walked to the highest point on the island but saw nothing of interest, just trees and scrub brush. Then, Andrew looked at the ground, and his blood ran cold. "Let's get back to the boat," he whispered to the Bos'n.

"What's the matter, Sir?" "Just shut up and follow my lead," whispered Andrew. Then he said in a loud voice, "All right, men, there's nothing here. Let's get back to the boat and tell the Commodore, this island is empty!" Andrew set a brisk pace back towards the longboat, with the sailors trailing behind him, confused.

"What's the matter, Sir?" "Quiet!" said Andrew, "just walk back to the boat and cast off. Whatever you do, don't run, and don't look back."

Andrew and the four now-worried sailors reached the boat and cast off, headed back to the HMS VALOR. "What was it, Sir?" asked the Bos'n. "Dragons," said Andrew quietly, "I saw dozens of dragon footprints in the sand when we stopped at the top of the island, and one set of the footprints was following us. The dragons must have learned the Concealment spell. I just hope they believed me and think they fooled us. Now, put your backs into it. I don't want to have to fight a dragon from a longboat." The sailors pulled hard for the ship and reached the VALOR in minutes. The Commodore was waiting when they came aboard.

"That was fast," he said. "What did you find?" "No fresh water, but lots of dragons, Sir," said Andrew. "Above the high-water mark of the tide, the island is covered with dragon footprints, and I'm pretty sure that one of them was following us under a Concealment spell." "What!" said the Commodore. Andrew nodded, taking a long drink from his water bottle, and then he said, "They're probably watching us right now, waiting to see what we're going to do."

"Recommendation?" "If I had to guess, they probably saw us coming, Sir," said Andrew. "I mean, it's probably impossible to sneak up on a bunch of Sea dragons by sailing up to their islands, circling them twice, then dropping anchor just off shore." The Commodore grunted his agreement. "So now what? We have orders to patrol these islands. We can't just run away." "Well, Sir, we sure don't want to fight them on land. We need the Seabows if we're going to have any chance." "Agreed."

"We need to lure them out somehow. I'm still convinced that there is a freshwater source on at least one of these islands. Otherwise, I don't think the dragons would stay here." "Which means if we do nothing, they can wait us out," said Commodore Matthews. "I'm not sure that's true," said Andrew. "They still need to eat. They probably come out at night to gather fish, and they might have to go a way out from the islands. If I was a fish, I sure wouldn't hang around here."

"So, what do you suggest?" asked the Commodore. "For right now, let's get out of here. I don't like being surrounded on three sides by land. Once we get out to sea, I'll try to think of a spell that might be useful. Failing that, we'll need more ships to blockade the islands, maybe the entire Navy," said Andrew. The Commodore gave the order, and within the hour, all four ships had left the cove and headed east, back into the open sea.

"Please allow me to show you to your room, Wizard Edward," said Mage Kathy, the Assistant Court Wizard. "It's down the hall, this way," she said, taking his hand. Edward was shocked by her touch but not alarmed. It occurred to him that he had not felt a woman's touch since his wife died several years ago. Kathy led him down the corridor from the King's private study to an elaborately furnished room that, while decorated with lots of gold leaf and finery, had obviously not been cleaned in some time, as evidenced by the dust on the floor and the furniture.

"This was the Franconian Ambassador's room," said Kathy. "I'm afraid that it hasn't been cleaned by the palace staff since he left abruptly several months ago. I'll ensure the staff cleans it thoroughly this evening during dinner. Will you dine with me?"

Edward thought carefully about the wisdom of dining alone (he assumed) with an attractive foreign magician, but his curiosity overcame his caution. "I would be honored," he said.

Kathy turned to leave, and Edward, surprisingly, decided that he did not want her to leave so soon. "Can you stay and talk with me a while?" he asked. "I wouldn't want to interfere with your duties, though," he temporized. "I'm sure you must have a lot to do as the new Court Wizard." Kathy laughed, "*I* will not be appointed as the new Court Wizard," she said. "For one thing, I'm only a Mage. The 'Assistant Court Wizard' title is just a formality. Most of my duties involve administrative paperwork and running errands for Wizard Louis."

Edward summoned a brief Wind spell, to remove the dust from the table and the two sitting chairs. He held one out for Mage Kathy. Kathy hesitated a moment, scanning the floor, then took the seat that Edward offered. "So, how much have I complicated your life by eliminating Wizard Louis?" Edward asked. Kathy laughed again, "Actually, you've made my life so much better than it was earlier today. Louis was a very demanding Court Wizard, and he didn't like hearing the word 'No.' I also believe that he's been trying to kill me lately." Edward looked puzzled and asked, "Why would he do that?"

"I believe that Louis has been reassigning magical support from our Army and Naval forces, supposedly looking for Dream Dust smugglers," said Kathy. "When I started to investigate, Admiral Vandall's secretary tried to push me out of my bedroom window in the tower; then I started finding poison in my food and water." Edward reached across the table and took her hand, "Well, he won't be doing anything like that anymore. I suspect the Franconian Court Wizard was attempting similar things. Wizard Victor terrorized the palace staff and most of the King's Ministers. I felt no remorse in removing him. So, tell me about the Kingdom of Baize; I know so little," said Edward, somewhat self-consciously releasing her hand.

"We are a Kingdom of 'haves' and 'have-nots,'" said Kathy. "In Baize, there is really no middle class. The wealthy run everything, and the poor struggle to survive." "What about the merchants?" asked Edward. "Most of the trade has been taken over by a few wealthy families, and the small shops are quickly bought out or taken over by the large trading houses. The military is always an option, but our soldiers make little beyond room, board, and clothing. Except for the officers, which, as you heard, all come from wealthy families."

"That explains why so many of your young people hope to have the spark of magic," mused Edward. "Exactly!" said Kathy. "There is no unemployment among our magicians. Those with the spark all find work either with the military, the crown, or even a wealthy family or merchant." "That explains much," said Edward. "In Franconia, those with the spark are often reluctant to enter the Wizards Academy, and our Regional Mages have to seek them out and, most often, bring them to the Academy unwillingly." "Our countries really are very different," said Kathy.

"Not really," said Edward, "most people just want to live their lives, find work they enjoy, make a living, find someone to spend their life with, and raise a family." "What about you?" asked Kathy. "Both my parents were magicians, so it wasn't a big surprise when they discovered I had the spark. I entered the Wizards Academy at eleven winters old. Nine years later, I came out a Sorcerer, having spent six years as a student and three years as a Mentor. I was assigned to the 10th Franconian Battalion in Westport. That's where I met my wife, Joyce."

"Oh, you're married," said Kathy. "No. My wife was murdered by one of Victor's henchmen while I was assigned to my post with the 11th Franconian Battalion in Prarrieville. I was investigating stolen weapons and got too close to the culprit. They killed my wife and tried to murder my son, Donovan, so I had to send him away to live with family in Southport until it was safe," said Edward. "Oh, Edward, I'm so sorry," said Kathy, taking his hand again.

"It was a long time ago, and the pain has eased somewhat. It helps that Donovan understands what happened and no longer holds me responsible for his mother's death. He's at the Wizards Academy now. So, enough about me, where are you from?" Edward asked.

"I grew up here in Baize. My father was a Mage, and my mother worked as a scribe, copying documents for the King and his Ministers. I practically grew up in the palace." "What happened when they discovered that you had the spark?" asked Edward. "My father was so happy because my future was secure. As a magician, I would have a career and not have to find some disagreeable husband to provide for me." Edward smiled and said, "Not all men are 'disagreeable.'"

"No, I suppose not, but around here, it seems that the more attractive you are, the more onerous the men who pursue you." "Then you must have had the most terrible suitors," said Edward. Kathy blushed. "Now that Louis is dead, what will you do next?" asked Edward. "I haven't had much time to think about it. Like I said, it's very unlikely that I'll be promoted to Court Wizard; that job is reserved for men. Is it the same in Franconia?" she asked.

"For the first time in history, the Franconian Court Wizard is a woman, Wizard Cassandra." "That's remarkable!" exclaimed Kathy. "Well, after I killed Victor, I recommended her to the King as the new Court Wizard, with maybe just the *tiniest* bit of Compulsion added in." "You used a Compulsion spell on your

King?" Kathy asked, shocked. Edward nodded. "I value ability and trustworthiness above any other characteristics in a magician. I couldn't think of a better candidate for Court Wizard than Mage Cassandra." "She was only a Mage?" "She was the Kingston Regional Mage, and she supervised three Sorcerers, one of whom turned out to be a dragon Changed One. She passed the Wizard's Test the day after her appointment as I knew she would," said Edward.

"You are a most unusual man, Edward," said Kathy. "You use Compulsion spells on your own King; advance capable women into jobs traditionally held by men; kill your enemies without mercy; defeat dragons; spare conquered cities; repair watering holes for foreign countries; and confront neighboring Kings without fear. Although, I do know that you have a most capable associate with you," said Kathy, looking at the corner of the room. Edward followed her gaze and said, "I guess you can come out now, Dirk." Dirk lowered his hood slowly. "Mage Kathy, may I present Senior Specialist Dirk, from 1st Company, Franconian Royal Expeditionary Force, Dirk, this is Mage Kathy." "I know who she is, Sir Edward. I'm not sure how she detected me," said Dirk, slightly bewildered.

"I didn't know you were here until we came into this room," she said, "it's the dust on the floor that gave you away. I saw your footprints in the dust, and I can just barely detect your Concealment cloak when you move. It's really quite remarkable." "I like this one, Wizard Edward. She's smart… like you. Since you appear to be in no danger from this lady," said Dirk, "I'll remove myself to the hallway in case there are any threats about." Dirk replaced his hood and stepped outside.

"I'm sorry for the deception," said Edward. "Even Senior Courier Keith doesn't know about Dirk. I asked him to follow us at a distance on the road." "Your bodyguard?" "Hardly," snorted Edward. "Dirk is 1st Company's Specialist/Assassin. His job is to eliminate sentries, spy out traps, and get into supposedly secure places. He is one of only eight such men in the entire Franconian Royal Guard. I thought he might be helpful here if I had to sneak into the King's sleeping chamber to deliver my message." Kathy laughed, "I would have paid gold to see that!"

"I'm just glad that Dirk didn't kill that Minister who was about to throw a dagger at me earlier. That would have been most unfortunate." "Knowing Minister Conklin, he would have missed and probably hit the King instead." Edward laughed, "So, what do you think the King will do now?" "He'll probably ask for your help. We've had trouble replicating the crossbow; at least Wizard Louis was unable to do so." "Being a dragon Changed One, he had reason to want those efforts to fail. Easily done. Anything else?"

"He'll probably ask you to go through the palace and root out any more Changed Ones before you depart," said Kathy. "Then you need to tell him to keep what happened to Louis quiet until tomorrow, or any Changed Ones will flee before we can catch them." "I hadn't thought of that. I'll go and warn him right now." "One more thing," said Edward. "Please tell the King that I may have a solution to the expanding Salt Flats problem."

Kathy rose from her chair, hesitated a moment, then impulsively kissed Edward on the cheek. "You solve that problem, and he may make *you* the Court Wizard of Baize."

Mage Kathy returned to her room. There was something about Edward that *excited* her. She hadn't felt this way about anyone before. Of course, she was grateful for his elimination of Wizard Louis, but she couldn't help feeling that it was something more.

"Is everything OK, Mage Kathy?" asked Stephen from the window. Kathy started, she had completely forgotten about Stephen, the apprentice magician from Middleberg who had come to her with a warning about Louis. "Yes," said Kathy. "More than OK! In fact, all of our problems with Wizard Louis have been solved!" "How was that accomplished?" asked Stephen. Kathy explained about the arrival of Wizard Edward and his news about the dragons. She also told him about how Edward had forced Louis to drink his own Death Serum, solving many of their problems.

"This Edward sounds like an incredibly powerful Wizard," said Stephen. "Yes, but he is also exceedingly kind. On his way here from Springfield, he restored and rebuilt all ten watering stations along the road. He also says that he has an idea of how we can contain the Great Salt Flats," said Kathy. "That would be amazing if he could do it," said Stephen. "Mage Elianna is from Springfield, and she often talks about the threat the Salt Flats pose to the Amber River." "Yes. I have no idea what his plan is, but I'm sure it will be *inventive*."

"Meanwhile, with Wizard Louis gone, I think it's time for you to be on your way back to Middleberg. Are you ready to depart?" "Well, you see..." said Stephen, hesitantly. "What is it?" asked Kathy. "I traded my horse for transport down the river, and I doubt that I have enough money to buy another horse or purchase river transport back to Middleberg."

Kathy smiled, "Easily solved. Let's head down to the dock and find out the cost of a one-way ticket to Middleberg. First, let me write out a note for Mage

Elianna." Kathy went to her desk and pulled out a sheet of parchment. Thinking quickly, she wrote:

Elianna,

Received your message. Much to tell you. Dragons can hear and understand human speech. They can also perform magic spells, including the Change spell. Louis was a Dragon, disguised as a human! He undoubtedly tried to poison you for being too efficient. Dragons can't use contractions, and they smell *reptilian*. No need to worry about Louis, a visiting wizard from Franconia unmasked and killed him. I am sure there are more dragons in Middleberg and elsewhere in the Kingdom. Be on your guard.

Kathy

Kathy rolled and sealed the message and reduced it in size, much as Elianna had done with her message. She handed the message to Stephen and bundled him off to the dock, where she was able to secure passage for him on a cutter that was sailing for Middleberg that evening. Kathy generously replicated ten silvers and five coppers for Stephen and sent him on his way.

"These are the nicest clothes I've ever worn," said Donovan. Rachel's father signed that he was pleased that Donovan approved of his new garments. Brian had made him three sets of clothes: a blue silk shirt with charcoal gray pants, a maroon wool shirt with silver-grey trousers, and a velvet, forest green shirt with tan pants. A heavy navy blue cape with red satin lining completed the ensemble. *I better not wear this green outfit around town very often,* signed Donovan, *or someone might mistake me for King Henry.* Brian doubled over and made a coughing sound; Donovan looked at Rachel inquisitively. "He's laughing. That's something I haven't heard in a long time."

Rachel's father retreated into the back room and returned with a package wrapped in paper, tied up with string. He handed it to Donovan with a smile and nodded at Rachel. Donovan understood immediately. He turned and handed the package to Rachel and said, "Happy Birthday." Rachel frowned and said, "My birthday isn't for another month." Donovan withdrew the package, saying, "OK, if you'd rather wait…" "Give me that present, you rogue! Now you'll just have to get me something else next month!"

She quickly cut the string and tore open the paper. Inside was a formal, peach-colored dress, with gold lace trim. The dress had an orange satin sash for a belt, and the shimmering skirt changed color from peach to orange to yellow, depending on how the light hit it. "Papa, this is magnificent!" she gushed. *I have always wanted to make you a dress like this*, her father signed. *But I never had the means. This color-changing cloth is very difficult to come by and very expensive. Can you afford it?* Signed Rachel. Brian smiled and signed that she had Donovan to thank, since he paid for the dress as a surprise when he ordered his new clothes. Rachel hugged her father tight, her eyes brimming with tears.

"We'd better make sure it fits," said Donovan. Rachel gave him a peck on the cheek, then disappeared into the back room to try on the dress. When she emerged, Donovan was speechless. This was one of the most beautiful dresses he had ever seen, and Rachel looked radiant in it. "What do you think?" she asked. Donovan struggled for words but finally said, "You look beautiful, but there's a problem." "What?" asked Rachel, scanning the dress for flaws. "You're going to need new shoes to go with that outfit. Your boots are great for the Academy, but they would clash with that dress. Fortunately, I know a good cobbler," he said, smiling.

Rachel and Donovan changed back into their normal clothes as they prepared to head back to the Academy. As they neared the door, they heard a boom of thunder and the sound of heavy rain striking the shop windows. "Oh, no!" said Rachel, "Our new clothes are going to get soaked!" "Not to worry," said Donovan, taking out his new cape and putting it on. "As long as you stay close to me, I think this will keep everything important dry." Donovan lifted up the right side of the cape, making room for Rachel, who snuggled under his arm and pulled the cape closed, protecting the packages of new clothing.

They left the shop and hurried towards the Wizards Academy, some blocks away. The new cape kept them dry, except for their heads, which quickly became soaked. Before entering the Gatehouse of the Academy, they ducked inside the cobbler shop, where Rachel was fitted for new formal shoes that would compliment her dress. The old cobbler was very excited to receive such an expensive custom order on such a rainy day. He told Donovan that it would take about six weeks for the shoes to be finished. While Rachel browsed among the shoes and boots displayed in the shop, Donovan took the cobbler aside and said that he needed the shoes for Rachel's birthday next month and slipped the old man an extra gold for the priority job. The cobbler expertly palmed the coin and quietly promised he would have them ready in three weeks.

The rain let up slightly as they left the shop and walked next door to the Gatehouse. Wizard Faith was waiting for them. "Ordering some new shoes?" she asked. "They're for Rachel," said Donovan, "a late birthday present, I'm afraid. I had no idea how long it takes to make shoes, or I would have ordered them sooner." Wizard Faith gave Donovan a knowing wink and opened the back door to the Academy courtyard. It was still raining, but now that they were inside the Academy grounds, they both erected weather shields, and Donovan walked Rachel to her room in the Mentor's quarters.

"I had a great time today. Your father is a very talented tailor." "Yes, he is," said Rachel, opening her door. "Now, why don't you come in and get out of those wet clothes before you catch a cold?"

The Compassion of Enemies

Mage Kathy

Chapter Thirteen:

FLOUR, SALT, AND SAND

"So, Mage Kathy, what are your impressions about the Franconian Wizard?" asked the King. They were seated in the audience chamber, with three dozen or so Ministers, Assistant Ministers, Deputy Ministers, Aides, Military Officers, magicians, and assorted strap-hangers in attendance. It seemed that everyone in the palace wanted to know about Wizard Edward. "Sire, I believe that you spoke wisely when you said that Edward would make a good friend and a dangerous enemy," Kathy began. "He is a most competent magician, and he uses the same spells that all Wizards know in creative ways to achieve ingenious solutions to complex problems. Consider, with only one Mage and fifty soldiers, he detected and killed seven Fire dragons, intent on ambushing his force. Then, he turned around and established a healing clinic for the citizens of Springfield. On his way here, he restored and repaired ten watering stations along the road between Baize and Springfield. This is a task that would probably have taken a dozen of our engineers along with some magical support, and he did it with no expectation of reward or payment. These are not the acts of an enemy."

"How do we *know* he supposedly restored these watering stations?" asked William, the Minister for Public Works. "I was with him," said Wizard Timothy. "As was Senior Courier Keith, and I assure you, Minister, those watering stations are in better condition than when they were constructed. What was most impressive, though, was the ease and speed with which Wizard Edward made the repairs." "How did he accomplish such a feat so quickly?" asked Wizard James, the presumptive new Court Wizard. "He began with a Dig spell, and used it to open a larger channel to the underground water sources, then combined the Sand and Adhesive spells to construct a wall around the new well," said Timothy. The assembled Ministers murmured amongst themselves. "I have never considered combining those two spells," mused Wizard James, "and you say it worked?" "Absolutely," confirmed Timothy, "Those sand walls were as hard as stone when Edward finished, and I judge that they will last for decades. As you know, the Sand and Adhesive spells take very little energy from the magician conjuring them. Using this technique, we could accomplish many of our planned city improvements, rapidly, at almost no cost to the crown."

Now, the King was interested. "Can you replicate this technique, Timothy?" "I believe so, Your Majesty. After the first time, I observed him most closely during his subsequent efforts." The Ministers began talking amongst themselves, speculating on all the ways that this new building method could be used. "Silence!" said the King. "Wizard Timothy, what will happen to these structures when Edward dies? Will his spells last?" "Yes, sire, those spells do not require maintenance by the magician. Once cast, the spell is complete and will endure indefinitely."

"Remarkable," said King Donald. "Mage Kathy, please continue. "Well, sire, I learned that Edward was once married but that his wife was murdered some years ago, on orders from the Franconian Court Wizard. He has one son, Donovan, who is currently a student at the Franconian Wizards Academy." "This Court Wizard, is he the one that Edward killed?" "Just so, Your Highness, but I believe that execution was done more to protect the kingdom, than out of any desire for revenge, although I doubt that Edward had any remorse about his actions." "I expect not," said the King. "Continue."

"There is little else to tell, sire. After all, I only spent perhaps a glass with him yesterday after our meeting in your private study." "But you had dinner alone with him last evening," said the King. "You are correct, sire," said Kathy, wondering which magician had been spying on her, "but we only spoke about trivial things: the weather, how magicians are trained here in Baize compared to Franconia, different types of food in each country, that sort of thing."

"You like him," said Donald. "I admit there is a certain *attraction* between us," said Kathy, "but I do not believe that it can lead to anything. He is a Franconian Wizard, while I serve the Kingdom of Baize." The King considered her words for a few moments, then said, "Very well, I would like you to continue your association with Wizard Edward. Learn what you can from him. There may be much he can teach us before I allow him to return to Franconia."

"*Allow* him, sire? I would strongly advise against any attempt to keep Edward here against his will." "A slip of the tongue, Kathy. We will certainly not attempt to keep him here against his wishes. However, if he could be *enticed* to remain for a short period, that could be most beneficial. If you take my meaning." "I do, Sire," said Kathy.

"Very well, is there anything else of importance that you learned from Wizard Edward?" "Sire, he did say that he may have a solution to the problem of the ever-expanding Salt Flats," said Kathy cautiously. "Indeed? One that we have not thought of? Not just using magicians to blow the sand back or contain it with walls?" "I believe so, sire, and as I said, he has demonstrated an ability to use magic spells in creative ways. He could be a great help to us, if properly motivated." "We will consider this carefully, Mage Kathy. Thank you for your insights."

"Now, is there anything else we have learned from the Franconians in the last few months? Wizard Timothy?" "Sire, one thing that I inquired about was how the Franconians defeated the dragons. Eventually, one of the soldiers told me that they used barrels of flour to incinerate two of the dragons that attacked their wagons," said Timothy. "Flour?" asked the King. "Yes, sire. According to the soldier I spoke with, they left several open barrels of ordinary flour in their wagons; when the dragons approached, Mage Curtis used a gust of wind to blow much of the flour into the air, then he ignited it with a Fire spell. The resulting fireball was apparently able to kill the two dragons that were about to attack the wagons."

"FLOUR?" "IMPOSSIBLE!" "PURE FANTASY!" exclaimed the assembled audience. The King held up his hand for silence, and the crowd quieted. "Are you certain it was ordinary flour, Wizard Timothy?" "Quite certain, Your Majesty. I inquired most insistently, and I spoke with several soldiers to confirm the tale after I heard it."

"Ahem, excuse me, Sire," said Stewart, the Assistant Minister for Logistics. "Yes?" said the King. "Sire,

Wizard Timothy is absolutely correct when he says that flour is extremely flammable. It burns faster than sawdust and would certainly cause a large fireball if a sufficient quantity were blown into the air and ignited." "Really? Could you demonstrate this effect for us?" asked Wizard James. "Of course," said Stewart, "all I would need is a small keg of flour from one of the kitchens. We should probably conduct the demonstration outside, though. It would undoubtedly set the curtains and furniture on fire if done inside." "Secure a keg of flour and meet us in the courtyard in one glass," said the King. "If anyone wishes to observe this demonstration, you are welcome, but it is certainly not required if you have other duties to attend to." The door to the audience chamber opened, and the ministers filed out, talking excitedly about new construction methods, exploding flour, and the Salt Flats.

Dirk knocked softly on the door to Sir Edward's room. "Come!" said Edward. The door opened, and Dirk lowered his hood. "Anything interesting happening, Dirk?" "Well, Wizard Timothy apparently learned about our exploding barrel of flour trick, and the King has asked for a demonstration in the courtyard in about a glass. That should be exciting," said Dirk. "The Minister of Public Works was very interested in your use of the Sand and Adhesive spells for construction repairs and buildings, and the King has asked Mage

Kathy to get close to you to entice you to extend your stay in Baize while they pump you for information. Oh, and the 'fix the Salt Flats' thing has most of them very excited, if doubtful." "I imagine so," said Edward. "I'm not sure my idea about the Salt Flats will even work, and it will take considerably more time and effort than simply repairing some small watering holes, but we'll see."

"What about the Mage?" "Kathy? I like her," said Edward, "and I don't think she's particularly fond of living in Baize. Maybe a 'Magicians Liaison Office' could be created so she could move to Franconia. It's a little early for those thoughts, though." "What are you going to do about the demonstration with the flour?" "I suppose I should go down and make sure no one injures themselves," said Edward. "Why don't you stay here and make sure no one tries to leave me any unpleasant surprises while I'm out? I'm sure you could use some rest."

"All right. What do I do if someone comes in?" "First, make sure it's not just the cleaning staff, then see what they do and get a good look at them so you can identify them for me later. Try not to kill anyone, please." Edward finished getting dressed, and then cast a Concealment spell before stepping into the hall. He proceeded to the courtyard, where a crowd had gathered to see if flour was really flammable.

A barrel of flour had been placed in the center of the courtyard, while the King and his Ministers stood back along the inner wall, well out of the danger zone. Some of the onlookers appeared to be awfully close to the barrel before Mage Kathy shooed them back. Kathy had obviously been chosen to disperse and ignite the flour, but Edward deemed that she was too close to the barrel for comfort. Moving swiftly, Edward moved next to Kathy and prepared to erect a protective shield over them both once Kathy ignited the flour.

"Ready, Your Majesty?" shouted Kathy. "Yes. Please proceed," said the King. Kathy sent a strong gust of wind at the open barrel of flour; the flour billowed into the air like a white cloud. Then Kathy said, "*IGNITOUS,*" while making the flicking gesture with her thumb. Edward simultaneously erected his shield. The resulting fireball almost filled the courtyard. The concussion knocked down several children who had gathered to watch, and the fireball ignited the clothing of some of the Ministers who were closest to the barrel. The fire sheeted around Edward's shield, which protected both himself and Mage Kathy. Without the shield, Kathy would have been badly burned.

Edward murmured, *"CODA,"* dropping both of his shields and pulling Kathy close to him. "You really shouldn't play with fire," said Edward sardonically. Kathy gasped and clung to him for support. "I had no idea it was going to do that," she said. The King and his Ministers approached cautiously. "That was extraordinary!" said King Donald, "and you ignited how many barrels against the dragons?" "I think each wagon had about ten barrels of flour," replied Edward. "It was an amazing fireball." "And it killed the dragons?" asked the King. "I watched the explosion with a Sight Enhancement spell from almost a mile away, and it appeared that the dragons inhaled the smoke and flames, which is what killed them. Dragon scales are not fireproof, but they are certainly fire-resistant," explained Edward. "I wish someone had told me you were planning this experiment. I would have been happy to demonstrate without putting anyone at risk."

"We didn't want to disturb your rest," the King assured him, "and some of the Ministers doubted that the flour would ignite at all or would be forceful enough to cause much damage," "I understand," said Edward graciously. "I myself had my doubts when one of our cooks told me how flammable flour is and how, in Franconia, we keep it well away from any open flames in our kitchens because of the danger. I'm sure your cooks know this as well. It's just that we never asked them." The King laughed, "That's true enough! Well, I think that's enough for now. Ministers, please return to your duties. General Diaz, it occurs to me that we might construct some type of flour hand-grenades in glass containers, which could be ignited by a magician. They might not kill a dragon, but they might give one pause."

General Diaz brightened at the thought. "I will direct the development of such a device immediately, sire! I will inform you when we have a working prototype." "Very well, said the King. "Be sure to consult a magician in the process." "Of course, Your Majesty," said the General.

"This has been an exciting morning," said Donald, "Wizard Edward, would you and Mage Kathy join me for luncheon? I find that I still have many questions." "I would be honored, Your Majesty," replied Edward.

As the people cleared the courtyard and headed about their daily business, Edward whispered to Kathy, "Whose idea was it for you to stand that close to the flour barrel before igniting it?" "I—, Wizard James suggested that I make sure to be close enough not to fail to ignite it with the King watching," said Kathy quietly. "Tell me about Wizard James," said Edward. "He will be the next Court Wizard. He has been the Army Chief of Staff for Magical Support for the last few years, stationed here in Baize at Army Headquarters. He is a competent Wizard, and I have never had cause to question his motives." "I see. Will he retain you as the Assistant Court Wizard?" asked Edward. "Probably not.

He has an assistant now, Mage Juliet, who he has worked with *closely* for the last two years, if you get my drift," said Kathy.

"I understand, and I would not fault him for that. So, if Mage Juliet replaces you as Assistant Court Wizard, what will you do next?" asked Edward. "I will most likely be assigned to one of the cities in Baize with the task of instructing and testing new magicians," said Kathy. "Will you have any say about which city you are posted to?" "I can ask, but there are no guarantees. It depends on which cities need Mages and the rotation of other magicians throughout the Kingdom." "I see," said Edward. "Why do you ask?" "I have an idea that I may propose to the King. I expect him to ask me about how to contain the Salt Flats, and I may have conditions for my cooperation."

"Conditions?" asked Kathy. "How would you feel about living in Springfield? Wizard Timothy is old, even for a Wizard, isn't he?" "Wizard Timothy is definitely old," Kathy said, stalling for time, "and I have never considered moving to Springfield. What do you have in mind?" "After the events of this morning, I'm not sure how safe you are in this city. I would remove you from danger if I can."

Before Kathy could reply, they were entering the King's private dining room. Edward was not surprised to see that Wizard James and one of the Ministers he saw yesterday would be joining them. Edward waited for the King to take his seat and say, "Please, everyone, be seated," before holding a chair out for Kathy and taking the seat next to her. The meal was excellent, if unfamiliar. It was some sort of meat with potatoes and a fruit compote for dessert. When the meal was over, the King said, "Wizard Edward, Mage Kathy has informed us that you may have a possible solution to our problem with the expanding Salt Flats. That is one reason I invited our Minister of Public Works, Minister William, to join us. As you can imagine, we are very interested in hearing any of your suggestions."

Edward nodded slowly, considering how to present his proposal in a way that would ensure success. Finally, he said, "Your Majesty, Minister William, first, I need to point out that I have never been to the Salt Flats and that all I know about them, I learned from Wizard Timothy on our journey from Springfield to Baize. As I understand it, the Salt Flats is an immense area of sand covered or mixed with salt, and when it rains, the rainwater expands outward, increasing the size of the Salt Flats once the water evaporates. I understand that you've tried employing magicians using Wind spells in order to blow the salty sand back towards the center of the Salt Flat area and that those efforts, and the construction of walls or other barriers to contain the Salt

Flats, have been generally unsuccessful. Have I summarized the situation correctly?"

"You have," confirmed the King. "Twenty years ago, my predecessor sent a hundred magicians to the southern and eastern edges of the Salt Flats to try and blow the encroaching salt back. They spent months on the task, and I'm sure they did their best, but their efforts yielded only minimal success. Today, the Salt Flats are bigger than ever and still expanding."

Edward nodded, "Do you have a map of the area? It would help me to visualize the situation." The King snapped his fingers, and a Page rushed out of the dining room to find a map of Eastern Baize. He returned quickly. Wizard James spread the map over the dining room table and secured the corners with an Adhesive spell. Edward nodded his thanks and scanned the map closely. "I presume that the Salt Flats are only expanding to the south and east," said Edward. "How could you know that?" asked Minister William. "By looking at the terrain," explained Edward, "the land in this area slopes south, away from the Caperian Mountains, and east away from this mountain range here," said Edward, pointing to the mountain range just to the west of the Salt Flats. "The water from the rain will flow downhill, towards the Amber River and Springfield."

"Very astute and correct," said Wizard James, "but what do you think we can do about it?" Edward paused before taking the leap. "Your Majesty, I may have a solution to this problem, but it will take magical resources and time. This is not something that can be remedied in a month or even a season. If you approve of my idea, I would be willing, with King Henry's permission, to supervise the project, at least initially, provided that I can have the assistance of a Baizian Magician of my choice."

"Anyone in particular?" asked the King with a knowing smile. "Sire, I only know three magicians in Baize," said Edward reasonably. "Wizard James here, who I believe is in line to be your next Court Wizard and is therefore unavailable; Wizard Timothy, who, while an able Wizard, is a bit old for such a physically demanding project, and he has other duties in Springfield, and Mage Kathy, who is the magician that I had in mind." The King considered the proposal for a minute, then said, "If Wizard James and Minister William feel that your idea has merit, I will agree to your terms. What do you have in mind?" asked the King.

"Your Majesty, yesterday I told you that the Royal Expeditionary Force crossed the Amber River and attacked the dragons that were waiting in ambush from behind. What I didn't tell you was how the Force got across the river," Edward began. "I assumed that you crossed at the ford," said the King. "That is what I believe the dragons thought we were going to do, Sire, and they had a Fire dragon flying over the Expeditionary Force to track our movements. Instead, under cover of darkness, the force moved north along the river road to a shallow part of the river. Mage Curtis remained alone with our three wagons. He cast a Seeming of the Expeditionary Force when he drove the wagons across the ford. Meanwhile, the Expeditionary Force crossed the river three hours north of the ford."

"How did you get fifty men across that river?" asked James. "I used a Dig spell to create a deep trench across the river and dumped all of the excavated sand and silt onto a sand bar on the downstream side of the trench. The soldiers galloped across the sandbar before the river filled the trench and washed out the sand bar. It all happened in a matter of minutes." "Ingenious," said the King, "but how does this help us with the Salt Flats?"

"Sire, I believe that it might be possible to excavate a large reservoir in the Salt Flats and use the excavated soil to construct walls around the giant hole we will dig. When it rains, the water will flow downhill into the reservoir, instead of expanding outward. If we make the reservoir big enough, you could even siphon off some of the collected saltwater and convert it to freshwater, which could be used for watering crops," Edward concluded.

The King remained silent for a time, considering this idea. Finally, he said. "What do you think, William?" The Minister of Public Works nodded and said, "Your Majesty, I think this might actually work! It would take a big, deep hole to contain all the water, and it would have to go all the way down to the bedrock, but I believe it's worth a try. But, as Edward very rightly says, this is a project that will take time and must be managed carefully." "James, what are your thoughts?" asked the King.

James thought for a moment, then said, "I agree that it's an interesting proposal, but the timing is not optimal, Sire. We are still on the brink of war with Franconia and these dragons. We do not have a hundred magicians that we can spend on this project." The King considered James's words and said, "James is right. I appreciate your insights, Wizard Edward, and your plan might work, but we simply can't spare the magicians at this time." Kathy looked crestfallen.

"I anticipated this very problem, Your Majesty, and I believe I have a solution that would allow this project to proceed without reducing your ability to provide magical support to your military forces," said Edward confidently. "And just how would this miracle be accomplished?" asked James skeptically. "As I understand it, Baize does not train young magicians with the spark at one central school, the way we do in Franconia, but rather, they are dispersed among your towns and cities where they are trained by local magicians," said Edward.

"That's essentially correct," said James. "So?" "So, send me these young, barely trained magicians, and we will make this Great Salt Lake," said Edward. "As you know, the Dig spell is one of the easiest to master, and it takes very little power from the conjurer. We could use these young magicians, who would be of little value in a battle, as a construction corps to dig a giant hole in the ground. We will also have time to teach them other useful spells, like Adhere, Wind, and shields," said Edward.

James's attitude changed immediately, "That's a brilliant idea!" he said. "I apologize, Wizard Edward. I had a suspicion that you were attempting to weaken our magical forces for the benefit of Franconia, but this idea is genius! We can build this reservoir, while giving some training to our young apprentice magicians and still maintain our magical forces in the field! You have my complete endorsement." The King smiled and said, "Well, Wizard Edward, it appears that we have a deal. Mage Kathy will accompany you to help with this project. What else do you need?"

Edward considered carefully, "Your Majesty, I appreciate your support. While this project will not tax your magical assets, there will be a need for provisions, tents, and transportation for these apprentice magicians. There could be considerable, non-magical expenses, and I will need the assistance of some of your engineers and builders."

"Of course, of course," said the King, "Minister William, you and your staff consult with Wizard Edward and Mage Kathy to determine what they will need in the way of resources and get me a list of their requirements, James, I need you to immediately send word for all our apprentice magicians to make their way to—Where do you think Wizard Edward?" "Springfield would be the most logical place, Your Majesty. From what I saw during my brief time in the city, there is plenty of room in the Army garrison, and it's close enough to the Salt Flats. Additionally, with Wizard Timothy's return, Mage Curtis and the remainder of the Royal Expeditionary Force must return to Franconia."

"Yes, of course," said the King. "When can you leave?" Edward was shocked by the question. "Your Majesty, I expect that it will take several days to put together a plan and identify the necessary resources for this project, but we could probably be ready to depart for Springfield sometime next week. I need to get a message to Mage Curtis in Springfield in case apprentice magicians begin arriving before we get there.”

William rose and said, “I will assemble my staff and begin gathering the supplies necessary for this project, Wizard Edward. Can we meet tomorrow to discuss any particular needs you might have?” “Of course,” said Edward. “Mage Kathy and I will come by your office after lunch tomorrow. Will that be soon enough?” Minister William said he would be ready for them tomorrow afternoon, and the King dismissed them to go and make their preparations.

After everyone had left the Dining room except the King and Wizard James, the King asked, “Do you really think this is going to work, James?” James thought for a moment, then said, “Wizard Edward is a most impressive magician, I must say. I have my doubts about how he’ll build such a massive hole without the sides caving in or the rain turning it into a mud pit, but the investment is minimal: one female Mage and some apprentice magicians, plus some provisions. I think it’s worth the risk. Besides, while Edward is working on this project, he’ll be working for us and not against us.”

As they left the Dining room, Edward said to Kathy, “I hope you’re not too upset that I asked for your assistance with this project. I know I didn’t ask you beforehand, and it must have been a surprise.” Kathy responded by giving him a passionate kiss. "I've only known you for two days, but I think I'd follow you anywhere," she said.

Chapter Fourteen:
HURRY UP AND WAIT

Donovan was awakened by a gentle tapping on the door. "Yes?" he asked. "Donovan, it's Leo. It's just after five." "Right. Thank you, Leo." Donovan heard Leo's heavy footsteps walking quickly down the hall. He rolled over, kissed Rachel on the neck, and said, "Great, now everyone in the Academy will know I spent the night here. I wonder how Leo found me." Rachel laughed softly, "There is very little that goes on in the Academy that the staff doesn't know about. Leo probably tried your room first, then came here. It's not a secret that we're dating."

Donovan pulled her close and whispered, "After last night, I'd say we're doing a lot more than dating." They kissed passionately, and then Rachel whispered, "Let's skip breakfast." Donovan shook his head and said, "Shame on you, a Mentor, trying to corrupt a lowly Level Three magician. You know I have Serums class first period, and we're making Love Serum again." "Maybe you're right," said Rachel, pouting. She threw off the covers and walked towards the shower. Donovan admired the view from the bed, then hurried to the shower himself.

Donovan arrived almost as breakfast was ending, and the other girls in his group snickered knowingly. "Did you sleep well?" asked Hope, mischievously. "Yes, we did," said Rachel, joining them at the table. Hope reddened. Without missing a beat, Rachel asked, "So, Laura, are you ready for your test tomorrow?" Laura was going to be given the Sorcerer's test this week. It always began on a Twoday morning, with the casting of a spell of the student's choice that had to last for three days. On Endday morning, if the spell was still active, the rest of the test commenced. If she passed, Laura would be promoted to Sorceress and either be assigned as a Mentor at the Academy or to another post in Franconia.

"I'm as ready as I'll ever be," said Laura. "Which spell will you cast?" asked Joyce. "I think I'll use a Tracer spell," said Laura, "I can easily hold that for three days." "I'm sure you'll do fine," said Donovan. "Any idea of what you want to do after you pass?" Laura shook her head. "I came to the Academy from Three Forks. The 6th Regiment is stationed there, and they have a Regional Mage's Office, but it's so cold up there in the winter, I'd rather go somewhere warmer, like Southport, Eastport, or Grotton."

"I hear that there's an opening in the Grotton Regional Mage's Office," said Rachel. "The Regional Mage was so angry with Sorceress Celeste for letting the young man she was transporting to the Academy get away that he said he doesn't want her back." "That's not fair," said Mary, "it's not her fault that the coach was attacked by brigands!" "Fair or not, that's what I heard," said Rachel. "I think Wizard Noland is going to take her back and make her the Mentor's supervisor, replacing Sorceress Karen."

"Then what happens to Karen?" asked Joyce. "She'll probably be assigned to the Regional Mage's Office in Smithville. That's where she's from, and she's been here for ages; first as a student, then a Mentor, then the Mentor's supervisor," said Rachel. Just then, the bell tolled for the first period, and the students quickly cleared their tables and headed toward the Lecture Hall.

As they entered the Serums classroom, Wizard Toffin was just putting on his cloak. "Ladies and Gentlemen," said the rotund Wizard, "we will not be making Serums today. Instead, we are going on a field trip to observe the effectiveness of the Serums you have produced in previous classes. Please return to your rooms, gather your cloaks and staffs, and put on your best outfits. We are going to court!"

Donovan selected the maroon top and silver-grey pants but chose to wear his travel cloak (his new cape was still damp from yesterday's rain). As the students assembled in the courtyard, Wizard Toffin gave them some instructions: "First, you are not to speak in the courtroom. We are there as observers *only;* second, you may get angry when you hear the charges against some of the defendants; there may be quite a few cases of child abuse, neglect, or the infliction of serious injuries between spouses. You are not there to render judgment or determine guilt or innocence; that is a matter for the court. You may disagree with some of the sentences imposed by the judge; again, it is not our place to comment or intervene. The Judges hear these cases every day and have an established system of escalating punishments. What may seem like a slap on the wrist for a first-offender, will result in a much more severe punishment for someone who has been charged with the same offense before. Does everyone understand?" The class murmured their understanding, now, not nearly as excited with this exercise as they had been a moment before.

The first case was simple adultery. A man with a wife and two children had been caught in an intimate embrace with another woman by his oldest child. The man had severely beaten the child in an attempt to keep him quiet. After hearing the evidence, the judge sentenced the man to a dose of Love Serum and a warning that this was his last dose of the Serum; the next time he was brought to court for a similar crime, he would be assigned to a Road Crew.

The man willingly drank the Serum and thanked the judge for his mercy. He left the courtroom arm-in-arm with his wife. "He'll be back," predicted Wizard Toffin, between cases, "This was his third offense. Each time he returns, he has another child." As the day wore on, there was a veritable parade of sorrow through the courtroom: beatings, adultery, child neglect, sometimes almost to the point of starvation, and, as Rachel had said, the husband was not always the abuser. The last case of the day was particularly heinous; the man was accused of sexually abusing both his wife and eldest daughter, who was only eleven. This was his fourth offense and the judge was having none of his excuses or pleas for mercy. "The defendant is sentenced to five years on the Road Crew; if he completes that sentence, he has an additional five years probation, during which, if he appears before this court again, the sentence will be death. Take him away."

As the Enforcers approached the convicted man, he drew a sharpened spike from his sock and lunged at the judge. *"LIGARE,"* shouted Donovan, making a fist with his left hand. The man froze, paralyzed, the spike inches away from the judge's throat. The judge recoiled in shock, and the Enforcers yanked the now-paralyzed man backward, dropping him onto the hard wooden floor. The Sorcerer from the Regional Mage's Office, who'd been flirting with the attractive court clerk when the incident began, offered his apologies to the judge. "Your Honor, I—" "Shut up, Sorcerer Chad! I've warned you before about being inattentive in court! This time, your dereliction of duty nearly cost me my life! You are dismissed. I never want to see you in my courtroom again!" shouted the judge.

The Sorcerer's shoulders slumped, and he began shuffling towards the door. As he reached for the doorknob, he suddenly turned towards the judge and shouted, *"TERMI—"* *"LIGARE,"* murmured Wizard Toffin, making the clenched fist gesture, and Sorcerer Chad was paralyzed before he could complete his killing spell. Chaos erupted in the courtroom. The judge banged his gavel until it nearly broke, "ORDER! ORDER! ORDER IN THE COURT!" he shouted. "Enforcers! Clear the courtroom of everyone except for the Convict, Sorcerer Chad, and the Wizards Academy students."

In short order, the Enforcers rushed the spectators, solicitors, and other court personnel out of the room. Once the room was cleared, the judge approached Wizard Toffin, "Jeffrey, you have my sincere thanks for your timely intervention. I knew that Sorcerer Chad was something of a scoundrel and a lady's man, but I never expected that from him, and who is this lightning-fast student of yours I have to thank for saving me from that first attack?" "Your Honor, allow me to introduce Level Three Donovan Francis," said Wizard Toffin.

The judge came over and shook Donovan's hand, "Thank you, young man, that was very quick thinking on your part. What made you anticipate the attack?" "I saw the man reach into his sock, Your Honor," said Donovan. "I've been in court all day, and no one else, not even those sent to the Road Crews or prison, responded by pulling up their socks." The judge laughed. "That's very observant, Donovan! So, what do you think we should do with these two?" the judge asked, pointing to the paralyzed convict and the Sorcerer.

"Your Honor, I'm not a solicitor or an expert in the law—" began Donovan. "Yes, I know, but you've been in court all day, and you've seen how most criminals are punished. So, let's start with him: convicted of sexual assault, fourth offense, sentenced to the Road Crew, then attempted to murder a member of the court. What do you say?" Donovan took a deep breath, then said, "Death."

"And this one: a member of the Regional Mage's Office, fired for incompetence, also accused of attempted murder of a judge?" Donovan hesitated, "Sir," he said finally, "if this had happened at the Wizards Academy, Sorcerer Chad would have his spark removed and be sent to the Road Crews. That's probably the appropriate punishment now." The judge smiled and said, "You're right on both cases. If you weren't a magician, you might have made a fine judge. Jeffery," he said, addressing Wizard Toffin, "I would never ask a student to carry out these sentences. Would you mind?" Wizard Toffin used a Death spell on the convict and an intricate Remove spell on Sorcerer Chad. Chad was led away by the Enforcers, still dazed and confused by what had happened.

"Well, this has been a trying day," said the judge with a wry grin, "I need to get home to the wife and kids. Thank you again, Donovan. You will be receiving a Special Commendation from the Superior Court of Kingston for 'Services Rendered.' Goodbye, Jeffery." "Goodbye Martin, I'll see you on Endday." The judge left, leaving the students alone with Wizard Toffin.

"Martin?" asked Donovan. "Yes," replied Wizard Toffin, "Martin is my brother. That's why we're allowed to observe cases in his courtroom. Although, after the news gets out about the events today, we may be invited by other judges."

They returned to the Academy just in time for dinner, and the entire Level Three dining room was buzzing with talk of the day's events. Wizard Toffin, of course, headed straight to the Headmaster to report on what transpired. "I never did like Sorcerer Chad," said Wizard Noland, "I was always getting complaints about him from his classmates about the unwanted attention he kept paying his female classmates. Donovan really paralyzed the convict?" "He did," confirmed Wizard Toffin, "he practically screamed the incantation, but I guess it was understandable given the circumstances." "I'll speak to him about it. It might serve to deflate his ego a bit after all of the accolades he's likely to receive after today," said Noland. "I can't remember the last time a student received a Special Commendation from the Kingston Superior Court." "I can," said Wizard Toffin, "it was Edward, for much the same action." "That's right, I had forgotten. That murderer tried to stab an Enforcer with a sharpened toothbrush." "I guess it runs in the family," said Wizard Toffin with a smile. "I'll send Donovan to see you right after dinner. That's if he can get his head through the doorway."

After dinner, Donovan headed over to the Headmaster's cottage. Jerry, Wizard Noland's houseboy, answered immediately. "Come on in, Donovan. I hear you had quite an interesting day in court," said Noland from the parlor. Donovan stepped in and took a seat in the armchair across from the Headmaster. "Yes, sir. It was a very depressing day, but then it got pretty intense after the last case." "So I heard. Now, first, congratulations on stopping the assault on the judge. That was quick thinking. Second, Wizard Toffin says that you yelled out the Paralysis incantation loud enough for the whole courtroom to hear. That is unacceptable. Do you know why?"

Donovan was taken aback by the rebuke but said, "Yes, sir. Because someone in the courtroom might have the spark and could try the spell and cause harm." "Exactly!" said Noland. "I understand that the circumstances were sudden and surprising, and it's only natural to be enthusiastic when conjuring a spell in defense of someone's life, but a magician must *always* remember to obscure the magical incantations." "I understand, sir," said Donovan.

"Now, it's unlikely that one of the few people in the courtroom actually has the spark, but you never know. Also, the Paralyze spell is not one of the more dangerous spells we worry about becoming common knowledge. So, all in all, you did very well today, but you could have done even better. There will be a short ceremony when we present you with the award from the court. I believe there is also a five-gold monetary stipend that comes with it. It might interest you to know that the last student to receive such an award from the Kingston Superior Court was your father, for his quick action in a similar situation. However, as I recall, he didn't scream out the incantation."

Donovan left the Headmaster's cottage slightly less pleased with himself than he had been when he entered, which, he decided, was probably Wizard Noland's intent. Rachel met him in the courtyard. "What's wrong?" she asked. "Wizard Noland just chastised me for shouting the incantation when I paralyzed the convict. I guess he's right, but it was a spur-of-the-moment reaction." "I understand," said Rachel. "I was going to mention it when we were alone tonight because I didn't want to embarrass you in front of the others."

As they strolled around the Academy, Donovan began to wonder where he was going to be sleeping. He didn't want to assume that last night's invitation was universal, nor did he wish to seem ungrateful or disinterested. Finally, he decided to just tear off the bandage and ask the question. "Rachel," he began, "I'm not sure how to say this. Last night was wonderful, and I want to stay with you every night, but I don't want to presume that it was an invitation to move in with you." Rachel smiled, "Hmm, you're not a Mentor, so I don't think you're allowed to move in with me," she said. Donovan's hopes sank. "However, you can certainly spend every night with me, if you wish." Donovan took her in his arms and said, "I absolutely wish."

The HMS VALOR bobbed on the open sea. Nearby, the other three ships in the squadron were conducting battle drills, loading and reloading the Seabows and crossbows, the Captains yelling for their sailors to work faster. Andrew paced the deck, trying to think of a spell that would be effective in luring the Sea dragons out, away from the islands where the small flotilla of ships could inflict some damage without being destroyed themselves.

Eventually, Commodore Matthews approached and said, "Have you come up with anything yet, Andrew?" "No, sir, not yet," replied Andrew. "We don't have enough ships to blockade the islands, and I'm not sure how we can lure the blasted creatures out into the open sea where we can mass our fires against them."

"Well, come on down to my cabin, and we'll talk and have some tea. Maybe something will come to you." They went below to the spacious cabin (for a warship). The Commodore struck a match and lit a small burner to warm the water in the tea kettle. Andrew sat thinking. It was maddening! So many magical spells, but nothing seemed to be useful in the current circumstance. Eventually, the water in the kettle boiled and the Commodore poured them both a cup of tea. "I suppose we could pretend that one of the ships was damaged and try to lure them into attacking," said the Commodore.

"I thought of that, sir, but the other ships would have to be so far away that the ship we use as bait could be sunk or heavily damaged before we got there." The Commodore just nodded his agreement. Andrew sat in the chair, drinking his tea, when he noticed the flame below the tea kettle. "Sir! I've got it! What if we sailed up to the southernmost island and set fire to it?" "Set fire to it? Can you do that?" "All Sorcerers have to be adept at igniting objects at a distance. Obviously, some of us are better than others and can cast the spell at a greater distance, but from half a mile away, I'm sure I can set fire to a palm tree. Once we get the fire going, it'll be self-sustaining."

"Do you think that will lure the dragons out?" asked the Commodore. "I'm not entirely sure," said Andrew, "but if I was a Sea dragon and you set my home on fire, I'd be mad enough to come out and try to stop you." "So would I," said the Commodore. "What do we need to do to prepare for the attack?" "Sir, I need all the other Sorcerers here to brief them on the plan and determine their abilities with fire; then, I can tell you how close we have to get to the island to make it work. Lastly, we need to work on speeding up our reloading of Seabows and practice shielding them between shots."

"Why would we need to shield them?" "Sir, these dragons aren't stupid. As soon as we start killing them with Seabows, they'll focus their attacks on them. If we lose too many of the Seabows, we might be in big trouble." "All right, I'll signal the other ships to send their Captains and Sorcerers here for a Council of War. We attack in three days!"

"I can make it, I tell you!" said Gek stubbornly. "No, you cannot. Not yet. Your wing is not healed enough yet. Believe me, Gek, I am as anxious as you to get to the islands, but I am not towing you halfway there if you suddenly cannot fly anymore!" said Azure emphatically. They had been on the beach for over two weeks now, and Gek was impatient to get Azure to the safety of the islands. She was getting heavier (and more argumentative) every day.

"Look, even if I cannot fly all the way there, I can swim the rest of the way!" said Gek. "No. Swimming is much harder than flying for you! Will you stop arguing with me? It is exhausting!" "I am sorry," said Gek. "I am just worried for you." "I know," said Azure, "and I appreciate that, but making your injury worse will not help us get to the islands any faster. We need to be patient."

"How much longer?" asked Gek. "It is a three-hour flight to Perfo from here. Once you can fly around for three hours, we can leave," said Azure. Gek had been making longer and longer flights each night. Last night, he made it almost two hours before he had to land because of the pain in his right wing. He knew that Azure was right, but he hated being the cause of their delay in getting back to the islands where Azure would be safe and could lay her egg.

"I will try again tonight," said Gek. "I think you should rest tonight. You flew too long last night and were whimpering in your sleep today. It was unbecoming." "If you insist," said Gek, his wing was really sore from the extended flight the night before. "But just for tonight. What would you like for dinner?"

"Fresh squid," said Azure. "What is a squid?" Gek asked, becoming more and more aggravated by Azure's weird food cravings. "They are multi-legged creatures with triangular heads, like octopuses with pointy hats. They are usually white or clear in color." "Where in the sea am I supposed to find them?" asked Gek. "They usually drift with the ocean currents," said Azure, "just swim out there and look around. I am sure you can find some."

"How many do you want?" asked Gek. "I guess that depends on how big they are," said Azure sweetly. "Just get me a mouthful," she said. "I am not really all that hungry tonight. I just need a snack."

Gek trudged down into the surf. *Squid! When would Azure stop with these weird food cravings,* he wondered, *and how was he supposed to carry a mouthful of squid back to her?*

Chapter Fifteen:
EXPLANATIONS

The second Company of the Royal Expeditionary Force rode into the Kingston garrison just after noon on Midweek. They proceeded at once to the stables to tend to their mounts. Major Gerald told Captain Fletcher to see tothe men, then release them until Firstday. Before departing to report to the King, he took Senior Specialist Lance aside and whispered, "Keep an eye on Corporal Sleet. I don't want him making trouble. I'll make the time off up to you later." "Anything you say, Major," said Lance.

The Major walked briskly into the palace, wound his way through the maze of corridors, and approached the Throne room, where the weekly Council of Ministers meeting was taking place. As the commander approached, the guards before the doors snapped to attention. "I need to report to the King and the Council immediately," said Major Gerald. The guards nodded, and one of them opened the door and announced loudly, "Your Majesty, Major Gerald, Commander of the Royal Expeditionary Force!" Gerald nodded his thanks to the guards and proceeded into the chamber.

The King rose to his feet and crossed the room. He extended his hand to Major Gerald; it was an extraordinary gesture from the King. "Major! How good to see you again! We feared the worst. Please, come in and have a seat. You must be exhausted." Major Gerald took an empty chair at the Council table, unsure of the reason for the King's concern. "Sire, I'm fine. The ride into Kingston this morning was easy and uneventful. I've come to give you a report of the Royal Expeditionary Force's punitive expedition against the Baizian city of Springfield."

"We heard that your force was ambushed, that there were many casualties, and that you were fleeing, while pursued by dragons and Baizian soldiers," said the King. "It's a miracle that you escaped alive." Major Gerald scratched his beard and said, "I'm afraid that you've been misinformed, Sire. While there was an ambush, we only lost two men and didn't encounter any Baizian soldiers at all." The King looked darkly at Minister Jasmine and said, "It seems that I have, indeed, been badly misinformed." Jasmine said quickly, "Sire, I told you earlier that some of my sources are not the most reliable of men..." "Enough!" said the King forcefully, "Major Gerald, please tell us what *really* happened on your way to Springfield."

"Of course, Sire," said Gerald. "The Expeditionary Force left Kingston and proceeded to Prarrieville, but two days into our journey, Wizard Edward noticed that we were being followed by a Fire dragon." "You're certain of this?" asked the King. "Very certain, Sire. The dragon was flying very high and ducking in and out of the clouds for cover, but Wizard Edward was using a Sight Enhancement spell to watch for trouble. Once he spotted the dragon, Sorcerer Curtis could see it too, but the dragon was too high for a man to see it with the naked eye."

"Did it *do* anything?" "No. Sire, it just followed us along the road," said Gerald. "In Prarrieville, there are two main roads leading to Colton and Weaton, respectively. However, Wizard Edward remembered a small trail used by smugglers, that he discovered during his posting to the 11th Battalion in Prarrieville. The path was narrow; it was just wide enough for our wagons, but it led directly to the ford across the Amber River and the road to Springfield. Knowing that you wanted this mission carried out expeditiously, we took the smuggler's trail, which cut two weeks off our travel time."

"A very wise decision, Major, go on," said the King. "Thank you, Sire. Well, as I said, the trail was narrow and wound through a forest, but we made good time. The Fire dragon stayed above us, following our every move. When we neared the end of the smuggler's trail, Sir Edward suggested that we stop for the night and plan our attack." "And what did you decide to do, Major?" asked Jasmine. "Wizard Edward took out his map and used a Seeing spell. Sire, you remember, like the one he used to determine the deaths around Farmdale." "Indeed," said the King, "and what did Wizard Edward discover?"

Gerald took a map out of his satchel and spread it on the table before the King. "We were here, Sire," said Gerald, pointing to the end of the smuggler's trail. "Here is the Amber River and the River Road that runs along the east side of it. Here is the ford across the river," Gerald said, pointing to the ford, "and then the road that leads from the ford to Springfield." "I see," murmured the King, "the road goes between these two hills; what are the red marks on the map?"

"Those are Fire dragons, Sire. There were three of them on each hill, waiting to ambush my force when we rode between the hills. The other dragon, the one that had been following us, was here," Gerald said, pointing to another red "X" behind where the force was camped. "Wizard Edward correctly predicted that this last dragon was going to block the road in front of us, and then the other six would attack us from the flanks." The assembled Ministers began talking amongst themselves, discussing what a sinister trap was laid for the Royal Expeditionary Force. Eventually, the King put an end to the speculation and said, "So, what did you do, Major?"

Major Gerald explained how the force left the cover of the woods and proceeded to the intersection of the trail and the River Road, just east of the ford across the river, and set up camp, as if they were planning to stay for a few days. "Why?" asked the King. "It was a trick, Sire," explained Gerald. "Once night fell, the entire force, except Sorcerer Curtis and our three wagons, rode north along the road. About three hours north of the ford, Wizard Edward found a shallow place in the river where he decided that we would cross the next night. It was approximately here," said Gerald, pointing to a spot on the map.

"Why didn't you cross immediately?" asked one of the Ministers. "It was getting light, Sir," said Gerald. "Instead, we backtracked to a farm we passed along the road and hid in a large barn throughout the day." "The dragons didn't detect the deception?" "No, Sire, you see, Sorcerer Curtis created a Seeming of the force at the campsite. He was able to create a reasonable illusion of the force, and because the dragon was so high in the air, it didn't detect the illusion." The King considered for a moment, "Is it possible, Wizard Noland? Could such a, what did you call it—a *Seeming*, fool someone?"

Wizard Noland considered the question, then said, "It's quite possible, Sire. The Seeming would be imperfect. It's impossible to make a Seeming of fifty men that would fool anyone up close, but if the dragon were flying high, it might not be able to discern the illusion." "Very well, please continue, Major." "Sire, Sorcerer Curtis remained in the camp throughout the day but monitored the progress of the Expeditionary Force through the use of a Seeing spell. He is one of the few magicians, along with Wizard Edward, who can conjure such a spell." "I know," grumbled the King. "If I had known that there were only three magicians in all of Franconia that could cast a Seeing spell, I wouldn't have allowed Sorcerer Curtis to accompany you."

"I think his ability to cast that spell is one reason that Wizard Edward selected him to come with us, Sire, and he proved invaluable." "I hope so," said the King, "go on." "As darkness fell, the Expeditionary Force left the barn and proceeded back to the river, to the place that Edward had selected. Edward then used a Dig spell to get us across the river." "A Dig spell?" asked Wizard Noland, "how did that work?" "Edward dug a large trench across the riverbed just upstream from a small sandbar. He dumped the sand, mud, and silt from the trench on top of the sand bar, creating a path across the river. The river flowed into the trench, and the water level downstream dropped to just a trickle. The Expeditionary Force galloped across quickly. It only took a couple of minutes to cross the river. After the water filled the trench, it resumed its course and washed out the temporary sandbar." "Ingenious," muttered Noland, "Edward always was sneaky."

"Then what happened?" asked the King. "Then we rode like mad through the night. We had crossed the river north of the hills where the dragons lay in ambush, and we circled around behind them and crept up on them during the night. The next morning, when Sorcerer Curtis used his Seeing spell and saw that we were in position behind the dragons, he tied the three wagons together, removed the canvas covers from them, and proceeded across the ford, while maintaining the Seeming of the Force. When he got to about here," said the Major, pointing to a spot on the road almost between the two hills, "he stopped, unhitched the horses, and took cover in a small clump of boulders."

"What happened next?" "The dragon that had been following us landed in the center of the road, blocking the path. Once he landed, Wizard Edward, myself, and the two Senior Specialists from the Expeditionary Force crept up behind him under a Concealment spell cast by Wizard Edward. When we were in position, he signaled Sorcerer Curtis that we were about to attack." "How did he do that?" asked Marshall Guzman, speaking for the first time. "Wizard Edward had Sorcerer Curtis put a Tracer spell on a coin and give it to him. Just before we attacked, Wizard Edward dissolved the Tracer spell, letting Sorcerer Curtis know to take cover."

"What did you do then?" asked the King. "We attacked, Sire, savagely. Oh, I forgot to mention that Wizard Edward and Sorcerer Curtis replicated crossbows for every man in the Expeditionary Force. As you know, swords and spears are useless against dragons. Anyway, our first volley killed five of the dragons outright and wounded the other two. One of them turned and blew fire all around him, killing two soldiers in 2nd Company. The wounded dragons then took flight and headed towards the wagons, where Sorcerer Curtis was still maintaining the Seeming. As they approached, he dissolved the Seeming and prepared our final surprise."

"What was that?" asked Marshall Guzman. "We had loaded each wagon with ten open barrels of flour, Sir. As the dragons approached, Sorcerer Curtis used a Wind spell to blow the flour into the air, like a giant white cloud. When the dragons entered the cloud, Sorcerer Curtis ignited the flour with a Fire spell. The resulting fireball was truly impressive, and it incinerated the two dragons who were intent on attacking the wagons. They slammed into each other and crashed down on top of the wagons, destroying them and killing two of the horses."

"You expect me to believe that you accomplished this using ordinary flour?" asked the King, incredulously. "Your Majesty," said the Minister of

Logistics, "flour is highly flammable, even more so than sawdust. There have been several accidents in the Kingdom, where unwise cooks have placed flour barrels too close to open flames in kitchens and been badly burned when the flour ignited." "And Wizard Edward knew about this?" asked the King. "No, Sire, he learned about it from Corporal Fry, one of my cooks, but he did some small experiments, then replicated thirty barrels of flour to place in the wagons. It was most effective," said Gerald.

"After the dragons were disposed of, Edward rode out and met Sorcerer Curtis on the road. Wizard Noland, I need to inform you that Wizard Edward conferred a battlefield promotion to Sorcerer Curtis, for exceptional valor in the face of overwhelming forces. He hoped that you would confirm the promotion." Wizard Noland smiled and said, "Sorcerer Curtis was scheduled to take the Mage's test the week after the force departed; that is undoubtedly another reason why Edward selected him to accompany the Expeditionary Force. I heartily endorse Wizard Edward's actions. Sorcerer Curtis Martin is hereby promoted to Battle Mage and it will be so noted in the Wizards Academy records."

The King smiled, then asked, "What happened next?" "Sire, we rode with all speed towards Springfield, expecting to encounter Baizian soldiers at any minute." "That's right, where were the Baizians during the dragon attack?" "Long gone, Sire. Just outside of the city, we were met by an old Baizian Wizard named Timothy, who surrendered the city to us without a fight." "Why would he do that?" asked Marshall Guzman. "Timothy said that the last Battalion of Baizian soldiers had left Springfield some months ago, headed for Westport, and that the city was utterly defenseless. He said that one old Wizard was no match for a force that could defeat seven Fire dragons. We rode into Springfield unopposed."

The King looked angrily at Jasmine and said, "You are to cease contact with the informant who gave you such poor intelligence immediately." Jasmine blanched, bowed her head, and said, "Of course, Your Majesty. I realize that I have failed you. Would you like my resignation?" The King thought for a moment, then said, "Not at present, but you need to do better in the future." "Of course, Sire," said a relieved Jasmine.

"So, what did you find in Springfield?" asked the King. "A defeated city, Your Majesty," said Major Gerald sadly, "There were only a few hundred hungry and despondent citizens left in the city. The Royal Expeditionary Force soldiers took over the administration of the city, restoring law and order to the streets, collecting taxes from the few remaining merchants who had stopped their payments in the absence of any authority. Mage Curtis and my two

Senior Healers set up a medical clinic in the city to tend to the sick and injured. Wizard Edward repaired the water fountain in the city square and repaired some buildings that were in danger of collapsing."

"You were sent to raid the Treasury. What did you find?" asked the King. "Sire, the Springfield Treasury only held a hundred silvers. Instead of taking the little remaining currency from them, I commandeered three new wagons to replace ours that had been destroyed by the dragons." "You feel that was sufficient?" asked the King. "Your Majesty, the people of Springfield are desperate. Taking more would have been cruel." The King considered this for a moment, then said, "Very well. Where are Wizard Edward, Mage Curtis, and the rest of your forces now?"

"Sire, Mage Curtis, and First Company remained in Springfield to maintain order until Wizard Timothy returns. Wizards Edward and Timothy went to Baize to confer with King Donald," said Gerald. The King's mood darkened. "Explain." "Sire, Wizard Edward believes, and I agree, that the dragons are attempting to get Franconia and Baize to fight each other; then, when we are weakened, they will attack us both." "How did you come to that conclusion?" the King asked. "Sire, all of the attacks so far have been by dragons, the attack on Riverside in Baize, Weaton here, and the attacks at sea. We have not engaged any Baizian forces in the field. It appears that the dragons are trying to provoke a fight between us for some reason. Wizard Edward is going to explain his reasoning to King Donald in an attempt to forestall any attacks on us by Baizian forces. I believe his theory is sound."

"That's preposterous!" said the Minister of Foreign Affairs. "This is a mission for someone with training in diplomacy, not a Battle Wizard!" Wizard Noland laughed. "Minister, Edward is more than capable of diplomacy when the situation calls for it. He is also capable of removing King Donald or any member of his court if he feels it necessary. I suspect that Edward is concerned that King Donald is receiving bad advice, possibly from a dragon Changed One, which would explain their bellicose attitude towards us lately."

The King paused and considered Wizard Noland's words. "We'll see. So, Major Gerald, you returned to Kingston with half your force. When will 1st Company return?" "It will likely be some weeks yet, Sire. It's a two-week journey from Springfield to Baize, and it took us almost three weeks to get here from Springfield, so Wizards Edward and Timothy should be in Baize by now. They may already be heading back to Springfield. I doubt Wizard Edward would stay in Baize more than a week," said Gerald.

"Very well," said the King. "I would promote you again, Major, but you already hold the rank of a Regimental commander. Instead, I am awarding the Royal Expeditionary Force the Distinguished Service Award. It comes with a two-gold bonus for you and all your men." "Thank you, Sire! The men will be most appreciative!" "If there is nothing else, this meeting is adjourned," said King Henry.

As the Ministers filed out of the throne room, Gerald approached Wizard Noland and Marshall Guzman and asked if he could have a word in private. Marshall Guzman led them to his office and sat down behind his desk," So, Major, what did you want to tell us that you didn't want the rest of the Council to hear?" Major Gerald handed Edward's note to Wizard Noland, saying, "Sir, Wizard Edward asked me to deliver this to you. I didn't read it, but I think I know what it says." "Really?" asked Wizard Noland. "Yes, Sir. Wizard Edward believes that Minister Jasmine is a dragon Changed One."

Marshall Guzman sat up straighter in his chair, "Is he sure?" "No, Sir, but those Fire dragons knew we were coming, and they knew it almost as soon as we left Kingston. There's also the fact that she doesn't use contractions and always wears a heavy vanilla scent." "That's pretty flimsy evidence, Major." "Yes, Sir, it is. But wasn't Minister Jasmine the one who insisted that we needed to launch a punitive expedition against Springfield? From what I heard today, she also falsely reported that my force had been ambushed and decimated. That's quite a coincidence, if you ask me," said Major Gerald.

"You may be right," said Noland, "and you are correct; this note has two words on it: 'Jasmine Onyx.' Edward may be wrong, but I trust his instincts on this. Henceforth, we need to be more careful about what we say around her. Is there anything else?" "Yes, Sir, two things; first, no one really asked me how my soldiers were able to sneak up behind those dragons. It's because Wizard Edward and Mage Curtis made Concealment cloaks for me and all my men." "You mean like those that Specialists wear?" asked Marshall Guzman.

"Yes, Sir. Just like them. Once we crossed the river, we all put on our cloaks. The dragons never saw us coming," said Gerald. Marshall Guzman whistled. "That could be a significant advantage! I thought those cloaks were incredibly expensive and hard to make." "Expensive, yes, but Edward figured out how to make them. It only took him a day to make one for every member of the Expeditionary Force. My Specialists were not too happy about it." "I can imagine," said Marshall Guzman, smiling.

"How did he do it?" asked Noland. "I think he cast a Concealment spell on the cloak, then added a Stamina spell, so that it would last, Sir," said Gerald, "otherwise the concealment effect faded in just a few seconds." Noland nodded, "Very clever." "Yes, Sir, unfortunately, the cloaks don't stop fire. I still lost two men, despite their cloaks." "Still, this could be a great strategic advantage for us," said Marshall Guzman. "Imagine, an invisible Army!" "It is certainly a revolutionary idea, and it may give us a decisive edge against the dragons," said Noland. "But, we certainly have to keep this a secret from Jasmine, at least until we know whether she's a Changed One or not." "Agreed," said the Marshall, "now I understand why you wanted to talk to us alone."

"There's one more thing, Sir. When we passed through Prarrieville, I recruited two replacement soldiers from the forces there. I'm worried that one of them, Corporal Sleet, maybe a dragon Changed One."

Celeste approached the Gatehouse to the Wizards Academy with great uncertainty. She was returning in disgrace, having been dismissed by the Grotton Regional Mage for her failure to deliver Jed to the

Wizards Academy. Mage Charles just wouldn't listen to reason; she tried to explain about the brigands and the trench dug into the road, which caused the carriage to catapult into the air, landing on its top and knocking her unconscious. When she woke, Jed and the bandits were gone. That wasn't the truth, but it was plausible, and she couldn't believe that she'd been summarily dismissed for what she considered an unavoidable incident.

As she approached the door, she wondered if anyone would answer, since it was Foursday and not Midweek, when new students were admitted. She knocked softly, almost hoping no one would answer. The door opened immediately, and Wizard Faith ushered her into the Academy. "Welcome back," she said, "are you hungry?" "No, thank you, Wizard Faith," said Celeste. "I suppose I need to speak to the Headmaster straight away." "He's expecting you. You know the way."

Celeste walked across the empty courtyard. She knew that all of the students were at their lessons because she had timed her arrival to avoid running into another Mentor or one of her former students as soon as she walked in the gate. It would be embarrassing enough later. As she stepped onto the Headmaster's porch, the door opened, and Jerry, the door warden, came out and said, "Go right in, Sorceress Celeste. He's expecting you."

Celeste entered the cottage and found Wizard Noland seated in a large, over-stuffed armchair in the parlor. "Come in and have a seat, Celeste. I know it's been a long journey." Celeste entered and sat down on the small sofa across from Wizard Noland. She sat with her hands in her lap, her eyes downcast. "Now, I want you to tell me the truth about what really happened to you on the road from Grotton and none of this nonsense about bandits," said Wizard Noland sternly.

Celeste looked up, hopefully, "You know?" she asked. "I know damn well that it wasn't bandits," said Wizard Noland angrily. "Celeste, do you know why you were dismissed from the Grotton Regional Mage's Office?" "Because I let the boy I was escorting to the Academy escape," she said. "No. You were dismissed because you lied to Mage Charles about what happened. He doesn't know exactly what happened, but he knows that you lied to him when you claimed it was bandits that attacked the carriage. You lost his trust, and he told me that he could no longer work with you," said Noland. "Now I want the truth." The *'or else'* hung in the air between them.

"You're right, Sir. It wasn't bandits. It was a dragon. You see, the boy I was transporting was a Great dragon, Changed One. Neither Mage Charles nor I detected him, since he said almost nothing to us the entire time we had him in custody. He just kept insisting that he didn't have the spark. I had him under a Paralyze spell, so he couldn't move. I sat on one side of the carriage, with my back to the driver, and he sat facing forward. I was telling him all about the Academy, how he would grow to like it here, and all the friends he would make, you know, trying to make the transition easier for him. You know how hard it is for 'drag-ins.'" Wizard Noland nodded, his countenance softening slightly. "Go on," he said.

"Suddenly, the driver went flying into the woods. I don't know what happened, but the horses went wild; they were galloping as fast as they could go, throwing the carriage from side to side, tilting it on two wheels. Jed and I were being tossed about inside, unsure of what was going on. I was so startled that I didn't release the Paralyze spell, and poor Jed was flung about the cabin without the ability to brace himself or protect his head as he was thrown about. Then, I guess the dragon used a Dig spell to create a trench in the road. The poor horses fell into it, breaking their legs and catapulting the carriage end over end until we came to a stop upside down."

"That must have been frightening," said Noland. "What happened then?" "I must have lost consciousness," said Celeste. "When I woke up, Jed was outside the coach, and the Paralyze spell was broken. Jed had a head wound, a shattered shoulder, some broken ribs, and internal bleeding. I tried to crawl over to help him, but my leg was broken. That's when I saw the dragon."

"Describe it," said Noland. "She was big, almost 35 feet long, the most brilliant aqua blue, and she was distraught about Jed's injuries; I think she was his mate. She just kept saying how sorry she was about causing the carriage wreck, that she was only trying to stop the horses, and that she didn't know what to do to help him." "I understand; what did you do next?" "I said that if she helped me out of the carriage, I would try to heal Jed. I didn't want him to die. I mean, he might have been a Changed One like Terry," she said.

"Continue," said Noland. "Yes, Sir. Well, I had some Healing Serum in my handbag, and I asked the dragon to get it for me. She transformed into a human girl, naked, with a blue streak in her blonde hair. She crawled into the carriage and retrieved my bag, and I gave Jed some Healing Serum. I think it stopped the internal bleeding and mended his ribs, but he was still in a bad way, so I cast a Healing spell. That closed the head wound, and he seemed to be breathing easier. Then the carriage driver came running up, shouting about the dragon and asking the girl why she didn't have any clothes on. She used a Sleep spell on him and he fell in the grass."

"I see. What did the dragons do next?" "Well, they had a brief discussion about whether they needed to kill me and the driver, but I convinced them that since I had just saved Jed's life, it wouldn't be very grateful of them." Wizard Noland smiled at that. "Eventually, they decided that I should be spared. They even gave me what was left of the Healing Serum so I could heal my broken leg. I asked them if they wanted to remain in human form, but they said no, but that in appreciation for my saving Jed, they named me a Dragon-friend, and said that they would try to spare me in the coming war. I asked them why there had to be a war, and they said that it was because humans were treacherous and untrustworthy."

"I understand why they might feel that way," said Noland, "What else?" "Well, the girl, her name was Azure, turned back into a Sea dragon, and Jed climbed on her back. Before they left, I advised Jed not to transform back into a dragon for a few days, since I wasn't sure how healing spells and Serums would work on dragons. I asked them how I should explain the carriage crash and whether I should tell anyone about them. They said it didn't matter to them, and I could tell whatever story I liked. Before they flew off, I asked Jed his real name, and he said it was Gek."

"I see. It seems the dragons were more inclined to tell the truth than you were. Why is that?" "Sir, Mage

Charles was so angry with me, I just couldn't bring myself to tell him that, not only did I let a dragon Changed One escape, but that I healed him. I'm not sure he would have understood." "You may be correct. Still, magicians do not lie to each other! You could have told him this story in confidence, and you might still have a job in the Regional Mage's Office."

Celeste nodded. "So, what happens to me now?" she asked. "That depends," said Noland, "How do you think we should explain what happened? Rumors are already circulating. Do we stick with the 'brigands story' or tell everyone the truth?" Celeste bowed her head and wept; it was a terrible choice. Finally, she said, "I tell the truth, Sir, and I apologize to Mage Charles."

Wizard Noland looked at her sternly and said, "If you had given any other answer, I would have removed your spark immediately and made you a gardener. Instead, you will stay here and supervise the Mentors. After some time passes, people will forget your mistake, and you will get a second chance outside the Academy."

Commodore Matthews

Chapter Sixteen:

DEATH, DEATH, AND MORE DEATH

After arranging to meet Kathy for dinner, Edward returned to his room, where he found Dirk pacing the floor. "Is something wrong?" Edward asked. "I think so," said Dirk. "Someone crept in here about two glasses ago and rummaged through your things. I don't know what she was looking for, but she was very careful to put everything back exactly as she found it." "Did she leave anything behind?" asked Edward. "Not that I could see," said Dirk, "but she was muttering to herself."

Edward sighed, "That sounds like a magician. Let's see what kind of spell she cast. '*MAGNUS,*'" Edward said quietly while steepling his fingers, a strong red glow encompassed the pitcher of water on the table. "Oh, my. Death Serum in the water pitcher. I must be making someone here very nervous. What did this woman look like?" "She had red hair, was tall for a woman, and was dressed in servant's clothes with an apron. She looked like she was about twenty winters old." "That sounds like a Fire dragon Changed One.

We'd better go and find her. Bring your crossbow and load it with the poisoned arrows. This could get messy."

Edward vanished the spelled water pitcher with a Remove spell, then headed out into the corridor. Being unfamiliar with the layout of the palace, he had no idea where to begin his search. He decided to find Mage Kathy. She might know who they were looking for and where to find them. He stopped the first palace servant he came upon and asked where he could find the Assistant Court Wizard. "Her office is down this hallway, sir. It's the fifth door on the left." Edward nodded his thanks and hurried along the corridor. He had a bad feeling about this.

When he reached the fifth door, he burst in without knocking. Mage Kathy looked up, startled, she had a quill in her hand, and several maps laid out on her desk. A glass of water sat on the edge of the desk. "Edward, what's wrong?" "Don't drink that!" Edward said, urgently. "It may be poisoned." "Poisoned!" "Yes," said Edward, as he used the Remove spell on her water glass. "Someone came into my room while I was out and put Death Serum in my water pitcher. I had Dirk guarding my things and I told him not to kill anyone. He didn't know she was a magician." "She?" "Yes, according to Dirk, she is a tall, red-haired woman, about twenty winters old, wearing servant's clothes with an apron. Do you have any idea who that could be?"

"That sounds like Marissa, but she's been here for years!" said Kathy. "Well, she's either a dragon Changed One, or someone with a grudge against Franconian Wizards. We need to find her. Now." "Of course, she's probably in the kitchen, follow me." They rushed through the palace, turning left, then right down a maze of passageways, and down several flights of stairs. As they reached the doorway to the kitchen, Edward held up his hand and said, "Dirk."

The Specialist crept into the kitchen like a breath of air, he touched Edward on the shoulder as he passed, letting him know as he entered. The kitchen was empty except for the body of Marissa, which was in the back corner of the pantry. "All clear," said Dirk. "She's in the pantry, dead." Kathy rushed forward to see, then turned and vomited into the sink. Edward laid a comforting hand on her back. "We need to tell the King. There are more Changed Ones in the palace."

The smoke rose from the southernmost Coral Island, reaching high into the sky. The thick smoke was pushed north, towards the other islands by the strong south wind. Commodore Matthews had deployed his ships in a line, a quarter of a mile south of the island. The HMS

VICTORY was in the lead, followed by the COMFORT, the VALOR, then the HMS VICEROY. Once in position, the magicians aboard each ship had begun setting everything that was flammable on the island on fire.

While Andrew and Sorcerer Roger aboard the VICTORY could ignite things from farther away, Sorceress Anne aboard the COMFORT, and Sorcerer Marvin aboard the VICEROY were at their limits. Casting the Fire spell on water was more difficult than when on land. So, Andrew and Roger were igniting the trees on the north side of the island, while the other two magicians concentrated on the south side. They wondered how long it would be before the dragons came out to fight.

They didn't have to wait long. It was only a matter of minutes after the first fire was conjured before five Sea dragons broke the surface of the water and headed for the HMS VICTORY. It was bedlam. Eventually, over fifty Sea dragons had joined the fight; some attacked from the air, others from the surface and some began ramming the ships from below. Sailors fired Seabow bolts to great effect, killing several Sea dragons with their first shots. Then the dragons began avoiding the deadly Seabows, attacking vigorously while the crews were busy reloading.

A Sea dragon swooped in from above and landed on the central mast of the COMFORT and began ripping the wooden mast to shreds. As the mast fell, crushing the Seabow below it, Sorceress Anne conjured a Blast spell that hurled the dragon off the mast and back into the sea. Dragons attempted to sweep the decks of sailors with high-pressure jets of water. Sailors responded with volleys of crossbow bolts, most of which missed their marks. Splinters of wood filled the air.

Another dragon rose up from the water beside the COMFORT, grabbed the shattered mast and flew into the air with it, ripping out lines and sails in the process. When the dragon got as high as he could fly carrying the heavy mast, he dropped it back onto the ship below. The mast came down like a spear, right on top of Sorceress Anne, it broke through the weather deck and the deck below, and punched a hole through the hull. As water rushed in, the crew abandoned ship, leaping into the water, which was teeming with angry dragons.

The VALOR moved forward to try and rescue the helpless sailors, with the VICEROY and the VICTORY providing covering fire from their Seabows and crossbows. Andrew moved to the railing, desperate to help the men in the water. Suddenly, two enormous Sea dragons erupted out of the water behind the VALOR. Together they began shooting high pressure jets of water at the sailors on the deck. The narrow jets of water cut through the sailors like a knife. Andrew moved forward and cast a shield to try to protect the exposed crew.

Then a strange thing happened; one of the Sea dragons looked down and noticed the ship's name on the stern. It immediately stopped its attack and screamed, "STOP! IT IS THE VALOR!" Unfortunately, the other dragon was so focused on its attack that it failed to heed the warning, and continued its assault on Andrew's shield, attempting to penetrate it with a tightly focused stream of water. In desperation, the first dragon moved between Andrew and the second dragon, the fine stream of water scoring its back, rending scales and splattering yellow dragon blood across the deck. Andrew, sensing an opportunity, dropped his shield and fired a strong Blast spell at the intervening dragon's exposed throat. Both dragons fell back into the water. Immediately, the dragon attack ceased and the remaining dragons fled back to the island.

As Teal sank to the bottom of the sea, his last thought was that he had saved his daughter's life.

Kathy and Edward raced through the palace, looking for the King. He was not in the Throne room, the audience chamber, his private study, or the Royal Dining room. In desperation, they headed for his sleeping chamber, where they encountered two palace guards. "Where is the King," asked Kathy, panting. The two guards shifted their feet, uncomfortably, then one, sensing the urgency, said, "He is in the Privy, Mage Kathy. He should be out in a moment." "We'll wait," said Edward. "Do you know if he's had anything to eat or drink in the last glass?"

"One of the Cook's assistants brought him a fruit tart a while ago," said one of the guards, "he rushed into the Privy not long afterwards." "Open the door, quickly!" insisted Edward. The tart may have been poisoned!" The guard hesitated briefly, then knocked gently and eased open the door. The King lay on the floor, convulsing.

Edward rushed in, pulling a vial of Healing Serum from his cloak. "Roll him over! Quickly!" The King was not a small man and it took both guards to roll him onto his back. Edward uncorked the vial and forced the King's mouth open. "It's Healing Serum, Your Majesty! Drink!" The King nodded weakly and opened his mouth. Edward poured the contents of the vial down his throat. The convulsions subsided immediately, but Edward conjured a Healing Spell, just for good measure. A few minutes later the King sat up and asked groggily, "What happened?

"The pastry was poisoned, Sire," said Kathy. "Fortunately, we came in time and Wizard Edward had a vial of Healing Serum handy." "Poisoned?" asked the King, "Who would do such a thing?" "Sire, was Marissa the servant who gave you the tart?" asked Kathy. "Yes. She said that she'd just taken a fresh batch out of the oven, and thought I'd like one. I can't believe it! Marissa has been with us for years! Why would she do such a thing?" asked the King.

"She was a Fire dragon Changed One, Your Highness," said Edward. Earlier today, while I was in the courtyard, she put Death Serum in the water pitcher in my chambers. I detected the threat and found Mage Kathy in her office. We went in search of Marissa and found her body in the kitchen pantry. She'd been killed with poison. We immediately came in search of you to ensure your safety."

"You have my thanks," said the King. "Nothing like this has ever happened in Baizc. How is it that I'm alive?" "Fortunately, you didn't eat the entire pastry, so you only ingested a small amount of the poison, and we reached you soon after. I'm grateful that your guards listened to reason and allowed us entry. I'm not sure the palace guards in Franconia would have been so accommodating," said Edward.

"So, Marissa was a dragon Changed One; then who killed her?" wondered the King. "There must be more Changed Ones in the Palace, Sire," said Kathy. "I assumed you would have searched yesterday, after what happened with Wizard Louis," said Edward, reproachfully. "We did," said the King, "but only the Ministers, guards, and anyone who had regular contact with me. We found none. Why would a dragon Changed One wish to pose as a servant?"

"Because servants have access to every room in the palace and they go about their work virtually unnoticed. No one would suspect a lowly cook's assistant, a chamber maid, or a gardener, but all of them roam the palace freely," said Edward. "Round up all the servants immediately," said the King. "Have them assemble in the courtyard. Make sure we find them all, I don't want anyone missing; and find Wizard James."

In short order, all of the palace servants were herded into the courtyard. They were confused and anxious. News of the attempted assassination of the King had spread like wildfire throughout the palace. As the King watched from the second-floor balcony, Wizards James, Edward and Timothy, and Mage Kathy roamed through the throng of servants, speaking to each one and using

Smell Enhancements. Despite their efforts, they detected nothing amiss among the servants. With the investigation complete, Edward asked the palace Senechal, Peter, who was in charge of all of the servants, if everyone was present. Peter looked around carefully, then said, "Sir Wizard, all of the palace servants are here, except the three night bakers from the kitchen, who I assume are asleep in their chambers." Edward looked at Peter darkly. "Dismiss these servants and bring the night bakers up here. This was a serious oversight."

Peter dismissed the servants to their duties and sent the Head Cook to bring the night bakers up to the courtyard, promising to give them some extra time off later to make up for the imposition. The three Wizards and Kathy went to speak to the King. "Anything?" he asked. "No, Sire," replied James, "but apparently, the three cooks who do the palace baking during the night were not present. Senechal Peter is gathering them now."

A few minutes later, three surly and confused servants were ushered into the courtyard by Peter. "Here they are, Your Majesty," shouted Peter. "Wizard James will be right down to examine them," said the King. Peter nodded his understanding, then took a seat on one of the benches that ringed the open area of the courtyard. Suddenly, the black-haired servant clapped his hands together and *rippled*, transforming into a Stone dragon. The dragon shot into the air, headed straight for the King. Edward conjured an enormous gale of wind, which blew the surprised dragon back into the ground and pinned him down. The dragon blew fire, but the inferno was caught up in the wind and pushed back at the dragon. The Stone dragon shrugged off the burning inferno and continued struggling to rise. "Blast spells, quickly!" Edward said to Timothy and Kathy.

Both Wizard Timothy and Mage Kathy fired Blast spells at the pinned dragon, but to no effect, the dragon's scales appeared impervious to the Blasts. James emerged on the first level and attempted a Sleep spell, which was equally ineffective. Edward was running out of ideas of how to kill this beast. Finally, he tried something new. *"DEFENDIO,"* he said, placing his hands together, then spreading them apart, pointing them towards the dragon. A protective shield appeared around the dragon. The dragon seemed confused, he struck at the shield with his talons, blew inferno at it, and attempted to fly through it. Nothing worked. The King looked confused and asked, "What are you doing, Wizard Edward? Why are you protecting the dragon?"

"I'm not protecting him, Sire, I'm *suffocating* him," said Edward through gritted teeth. A few moments later, the dragon began to feel the effects of the lack of air. It thrashed, hammered the shield with its tail, tried to bite through, or dig under. Nothing worked. Eventually, the dragon collapsed. Edward held the shield for several long minutes, wary of any trick by the dragon. After a time, it was clear that the dragon was dead. Edward released the shield, and sagged forward, clutching the railing. "Edward!" shouted Kathy. "I'm all right, Kathy, just a bit tired from holding the shield against such a forceful attack. I've never tried that before."

Wizard James came rushing up the stairs, "Is it dead?" he asked. "Yes, I believe so," said Edward, "Stone dragons are harder to kill than Fire dragons. I'm not sure if even the crossbow bolts would penetrate those scales, if Blast spells didn't work." "But, didn't a Sorcerer kill a Stone dragon in Weaton?" asked the King. "Yes," said Edward sadly, "but it was fired into the beast's forehead at point-blank range, and the Sorcerer who did it died on the spot from the energy drain."

"What made you think of using a shield?" asked James. "We teach our students that one way to extinguish a fire is to enclose it in a shield, depriving the flame of air. It's not the easiest, or most effective way to put out a fire, but it works. I'm not sure what else would kill a Stone dragon. A Death spell would likely kill the conjurer; maybe you could use a Change spell and turn it into a rock or something, or maybe Paralyze.

I've never fought a Stone dragon before," said Edward tiredly.

"Well," said the King, "You saved my life twice in one day, Wizard Edward. I'm in your debt." "I'm just glad I was able to help, Your Majesty," said Edward. "Now, if you'll excuse me, I need to go lay down somewhere and rest." "Of course," said the King, "thank you again." Edward nodded his acknowledgement and headed back toward his room with Kathy following. "You really are making quite a name for yourself in Baize. I can't remember the last time someone saved the King from an assassination attempt, much less twice in one day," said Kathy.

"That Stone dragon was awfully brazen. He should have fled immediately after killing Marissa. I wonder why he took the chance and stayed," said Edward. "He must have thought that both you and the King were dead," said Kathy. "Maybe," said Edward with a yawn, "but I'm not convinced. If I had to guess, there are probably more Changed Ones in town. Watch your back." "I will," said Kathy. When they reached his room, Kathy gave him a peck on the cheek and said, "I'll see you at dinner."

Dirk rose from the chair he had been napping in as Edward entered. "Everything alright?" he asked. Edward shook his head. "We found a Stone dragon,

Changed One, in the palace, disguised as a night baker. He undoubtedly killed Marissa after she attempted to poison both me and the King. We got to the King in time, and I gave him some Healing Serum. He's going to be fine." "What about the Changed One?" asked Dirk. "He transformed into a Stone dragon and attacked us," said Edward, wearily. "It was incredibly hard to kill. I'm not sure crossbow bolts will penetrate Stone dragons; Blast spells certainly didn't."

"Then how did you kill it?" "I put a shield around it." "I don't understand," said Dirk. "I put the shield *all* the way around it. Once it used up all the air inside, it suffocated." Dirk whistled. "That's a neat trick." "I suppose. Anyway, I need some sleep, and I know you've been up for too long also. Why don't you put the chair in front of the door and go back to sleep while I take a nap," said Edward. "Good idea," said Dirk. In moments, both Wizard and Specialist were sound asleep.

It was Endday, and Donovan decided to take Rachel to The Happy Maid Tavern for lunch. As they entered, Donovan spotted a familiar face. "Lance! When did you get back? Is my father with you? How did you kill seven

Fire dragons?" asked Donovan. Lance smiled, "So many questions, my friend. The 2nd Company returned to Kingston on Midweek; no, your father was not with us, and before I get into the rest, who is this lovely young woman?"

"I'm sorry, this is Rachel Turner, my girlfriend and Mentor; Rachel, this is Senior Specialist Lance from the Royal Expeditionary Force," said Donovan, belatedly. "It's nice to meet you, Rachel. Turner—are you related to Brian Turner, the tailor?" asked Lance. Rachel looked surprised, "He's my father," replied Rachel. "He's the best tailor in Kingston," said Lance. *Please give him my regards,* Lance signed. *I will certainly do so,* signed Rachel, surprised. *We are going to see him after lunch.* Lance continued signing, *I hope you are keeping an eye on my friend here, he is always getting into trouble.* Rachel laughed.

"OK, enough of that," said Donovan. "Stop hitting on my girlfriend." Lance laughed and replied, "All I said was—" *I know what you said,* signed Donovan. Lance smiled and signed, *So, you are learning more than just magic. Good for you.* "I didn't know you knew sign language," said Donovan. "My mother was deaf," said Lance, "so I have a special empathy for the hearing impaired. I seek out and patronize their businesses. I've bought many fine items from your father over the years," Lance said to Rachel.

"But enough about clothes," said Lance, looking at Donovan. "How did you know about the dragons?" "While you were gone, Minister Jasmine reported to the King that the Expeditionary Force had been ambushed by Dragons and Baizian soldiers and nearly wiped out; you were supposedly fleeing, pursued by dragons. When Wizard Noland heard this, he asked me to try a Seeing spell to locate you and my father. The map showed one company of the Expeditionary Force in Springfield; one on the way to Prarrieville; my father on the road to Baize; and the echoes of seven fire dragons in the hills astride the road to Springfield."

Lance grinned, "And you didn't think you had the spark." Lance winked at Rachel, then told Donovan the tale of the mission to Springfield, how Edward detected the ambush with the Seeing spell and fabricated concealment cloaks for everyone in the Expeditionary Force, the resulting battle, what they discovered in Springfield, and the purpose of Edward's journey to Baize.

"So, my father thinks that the dragons are trying to provoke a fight between Franconia and Baize. Why?" "So that after we fight each other, soldier against soldier, magician against magician, both countries will be weakened when the dragons attack." "Of course. It's so simple. But why now?" wondered Donovan. "Maybe there are too many dragons now to hide," speculated

Rachel. "That might be it," confirmed Lance, "but whatever the reason, your father went to Baize to convince King Donald not to go to war with Franconia."

"Do you really think he can do that?" asked Rachel. "Trust me," said Donovan sarcastically, "my father can be very persuasive." Lance and Rachel laughed. "So, how are you finding life at the Academy? I understand you're already a Level Three," said Lance. "It's challenging, but there are certainly some perks," said Donovan with a sidelong look at Rachel. She slapped the back of his head.

"Well, I must be off," said Lance, "while I'm glad to see you, Donovan, I'm really watching Corporal Sleet over there," he said nodding at the Corporal who was sitting at the bar. "Why, what's he done?" whispered Donovan. "Nothing so far as I can tell, but the Major has his suspicions," said Lance, rising from the table. *It was nice to meet you Rachel,* Lance signed. *Try to keep him humble.* Rachel signed back, *As if.*

Lance slipped out of the Tavern quietly, following Corporal Sleet. Donovan and Rachel settled down to order their food. "So, I'm a 'perk,' am I?" Donovan gulped, "How about the most amazing, beautiful, passionate perk in the world?" "Better," said Rachel. After lunch, the two lovers headed over to her father's tailor shop. As always, Brian was very happy to see them.

Rachel told him about meeting Specialist Lance and her father signed that Lance had been patronizing the shop for years. In fact, he had made the concealment cloak for him and for Dirk, the other Specialist in the Expeditionary Force. *How do you make them?* Signed Donovan. *I thought they were magical. They are,* signed Brian. *I purchase the cloth from a magician, then fashion it into a cloak.*

Just then, Donna, Rachel's mother, arrived, and the two women went upstairs to unpack the groceries and chat over tea. Donovan sat with her father for a while, watching him work. When Brian took a break from his work, Donovan signed, *Rachel needs a cloak, so the new dress you made her will not get wet when we go out. How long will it take you to make one?* Brian smiled and signed, *It's funny, you should ask. I have a woman's formal cloak right now that would be perfect for her. The Lady I made it for left town suddenly, and I have not heard from her for months. Fantastic,* Donovan replied, *How much do I owe you for it?*

Brian hesitated, finally signing, *It cost me two golds to make, but I can sell it to you at a discount. No,* signed Donovan. *Here are two golds and two silvers,* he signed, handing him the coins. *Can you keep it here?*

It's a Birthday present, signed Donovan. Brian smiled and nodded.

As they returned to the Academy, Wizard Faith said, "There you are! Wizard Noland has been waiting for you. Hurry over to his cottage. Wondering what this could be about, Donovan and Rachel rushed across the courtyard and knocked on the Headmaster's door. Wizard Toffin unexpectedly opened the door. "Here they are, at last!" said Wizard Toffin, hustling them into the parlor. Seated on the sofa was Judge Martin Toffin from the Franconian Superior Court. He rose as Donovan entered the room.

"Ah, there you are, my boy!" said the Judge. "I just came by to deliver your Special Commendation letter and the five-gold reward that goes with it. I wanted you to have it as soon as possible since I know that most students are generally short on coins." "Thank you very much, Your Honor. I certainly never expected anything this quickly." "Not at all, not at all," said Judge Martin, shaking Donovan's hand vigorously. "If there is ever anything I can do for you, please don't hesitate to ask."

Donovan walked the Judge to the door, casting a Silence spell around them as he walked, "Actually, sir, there is a favor I would like to ask. You see, next week is my girlfriend's birthday, and I know that the Royal Ball is the following week. I was hoping to take Rachel to it, but I'm not sure how to get an invitation." The Judge brightened measurably and said, "Donovan, you would be doing me a great favor if you would take *my* invitation. You see, my wife hates those things, and we have the children. *I* would consider it a favor if you took the invitation off my hands." "Seriously? I would be very grateful," said Donovan. "Think nothing of it. I'll send the invitation back with Jeffrey, I mean Wizard Toffin, next Endday." Thank you very much," said Donovan, dropping the Silence spell.

"Well, goodbye, goodbye. I'll see you next week, Jeffrey!" said the Judge heading for the Gatehouse. Once he was out of the Academy, Donovan turned and asked Wizard Noland, "Sir, do we really have to have a ceremony?" Wizard Noland smiled and said, "Of course we do! Accomplishments must be celebrated. Accordingly, there will be a brief ceremony in the Level Three common room after breakfast tomorrow morning. Don't be late—either of you."

As they entered the Mentors dormitory, Rachel asked, "What 'invitation' was the Judge talking about? And why the Silence spell?" Donovan sighed, "I forgot you read lips. I asked him, as a favor to me, to procure invitations for us to the Royal Ball the week after your birthday. I was trying to surprise you," said Donovan. "The Royal Ball! That would be wonderful! But my shoes—" "Will be ready next week," said Donovan.

"Surprise!" "How did you manage that?" Rachel asked, suspiciously. "I used a Compulsion spell on the Cobbler," joked Donovan. "YOU WHAT?" said Rachel, becoming angry. "Calm down, I was only joking. Actually, I just gave him an extra gold, and he said your shoes would absolutely be completed in time for your birthday."

As they entered Rachel's room, she asked, "Any more Birthday surprises for me?" Donovan thought for a moment, then said quietly, "Two, actually, and one for your father." "My father?" asked Rachel. "Yes," said Donovan, "but it's a surprise."

Chapter Seventeen:
SMOKE ON THE WATER

It was just past noon when Edward and Kathy walked into Minister William's office. There was a large conference table in the center of the room and it was festooned with various maps of the Great Salt Flats and the surrounding area. The Minister and several civic engineers were present, all with the same objective: to prove Edward wrong. "It just can't be done!" insisted Carl, the Assistant Minister for Water and Sewer in Baize, "As soon as you dig this hole, the surrounding sand is going to slide right back in. You might succeed in making a depression in the sand, but the walls just won't hold!" The other engineers nodded in agreement.

"How deep is the sand?" asked Edward. The question stumped the assembled engineers. "Gentlemen, I agree that if the sand goes all the way down to bedrock, this will be a daunting and maybe impossible undertaking. But what if there are only a few feet of sand on top of soil and rock? We could easily remove that much sand and dig in a firmer substrate that will not collapse."

The engineers paused and considered Edward's words. "I suppose it's possible," said Carl, "we've never really dug down to see how deep the sand goes, and with the expansion over the years…" "Exactly!" said Edward, "and given how far the sand has been pushed out by the rainwater, it should be shallower than when it started. I mean, it's not like the sand is multiplying; it's just spreading out. And it can't be very deep around the edges." The engineers conferred amongst themselves quietly. Finally, Carl said, "Sir Wizard, you make some very good points that we had not considered before. Do you have a background in Geology, by any chance?"

"No, but during my time in service to the crown of Franconia, I have constructed dozens of wells and aquifers. I know that sand can be a problem, but that there is really not that much sand deep underground. It's mostly on the surface." Carl actually smiled, "You are correct. The sand might be deep, but it is undoubtedly resting on a harder layer of soil below."

"So, Mage Kathy and I discussed this last night. We think the first thing to do is define the boundary you want for this reservoir. We will need survey teams to lay out the limits of the hole. In case you don't know, when a magician uses a Dig spell, they can either vanish the soil that is excavated or move it to wherever they want. So, as we excavate the dirt and rock along the outer edge, we will use it to make a wall above the hole using the Adhesive spell. The walls will be sheer on the inside and slope gradually on the outside. The form should not have any corners but have rounded sides to ease the water pressure on the walls. We believe that we need to start digging at the eastern and southern edges and work our way north and west. We build the wall as we go. This will stop the Salt Flats from spreading east and south while we work, using the Dig spell and vanishing the spoils; there will be no need to haul them away as happens with conventional construction projects."

Minister William nodded his head, "I agree about starting in the east. How big do you think the reservoir should be? A five-mile-wide reservoir will hold an awful lot of water," said Edward. "How large an area does the Great Salt Flats cover?" "As near as we can determine, the Great Salt Flats is currently square-shaped, about fifty miles on each side."

"How deep is it to bedrock?" asked Edward. "Who would know?" replied Carl. "I mean, generally, in Baize, how deep do you have to dig to hit bedrock?" asked Edward. "I believe it's about a hundred feet," said Minister William. "So, we dig a U-shaped hole, fifty miles wide at the bottom, with twenty-five-mile sides, like a cup, and we make it a hundred feet deep, and we use some of the spoils to create a wall around the edges." "That will take forever!" said one of the engineers. Edward nodded, "If we were digging by hand, I agree, but you forget, gentlemen, we're using magic. I can personally dig a ten-foot by ten-foot hole, a hundred feet deep, in about ten minutes without breaking a sweat. Now, your apprentice magicians won't be able to dig as fast as I can, but there should be a hundred of them!"

"What happens when it rains?" asked one of the engineers. "Once we get the outer walls built, they will not collapse. The amount of sand and dirt is unchanged; there is just water mixed in. Magicians can either heat the water to steam or freeze it to ice. The work does not stop for rain, sleet, snow or ice. We keep digging, all day, all night, with shifts of magicians."

"Where will you be?" asked Minister William. "Initially, I will be on the eastern side, digging, building walls, and training apprentice magicians. I will not be able to stay forever, since King Henry may recall me to Franconia at any time." "What about the dragons?" asked another engineer. "That's a question I can't answer," said Edward. "I don't know why the dragons would care if we dig a hole in the Salt Flats; it's certainly no threat to them."

"So, what do we need to do now?" "Now, you need to plan the greatest engineering project in Baizian history," said Edward. "How many apprentice magicians are coming? How many wagons do we need?

How many tents? Cots? How much food and water? Fodder for the horses? How many blacksmiths to repair broken wagons? There are a myriad of things you need to plan for, and not much time. You also need to consider how much salt you want to leave outside the reservoir. I understand that the salt trade is a major export for the country. I can't give orders here. You'll need the King's approval, and I doubt that he's grasped how complex and expensive an operation this size is going to be. I plan to leave by the end of the week to meet the apprentice magicians in Springfield."

Kathy and Edward quietly left the Minister's office. Inside, the various engineers, city planners and logisticians were scurrying about, making lists of supplies, estimating costs and manpower requirements, and preparing orders to commandeer wagons and other supplies from all across Baize. As they walked back to her office, Kathy said, "That was your best magic trick yet." "How so?" "You took a room full of engineers and bureaucrats who were dead set against your idea and convinced them it would work and inspired them to action. I'm not sure that's ever been done before in the History of Baize." Edward blushed at the compliment and said, "The King is going to have kittens when he sees the bill. This is not going to be cheap."

Kathy laughed and said, "Nothing worthwhile is. This could change the entire landscape and commerce for eastern Baize. Do you really think it'll work?" "It will work as long as the sand is not more than fifty feet deep and the bedrock is really only a hundred feet down. It will also depend on the skill and motivation of these apprentice magicians. They are the key. I can't dig the entire reservoir myself."

Andrew rushed about the deck, tending to wounded sailors. He left those in the water to be fished out by sailors whom he had already healed or who were uninjured. He found the Commodore, slumped against the railing near the starboard Seabow, a deep gash in his thigh. "Hold on, sir, I'll have you healed in just a minute," said Andrew, as he knelt by his side. The Commodore winced as Andrew pulled back the cloth of his tattered pants, exposing the wound. It looked like the damage was caused by one of the high-pressure jets of water; only this one had nicked the femoral artery, and blood was pumping out with each beat of the Commodore's heart. "I'm going to lose the leg, aren't I?" he wheezed. "Not if I can help it," said Andrew. "Here, drink this quickly," he said, handing over his water bottle, which was filled with Healing Serum.

The Commodore drank deeply, and the wound in his leg closed almost instantly. Just to be safe, Andrew muttered, *"SALVARE,"* while holding both hands over the wound. The Commodore's color returned, and he sat up straighter. "It's healed! I feel better than I have in years!" He started to rise, but Andrew pushed him back down onto the deck. "Not so fast, Commodore. You need to sit quietly for at least a glass while the Serum and the spell finish healing you. You get up too soon, and that cut will pop open again, and I'm trying to heal everyone just once."

The Commodore nodded his understanding and thanks, and Andrew moved off, down the deck, looking for more injured sailors. He was getting light-headed from all the exertion: the fire, the battle, and now the healing. He needed rest, but he knew that if he stopped, sailors would die that he could save. It also seemed that everyone on board had some injury or other, and those with minor cuts or bruises were asking for his help when there were others with greater needs.

Finally, he grabbed the Bos'n and asked him to start screening the wounded, so that Andrew could help those most in need first. A gray fog started to cloud Andrew's eyesight and he began to get tunnel vision. Knowing that he was on the verge of passing out, Andrew looked around quickly and snatched the water bottle from the Bos'n's belt. He uncorked the water bag and drank deeply, then spritzed it out quickly. The bag was filled with rum. "Get me some water immediately, before I pass out!" said Andrew, "and then send someone to my cabin. Under my bunk is a chest full of Healing Serum. Have it brought up here quickly."

The Bos'n walked over to a sailor who was draped over the railing, clearly dead, and removed his water bag. He ran back to Andrew and gave it to him, "Sorry, Sir Mage. The rum was purely medicinal, to stave off infections." Andrew took a sip from the offered water bag, making sure it was water this time. Then he emptied the bag. His light-headedness began to subside. The Bos'n offered him some hardtack, a thick cracker, but Andrew shook his head. "Eating will only make me sick. I just need water, and my Serum chest. How many more wounded, do you think?"

The Bos'n looked around, scanning the deck. "I think you've already gotten to most of them, sir. There might be a couple below deck that I can't see from here." "Signal the other ships, and find out if either of them need magical assistance. I'm about done in, but I have plenty of Healing Serum." The Bos'n hurried off to relay the message.

As sailors from the COMFORT were hauled aboard, it seemed like most of the injuries were shock, and Healing Serum did nothing for shock. There were a few cuts and bruises, and one sailor's arm had been bitten off at the elbow, but while Andrew got to him in time and closed the wound, there was no replacing the hand and forearm.

The ship was a mess, with deep gouges along the deck, splintered railings, and one mast was nearly cut in half. The crew rushed to splice timbers to the mast and repair the damage that they could. Andrew staggered to the lower decks to check the hull. There were only a couple of places where water was coming in, and they were easily repaired with Enlarge and Adhesive spells.

After seeing to the hull, Andrew returned to the deck and sought out the Commodore (who had moved from where Andrew left him). When he found him, Andrew said, "Sir, once we've recovered all of the men from the water and any of the bodies that we can, I suggest we put some distance between ourselves and these islands." "Why? We've won!" said the Commodore. "No, Sir. We didn't. They just left after I killed that big one. I suspect he may have been their leader. But we didn't drive them off; they just left. They could come back at any time."

"Why didn't you say so?" yelled the Commodore. "ALL HANDS, MAKE SAIL! STEER COURSE 1-8-0!" Sailors rushed to do his bidding, raising as much sail as they could safely, with the damage masts. The three surviving ships turned south, away from the Coral Islands. After sailing for two hours, the Commodore ordered what was left of the squadron to heave-to and anchor. He ordered the ship's Captains to get a count of the injured, missing and dead.

A glass later, the count came in. Ten sailors on the HMS VICTORY had been killed, twenty were wounded (but healed), and five were missing, The HMS VICEROY had seven dead, eleven wounded and two missing, The HMS COMFORT lost half her crew, fifty dead or missing, and six more were wounded. Aboard the HMS VALOR, there had been five sailors killed and twenty-seven wounded; there were none missing. That made 79 dead or missing, almost a full ship's complement. Among the magicians, Sorceress Anne was missing and presumed dead, but the other two Sorcerers were alive, although one was unconscious as a result of expending too much power healing sailors on the VICTORY.

The Commodore ordered a watch set, with the rest of the men allowed to get some sleep. Repairs would begin in earnest tomorrow morning. As the men settled down to sleep, Commodore Matthews beckoned Andrew to join him in his cabin. "What happened there at the end?" he asked. "Did I hear one of the dragons say something?" "Yes, Sir," replied Andrew, "and it's got me very curious. The biggest dragon, the one that attacked the VALOR from astern, looked down at our hull, then shouted 'Stop. It is the Valor!' At the time, the second dragon was trying to penetrate my shield with a fine jet of water, and appeared to ignore the first dragon. So, the big one moved between me and the other dragon, blocking the attack with his body, like he was trying to protect me. I fired a Blast spell into his exposed throat, which I assume killed him. Then all of the dragons suddenly dove underwater and left."

The Commodore yawned, clearly exhausted. "We can talk about this more tomorrow, Sir. You need some sleep." The Commodore nodded, and said, "You too, Andrew. That's an order."

As Donovan cleared his breakfast tray and prepared to head to Serums class, Wizard Noland stepped into the Level Three Common room and said in his deep voice, "Ladies and Gentlemen, may I have your attention, please? This morning, it is my pleasure to present a Special Award to Level Three Donovan Francis. Donovan, come here, please." Donovan moved to stand beside Wizard Noland, slightly embarrassed by the attention. Wizard Noland began reading from an elaborately written and decorated scroll of parchment:

On Firstday, the second week of Octi, while observing the proceedings of the Superior Court of Kingston, Master Donovan Francis, sensing that a four-time convicted criminal was about to assault the Judge, immediately paralyzed the convict, saving Judge Martin Toffin's life. In recognition of this heroic and selfless act, he is hereby awarded this Special Commendation from the Kingston Superior Court. Master Donovan's actions reflect great credit upon himself, his Mentor, and the Franconian Wizards Academy. Signed, King Henry XI, Supreme Ruler of Franconia.

Wizard Noland presented the scroll to Donovan and clapped. The other Level Threes all joined in with their applause, much to Donovan's embarrassment. When the clapping stopped, Wizard Noland said, "All right everyone, off to Serums class with you." As the other Level Threes filed out of the common room, Donovan approached Wizard Noland, "Excuse me, sir, I learned something in town yesterday that I need to talk to you about. Can I come by your cottage after dinner this evening?" "Is it something urgent?" asked Wizard Noland. "Not really, Sir. It's just something that might help us against the dragons." "Then I will be very interested to hear it. Will your Mentor be joining us?" "I'd appreciate it if we could speak privately, Sir. Otherwise, there could be a conflict of interest." "Now

I'm intrigued," said Noland. "I will expect you after dinner. Alone."

"Report," said Major Gerald. "Sir, there's nothing to report. As far as I can tell, Corporal Sleet is just another horse jockey;" said Senior Specialist Lance. "You mean cavalryman. So, he hasn't done anything suspicious in the last three days?" "No sir. On Midweek he went to the Happy Maids Tavern for a drink and a meal. He didn't get drunk or cause any commotion. He walked around the city for a while, then headed back to the barracks. On Foursday he tended to his mount, cleaned his gear, and spent the rest of the day in the garrison, sleeping, I guess. On Endday he went out again, but just to the usual places, a couple of taverns, he did some shopping, tried unsuccessfully to pick up a girl, then returned to his room."

"All right, maybe I'm wrong about him. Take the next three days off. I don't know how long we're gonna be here, but I don't expect it'll be long. For the next three days I'm gonna have the men focus on repairin' and maintaining their gear. On Foursday I wanna start some trainin' with the new cloaks. We'll ride to the outskirts of town for that." "What about the two new men?" asked Lance. "I'll go talk to Wizard Nolan at the Academy, maybe he can make two more cloaks for us. They open on Midweek, right?"

"Yes, sir. The entrance is the grey building between the cobbler shop and the bakery on Prince Street. You have to get there before noon or they won't open the door." Gerald scoffed, "Wizards!" "You might see Donovan while you're there. I ran into him on Endday. He seemed to know that we were back, and was curious about his father," said Lance. "I imagine," said Gerald. "I'll ask to see him if I have time. So, what are your plans for the next three days?" "I need some new boots. Other than that, I'll just stay around town and relax."

Anne broke the surface of the water gasping for air. She was alone but alive. When the mast had fallen on her, she poured all her strength into her shield, which surprisingly had held as she crashed through both decks of the ship and the keel. Fortunately, she'd managed to get out from under the mast before it embedded itself in the sea floor, and get far enough away so that when the HMS COMFORT went down, she wasn't trapped beneath her. Unfortunately, she was still deep underwater. Too deep to release her shield and swim to the surface—she would have been crushed by the water pressure or run out of air before she made it. What a predicament! She had no way to propel her bubble-like shield and she knew that she would eventually run out of air.

Her rescue came from the most unlikely creatures. Dolphins. A school of them decided that she was some sort of undersea toy, and they began pushing her shield with their noses, or swatting it with their tails. It was fortunate that they were pushing her towards the surface instead of deeper into the water. After a while, they got tired of the game and began to swim away, while she was still too deep underwater. In desperation, she conjured a Tether spell and attached it to one of the dolphins, knowing that they were air-breathing creatures, and would have to surface eventually.

Holding two spells at once was draining, and Anne was already weary after the fight with the dragons. Fortunately, as the dolphin pulled her toward the surface, she needed less power for her shield as the water pressure lessened. Finally, she was close enough to the surface to release the Shield and Tether spells and swim for it. Normally, she was a strong swimmer, having grown up in Grotton, but it took all her will power to get to the surface.

After the darkness of the sea, the bright sunlight was dazzling. She looked around but, as she expected, the other ships were long gone. Her only hope was to get to the island, but that thought terrified her. According to Mage Andrew, the islands were teeming with dragons, and after setting the island on fire; they were probably very angry dragons. With no other options, Anne conjured a Stamina Enhancement and began swimming towards the island, which was only visible because of the clouds of smoke still rising from it. As she drew near, she decided that once she made it to shore, she would cast a Concealment spell and try to hide from any dragons that were still on the island.

Her feet touched the sandy bottom, and she waded through the surf onto the beach and cast her Concealment spell. It was too much. Anne fell unconscious on the beach.

They left at moonrise, headed for Perfo, where they expected to find Cobalt. It was also the closest island, so Gek would not have to fly as far with his injured wing. They planned to fly north to Acropo the next night and see Teal and the others in the Sea Dragon Clan. As soon as they took off, it was obvious that the flight was going to take longer than they anticipated. Gek was moving slowly, and Azure's pregnancy was slowing her down as well. After only two hours of flight, they were both exhausted, so they decided to try swimming for a while, hoping it might be easier. They were wrong.

Gek, never the best of swimmers, found the drag on his injured wing to be incredibly uncomfortable, and Azure grumbled that she felt like a whale in the water. They managed only a short distance before they stopped to rest, bobbing on the waves like jellyfish. As they were about to take flight again, they spotted three seemingly deserted ships, or at least with only a few humans moving about on the deck. "We should attack them," said Azure. "Stop it," said Gek. "We have had this discussion before. We are not going to attack any ships while I am injured and you are pregnant. We need to put some distance between us before we take off again."

Azure grudgingly agreed, and the two dragons dove under the surface and swam for as long as they could stand it. When they surfaced, the ships were far behind them, still unaware of their presence. It took the rest of the night to travel the relatively short distance to Perfo; fly, then swim, fly, then swim. As the sun crested the horizon, they saw the smoke.

"Perfo is on fire!" screamed Azure, "Hurry!" They took flight again, making their best possible speed to the island, which appeared like a charred, black smudge on the water. They flew directly to Cobalt's cave, but there was no one home. Azure wanted to fly to Acropo immediately, but Gek put his claw down. "No. No. No! We just flew and swam all night to get here. We both need rest. We will sleep here today and leave at sunset. Cobalt is probably on Acropo with Teal and the rest of the Clan." Azure wanted to argue, but she realized that Gek was right, she was exhausted. "Very well. But I want some crabs for lunch!" "Fine. Just let me rest for a while, then I will go down to the beach and get you some crabs," said Gek, tiredly.

They slept restlessly, despite their fatigue. Gek was still injured and Azure was still pregnant, and the cave smelled of smoke and burnt eucalyptus leaves. A little before the sun reached its peak, Gek decided to head down to the beach to gather some stupid crabs for Azure. He left the cave and flew the short distance to the beach where he found Anne lying unconscious on the sand.

"So, Donovan, what have you thought of that might help us fight the dragons, that you didn't want Rachel to hear about?" asked Wizard Noland. They were seated in the Wizards office, not the parlor where they usually met to discuss things. "Well, sir, last Endday Rachel and I went into town and I ran into Specialist Lance from the Royal Expeditionary Force," said Donovan. "Yes. They returned on Midweek. I was at the Council meeting when Major Gerald arrived and gave his report to the King about their mission to Springfield."

"Yes, Sir. Specialist Lance told me that my father and Mage Curtis created Concealment cloaks for every member of the Royal Expeditionary Force, and that was how they were able to sneak up on the dragons." "I've also heard that. Marshall Guzman is very excited about the potential of equipping the entire Royal Guard with them. But we're keeping that a secret."

"Because you think Minister Jasmine is a Changed One?" Wizard Noland frowned. "What ever gave you that idea?" he asked. "Sir, isn't she the one who told the King that the Royal Expeditionary Force had been ambushed and nearly wiped out?" Noland nodded grimly. "So, either she's in league with the dragons, or really incompetent," said Donovan. Wizard Noland shifted uncomfortably behind his desk. This was clearly not a conversation he wanted to have with a Level Three student.

"What does this have to do with Concealment cloaks?" Noland asked. "Well, Sir, I was thinking, what if we made them for all of the magicians? I mean, then a Sorcerer wouldn't need a Concealment shield, and could save their spell for something else." Noland smiled. "Now *that* is a truly excellent idea! I can't believe that I didn't think of it myself. Why didn't you want Rachel to hear your idea?"

"Sir, her father is Brian Turner. He's the tailor in town that makes the Concealment cloaks for the Specialists. He told us last Endday that he gets the cloth from a magician and turns it into cloaks, but they're very expensive. With Rachel being my girlfriend, I didn't want anyone to think that I was just trying to drum up business for her father. I also didn't want to get her hopes up if you thought it was a conflict of interest."

"Hmm, I see what you mean, but since her father is already the only tailor making the cloaks, I think it would be all right. However, since *we* will be making the cloth here at the Academy, the price of Concealment cloaks is going to go way down. Especially if the King orders entire military units outfitted with them, I'm not sure one shop will be able to produce all of the cloaks we may eventually purchase." Donovan's smile faded. Wizard Noland laughed at his expression, "Take heart, Donovan. I'm sure we can work something out with Mr. Turner. Perhaps we can make him the official tailor to the Wizards Academy and employ him to make all of *our* cloaks. Regardless, we're going to have to keep this a secret for a while. Once we start equipping soldiers with invisibility cloaks, every brigand in Franconia will want one."

Donovan left Wizard Noland's cottage very pleased with himself, even if Wizard Noland had cast a Secrecy spell on him not to reveal their plan to award Rachel's father a big contract for cloaks. He met Rachel as she was leaving the Lecture Hall. "What were you doing in there at this time of night?" he asked. "Mandatory Mentor training," said Rachel crossly. "Can you believe it?"

Sorceress Anne

Chapter Eighteen:

ENTANGLEMENTS

"Celeste?" asked Gek. "What are you doing here?" Anne came around slowly. She was still exhausted from her ordeal and didn't realize who was speaking. "My name is Anne," she said hoarsely, "Celeste is my twin sister." Gek stood there, stunned. He had no idea what to do now. As Anne struggled to turn over, he said, "Wait right here, I will bring help." Moving off out of Anne's line of sight, Gek flew back up to Cobalt's cave and roused Azure.

"How many crabs did you bring me," asked Azure, hungrily. "None," replied Gek. "I found a human female on the beach. She says that she is Celeste's twin sister, Anne." Azure groaned, "So, I suppose we should not kill her either. Why is it that we keep running into humans that we are not allowed to kill?"

"I do not know," said Gek, "but if we leave her alone on the beach without water, she will probably die; and if another Sea Dragon comes along, they will most likely kill her." "I suppose we should bring her up here, out of the sun, give her some water, and hear what she has to say for herself," said Azure. "Human form or dragon?" asked Gek. "If we appear in dragon form, she will probably attack us. Why don't you change into human form and talk to her. Then bring her up here." "That's a long climb for a human," complained Gek. "I am sure you can make it," said Azure. "I was thinking of Anne," said Gek. "Sure you were. Well, if she is unable to make the climb, you may have to transform into a dragon and carry her up here."

Gek grumbled about doing all the heavy lifting lately, but he retrieved his still bloody shirt and pants and flew back down to the beach. He landed out of sight, transformed (painfully), put on his torn and ragged clothes, and walked up the beach to where Anne was now sitting up. "Hello," said Gek. "Hello," said Anne softly, "Do you have any water?" "No, but there is a fresh-water spring in a cave at the top of this hill," said Gek. "I could take you there and you could rest in the shade." "First, tell me why your shirt is all bloody," said Anne.

Gek thought quickly, then said, "I was injured a short time ago. I was healed by a magician, but I have not had a chance to purchase new clothes." "I see," said Anne. "And what are you doing here, alone, on this dragon-infested island?" Gek took great offense at the term *infested*, but decided that Anne must be in shock, so he replied, "You ask a lot of questions for someone who needs my help." Anne smiled through her cracked lips," I suppose you're right. Where is this cave?"

They trudged up the sandy hill, stepping around the charred brush and blackened trees. Neither of them spoke as they climbed, each lost in their own thoughts. Gek was desperate to know what could have caused such a fire on a basically deserted island, while Anne wondered what a man was doing alone on the island and how he had survived both the fire and the dragons.

As the slope got steeper, Anne struggled to make the climb; she fell several times, rose and kept climbing. Eventually, Gek draped her arm around his neck and helped her complete the journey to the cave near the summit of the hill. "You smell funny," murmured Anne. "So do you," replied Gek, "and you are welcome. We made it." They entered the mouth of the cave and Anne collapsed on the floor, spent.

Gek noticed that Anne had a water bag attached to her belt. He removed it and went deeper into the cave to fill it from the spring. He returned and revived Anne, handing her the water bag. Anne drank deeply and nodded her thanks. "What is this place?" she asked. "It is just a cave in the hillside," said Gek, "but it has a spring inside." "Do you live here?" asked Anne. "No," said Gek, "a friend does." "How do you avoid the dragons?" "What dragons?" asked Gek innocently.

"Hummph," said Anne. "These islands are teeming with Sea dragons." "Why would you say that?" asked

Gek. "We sent a landing party ashore on the northern island, and they found hundreds of dragon footprints in the sand." Gek thought a moment, then asked, "How many feet does a dragon have?" "Four, I guess," said Anne, "Why?" "Well, a four-footed dragon would make a hundred footprints in only about twenty-five steps, right?" Anne thought for a minute, then said, "You may be right. I wasn't the one who saw the footprints; it was Mage Andrew."

Gek recoiled, shocked, "From the HMS VALOR? I thought that ship was in the southern ocean!" "It was," said Anne, "but the Admiral reassigned it to the First Fleet after the dragon attack on Sundock that sank so many of our ships. How do you know Andrew?" Gek temporized, "I met his parents once. I have never met him, but I heard he was assigned to the VALOR."

Anne yawned, "I'm sorry, I just can't keep my eyes open any longer. I'm so tired. Is it OK if I sleep here for a while?" "Sure," said Gek. "Sleep as long as you need." Anne nodded, then curled up on the floor and was asleep almost instantly.

Gek moved deeper into the cave, to where Azure was waiting. "Now what?" asked Gek. "We can't just leave her here alone. If Cobalt comes back and finds her, he will kill her." "She will probably sleep until morning. We could fly to Acropo and be back by then—" "No. *I* should go and come back. You should stay here with Anne." "But—" "No 'buts,' Gek," said Azure. "It is the right decision, and you know it. I will leave at sunset. Now, go back and get me those crabs, and do not pick up any more strange women while you are out."

"Have you seen the projections?" King Donald asked James, his newly appointed Court Wizard. "Yes, Sire, I received the report," said James. "And?" "And I believe that the estimates are probably low. I suspect that your Ministers and engineers have undoubtedly underestimated the costs of the project in order to get your approval to begin. They'll come back with cost overruns and schedule delays later, once it's too late to turn back."

"You're saying that *a thousand golds* is an underestimate?" asked the King. "I'm saying that that's a possibility, Sire. On the other hand, Wizard Edward may surprise us again and complete the project ahead of schedule and under budget. He certainly has a way of getting things done," James acknowledged, somewhat grudgingly. "The Minister's engineers were dead set against this plan initially, but Edward has inspired them.

Now, they can't wait to get started. That's an amazing achievement when it comes to civil servants."

"You're right about that," said the King. "Is this worth a thousand golds?" "Sire, if Edward and the engineers can stop the spread of the Salt Flats and create a giant saltwater reservoir that we can draw water from and convert to freshwater, it will be an achievement worth ten times that amount, and you'll be remembered as one of the greatest Baizian monarchs ever."

"And if it fails?" "Then we blame Edward, a convincing schemer from Franconia that promised more then he could deliver," said James. "So, you think we should proceed?" "I do, Sire. Besides, they will not need all of the gold right away, we will finance the effort in stages. That way, if they fall behind schedule or their costs grow too much, we can always terminate the effort." The King smiled. That was a reassuring thought. "What about Mage Kathy?" asked the King.

"Hmmph," said James, "I think she's smitten with Wizard Edward. It's almost unseemly, the way she hangs by his side every minute. They're almost inseparable." "Can we use that to our advantage somehow?" asked the King.

"If Edward is as taken with Mage Kathy as she is with him, it might be possible to convince him to remain in Baize for an extended period of time. However,

Edward has a son in Franconia, which complicates matters somewhat." "Are father and son close?" "I believe so, but the son, I believe his name is Donovan, will likely be confined to their Wizards Academy for some years yet," said James. "Plenty of time," said the King. "Romantic entanglements have been known to be consummated in much less time than that. Very well, I will approve the project and allocate 250 golds as an initial outlay, with similar amounts invested quarterly. After a year, we will inspect the progress and determine if additional funds should be allocated to the effort." "By your command, Sire," said James.

As the King and Wizard James left the throne room, Specialist Dirk slipped out the back door to report the results of the meeting to Edward.

Andrew rose before the dawn. He was anxious to begin the repairs to the VALOR and see how much damage the VICEROY and the VICTORY had sustained in the attack. He walked up on deck to find the Commodore already barking orders to the crew. "Good morning, Andrew. How did you sleep?" "Like a log, sir," replied Andrew. "I guess I was pretty tired. How's the leg?" "Better than it was a week ago," said

Commodore Matthews, "my knee had been acting up, but now it's good as new! It was almost worth getting injured." Andrew laughed. "I guess I never thought of that, you see, Healing Serum isn't specific to the wound, it heals every ailment or injury in the body. Maybe we should prescribe it for all military officers over forty."

"So, how's the ship?" asked Andrew. "Most of the damage seems to be confined to the area around the Seabows," replied the Commodore. "It seems the beasts recognized the danger they posed right away and focused their attacks on them. It was fortunate that the magicians were stationed nearby and erected shields between shots. We just had more Seabows per ship than magicians." "You're right Sir, and I don't know how to fix that. It's not like we have enough magicians to assign four to each ship in the fleet. If anything, we need more Seabows, maybe as many as six per side," said Andrew.

"We don't have the crew for that," said the Commodore. "Well, we do now, with the sailors from the COMFORT, or we would have, except for the casualties. We might outfit two of the ships with six Seabows each, but with one less ship, we're likely to see more dragons per ship the next time." "I guess that depends on what their casualties were," said Commodore Matthews. "How many dragons do you think we killed?" Andrew thought for a moment, replaying the battle in his mind. "I would say we killed about fifteen dragons, and probably wounded another fifteen or so. I don't know how quickly dragons heal or if they know any healing spells. They certainly can't make Healing Serum."

"How many dragons do you think attacked us?" "Probably at least forty, maybe as many as fifty, it was hard to keep track of those that stayed underwater." "So call it fifty, and we killed or wounded about thirty. That should give them pause before they attack again." "I hope so, Sir. The problem is, we don't know how many Sea dragons there are! If there are hundreds of them, thirty casualties is a drop in the ocean."

"If there are hundreds, why did only about fifty attack us?" "Maybe only the adult males attacked. There would certainly be a number of females and young dragons that would remain behind," speculated Andrew. "There are too many unknowns. We could be on the verge of a decisive victory, or have just fought to a draw in the opening battle," said the Commodore. "I think we won this battle, Sir, I mean, *they* withdrew, not us." The Commodore smiled, "I like the way you think, Andrew. Now, how soon can you make us some more Seabows?"

Azure departed at sunset. She slipped out of the cave while Anne was still sleeping, and flew as fast as she could to Acropo. When she reached the island, she dove underwater and swam down to the underwater entrance to the Sea Dragon Clan's lair. When she emerged from the grotto, she found a cave of despair. There were wounded and dying Sea Dragons everywhere, every passage and cavern was crowded with injured dragons, most of whom were pierced with long iron spears that entered one side and came out the other. Some dragons were pin-cushioned with smaller iron arrows that Azure assumed were from the crossbows that Gek had told them about.

Azure went from room to room, calling for her father. Eventually, she reached the council chamber and found Cobalt in a heated discussion with several uninjured dragons. "I said, NO!" shouted Cobalt, "It is too dangerous right now. We need to regroup and assess our losses. We need a new strategy for dealing with these new weapons."

Azure approached and said, "Cobalt, where is my father?" Cobalt ceased his argument with the other dragon when he heard Azure's voice. "Azure, I am so sorry. Teal was killed in the attack. We did not realize that the VALOR was one of the ships attacking us until it was too late. Teal flew in front of another member of the Clan who was attempting to eliminate the magician Andrew. He took a blast in the chest and was killed. Once we realized that the VALOR was present, and Teal was lost, we retreated back here. Again, I am so sorry for your loss."

Azure wept bitter tears, she was so angry with Ard for casting that stupid Binding spell. If not for that, Teal might still be alive. Cobalt took her under his wing and walked her into a small, empty chamber so that she could be alone with her grief. Finally, the tears stopped and Azure asked, "How many of the Clan were killed?" Cobalt sighed, "Too many. I am still waiting for a final count, but at least seventeen of the Clan were killed, and we have almost thirty injured, and I do not know how to help them! The small arrows can be removed and the wounds patched with seaweed, but did you see the big arrows? They were new, and unexpected. They punched through our scales with ease. The tips are barbed, and when we try to remove them, they cause fatal damage. I do not know what to do, other than make the injured as comfortable as we can and wait for the end. I wish the Sleep spell would work on Dragons. At least we could reduce their suffering."

Azure thought for a moment. Though she was angry, there was a glimmer of hope. She beckoned Cobalt near and whispered, "I may know a way to help the injured. When Gek and I landed on Perfo this morning, we found a female magic-user lying on the beach. She is the sister of the magic-user who saved Gek's life on the mainland. Gek is with her in your cave now. If we can convince her to help, she might be able to heal some of the injured." Cobalt shook his head in confusion, it was just too much to take in at once. "Gek was injured on the mainland? When was this? How was he injured? Why would a human help a Dragon?"

Azure took a calming breath and quickly explained what happened; how Gek was taken while he was in human form, her disastrous attempt to rescue him, and the actions of magician Celeste. Cobalt was still confused, "Why was Gek walking around in Grotton in human form?" he asked. "He was just going in for a quick look to make sure the HMS VALOR was still in port. On his way back to where I and the other Changed Ones were waiting for him, he was grabbed by the Regional Mage and put in a coach headed to the wizard's school in Kingston. I had to prevent them from putting him in that place," said Azure.

"And you think there is a chance that you can get this female magic-user to help us? Just because her sister helped Gek when he was in human form? That seems a stretch," said Cobalt. "What other choice do we have? To just let them all die? Besides, Celeste recognized that we were Changed Ones after she healed Gek. She asked why we had to be enemies. It may be that her sister feels the same," said Azure.

"I will ask the Clan," said Cobalt. "I have been named Clan Chief, at least temporarily. I will return shortly. Please wait here." Cobalt left Azure alone in the chamber, she wept for her father and realized that he had died to save her, because if Andrew were killed, she would die also, since she was subject to Ard's Binding spell. Azure heard Cobalt speaking in the other chamber, and a rumble of disagreement, along with a chorus of Dragons who were so desperate that they would agree to almost anything to help their loved ones. After a spirited discussion, Cobalt returned.

"You may go and fetch the female magic-user and see if she will help us. The vote was far from unanimous, but the females of the Clan are desperate for any chance to save their mates, and we all remember the story of Wizard Amanda. Perhaps this magic-user will be of similar mind." As Azure rose to leave, Cobalt said, "One more thing, if this magic-user will not consent to help us, you are to kill her immediately." "I understand," said Azure.

Azure flew back to Perfo as fast as she could, knowing that any delay could mean death for an injured Sea Dragon. She landed in front of Cobalt's cave and called softly for Gek. He came out immediately, looking about frantically. "Did you see her?" he asked. "Who, Anne? No. Why?" "Because she is gone," said Gek.

It was finally Endday, and Rachel's birthday. As soon as she awoke, she demanded her birthday present from Donovan. Reaching under the bed, Donovan produced a box wrapped in colored paper. "Happy Birthday!" he said, relieved that he had snuck out the day before to pick up the shoes from the cobbler next door. Rachel picked apart the ribbon encircling the box, then carefully unwrapped the paper. The shoes were magnificent, they were open-toed sandals with peach-colored straps adorned with rhinestones. They sparkled in the light. Rachel put them on and paraded around the room, admiring the fit and sparkle. Donovan watched closely, only he was not looking at the shoes.

"They look gorgeous," he said, "and the shoes are nice too." Rachel strode quickly to the bed and gave him a passionate kiss. She sat down, took off the shoes, and hurried into the shower. Donovan followed a few seconds later.

After breakfast, it was time for Endday testing, this week the Level Threes had been working to master the Replication spell. After the other three Level Three students had demonstrated the spell to Rachel's satisfaction, she asked Donovan what he would like to try and replicate. Donovan walked behind a tree and emerged with what looked like a Specialist's Concealment cloak. At least it shifted colors as Donovan moved it about. "Why this item?" asked Rachel, "and where did you get it?" "I borrowed this one from Wizard Noland," said Donovan mischievously, "and it's part of your Birthday present." "Um—it's very nice," said Rachel, unsure of how to respond. "But why would I need a Concealment cloak?" "After our talk with Specialist Lance last week, I approached Wizard Noland and proposed the idea that all magicians should have a cloak like this, once they pass the Sorcerer's Test. It would save magicians from having to use a Concealment spell, if they had one of these. Then they could cast another spell instead."

"That's a brilliant idea!" said Rachel, "but what does that have to do with my Birthday?" "Well, since your father has the only shop in Franconia that makes Concealment cloaks—" "You mean, my father is going to get a contract for several hundred of these cloaks?"

asked Rachel, excitedly. "Yes," said Donovan, "but a magician still has to cast the Concealment and Stamina spells on the cloth first, then the Academy will give the cloth to your father to make the cloaks. He won't be able to charge as much, because he'll be getting the cloth for free, but he'll still get several hundred orders for cloaks."

"That's incredible!" said Rachel. "Does he know?" "Not yet," said Donovan. "I thought maybe you'd like to tell him."

Despite their desire to rush over to Brian's shop, Donovan still had to demonstrate the Replicate spell, and replicating a Concealment cloak was proving to be next to impossible. "I don't understand it," said Donovan, after the third failed attempt, "why won't this darn spell work?" "Because, in addition to the Concealment and Stamina spells I put on the cloak, I added a Secrecy spell to prevent anyone from replicating the cloak," said Wizard Noland, suddenly appearing beside them. Both Rachel and Donovan jumped in surprise.

"Wizard Noland," said Rachel, "Donovan was just telling me—" "I know what he told you," said Noland, "I've been here the whole time. I just came over to see if the Secrecy spell actually prevented replication. I'm delighted to see that it works. You see, once these cloaks get out, someone is going to try and replicate them, and we can't have that."

"Sir, is it true that you're going to award my father a contract to make all of the Concealment cloaks for the Academy?" asked Rachel. "Yes. In fact, here's the contract. I'd appreciate it if you could have him sign it today, so we can begin making cloaks. You know that Laura passed her test recently, so she'll be the first to receive one of these cloaks," said Wizard Noland, handing over a rolled-up scroll.

"We'll leave right after Donovan demonstrates the Replicate spell, sir," said Rachel. "I'm impressed by your diligence, Rachel," said Wizard Noland, "I half-expected you to rush off to town without testing Donovan, once he told you about the contract for the cloaks, but having watched him for the last few minutes, I can tell you that if this had been any normal item, his Replication spell would have worked perfectly. Donovan, you have passed your Endday test and may go into town at your leisure."

Donovan looked at Rachel and said, "You heard the Headmaster, let's get going." As they turned to depart, Wizard Noland said, "By the way, Happy Birthday, Rachel. Make Donovan take you to the King's Table Tavern for dinner today. It's much better fare than The Happy Maid Tavern."

They left the Academy and headed directly to her father's shop, arriving well before noon. As they entered, Brian and Rachel's mother both came out and greeted them warmly. Brian went into the back room and emerged with two packages for Rachel. *Happy Birthday, Dear*, he signed, *this present is from me and your mother*. Rachel opened it greedily, it was a small box that held a magnificent pearl necklace with matching earrings. *Oh, father they are lovely,* she signed, *but can you afford such an extravagant gift?* Brian smiled and signed *Your boyfriend is such a poor negotiator that I was easily able to splurge on this gift for you.* Rachel laughed and Donovan signed, *Next time, I will ask for the boyfriend discount!*

Brian laughed and handed Rachel the other package. *This is from Donovan,* he signed. The cape was stunning. It was a rose-gold color and unlike Donovan's heavier cape, this one appeared to be made of shimmering silk. "Father, it's beautiful," said Rachel, "but isn't this the cape you made for the Dutchess?" *Yes, it is,* he signed, *but she disappeared from Kingston. When Donovan asked me to make you a cape to match your new dress, I sold him this one. But, this cape cost more than the dress!* signed Rachel. *So, try to keep it out of the mud,* interjected Donovan. Brian doubled over laughing, with his strange, coughing laugh.

Then you better hope it doesn't rain next Endday, or you'll have to carry me to the Ball, Rachel signed. Brian looked impressed, *You're going to the Royal Ball? Isn't that by invitation only? Yes,* signed Rachel, *Donovan finagled an invitation. I think this one's a keeper,* signed Brian. "OK," said Donovan, "my brain is melting because you two are signing so fast, and I certainly didn't forge the invitation. Everyone except Donovan laughed. "The word was 'finagled,' not 'forged.' I would never accuse you of forgery," said Rachel.

"So, now that the Birthday presents have been given and opened, why don't you give your father the 'other thing'?" *What Other Thing?* asked Brian. Rachel handed over the contract. *Wizard Noland asked me to give this to you. It is a contract to make Concealment cloaks for every magician who graduates, or has graduated, from the Wizards Academy.*

Brian took the contract with shaking hands, *Are you serious? This could be worth hundreds of golds!* "Before you get too excited," said Donovan slowly, "we will make the cloth at the Academy and give it to you. You will make the cloaks and sell them back to the Academy, at a greatly reduced price." *Of course,* signed Brian, *but one of my normal cloaks still costs about five silvers. How many magicians are there?* Donovan thought back to his Level One History class and signed,

I think the number is currently about a hundred and forty.

That's seventy golds, right there! signed Brian. *Plus, the new business as more students graduate!* "Papa, can you make that many cloaks? You may need to hire some helpers," said Rachel. Brian waved away the question, *Cloaks are easy,* he signed. *I'll make a pattern for each size: Small, Medium, Large, and Extra Large. Then all I have to do is cut the cloth, hem the edges, then put in some buttons to keep it closed. I could make a dozen in a day.*

Then I guess all you need to do is sign the contract and you are the Official Tailor of the Franconian Wizards Academy, signed Donovan. Brian took the contract and read it over carefully. It was a straightforward firm, fixed-price contract. Brian would be paid five silvers for each cloak, regardless of size, and would deliver them to the Academy Gatehouse as soon as he had a batch of ten cloaks completed. He would receive five golds for every batch of cloaks. Once all of the existing magicians in Franconia were outfitted with cloaks, the Academy would order five of each size to keep in stock. Brian would receive additional orders as the need arose.

The final clause in the contract was that Brian was not allowed to supply Concealment cloaks to anyone other than the Wizards Academy. Brian signed the contract and handed it back to Rachel with tears in his eyes.

After they left the tailor shop, as suggested, Donovan escorted Rachel to the Kings Table Tavern for dinner. As they stepped inside, the Head Waiter asked if they had a reservation. Donovan was crestfallen, and said that Wizard Noland should have mentioned that they needed a reservation before suggesting they come here for dinner. "Wizard Noland? Are you Donovan? Please follow me sir, your table is right this way." They followed the waiter to a secluded corner booth, with heavy curtains that could be drawn for privacy. Donovan whispered in Rachel's ear, "I guess I'm not the only one who's sneaky."

"Were you followed?" asked Jasmine. "Of course I was," replied Corporal Sleet. "Specialist Lance has been following me wherever I go lately. But I lost him in the marketplace. Besides, I have not caused any mischief since I broke the wagon wheel outside Prarrieville. I think Major Gerald was getting suspicious."

"So, what do you have to report?" asked Jasmine. "It seems that Wizard Edward made Concealment cloaks for the entire Royal Expeditionary Force. That was how they were able to sneak up behind our cousins outside Springfield." "Indeed. I wonder why Major Gerald left that bit of information out of his report to the King." "Does he suspect you?" asked Corporal Sleet. "After prematurely reporting the Royal Expeditionary Force's demise, I have certainly lost some credibility with the King," mused Jasmine. "Major Gerald may have his suspicions, but he has no proof to incriminate me."

"Would you like me to eliminate him?" "Not yet. It may become necessary soon, but he is still a useful tool. That may change suddenly if he forces my hand. Is there anything else I should know?"

"Major Gerald has informed Marshall Guzman about the cloaks. The Marshall is considering ordering them for the entire Royal Guard." Jasmine frowned. "That would be a definite complication for us. Has he made a decision yet?" "Not that I know of. As I understand it, the cloaks are very expensive, five golds each. That big an expense would probably put a big dent in the Treasury." "Bankrupt it, is more likely. I have been steadily draining it to weaken Franconia. It is amazing that the Minister of Finance has not reported the situation to the King yet."

"Perhaps he fears that he will be blamed for the theft," said Sleet. "That is possible, and will be a delightful bonus when the loss is eventually discovered," said Jasmine. "If Marshall Guzman proposes buying several thousand Concealment cloaks, the situation may come to light very soon," said Sleet. "You are correct. We must eliminate the Marshall before that happens. He has been too efficient for too long," replied Jasmine. "How would you like me to proceed?"

Jasmine thought for a moment, then asked, "Have you been issued a Concealment cloak yet?" "No, but I understand that I will receive mine on Midweek." "Excellent!" said Jasmine. She extracted a single purple berry from a hidden pocket inside her shirt, handing it over gently, along with a small brass key, she said, "This is a Nightshade berry. It is deadly poison. Using your new cloak, and this key, I want you to infiltrate the Royal Ball on Endday. Place this berry in Marshall Guzman's wine, then make your escape." "What does the key open?" asked Sleet.

"Come with me and I will show you." Jasmine walked around the palace walls until she came to a small door on the west side. "This is the door that the cooks and servants use to remove the rubbish from the palace. Enter here. It will be heavily trafficked during the ball, so be cautious entering. You may kill anyone you wish on your way out, but I do not want an alarm raised before you place that berry in the Marshall's wine. Do you understand?" "Clearly. How long will it take for the poison to act?" asked Sleet.

"That depends on how much the Marshall has eaten. It could be very fast, or delayed some hours if his stomach is full." "I understand," said Corporal Sleet. "Understand this as well, if you succeed, you will be rewarded. If you fail, I may have to kill you."

Dirk slipped back into the room quietly. Edward was sitting at the desk, studying lists of provisions, and plans prepared by the Baizian engineers. "Where have you been?" Edward asked. "Oh, just nosing about." Edward snorted, "If I know you, you were nosing about in the Kings private chambers. Did you learn anything useful?" "The King is going to approve the Salt Flats project and allocate 250 golds per quarter for the construction of the reservoir. After a year, he is going to check on the progress and see if the effort should continue. He wants you to leave within a week," said Dirk.

Edward thought about this for a moment, then smiled, "You know, that might just be enough. That is, if these Baizian apprentice magicians work hard and don't give me any trouble." Dirk laughed, "Sir Wizard,

I'll wager you can handle a few troublesome apprentices." "I can, but that's not what I mean. These young magicians are going to have to work *hard*, in grueling conditions. I can't be everywhere and if they start slacking off, they'll delay the project, incurring additional costs. Digging holes and making walls is going to get very boring, very quickly. I will need to come up with something to keep them interested and engaged," said Edward.

"Speaking of 'interested and engaged,'" said Dirk, "your relationship with Mage Kathy has not gone unnoticed." "Really?" said Edward, "and what is the King's position on it?" "Both the King and Wizard James are hoping to encourage it. I believe their exact words were that a 'romantic entanglement' could be a great benefit to Baize, if it enticed you to remain for an extended period of time." Edward was both relieved and concerned. "I'm relieved that they're not going to place any obstacles in our path, but I'm not sure King Henry will approve of my remaining in Baize for very long."

"So, what are you going to do?" asked Dirk. "I'm not entirely sure. Kathy gets a vote too. I'll certainly have to take her wishes into account." "Who's wishes?" asked Kathy, entering the room without knocking, a very *familiar* act, thought Dirk. "Why yours, of course my dear. Specialist Dirk has just informed me that the

King plans to approve the project, give us gold, and 'shoo' us out of town by the end of the week."

"That's wonderful! I was sure he was going to balk at the cost," said Kathy. "Apparently, he's going to allocate 250 golds each quarter, then inspect our progress at the end of the year." "Will that be enough?" "It will be more than enough, if we can keep the apprentices working diligently. If they start slacking off, and we fall behind schedule, it will assuredly not be enough." "I see. How will you keep them motivated?"

Edward considered the problem for a moment. "We'll form them into teams, and have competitions between them, 'how many yards of trench did each team dig this week? How far did they extend the walls? That sort of thing. There will have to be prizes or awards for the winning teams each week." "What sort of prizes?" asked Kathy. "Coin is usually a motivator, or better rations, even medals or ribbons have been known to motivate men; maybe some time off, but the work must continue non-stop if we are to meet our deadline."

"That sounds like an excellent plan, but I will ask again, who's wishes must be 'taken into account'?" Dirk rose and excused himself, granting Edward some privacy for what was going to be a delicate conversation. "I'll be outside if you need anything," he said, closing the door softly. Kathy looked at Edward questioningly. "Dirk overheard the King and Wizard James discussing our obvious attraction to each other. They opined that a 'romantic entanglement' between us should be encouraged, if it resulted in my remaining in Baize for an extended time. My comment to Dirk was that such an 'entanglement' would have to take your feelings and desires into account," said Edward gently.

Kathy sat silently for a moment, and Edward feared that he had misinterpreted her attention as more personal than she intended. When she rose and headed for the door, Edward's heart sank, but she stopped and locked the door. As she began disrobing, she said, "I will show you my feelings and desires, Edward."

"What do you mean, 'she's gone'? Where could she go?" asked Azure, frantically. "I fell asleep in the cave, when I woke up a few minutes ago, she was gone. I just finished searching the cave and she is not in here," said Gek. "What is wrong?" "Too much! Teal is dead, killed by the humans, and many of my Clan are injured and dying. They all fled to Acropo. I convinced Cobalt that Anne might be persuaded to heal them. We have to find her quickly!"

Gek was shocked by the news, and overcome with guilt, at having let Anne slip away while he was sleeping. "Well, she cannot have gone far. The only water on the island is in this cave. We could just wait here until she returns," said Gek reasonably. "No! dozens of my kin could die before she returns!" "What do you suggest?" "I could fly around the island and search for her," said Azure. "If Anne sees a Sea Dragon flying around, she will undoubtedly hide from you." "Then I can change into human form—" "And what, waddle around, naked, in the hot sun, looking for her? I do not think that is a good idea," said Gek. Azure began to weep in frustration. She knew that Gek was right, but she had no other ideas. They sat, side by side, looking out at the ocean, searching for inspiration.

"If you want my help," said Anne, dropping her Concealment shield, "we will need to make an agreement and I will insist on a Binding spell."

Chapter Nineteen:

SECOND CHANCES

The agreement was simple. Every dragon that Sorceress Anne healed had to agree to a Binding spell, never to attack humans again. Anne was insistent; she was not going to heal a dragon just so it could go out and try to kill her friends again the next day. The dragons also had to agree to take her back to the mainland unharmed when she was done. She did not want to be the only human on an island chain populated exclusively by Sea dragons.

Gek and Azure promised to present her conditions to the Sea Dragon Clan. They could not assure her that any of the uninjured dragons would consent to the Binding spell. In fact, they were pretty sure that they would not. Also, since neither Gek nor Azure needed healing, they would not promise never to attack humans either, they would only swear to take her to Acropo, and then return her to the mainland, unharmed, after she presented her conditions to the Clan.

After Binding them to their promise, Anne watched with fascination as Gek transformed into a Great Dragon. Gek said that he would be happy to give Anne a ride, but that his wing had been injured a few weeks ago and was not yet fully healed. Before departing,

Anne asked, "How do you know Celeste?" Gek and Azure looked at each other, unsure of how much to tell Anne. Finally, Gek said, "A few weeks ago, I was in human form in Grotton when I was grabbed by Regional Mage Charles. Celeste was assigned to transport me to the Wizards Academy in Kingston. Azure intercepted the coach enroute and rescued me, but I was injured when the carriage overturned, that is why my shirt is bloody. Celeste healed me, but realized that I was a Changed One. For saving my life, we named her a Dragon-friend and vowed to spare her life. That is why I mistook you for her when I saw you washed-up on the beach."

"So it wasn't brigands," said Anne softly. "Excuse me?" said Gek. "Celeste told everyone that it was brigands that attacked the coach. The Regional Mage was so angry with her that he sent her back to the Wizards Academy in disgrace." "Sorry about that," said Azure. "Although we did tell Celeste that she could tell everyone that it was a Dragon that attacked the coach. I wonder why she did not report us?" "She probably thought that no one would believe her," said Anne. "Most people still believe that dragons are mythical." "Humph," was all Gek had to say about that.

As Anne approached Azure, she said, "I don't believe we've been introduced, I'm Anne Mace." "My name is Azure, and you should know that two days ago, your human shipmates killed my father. I appreciate your willingness to help us, but I am not fond of humans," said Azure. "I understand," said Anne, "If our places were reversed, I would probably feel the same way."

Anne climbed onto Azure's back and grabbed on tight, "Ready," she said. Gek and Azure leaped into the sky, making their best possible speed to Acropo.

"Hello, Wizard Loren," said Celeste, timidly. "Celeste, my dear, it is so good to see you again. I hear you had quite an adventure," said Loren. "If you call almost being killed by a Sea dragon and adventure," said Celeste. "Well. You were obviously not the intended target, or you would not be here." "You're right about that, Azure was just trying to rescue Gek," Celeste confessed. "The Great Dragon? Yes, I have heard about him, though I did not know his name. He certainly gets around."

"What do you mean by that?" asked Celeste. "Why, he was here in Kingston. Stuart met him and Azure. They had come to protect Donovan." "Why would dragons want to protect Donovan?" "Oh, some nonsense about his being a descendant of Wizard

Amanda, and the Dragons owing him a debt. I believe there was even a Binding spell involved. Such a shame too, I had big plans for that young man." "You're saying that the dragons are sworn not to harm Donovan?" asked Celeste, shocked. "Yes. Well, at least those members of the Dragon Council who were bound to the oath." "So, Donovan is a descendant of Wizard Amanda," mused Celeste. "Oh, not just him, Sorcerer Andrew too. Did you know those two are cousins?"

"No. I had no idea." "Neither did we, but that old scoundrel, Ard, he found out somehow. Then came scurrying back to tell us." "Where is Ard now?" asked Celeste. "No idea. He is so old that it takes him forever to get anywhere. For all I know, he may be headed back to the rock quarry for the next meeting of the Dragon Council," said Loren. "The one on the eastern shore?" asked Celeste, innocently. "No, dear, the one on the Amber River, just north of Colton. That is where we always meet, since the Fire and Stone Dragons are supposed to stay on the west side of the river."

"I still don't understand why the dragons wanted Franconia and Baize to fight each other," said Celeste. Loren scoffed, "Silly girl, the answer is obvious, it is so that you would both be weaker when we attacked. Oh, my. This is an interrogation, and I have just spilled the proverbial beans. Well done, Celeste! I did not think you had it in you." "I wasn't sure myself. Thank you, Loren."

Celeste left the room where Loren was being held. She met Wizard Noland in the hall outside. "Did you hear all that?" "Indeed. You got more out of her than any of us have learned in all the months of her captivity. She seems to have forgotten that her water is always laced with Truth Serum. Now we know where the Dragon Council meets, should we ever decide to make an appearance, and that the members of the council promised not to attack Donovan or Andrew. That explains much. I must send a message to the Admiralty immediately. We may be able to use this information to our advantage," said Noland. "Well done, Celeste. I do not regret giving you a second chance."

"Here are your Concealment cloaks," said Major Gerald, presenting the new cloaks to Corporal Sleet and Sergeant Cooper. "If you lose or damage them, they cost five golds to replace. That means you'll be working for free for almost a year. Next, remember where you put them! If you lay them down on the ground, you may never find them again. Most of the men turn them inside out when they're not wearing them. They're much easier to see that way. Got it?"

The two newest members of the Royal Expeditionary Force nodded their understanding and took their new cloaks from Major Gerald eagerly. "Another thing," said the Major, "these cloaks will make you almost invisible, but they will not stop arrows, swords or fire. Remember that. Now let's move out."

The Force rode to the outskirts of Kingston where they began a series of maneuvers. They played an advanced version of hide-and-seek, where one squad, wearing their Concealment cloaks, tried to sneak up on another squad that was dressed 'normally.' The soldiers were very impressed with the cloaks and the potential they had. After a few hours of these exercises, a somewhat grumpy Specialist Lance approached the commander. "So, what do you think, Lance?" asked Major Gerald. "Well, for one thing, you're going to have to make a new regulation about not allowing people to sneak up on you, or you're going to be very jumpy." "That's true enough. What else?" "The cloaks are great for dismounted operations, which is what Specialists mainly do, but for mounted missions, they're not much use. Take a look over there."

Major Gerald looked to where Lance was pointing, and saw the problem, there were eight, seemingly riderless horses racing across the field. You couldn't see the men, but the cloaks were too short to cover the mounts. "Why didn't we notice that before?" asked Gerald, rhetorically. "It's because we snuck around behind the dragons at night, sir. In the darkness, they couldn't see the horses. We're going to need something made out of this cloth to cover the horses if we're going to conceal the whole Force."

"You're right about that. Damn! If a cloak for a man costs five golds, how much more is a horse cloak likely to cost?" "Probably two or three times the cost, say ten to fifteen golds each, I expect," said Lance. "I'll need to talk to Wizard Noland again. Maybe he can find a way to make 'em cheaper," said Gerald. "Equipping an entire Cavalry Company is going to be very expensive. I don't know how I'm gonna sell this idea to the King, or the Marshall for that matter." "Maybe Wizard Noland will have an idea. He's pretty smart." "I hope so," said Gerald, "Otherwise, these cloaks will be restricted to the infantry."

"We should probably order a few spare cloaks, sir. For when someone loses theirs. Despite your warning, I guarantee you, someone is going to lose or damage one." "I know, we also need to find a way to make sure no one sells theirs on the black market. I'll probably have to institute a weekly inspection to make sure none of them disappear."

They arrived on Acropo two hours after departing Perfo, and were faced with a dilemma. *How were they going to get Anne inside the underwater cave?* They landed atop the cliff above the cave's entrance and discussed the matter. "The entrance to the Clan's living area is reached by an underwater cavern," said Gek. "How long can you hold your breath?" he asked Anne. "Only about a minute," she confessed. "Will that be long enough?" "Maybe not," said Azure, remember, we jump off from here and our momentum carries us deep enough under the water to reach the entrance. I doubt she can hold on during the impact with the water."

"Can you just land on the water and swim down?" "Of course, but that takes much longer." Anne pondered the problem, then came up with a solution. "When the mast from the ship landed on me and drove me deep underwater, my shield protected me and I was able to breathe the air inside. Maybe I can cast a smaller shield around my head and that will give me enough air to breathe while we swim to the entrance."

"We should probably do some tests before we go all the way in," said Azure. "I appreciate that," said Anne, "I've never tried this before." "Gek, can you go in and let Cobalt know we are here? You should also let him know about Anne's conditions. I warn you. It is not a pretty sight down there." Gek swallowed hard, and steeled himself for what he was about to witness. Then he said, "Be right back," before launching himself off the cliff, The impact with the water did *not* feel good on his injured shoulder, but he pushed on, entering the underwater grotto as he had many times before. As his head broke the surface, he heard the cries of the wounded and dying dragons, and the lamentations of their mates and children. It was heart-wrenching.

As he emerged from the water, Cobalt was there, waiting anxiously. "Did she agree? Did you bring her?" Cobalt asked desperately. "Yes, and Yes," replied Gek, "but she has conditions." "Of course she does," grumbled Cobalt. "What does she want? Gold? Treasure?" "No," said Gek. "She wants a promise that any dragon she heals will never attack a human again. She insists on a Binding spell on it. She also wants to be returned to the mainland unharmed after she is done."

"THAT IS UNREASONABLE!" shouted Cobalt. "The Clan will never agree to those terms!" "I am sorry. Those are her conditions. She says that she will not heal a dragon just so they can go out and kill some of her friends tomorrow. I understand her reasoning." Cobalt calmed down and considered his options. It was unlikely that he could compel a magic-user to heal his injured family against her will. Killing her would be easy, but it would not help the dying dragons.

"I will discuss it with the Clan. Anything else?" "Anne agrees that any dragon who does not need healing does not need to commit to the Binding spell. Azure and I both declined, perhaps it would be best if the uninjured of the Clan move to the deepest part of the cavern system, so she does not see them," said Gek. "A wise precaution. Where is she now?" "She is on the surface with Azure, working out a way to get in here without drowning. Few humans can hold their breath for long enough to make it in here." Cobalt grunted his agreement and headed into the cave complex. Gek heard him discussing the situation with the Clan. It was a contentious conversation. Finally, he heard dragons shuffling off, down into the depths of the cavern system, out of sight.

Cobalt emerged a moment later. "Some of the Clan will agree to the conditions, and some of those with less severe injuries will not. I have sent all of those who will not agree into the lower levels, and ordered the most severely injured brought up, closer to the entrance. We must hurry. Some are near death."

Gek dove into the grotto, swimming as fast as he could with his injured wing. When he broke the surface, he found Azure and Anne waiting. "Will it work? We have to hurry," said Gek. "I think so," said Anne. "What did they say?" "The most severely injured are being brought up to the area closest to the entrance, those unwilling to promise not to attack humans are moving to the lower levels of the cave system and will not see you. Are you ready?" asked Gek. Anne nodded and conjured her shield spell. A shimmering blue bubble encompassed her head. She patted Azure on the neck to indicate she was ready.

Azure dove beneath the water, swimming strongly towards the mouth of the underwater cave. A few minutes later, she broke the surface of the water and climbed out onto the ledge. Gek followed soon after. Anne hopped down off Azure's back, released her shield, and used a quick Wind spell to dry her clothes. She had no intention of healing dragons while soaking wet.

Cobalt met them in the passageway. "I am Cobalt, Chief of the Sea Dragon Clan. Welcome Anne. Thank you for agreeing to help us." "I am deeply sorry that we have become enemies, Cobalt. I will do what I can to help your injured. Please take me to them." Cobalt led the way into the first chamber, where a Sea dragon lay impaled with a Seabow bolt through his lower abdomen,

Anne thought, (it was difficult to tell with dragons). Anne used the Remove spell to dissolve the iron bolt, then tried a healing spell. The bleeding slowed, then stopped. Anne used an Adhesive spell to seal the edges of the wound shut. She gave instructions that the dragon should be given water, but no food for at least a day.

The rest of the night and into the morning, Anne moved through the caverns, healing arrow wounds, broken bones, and blast injuries. She wished she had some Healing Serum but had no idea how much Serum it would take to heal a dragon. She worked tirelessly, using a Stamina spell when her fatigue began to overtake her. She drank water from her bottle when she began to feel lightheaded. As she went about her task, Cobalt watched from the shadows.

When the last dragon that could be healed was tended to, Anne sank to the floor, exhausted. Cobalt emerged from the passageway and said, "You have done a great service for the Sea Dragon Clan. As your sister is, I name you Dragon-friend, and under our protection. Rest well, Anne. You will sleep safe tonight. You have my word." Anne laid her head down and fell into a deep sleep.

Cobalt went down the passageway to where Gek and Azure were waiting. "Is she finished?" asked Azure. "Yes. She saved all but the two most gravely injured. It was amazing; she was so weary, but she would not stop. She is sleeping now," said Cobalt. "What will you do now?" asked Azure. "I have been watching Anne for hours, and I think I have learned the commands and gestures for some new spells. I will go below and try them on the members of the Clan who would not consent to Anne's terms. Maybe I can heal some of them."

"I could change back into human form and try them," said Gek. "Can you make all the gestures?" "The spell she used to dissolve the arrows involves a gesture that is not natural for a dragon. Your help may be needed. Azure, how are you? You look unusually tired."

"I am tired all the time lately, and hungry for strange food. Are there any Barracuda in the food stores?" Cobalt looked at her closely for the first time. "You are pregnant! Congratulations! Why did you not say something sooner?" "We had more pressing problems than my condition, and as Gek can tell you, I am not my jovial self lately." Gek wisely remained silent.

Cobalt led them down the passageway to the lower levels where the other Sea Dragons were waiting. Cobalt said, "The human magic-user has kept her promise and healed all the wounded upstairs. I have watched her closely and will attempt to conjure some of the healing spells I saw her employ. If I am unable to perform the gesture required for the spell to work, Gek here has volunteered to change into human form and try the spell. Lastly, I named Sorceress Anne a Dragon-friend for her help. She is to be protected."

Cobalt walked among the wounded, and amazingly, the healing spells worked. This was a great thing for the Sea Dragons. Also, as expected, the 'flicking' motion required for the Remove spell was not possible for a Dragon. Gek transformed and used the spell successfully to remove several Seabow arrows from wounded Dragons. When all of the Dragons had been healed, Cobalt ordered them to remain below, so as not to let Anne know their number. She was still a human, after all.

Cobalt, Azure and Gek moved to the chamber previously occupied by Teal. As they entered, another Sea Dragon rose from where she had been sleeping on the floor. "

"Hello, Azure," she said. "Hello, Aqua," replied Azure coldly. "Gek, this is Aqua, my mother."

Endday testing had been exceptionally easy this morning, probably because Rachel was in a hurry to get into town to have her hair, nails and make-up done for the ball that evening. Donovan had grumbled, claiming that she didn't need any make-up, her hair looked great as always, and what did it even mean to get one's 'nails done'? His objections were overruled, and Rachel gave him a quick peck on the cheek as she practically sprinted for the Gatehouse.

Left alone, Donovan was unsure what to do with himself. He returned to his room and took a shower. When he was finished, he decided to go into town for lunch. Rachel said that she would not be back until that evening, just before they had to leave for the Royal Ball. After confirming his last surprise for Rachel with Wizard Faith, he headed out into town. He decided to check on his house and pick up some money for the evening. He grabbed some silver and a couple of golds, just in case.

The whole city was buzzing about the Ball. Shops were doing a booming business, especially the florists. Donovan slapped his head; he had forgotten a corsage for Rachel. He rushed into the nearest florist and picked up a modest arrangement of two pink roses surrounded by something called 'baby's breath.' The corsage in hand, Donovan continued his walk. As he passed the barber shop/dentist, he decided that a shave and a haircut might be appropriate, so he went in. *How did he want his hair cut? What a stupid question! With scissors, of course.*

The barber laughed at the joke he had undoubtedly heard a thousand times before and asked what *style* Donovan wanted for his hair. Donovan informed the barber that he was going to the Ball that evening and wanted something appropriate yet conservative. He just wanted a man's haircut. The barber showed him several sketches of different styles, and Donovan selected the one that looked the least ridiculous. As the barber proceeded with the haircut, he commented about the state of Donovan's fingernails and asked if he was sure that he didn't want a manicure as well.

Donovan looked at his nails. They were a bit jagged and uneven. Fine, trim the nails. A glass and a half later, Donovan emerged from the shop looking splendid (he thought). He stopped in at The Happy Maid Tavern for lunch and, as usual, found Specialist Lance sitting alone in a corner booth. Donovan walked over and took a seat.

Lance took a close look at Donovan and said, "I didn't know that Academy students were invited to the Royal Ball." Donovan grinned, "Sharp as ever, I see. What gave me away, the haircut?" "No. The corsage. It must be for Rachel. I assume she's off somewhere getting prepped for the Ball." "Right again," said Donovan. "Have you ever been to one?" Lance snorted,

"A mere Specialist, be invited to the Royal Ball? Never in a million years. I think the lowest-ranking guardsman there will be the Marshall. Oh, there'll be some of the palace guards there, but they're just for security. They will not be dancing or hobnobbing with the guests." "Dancing?" asked Donovan, panicked. "Of course, dummy. After all, the Ball is one big formal dance. Didn't you know that?"

"I need to learn how to dance. Right now. Where can I learn?" Lance laughed out loud. "You've certainly waited until the last minute, my friend. Come along with me. I will take you to Madam Finch's dance studio. I just hope she has time for you today."

They left the tavern and headed down the street. Donovan asked if Lance was still following the new Corporal. "No, the Major decided that it wasn't necessary. He seems fine, just a bit of a loner. Ah! Here we are." They entered a nondescript store front with a sketch of a couple dancing hanging over the front door. An attractive brunette came out to meet them. "Lance!" she said, coming up and giving him a kiss on the cheek. "Have you finally come to sweep me off my feet?" Lance blushed, something Donovan had never seen before, "Not yet, Megan. Soon, but not yet. May I present Master Donovan Francis? Donovan is a student at the Wizards Academy and has somehow wrangled an invitation to the Royal Ball tonight. He just learned about a quarter-glass ago, that a Ball is a dance. He needs a crash course in ballroom dancing."

"Now? But the Ball is tonight!" said Megan. "You can't be serious!" Lance laughed again, "You don't need to make him an expert; just teach him the basic steps for a waltz and a foxtrot. He's a quick learner, if a bit naïve." Megan took Donovan's hand and immediately led him into the dance studio, which was really nothing more than a large open space with mirrors along one wall.

Over the next three glasses, Megan gave Donovan his first dance lesson. The most important thing, Megan informed him, besides knowing the steps, was to *lead* his dance partner by signaling where he was going next by applying subtle pressure on her waist. That, and not stepping on her toes. Donovan started wondering if he could conjure shields around his feet. Rachel would definitely not appreciate it if he stepped on her new shoes or her newly manicured toes. He paid Megan a gold for her time, which she said was way too much, but Donovan insisted, given the late nature of his arrival.

Donovan left the studio and headed back to the Academy, realizing that he had spent almost all day getting ready for the ball. "Shine, Sir?" asked a young man on the street corner. "Excuse me?" said Donovan. "Would you like your boots shined? It looks like you're going to the ball tonight. It wouldn't do to arrive with unpolished shoes." Realizing the boy was right, Donovan paid a silver to have his boots buffed to a high shine. They probably never looked better, he thought. Now, he really must get back to the Academy and get dressed for the ball.

After putting on the green velvet outfit and the cape, Donovan decided that he looked rather dashing. He retrieved the corsage for Rachel and headed over to her room in the Mentor's quarters. As he crossed the courtyard, he saw Wizard Noland in his formal clothes and robe, striding quickly towards the Gatehouse. A couple of students made wolf-whistles at Donovan as he passed. He arrived at Rachel's door and knocked. "I'll be out in a minute!" Rachel said through the door.

Donovan waited in the hall for several long minutes, pacing and wondering if the carriage he had engaged would wait for them. Finally, Rachel emerged. She looked beautiful, but Donovan didn't have time for compliments. He took her arm and hurried towards the Gatehouse. "Slow down!" said Rachel, "What's the rush?" Not wanting to spoil the surprise, Donovan slowed his pace and said, "I just don't want you to be late to the Ball." As they left the Gatehouse, a gleaming carriage was waiting for them. It was white with gold accents. The red-clad driver opened the door as they approached. "What's this?" asked Rachel. "This is so you don't have to worry about dragging your new cape in the mud," grinned Donovan.

The coachman helped Rachel into the carriage. Donovan slipped him a gold for the ride and entered behind her. Once inside, the carriage moved off at a slow, even pace, so as not to jostle the couple inside. As they rode through town, Donovan produced the corsage. Rachel said, "So, you did remember." She smiled as she allowed him to attach it to her dress. The box contained two straight pins, but Donovan, not wanting to damage the dress, used an Adhesive spell instead.

Rachel smiled and said, "I see you got a haircut and a manicure today, and even had your shoes shined. What did you do with the rest of your day? "I went into town and picked up your corsage, then went to the tavern for lunch. Every place was so busy, after I got my haircut, I didn't have time for much else," Donovan lied. "How did your day go?" Rachel said, "Oh, the stylist was ridiculous! She actually wanted to put feathers in my hair! The idea! Then she suggested blue highlights! As if I was a Sea dragon Changed One," she whispered. "Then the nail salon wanted to paint my nails black. Black! Can you imagine? At least the make-up artist did a passable job. Don't you think?" Donovan decided that there was no right answer to that question, so he took the diplomatic way out, and said, "You always look beautiful." He leaned in for a kiss, but Rachel pushed him away. "Not now. You'll ruin my make-up!" It was at this point that Donovan realized that it was going to be a very long night.

"Your mother?" asked Gek. "Yes," said Aqua, "it is nice to finally meet you, Gek. I have heard a great deal about you." "I wish I could say the same about you," stammered Gek, looking at Azure. "Aqua abandoned me shortly after I was born," said Azure harshly, "While she is technically my mother, *I* do not consider her family."

Gek looked between mother and daughter, unsure what to say. Finally, Aqua broke the uneasy silence and said, "Azure, you should know that dragons do not mate for life. That is because of our long lives. Teal and I stayed together for almost two hundred years. After that, Teal began to have a 'wandering eye,' and to be fair, so did I." Azure snorted, "A 'wandering eye'? You moved out and left us alone!" "Yes, I did. Because Teal kept bringing his new 'friends' over to visit while I was away, you were too young to notice, but I could not bear the shame any longer," said Aqua softly.

"It is not uncommon among Dragons, Azure. Right now, you and Gek are happy and cannot imagine being with anyone else. I hope you still feel that way in a hundred years. After a century together, dragons often desire *variety*." "Why are you here now?" asked Azure, still angry.

"I was mourning Teal, my mate for almost two hundred years. While we lived apart, Teal and I were still friends. As I said, it is not unusual," said Aqua. "But to abandon your child?" "Did you lack for care? Were you abused or neglected? No. There were always others around to care for you. Think back on the regular succession of nannies and other female caregivers, and you may understand why I never returned."

Azure was silent, thinking. Aqua was right about one thing, there had been a great number of other Dragon females sharing their chamber as she was growing up. Maybe she had misjudged her mother, and over-esteemed her father. "I will consider your words," Azure said. "You may stay here if you wish." "You will give birth soon," said Aqua, "in a month at most. You should remain close, for when the time comes." "I have one more trip I need to make, then I will return. I hope to see you then."

Anne woke up to something tugging on her pant leg. She roused and found herself face to face with a baby Sea dragon. He (or she) had wandered away from her mother and wanted someone to play with. Anne picked up a coconut that was laying nearby and rolled it across the cavern floor. The baby dragon chased after it and brought it back. A spirited game of 'fetch' ensued. Eventually, the baby grew tired of chasing the coconut. Anne conjured a Seeming of a ball and tossed it towards the baby. When the dragon reached out its claw for the ball, it vanished in a flash of light. The baby squeaked with delight. Anne sat on the floor, playing with the baby dragon for almost a glass before a voice behind her said, "In all my long life, I never imagined that I would see a human magic-user playing with a baby dragon."

Anne turned to find Cobalt and Azure standing in the passageway. "He's adorable," said Anne, "is it time for me to go?" Cobalt nodded and led Anne to the grotto. "Before I go, can you tell me why we have to be enemies?" Cobalt thought for a moment, then said, "How can you ask that, after the events of the past few days?" Anne persisted, "At least tell me why, after so many years, dragons suddenly started attacking humans."

"It all started when humans killed my mate, Gek's mother," said Cobalt. "A regrettable incident, surely," said Anne, "but why the attacks at sea? We did not attack you until after dragons began attacking our ships, then the port at Sundock." Cobalt shifted from foot to foot, "It was the will of the Dragon Council. We need room, and food to survive. Liza, my mate was simply trying to feed her son when she was attacked and murdered. If Gek had been found, he would have undoubtedly been slain as well. Do you deny it?"

"No," said Anne, "but we might have reached an agreement before all the bloodshed. We might still." "Humans betrayed the last agreement," said Azure. "I know," replied Anne, "but we could always try again. A second chance, if you will." Cobalt considered her words, then said, "You are kind-hearted, Anne, but you do not speak for your race. If a truce is to be agreed to, someone with more authority than you will have to agree to it. If such a time comes, you know where to find us. If humans attack our islands again, we will respond accordingly. As Chief of the Sea Dragons, I will order my Clan to cease the attacks on your ships, at least temporarily, unless they attack us first. I have no control over the Snow, Fire, Stone and Great Dragons, they will do as they feel they must."

"I understand. Thank you, Cobalt. I will carry your words to my people." With that, Anne climbed on Azure's back and conjured her shield. "Farewell." Azure and Gek dove into the water and swam out of the cave. They landed on Acropo and Anne released her shield, and dried herself off. "Where would you like us to take you?" asked Gek. Anne thought for a moment, then said, "I know our agreement was for you to take me to the mainland, but if I am to try and stop our ships from attacking you again, I need to get back on board the VALOR and speak to the Commodore."

Donovan decided that he was *never* going to another Royal Ball, ever. It started all right, first there was the receiving line. They waited to be announced, "Sorceress Rachel Turner and Master Donovan Francis," then they had to shake hands with a dozen Ministers, Cabinet Officials, and finally, the King. "Welcome to the Ball. Your gown looks lovely," said the King. "Thank you, Your Majesty," Rachel replied.

The band struck up the music and they danced. Rachel was very impressed that Donovan knew the steps and how to dance. She was very glad when he didn't step on her toes. After the second dance, the Minister for Commerce tapped Donovan on the shoulder and asked if he could 'cut-in.' Rachel nodded, and so began a seemingly endless line of Ministers, nobles, and Cabinet members who all wanted to dance with Rachel. Even the King. Donovan couldn't seem to get back in the rotation. Eventually, he gave up and headed to the refreshment table.

The table was filled with champaign, red and white wines, and an assortment of unrecognizable appetizers that looked a lot like raw meat on a cracker. Unimpressed, Donovan scanned the room, looking desperately for anyone besides Rachel that he knew. He saw Wizard Noland across the hall, leaning against a column, looking very bored as the Minister for Public Works was badgering him about how the Academy students could do more for the crown than clear rockslides and perform snow removal. Wizard Cassandra stood next to the King, obviously providing magical security for him.

As predicted, the only man in uniform was Marshall Guzman who was looking equally bored as he stood near the drink table. Donovan headed over to talk to him, thinking maybe they could discuss Concealment cloaks. "Marshall, it's good to see you again," said Donovan. "You may not remember me—" "Master Donovan! How good to see you!" "You remember me?" asked Donovan. "You're the one that threw that dragon's head at the King's feet. One does not forget something like that. Are you enjoying the ball?" "Hardly," murmured Donovan, "everyone here seems to want to dance with my date." The Marshall laughed gently. "Yes. That does seem to happen quite often at these things. Unless… your date is old, fat, or unattractive. Tell me, how are things at the Academy?"

"They're going very well, sir. Thank you for asking. Has there been any further word about my father?" "No. He is still in Baize, I believe, trying to convince King Donald that we are not behind the dragon attacks on his country. I hope he succeeds. We have enough problems without the Baizian Army attacking." The Marshall moved down the table and selected a glass of red wine.

Out of the corner of his eye, Donovan detected a slight shimmer to the air, as if someone was approaching under a concealment. Donovan turned, wondering if it was just Specialist Lance under his cloak, providing some sort of security for the Marshall. He was about to say something when he noticed that a small splash appeared in the Marshall's wine glass, as if someone had dropped a pebble in it. Just then, Minister Jasmine shouted, "A TOAST, TO OUR HOST, KING HENRY, MAY HE LIVE FOREVER!"

The concealed individual began moving away rapidly as the Marshall raised his glass for the toast. Donovan immediately placed a shield over the top of the glass, and conjured a Tether spell around the fleeing assassin. "What the—" "Don't drink that, sir! I'm pretty sure it's poisoned," shouted Donovan, as he raced to the tethered man who was struggling to escape. Donovan reached him and pulled down the hood of his Concealment cloak, exposing Corporal Sleet.

Pandemonium broke out among the guests, as men fled, women fainted, and palace guards rushed forward. "What's going on? What is the meaning of this?" demanded the King. "Sire," said Donovan, "I believe this man is an assassin, and that he just put some kind of poison in Marshall Guzman's wine. I noticed someone approach under a concealment, but I thought it was a Specialist I know from the Royal Expeditionary Force. As I turned to greet him, I saw a small splash in the Marshalls wine. Then this man quickly tried to run away before I Tethered him."

"Who are you? What are you doing here?" demanded the Marshall of the tethered Corporal. Wizard Noland approached quickly and the assembled guests parted for him. He examined the Marshall's wine glass and smelled it briefly, "Nightshade. Marshall, your wine is indeed poisoned," said Wizard Noland, placing the glass back on the refreshment table. "It's fortunate that Donovan was near and attentive. Does anyone know this man?" "Sir," said Donovan, "I recognize him. That's Corporal Sleet, one of the newest members of the Royal Expeditionary Force."

"No," said Noland quietly, sniffing the air, "this is a dragon Changed One. Keep him bound tightly so he can't transform." Donovan nodded. "Your Majesty," said Wizard Noland, "I strongly suggest that you dismiss your guests while we sort this matter out." "Of course, Wizard Noland," said the King. "Ladies and Gentlemen, I must unfortunately declare this Royal Ball concluded. Please make your way to the exits and depart immediately."

As the crowd headed for the doors, Rachel moved to Donovan's side, he noticed that she was missing a shoe. Wizard Noland beckoned Wizard Cassandra over. "Do you have any Truth Serum handy?" he asked. "I have some in my quarters," said Cassandra, "I'll be right back with it." Wizard Noland nodded and Cassandra departed rapidly. "What are you going to do with him?" asked Marshall Guzman. "We need to get some Truth Serum in him to determine who hired him, and why you were targeted," said Noland.

"Donovan, hold him steady." Wizard Noland threw back the Concealment cloak and efficiently removed both of Corporal Sleet's hands. "There. That will keep him from transforming into a dragon, or conjuring any spells. Donovan, you may release your Tether." The instant that Donovan released the Tether spell, Corporal Sleet lunged at Rachel, and Donovan moved to interpose himself between them. The Corporal dodged to the left, seized the poisoned wine glass between his stumps and took a deep drink. He gasped, convulsed, and fell to the floor dead.

"Damn," said Noland, "I forgot about the wine. I never expected that." When Wizard Cassandra returned, the palace guards were removing the now headless body of Corporal Sleet. The King was shaken by the ability of an assassin to get so close to him. Fortunately, he did not ask about the Concealment cloak, but Donovan thought the chances of procuring them for the entire Army were probably dashed now.

Donovan and Rachel rode the carriage back to the Academy in silence. This had not been the night either of them had hoped for. Finally, Donovan asked, "Are you mad at me for some reason?" Rachel looked at him coldly, and said, "Only because you let that assassin get to the poison." "He lunged at you!" said Donovan. "I am a Sorceress! Do you seriously think I couldn't handle a skinny man with no hands? You embarrassed me in front of Wizard Noland!" "I'm sorry! I was just trying to protect you!" said Donovan desperately. "I know. That's the problem," said Rachel.

Chapter Twenty:
COMMITMENTS

"How are we supposed to get you back to the ship?" asked Gek. "I'm not sure yet. Let's head back to where we met. Maybe I'll think of something before we get there," said Anne. Anne climbed aboard Azure and they flew south toward Perfo. Anne decided that flying on a dragon was much more fun than riding on one underwater. The view was spectacular, and the feeling of the wind in her hair was exhilarating. She wished the ride would last, but after two short hours, the dragons landed back on the charred terrain of Perfo.

"So, have you thought of a way for us to get you back to the ship?" asked Azure. "Maybe," said Anne, "if you get me close enough and set me down in the water, I can swim to it and call for help. I'm a good swimmer." "No good, "said Azure. "The sky is much too clear today. The humans would spot us from fathoms away. We normally only fly during the day when there are clouds to hide in. We could wait until dark and make the attempt."

"I'm not sure I like that," said Anne. "For one thing, there are fewer sailors on duty at night, and it would be a lot harder to see me. I could drown before anyone noticed me." The three sat in the sand, lost in thought, considering the problem. Then Anne had an idea. "Do you know the Concealment spell?" Ard and Azure looked at each other, unsure of how much to tell Anne about which magic spells Dragons could and could not do. Finally, Azure admitted that they knew the Concealment spell, but that it did not work underwater. It only created a bubble that prevented swimming.

"What about in the air?" asked Anne. "Does it work while you're flying?" "I have no idea," said Gek. "I have never tried it while flying. I was afraid that it would not work." "I suppose you could try here, on land, then try to fly and see if it works." Azure agreed that it was worth a try, thinking that it would also be a great way to sneak up on humans if it worked. Gek cast the spell and took flight. The spell worked and he was able to fly without too much difficulty. On the ground, Azure and Anne scanned the sky for him. "There he is," said Anne, pointing. "You can barely make out the distortion in the air as he flaps his wings."

Anne tracked Gek as he circled the island and was looking right at him after he landed and the Concealment spell faded. Gek walked over and said, "It works, but it is a lot harder to fly than it normally is. The spell takes energy and tires you out. It seemed to get worse the longer I flew." "Spells normally take energy from the conjurer," said Anne. "I hadn't considered that. Maybe we should think of something else."

"What if we flew most of the way there, then cast the Concealment spell once we are in sight of the ships?" "Can you cast the spell while you're flying?" asked Anne. "I know the gesture. Wouldn't that effect your flying?" "It should only be for a second," said Gek. "Let me try." He took off again, circling the island, when he reached a good height, he suddenly disappeared. They tracked his distortion until he landed and the spell dissipated. "It worked!" Gek said, excitedly.

"Let me try," said Azure. She took off, then cast the spell, but immediately began descending. She landed with a THUMP in the sand and sat still, panting until the spell wore off. "I am not sure I can do this," she said. "The strain is too much, even without Anne on my back. With her extra weight, I will never make it." Anne approached cautiously, "What's wrong? You look much more fatigued than you did yesterday." "I am pregnant," said Anne, "and according to my mother, the birth will happen soon. In the next few weeks I will lay a Dragon egg that will have to be kept warm and protected. That is why we were going to my home on Acropo."

"Congratulations!" said Anne. "I'm very glad that you weren't caught up in the battle and injured." Azure remained silent, unsure of how to reply to that comment. "I have an idea. Gek, what if *I* cast the Concealment spell? That way, it wouldn't draw any energy from you. If you don't think it will work, I suppose I can just stay here and signal the ships when they return."

"Are you sure they will come back?" asked Azure. "Yes. Commodore Matthews is not one to give up so easily. He will return and have his magicians set fire to both of the other islands if that's what it takes to win a decisive victory." "And you think you can stop him?" "I think I can *convince* him that a truce serves us both better than continuing to fight needlessly. Frankly, King Henry sees no value in these islands, except perhaps for the sheltered cove on—Acropo? Acropo. Our fishing fleet seldom ventures this far north. There are plenty of fish closer to our ports."

"I hope you are right," said Azure. "Gek, can you try flying with Anne? She is not very heavy." "I will try. If this works, I will be back in about two hours. Wait in the cave. I shall return." Anne climbed onto Gek's back, trying to avoid touching his injured right wing. "Goodbye, Azure. It was nice to meet you. I hope to see you again sometime." "Goodbye, Anne. For a human, you are not a bad sort."

Gek took off into the air, flying south, while he had an injured wing, he flew faster than Azure did, and Anne had to maintain a firmer grip to stay on. After a little over an hour, they spotted three ships, sailing north. "There they are," said Gek and Anne simultaneously. Anne cast a Concealment spell over both of them and Gek began to descend gradually. About two hundred yards from the lead ship Anne said, "I will jump off here. You will need to cast your own Concealment spell once I hit the water. If you ever need to contact us, just hold a big white cloth in your claws. That is the human sign for asking for a parlay." Gek nodded his understanding. "Goodbye, Gek," said Anne as she leapt into the sea." Goodbye, Anne. Say 'Hello' to your sister for me," said Gek as he cast his Concealment shield and soared back into the sky, heading north to Azure.

Tap, Tap, Tap, "Donovan, It's Leo. It's a little after five," said Leo, from the other side of the door. "Thanks, Leo. I'm up, but I don't think I'll be coming down to breakfast today. I'll probably be sleeping back here for a while," said Donovan sadly. "I know. Rachel told me when I knocked on her door a few minutes ago. I'm sorry it didn't work out. I know you liked her," said Leo, before heading back downstairs to the kitchen.

Donovan shook off his sadness and headed for the shower. He just couldn't understand how things with Rachel had gone so wrong, so quickly. The Royal Ball last night was a blur. First the feelings of jealousy as Rachel danced with dozens of other men, after only two dances with him; the detection and apprehension of the assassin who tried to poison Marshall Guzman; Wizard Noland removing the dragon Changed One's hands; his charge at Rachel; Donovan moving in front of her to protect her; and the Changed One slipping past him to grab and drink the poisoned wine, and then dying before he could be questioned.

Rachel had been furious during the carriage ride back to the Academy. She had accused Donovan of dismissing her abilities as a Sorceress, thinking she needed protection against an unarmed man who had just had his hands forcibly removed. Nothing Donovan had said had made any difference. When they entered the Gatehouse, Wizard Faith asked how the Ball was and Rachel simply replied that it was 'eventful,' and that Faith could read all about it in the morning papers.

Donovan walked Rachel back to her room where she slammed the door in his face. Donovan was hurt, angry, and confused. He thought he'd be lauded as a hero who saved Marshall Guzman's life. Instead, he was an "inconsiderate glory-hound, who thought of Rachel as no better than a Tavern Maid," (her words, not his). He returned to his room, threw his new dress clothes on the floor in the corner and went to bed. He did not sleep well.

The rest of the week was miserable. It seemed that everyone knew about his and Rachel's break-up; and none of his female classmates had any sympathy for him. The news of the attempted assassination of the Marshall at the Ball was all over town, but Donovan's name was suspiciously absent from the account of the incident. The King had of course ordered Minister Jasmine to conduct an investigation. Major Gerald had some explaining to do about how an assassin had gotten his hands on a Concealment Cloak, and how a dragon Changed One had infiltrated his command.

Donovan suspected that the idea of outfitting the rest of the Royal Guards with Concealment Cloaks had died with the assassin; the Royal Expeditionary Force would be lucky to keep theirs. Wizard Noland had not spoken to Donovan since the Ball. This wasn't unusual, they seldom spoke, but Donovan could have used some friendly advice.

As expected, Endday testing was horrible. "Unacceptable. This Death Serum is pale purple. It should be clear. Do it again," said Rachel, in full-Mentor mode. Donovan returned to the Serums classroom and started over. His next attempt supposedly

had a slight odor, and was also deemed 'Unacceptable."
Donovan resented the fact that his Serums were
definitely better than his female classmate's Serums,
but they had passed, and were released for Endday
activities.

Donovan's third and final attempt at Death Serum
was perfect: odorless, colorless, and lethal. Rachel
grudgingly agreed it was 'acceptable,' but by then it was
evening and the dinner bell rang as Donovan was
cleaning up his Serum equipment. No Endday activities
today.

The following week was no better, During
Twoday's Martial Arts class, Donovan had tried to go
easy on Rachel. She had knocked him unconscious and
he woke up in the infirmary. During the Martial Arts
class on Foursday, Donovan had returned the favor and
later felt terrible about it. Endday testing involved
demonstrating the Replication spell; and again,
Donovan's best efforts were deemed wanting. The
crossbow was too long, or too heavy, or too noisy, or
the firing mechanism was too stiff. Again, the dinner
bell rang before Donovan replicated a crossbow to
Rachel's satisfaction. This could not go on. Donovan
was seriously contemplating asking for a new Mentor.

In desperation, he approached Wizard Daniel after
dinner on Firstday. He knocked on Daniel's cottage

door, which opened immediately. "Sir, can I speak with you? I don't know who else to talk to." "Is this about Rachel?" Donovan nodded glumly. "Come on in." Having never been in Wizard Daniel's cottage before, Donovan was struck by the array of weapons displayed on the walls. There were swords, shields, maces, and all manner of knives and daggers in various display cases.

"Sir, I just don't know what to do anymore!" said Donovan. "Rachel has become unreasonable! Nothing I do is good enough, no Serum perfect enough, no spell cast precisely enough, I'm at my wit's end!" "I see," said Daniel. "Well, to be fair, Serums are *supposed* to be perfect, and spells too. Could it be that you've been given special treatment previously?" Donovan was shocked by Wizard Daniel's question. He'd always been top of his class in everything, spells, Serums, and Martial Arts, until two weeks ago.

"Sir," said Donovan, choosing his words carefully, "It may be that Rachel didn't scrutinize my work as closely when we were dating as she is now. But I judge my abilities as better than my classmates, and they have not been subjected to the criticism I have received lately." "I see," said Daniel, "so you think you are being treated unfairly, as compared to your classmates?" "Absolutely," said Donovan.

"And you're absolutely correct," said Daniel. "What? You admit it?" asked Donovan. "Of course, all of your instructors know it." "I don't understand," said Donovan. Wizard Daniel sighed. "I'll try to explain. How long did you spend as a Level One?" "About six months," said Donovan. Daniel nodded, "And Level Two?" "About a year and a half." "And how long do you think you have left as a Level Three?" "At this rate? About five years!" said Donovan.

Wizard Daniel chuckled. "Stop the theatrics, please. Before Rachel started being so hard on you, how long did you believe you had left before you were ready for the Sorcerer's Test?" Donovan paused to consider the question. "Six months, maybe sooner." "Exactly!" said Daniel. "Exactly what?" asked Donovan. "Donovan, you are about to complete the course of training at the Wizards Academy in less than four years! That's never been done before! Even Wizard Noland and your father took a little over six years to graduate! The reason your classmates are held to a less demanding standard is that they'll be here for years longer than you. We can't deny them Endday activities for years! They'd become despondent and argumentative. You're causing a great deal of trouble for us, unintentional as it may be."

"Consider this: you were in court when a convict attacked the judge and you stopped him. How many other magicians were in that room? As I understand it, one Wizard, two Sorcerers, one of who's duty it was to protect the judge, and about twenty-five other Level Three students, yet it was you that acted and prevented the attack. You may have shouted the incantation, but you saved the judge, no one else. You recently saved the Marshall of Franconia, by detecting and detaining an invisible assassin, and you kept the Marshall from drinking poisoned wine. You have the unique ability to *act* quickly and decisively, which has served you well so far." "Sir, I—" "Let me finish," said Daniel. "You're about to become a Sorcerer in record time. What do you think is going to happen next?"

Donovan thought about the possibilities. Finally, he said, "I'm about to become a Mentor." "No. You have too much ability to remain here with a war going on. You will be assigned to the military and sent to fight dragons and/or Baizians." "But I'm not ready!" "Which is precisely why Sorceress Rachel has been ordered to push you, to make sure you make every Serum exactly, cast every spell precisely, defend yourself perfectly. Because very soon, you'll be in the 'real world,' with no more do-overs, no more second chances. Everything will be life or death, do you understand?" Donovan was stunned and terrified by Wizard Daniel's words.

"Now, the timing of Wizard Noland's order to Rachel is unfortunate. I understand that you had a break-up after the Royal Ball. Can you tell me what happened?" Donovan related the events of the Ball, and Rachel's accusation that he didn't respect her abilities as a Sorceress." Daniel nodded in understanding. "Donovan, this is a common problem with romantic relations between magicians, but we seldom discuss it. You see, in a relationship between magicians, one partner is almost always more powerful than the other. No two magicians are ever evenly matched. One individual always has some spells they can conjure faster, hold longer, or use more creatively. This inequality is a constant source of friction between romantically involved magicians, *at every level*. It's probably particularly annoying for Rachel."

"But I love—" "It doesn't matter how you feel. It matters how *she* feels. She is your Mentor, your superior, a recognized Sorceress; yet you moved to protect her from someone who wasn't really a threat. How would you feel if your places were reversed?" "But I meant no insult!" pleaded Donovan. "I'm sure you didn't, but she was hurt nonetheless."

"So, what do I do now?" "First, you accept that she is going to push you for perfection in everything you attempt. She has to. Wizard Noland has ordered her to do so in order to prepare you for the Sorcerer's Test. He also believes that she might have gone easy on you because of your past relationship. That is a mark against her, and she's been counseled not to let it happen again, or you'll be reassigned to a new Mentor."

"How do I fix this?" asked Donovan. "You need to talk to Rachel, and you need to be honest with her and tell her you understand why she's been so demanding of you lately, and that you'll work harder. Beyond that, I can't advise you. You need to decide how you really feel about her, and determine if you two can make it work. I wish you luck."

The water was colder than Anne remembered. She waved for help and yelled, but no one on deck seemed to hear her. This was not going as planned. In desperation, she conjured a Seeming and hurled it at the sailor on deck, when it struck him, it vanished in a flash of light. That got his attention (finally). "MAN OVERBOARD!" the sailor screamed. The deck crew sprang to life, "MAN THE LIFE RINGS! LAUNCH THE LONGBOAT! HURRY NOW! PREPARE TO COME ABOUT!" The HMS VALOR began to turn slowly, almost swamping Anne with its wake. Fortunately, a life ring landed close by and she was able to swim to it and hold on. A few minutes later, the longboat pulled alongside her and the sailors quickly pulled her aboard.

When the longboat was hoisted aboard, Andrew was the first to greet her. "It's Sorceress Anne!" he shouted. Surprisingly, the crew gave out a shout of celebration. "Anne, we thought you were lost! Have you been in the water this whole time? We thought you were crushed by that mast!" said Andrew. Anne climbed out of the longboat and again used a warm Wind spell to dry herself off. She realized that she was getting pretty good at that spell combination.

"We need to turn around and go back to Sundock," said Anne. "I need to speak to the Commodore at once." "Turn back? I don't understand," said Andrew. "I will explain everything. Just get me some hot tea and a biscuit, please. I'm famished," said Anne wearily.

A few minutes later, Anne was seated in the Commodore's cabin with Andrew, a hot cup of tea in her hand. The Commodore was very glad to see her. "We thought you were done for," he said. "How did you survive that mast falling on you? It went all the way through the hull!"

"I know, and it took me with it," said Anne. "I poured all my power into my shield when I saw the mast coming. I don't know how, but the mast pushed me right through both decks and the keel. After punching through the hull, the mast tilted as it fell to the seabed, or I would never have survived. As it was, I was deep under water. I expanded my shield as far as I could, hoping I would float to the surface, but I was too deep."

The Commodore grunted and said, "So how did you survive?" "I got caught in an undersea current that pushed me towards the islands," explained Anne, "but I was still too deep to make it to the surface if I had released my shield. Then a school of dolphins, of all things, thought I was some sort of plaything. They started pushing me with their noses and tails, forcing me toward the surface. Eventually, they got tired of the game and started to swim off, so I tethered one of them. I knew that they were air-breathers. Once the dolphin towed me close enough to the surface, I released my shield and swam for it."

"That's incredible!" said Andrew. "Well, what happened once you reached the surface?"

"You were gone by then," said Anne, "but I could see the smoke rising from the island, so I swam for it." "Weren't there dragons on the island?" asked the Commodore. "I really didn't have much choice you know. I figured that once I reached the island, I could cast a Concealment shield and try to figure out what to do next. It didn't work out as I planned. Once I reached the beach, I tried to cast the Concealment spell, but the power drain was too much and I fell unconscious."

"I can imagine," said Andrew. "Between the shield, the Tether and the swim to shore, I'm not surprised you were too exhausted to conjure a Concealment shield. What happened next?"

"I woke up when I heard someone call me 'Celeste,'" she said. "Celeste? Who the devil is Celeste?" asked Commodore Matthews. "My twin sister," said Anne. "Anyway, I said, 'No, my name is Anne. Celeste is my twin sister.' Then the voice said, 'Wait right here, I will go and get help.'"

"Why would someone go get help instead of just helping you?" asked Andrew. "That doesn't make sense." Anne continued, "I must have fallen back to sleep on the beach. When the voice returned it was a young man, maybe twenty years old. He was wearing tattered clothes that were covered in dried blood. He told me that there was a cave at the top of the hill with a freshwater spring in it, and that I could rest there. He helped me climb the hill to the cave, and filled my water bag."

"Then what happened?" "Well, I was very curious about how one man could survive alone on a dragon-infested island. Especially one that was burned from stem to stern," said Anne. "So, I pretended to fall asleep and then I heard them talking; as I suspected, they were dragon Changed Ones."

"Dragons!" exclaimed the Commodore, "and they let you live?" "Yes," said Anne. "It has something to do with owing a debt to my sister. Anyway, one of the Sea dragons, Azure, went off to the northernmost island to see what had happened to the dragons that normally lived on the island that we burned. She returned a few hours later and was almost hysterical. Apparently, the dragons fled to their main sanctuary after the battle, and there were a lot of injured and dying dragons. It seems that while dragons know some magic, they do not know any healing spells. Azure was desperate for me to help them."

"You didn't, of course," said the Commodore. "Yes, I did," said Anne, earning a scowl from the commander. "But I made them agree to a Binding spell that any dragon that I healed would never attack a human again." The Commodore interjected, "What's a Binding spell?" "It Binds a magic-user to a promise. Once given, it's unbreakable, even if the magician who cast it dies," explained Mage Andrew. "And just what happens if one breaks a Binding spell?" "They die. Immediately," said Anne.

"And just how many dragons did you heal?" asked Commodore Matthews. "I healed thirty-three dragons, and two died of their wounds. I overheard them say that they lost an additional seventeen that did not make it back. That means that fifty-two Sea dragons are out of the fight. There were some uninjured dragons who wouldn't agree to the Binding spell, but I don't know how many. They kept out of sight." The Commodore whistled. "I may not approve of your healing our enemies, but if it's true that those you healed cannot attack us again, I call that a victory!"

"There is more, Commodore. I have reached a temporary truce with Cobalt, their new Clan Chief. He has agreed that his Clan will not attack our ships again as long as we do not attack them. He cannot speak for the other dragon clans: Snow, Fire, Stone and the Great Dragons, but the Sea dragons are no longer a threat as long as we do not attack them."

"We never attacked them!" said the Commodore. "They started this fight!" "I know," said Anne, "and after the last battle, I think they regret it, bitterly."

After leaving Wizard Daniel's cottage, Donovan walked directly to the Headmaster's house. He needed to talk, and he needed some advice. He knocked on the door and after a few moments, Wizard Noland opened the door. "Come in, Donovan. I've been expecting you." "You have?" asked Donovan, confused. "Yes. Have you come to ask for a new Mentor?"

"No. I would never ask for that, Sir." "Even after the hell Rachel has put you through for the last two weeks? Yes, I know about that. In fact, I'm the cause of it." "Yes Sir. I know. I have just been talking to Wizard Daniel. He explained it to me." "I see, so why are you here?"

"Sir, do you really think I'll be ready to take the Sorcerer's Test soon?" Wizard Noland sat in thought for a moment, wondering what to say. Finally, he asked, "Do you know what the King asked me after the Royal Ball?" Donovan shook his head. "He asked me why such a talented magician as you was not already a Sorcerer, and why I was keeping you at the Academy needlessly." Donovan was shocked by this news, "But, Sir, I've only been a Level Three for—" "Seven months and two weeks. I know. That's part of the problem. You have absorbed almost all we can teach you, and more. I understand that you can actually cast two spells at once, if only for a short time. You're extraordinary. But you're not perfect! You shouted an incantation in public, your Serums, which are probably good enough, are not yet always perfect. Your Martial Arts skills are almost on par with Wizard Faith's, yet Rachel knocked you unconscious two weeks ago! Do you understand what I'm saying?"

"You're telling me that I need to work harder to be perfect, not just better than my classmates," said Donovan. "Exactly! And I'm afraid that I can't keep you here much longer." Donovan sat in thought for a few minutes, considering Wizard Noland's words. Eventually, he said, "Sir. There's no denying that I'm in love with Rachel. I know that you've got concerns that she's gone easy on me during my training because of our relationship. I assure you that that's not the case. If anything, I've been more distracted lately by our separation than I was before."

"I thought as much when you ended up in the infirmary," said Noland with a smile, "and I agree that I may have been mistaken when I accused her of going easy on you. But the fact remains, she has to push you, hard." "I understand, Sir. I promise to work harder, but I plan to propose to her soon."

Wizard Noland smiled, "I thought as much. Your father is not here, but if he was, he would ask, 'Are you certain about this?'" "More certain of anything in my life," said Donovan forcefully. "Then you have my complete support. Is there anything I can do to help?"

Donovan was stunned by Wizard Noland's offer. He said, "There is one thing, Sir. During all the commotion at the Royal Ball, Rachel lost one of her shoes. I need to find it or have another one made. Is there a 'Lost and

Found' in the palace?" Noland laughed, "No, but I'm pretty sure I know who has her shoe. One of the Ministers has a shoe fetish, and the scoundrel has a habit of collecting women's shoes during Royal Balls and other Regal events. I'll have the shoe back for you by tomorrow. What does it look like?" "It's an open-toed sandal, peach-colored, with rhinestones," said Donovan. "Easily fixed," said Noland. "What else?" "I need to leave the Academy after dinner tomorrow and go into town; then, I need to open the portal at the boat dock. I promise not to run away."

Wizard Noland smiled understandingly, "Is it a scavenger hunt you're planning?" Donovan was shocked at Wizard Noland's perceptiveness, "More like a treasure hunt, I hope," said Donovan. "Very well, I hope you know what you're doing. If it eases your mind, Rachel was most upset with me for making her be so demanding of you. She cares a great deal for you."

"I hope so," said Donovan. "Sir, Once I pass the Sorcerer's Test and I'm assigned to the military, what will happen to her?" "Believe it or not, I have given this some thought already. Once you pass the test, you will be assigned to the 3rd Franconian Regiment in Fairview, and Rachel, if you two are still together, will be assigned to the Fairview Regional Mage's Office."

As Mage Kathy hurried out of Edward's room, Dirk whispered, "You missed a button." Kathy blushed and adjusted her blouse without stopping or commenting on Dirk's observation. Dirk waited outside the room for a few minutes to give Wizard Edward some privacy and to clean up and re-make the bed. When he deemed that enough time had passed, he knocked quietly on the door. "Come in, Dirk. Thank you for waiting. I expect the King and Wizard James will be summoning me soon. I have a question. Do you think I should reveal your presence to them?" "Why would we do that, Sir?"

"Well, sooner or later, they're going to learn about 'Specialists" and their cloaks. At that point, the King will wonder whether I had a Specialist with me when I visited and what he might have snooped out. He might also wonder whether Kathy, I mean Mage Kathy, knew about you, and that would put her in an uncomfortable position."

"I see what you mean, sir. How do you think King Donald will react if you tell him?" "He'll undoubtedly be surprised and a little suspicious. He will also start snooping around to find out how your cloak works, how many invisible soldiers we have; stuff like that. We also have to consider Wizard Timothy. After all, he never mentioned you either."

"It's your decision, sir, but I'm all for telling them." "Why?" "It might keep them from plotting anything if they think there might be a Specialist listening in on their conversations." "You're probably right. We'll let them know at my next meeting with the King. I just hope Kathy understands and acts surprised."

A few minutes later, Mage Kathy knocked on the door. Edward rose and let her in, and she said, "The King has asked to meet with us. I think he's going to tell us that he approves of our plan and wants us to get moving as soon as possible." "I expected as much. Before we go, I wanted to warn you that I believe it's best to inform the King about Specialist Dirk. I'm afraid it might cause issues if it's discovered later." "You're probably right. The King may not like it, but at least he'll see that you're being honest with him. What would you like me to do?"

"Act surprised. It might look bad for you if you had to admit that you knew about him before and never said anything." "Thank you. I'll do my best. We should go now."

The two magicians and the cloaked Specialist walked down the hall to the King's private study. The King, Wizard James, and Minister William were seated at the conference table when they entered. "Come in," said the King. "Wizard Edward, Minister William and Wizard James are most impressed with your proposal. I've given it a lot of thought, and I've decided to allot 250 golds every three months to this effort. After one year, I'll travel to Springfield to review your progress. If additional work is still needed, we'll decide on the best course of action then."

Edward pretended to consider the offer for several moments, then said, "I think that is a wise decision, Your Majesty. And, if all of the variables work out, we may be done by the time you arrive." "What specific 'variables' are you concerned about?" asked James. "The number and skill of the apprentice magicians; the depth of the sand; the distance to bedrock; the weather over the Great Salt Flats for the next year; and how long King Henry will allow me to remain in Baize," said Edward.

"The number of magicians will be a constant, but I don't know their skill level or their strength yet. The sand will be shallower around the edges and deeper in the middle; the distance to bedrock should be generally consistent. The weather is unpredictable, as is King Henry sometimes." King Donald smiled, "It has ever been so. So, how will you proceed?" "Once we know how many apprentice magicians we have, we will divide them into teams of six. Two to Dig, two to hold a shield against the edge, and two to use the Adhesive spell to form the dirt into a wall. The apprentices will rotate through each job until we determine their individual strengths. Then we use the strongest diggers, shield holders and adherers. I will arrange competitions between the teams and award prizes to the teams that demonstrate the most progress each week," said Edward.

"What sort of prizes?" asked Minister William. "In the beginning, it will probably be ribbons or medals of some sort; we may move to time off, special rations, or even coins, depending on what is more desirable. This will be grueling work, and the construction will not stop. We will work in three eight-hour shifts, five days a week, and will not stop until the reservoir is complete." The King nodded approvingly. "When can you leave?"

"We can probably leave by the end of the week if the apprentice magicians in Baize are prepared to depart by then. Do you have some way to communicate with Springfield? It would be best if I could alert Battle Mage Curtis and have him prepare lodging for the magicians and the engineers. It will be quite a shock if any arrive unannounced before we get there." Wizard James spoke up, grudgingly, "Yes, we normally use Messenger Hawks to communicate between cities." "We do the same," said Edward. "Unfortunately, with Wizard

Timothy here, I'm not sure who we can send the message to," said William.

"I believe that there is one hawk trained to deliver messages to the Town Council. Will that work?" asked Wizard James. "Certainly," said Edward. "I'll prepare a message and give it to Mage Kathy within the glass." "We'll send Messenger Hawks to all of the other cities and towns in Baize, directing them to send their apprentice magicians to you in Springfield. When will you begin digging?" asked the King. "The first step will be for the engineers and surveyors to lay out the boundaries of the reservoir. We'll start with a giant "U" shape, then excavate the middle. I expect the surveyors to have enough laid out for us to start digging once the magicians arrive. We'll begin as soon as we're able and not wait for those who have to come from a greater distance."

"That sounds like an excellent plan," said the King. "Is there anything else?" Edward steeled himself and said, "Yes, Your Majesty, I have a confession to make, and I must apologize for the deception. Sire, the Franconian Royal Expeditionary Force, has two individuals who are called 'Specialists.' Their tasks are to eliminate sentries, spy out enemy positions, and access locked rooms. They are equipped with Concealment cloaks which render them practically invisible, even from magicians. I must admit that I brought one of them along with me. Specialist Dirk here—," Dirk lowered his hood to the astonishment of the King and his advisors, "has been guarding my quarters while I've been here. It was he who observed the cook's assistant, Marrissa, putting Death Serum in my water pitcher, and it was Dirk who told me of your demonstration with the flour barrel. Without his warning and my attendance at the demonstration, Mage Kathy would have been accidentally burned by the fireball. I know this may seem like I was spying on you, but I swear that Specialist Dirk has not been snooping about the palace, trying to gain intelligence for Franconia. I will submit to Truth Serum on that issue if you wish."

The King looked troubled, and James was angry. Minister Williams looked more curious than angry, and Kathy tried to keep a straight face. "Why didn't Wizard Timothy inform us about this Specialist?" asked the King. "I asked him not to, Sire." "And Dirk has been with you, guarding your back, this whole time?" "Yes, sire, except when he was sleeping." "Amazing," said Minister William.

"Why didn't Dirk stop Marrissa before she poisoned your water?" asked Wizard James. "I gave him strict orders not to kill anyone but to observe closely and provide me with a description of anyone who entered my room," said Edward. "Why are you telling us about him now?" asked the King. "Sire, I will be working closely with Baizians for the next several months at least. It's likely that the Specialist's presence will be detected at some point. I didn't want this to come up without the opportunity to explain."

"Specialist Dirk, I will ask you the same question I asked Wizard Edward when he arrived: How many Baizian citizens have you killed?" Dirk hesitated, but Edward nodded, "Your Majesty, during our stay in Springfield, Specialist Lance and I eliminated six criminals who were intent on attacking our visible law enforcers in the city. Additionally, I personally eliminated two of the leaders of the criminal gangs that were active in the city."

"Wizard Edward, are you prepared to share this cloaking technology with us?" asked Wizard James. "Not at this time, sir. The manufacturing process for Concealment cloaks is a carefully guarded secret in Franconia. As you can imagine, criminals and brigands would pay dearly for such cloaks, and the consequences would be severe for law-abiding citizens. There is also the concern that assassins could target the crown." The King nodded, understanding the danger.

"However, there is a good chance that, if relations between our two kingdoms improved, a small number of cloaks might be made available for purchase. Not the production process, you understand, but the finished product." "An interesting suggestion, Wizard Edward, and one I will certainly discuss with King Henry at the appropriate time. I appreciate your honesty in this matter and I don't think Truth Serum will be required this time. I will, however, ask that Specialist Dirk remain in your quarters at all times, unless he is uncloaked."

"I understand completely, Your Majesty. If there is nothing else, we will retire to my quarters." Edward and Dirk (uncloaked) departed and returned to his quarters.

"A most interesting and cautious man," observed the King. "He has certainly inspired my engineers, sire," said William. "I have never seen them so enthusiastic about a civic project." "Indeed," said James, "and I admit that he didn't have to reveal his bodyguard to us. They could have just left, and we would have been none the wiser." "What do you think, Mage Kathy?" asked the King.

"I think that without Specialist Dirk, Wizard Edward might have been poisoned, and we would be unaware of the Stone dragon in our midst," said Kathy. "Indeed," said the King. "Edward has proven to be a most honorable man. What do you think of him, Kathy?" "I have only known him a few days, sire, but I like him very much. I must admit that I'm looking forward to spending more time with him as we construct the Great Salt Reservoir."

"If this project succeeds, I will consider releasing you from your service to the crown if you wish to continue your association with Edward. But that implies that he remains here long enough to complete the project, if you take my meaning," said the King.

Donovan breezed through his Endday testing, which was the Blast spell this week. He successfully pulverized several stones, boulders, bricks and even a marble column. When the last spell was perfectly executed, Rachel said, "Pass. You are released for Endday activities." "Thank you," said Donovan, "If you'll excuse me, I have some things to take care of in town." Donovan practically sprinted for the Gatehouse while Rachel watched despondently, wishing he would turn around and ask her to accompany him. She walked slowly back to her quarters, fighting back tears.

When she arrived at her door, there was a roll of parchment stuck to her nameplate with an Adhesive spell. Confused, she used a Remove spell and unrolled the parchment. It read:

You lost a shoe,
And a boyfriend, too.
To reclaim one or two,
You must follow the clues.

I fell hard for you,
And woke up in a strange bed.

Rachel thought, pondering the riddle, then raced for the infirmary. As she entered the ward, she expected to find Donovan waiting. Instead, there were only rows of patients, sick or injured students or staff. She looked around, confused, and then she spotted an empty bed with an exact replica of the carriage they took to the Royal Ball sitting on it. She reached out to pick it up and it vanished in a flash of light, a Seeming. Inside the Seeming was her missing shoe from the Royal Ball and another note. This one said:

What has shoes they never take off?

Horses! Rachel left the infirmary and ran across the courtyard, headed for the stables. As she entered, the Ostler gave her a wink and nodded toward the stall with her favorite Chestnut, Ginger. She opened the stall door to find Ginger saddled with another note tied to the saddle horn. This one said:

Horses are for riding.

What else can you ride around here?

This one was harder, and Rachel had to think for several minutes before she had the answer. You could ride *boats* from the Academy marina. She walked Ginger out of the stables and took off at a fast trot for the marina. When she reined up and looked around, there was another note, tied to the hitching post.

Only a few can enter here,
Wizard Faith is aware, my Dear·

What the heck did that mean? Rachel guessed it meant that Faith knew that someone would be opening the portal and would not come running to catch a student trying to escape. She opened the portal and walked onto the dock, checking each boat carefully. Nothing. She paced back and forth in frustration. As she stepped off the dock, she noticed an "X" on the ground and a message written in the dirt.

Dig right here, but not too deep,
I wouldn't go down more than two feet.

Rachel used the Dig spell, gently and found a metal box. Inside was another note.

Mira's playground is fun for all,
Surely, much better than a Royal Ball.

Rachel remounted the horse and headed for the Enhancements Training Area, hoping that there were not too many more stops on this merry-go-round. When she arrived at the Enhancements area, she realized just how big the area was. *How was she supposed to find anything in here?* The Enhancements area was covered with knee-high grass with boulders strewn about haphazardly. She rode around the area, searching diligently. Then she noticed an enormous boulder with the words "UNDER HERE" written on the side. Rachel tried a Wind spell, but the rock remained in place. She considered using a Strength Enhancement but decided that even that might not be enough. She dismounted and conjured a strong Blast spell. The boulder shattered, leaving a small cavity underneath it with another metal box. This box held a much longer message.

Rachel,

Only a gifted Sorceress could have reached all of these clues· I never doubted you, but as someone who loves you, I will always defend you from anything that threatens you, be it a dragon, a brigand, or a small child with a stick· Never expect me to do less, for I will risk no harm to you· I know what Wizard Noland said to you, and I have assured him that, as my Mentor, you have never accepted anything less than my best effort·

(Sorry, I couldn't make this rhyme·)

D·

Rachel wept after reading the message. *But where was Donovan?* She expected to find him waiting at the end of this scavenger hunt. One of her tears fell on the parchment, and additional words appeared:

Your true love is waiting,
Stop hesitating·
What are you, deaf?

Deaf! She knew where he was! She remounted and galloped back to the stables, right across the Academy courtyard, startling several of the students and staff. She leaped off Ginger, tossed his reins to the stable boy and ran for the Gatehouse. As she arrived, Wizard Faith said, "Slow down, Rachel. He'll be there."

Rachel rushed through town, arriving at her father's shop and throwing open the door. Both her father and mother were there, sitting at the work table. *Where is he?* She signed. *Donovan? He was here a minute ago,* signed her father. *He left this for you,* her father signed, handing over a small box tied with a string. Confused, Rachel untied the string and opened the box. Inside was a velvet ring box. She opened it to find a gold engagement ring with a large pink diamond. As she stood there, stunned, a familiar arm wrapped around her waist and Donovan said, "Tag. You're it."

Chapter Twenty-One:
MESSAGES

Edward sat at the desk in his quarters, wondering how to word his message to Mage Curtis. He needed to convey what was happening but assumed that the message would be read by Wizard James and King Donald before being sent. Mage Kathy had provided the message parchment. It was about the length and breadth of his hand. That made sense; a Messenger Hawk could only carry so much weight. Finally, Edward wrote:

Mage Curtis,

I have met with King Donald and convinced him of the danger the dragons pose to both our Kingdoms. I hope he will recall some of his troops from the border and re-establish relations with Franconia. I will be leaving here in three days with a contingent of apprentice magicians and Baizian Engineers. I have tentatively agreed to assist King Donald in a project to stop the spread of the Great Salt Flats. The Salt Flats have been expanding every season, and if they reach the Amber River, it will be an environmental and economic disaster for both Franconia and Baize. I hope that King Henry will allow me to remain in Baize for a time to address this mutual problem. Please prepare Springfield to receive approximately one hundred workers. Once I arrive in Springfield, I believe it would be prudent for you and the remainder of the Expeditionary Force to return to Franconia immediately.

Wizard Edward Francis

After finishing the message, Edward set it aside to allow the ink to dry. "So, Dirk, what am I forgetting?" asked Edward. Dirk thought for a moment, then said, "If you're going to be throwing around that much sand, salt, and dirt, you'd better bring bandanas for everyone. Even using magic, the wind is going to blow that stuff everywhere. You'll probably want some kind of protection for your eyes as well." "Those are two excellent suggestions," said Edward. "I must admit, this is the biggest project I've ever attempted."

"I'm sure you'll figure out how to get the job done, Sir. You always do." "Yes, I know, but this time it's different." "How so?" "This time, I'm a foreign Wizard in charge of Baizian workers and magicians. If I have to quell a rebellion or push through a work stoppage, I'm not sure how much authority I have to keep everyone in line." "What about Mage Kathy?" "Hmmm, well, yes, technically, either she or Wizard Timothy will have the authority to keep the workers in line," said Edward.

"You expect trouble?" "I expect grumbling," said Edward, "this is going to start out as an exciting adventure for these apprentice magicians, and then it's going to turn into drudgery. I also expect the Springfield merchants to try to overcharge us for everything from tools to rations. If the costs go too far over budget, the King will terminate the project and blame me."

"You?" "Yes, me. That's undoubtedly why they put me in charge, so that if the project fails, it will be the fault of the 'Franconian Wizard,' not anyone from Baize, except maybe Kathy and Timothy." "Then why did you agree to head up the project?" asked Dirk. "Two reasons: First, if the salt gets to the Amber River, it's going to kill all of the fish downriver from where it enters, to the sea. That will destroy most of the commerce in Weaton and severely impact Westport. Second, if the economy of Baize gets desperate, they may attack Franconia. We should avoid that if at all possible."

"So, it's not just an excuse to spend more time with Mage Kathy?" Edward snorted, "Kathy is a competent Mage and a wonderful woman, and I'm very fond of her. But I didn't sign up to dig holes in a desert for a year just to spend time with a beautiful woman." "The King would be very disappointed to hear that," said Kathy, dropping her Concealment shield. Both Edward and Dirk jumped.

"I must be slipping," said Edward. "How long have you been standing there?" "Well," said Kathy with a sly grin, "I never left the room after giving you the parchment for the Messenger Hawk." "I think I'll go check the corridor," said Dirk diplomatically as he slipped out the door. "You really see problems with the project?" asked Kathy. Edward sighed, "I always anticipate problems when I have to deal with merchants." "You worry that they'll overcharge us?" "I'm certain they'll try. That's why we'll have to be extra vigilant during the early months of the project. If the merchants learn that there are penalties for overcharging the crown, we'll have much fewer problems."

"I'm confused. Are you worried that they'll charge us a gold for a five-silver barrel of flour?" asked Kathy. "No, that they'll charge us a copper for a horseshoe nail." "I don't understand," said Kathy. "How much does a horseshoe nail cost?" asked Edward. "I have no idea, but judging from your comment, I expect it's less than a copper." "In Franconia, I can buy 100 horseshoe nails for a silver. That's *ten* nails for a copper. If we pay a copper for every nail, we'll be out of golds in a month."

"I see," said Kathy, "so we have to scrutinize every invoice and receipt." "Exactly!" said Edward. "Another problem will be the lack of vendors. You told me that the small traders are usually swallowed up by the big merchant houses. That means less competition, which means higher prices. We'll need to encourage small businesses and try to help them so they're not bought out by the big firms." Kathy looked thoughtful. "If this works, you could create a middle class in Baize!" "Initially, only in Springfield, but the idea could spread to other cities," acknowledged Edward.

"Do you know a good accountant?" asked Edward. "I *am* a good accountant," said Kathy. "That's been my job for most of the last two years here in Baize." "Do you have a good staff?" "I think so." "Bring them along," said Edward.

Rachel leaned back into Donovan's embrace. "What does 'It' mean?" she asked. "It means that if you accept that ring, you're my future wife," said Donovan, hopefully. Rachel looked at her parents, sitting across the table from them. Her father signed *I told you he was a keeper.* Rachel turned, facing Donovan, "When did you have time to set all this up?" "Well, I visited the jeweler after dinner on Midweek, after I asked your father's permission to marry you, then I spent most of last night hiding clues." "How did you open the portal at the Academy marina?" Rachel asked. Donovan grinned, "I've known how to open that since I was a Level Two. I just needed to inform Wizard Faith so she didn't come running."

"Wait—Wizard Faith let you leave the Academy grounds on Midweek?" "Sure, after I got permission from Wizard Noland. He and I had a long talk on Twoday evening," said Donovan. "About what?" "Well, he asked me if I had come to request a new Mentor," said Donovan, "which I assured him I would never do. Then he explained to me why he had insisted that you be so tough on me for the last two weeks." Rachel nodded, "I'm sorry, but—" "I know why," said Donovan.

"Anyway, after our talk, I told him that I planned to propose to you, and he asked me if there was anything he could do to help. I mentioned your lost shoe, and my need to leave the Academy for a short time on Midweek." Rachel smiled and said, "You seem to have planned this all out splendidly." "Yes, but I'm still waiting," said Donovan. "For what?" "How about an answer." "You haven't asked me a question yet," said Rachel. Donovan slapped his forehead, took the ring from the box, got down on one knee and said, "Rachel Turner, will you marry me?"

Rachel nodded, too choked up for words, and Donovan slipped the ring onto her finger. It was a bit too large, but a quick Reduce spell and the ring fit perfectly. "You must have practiced that," whispered Rachel. "Of course I did," said Donovan. "It's the most important spell I've ever cast."

"I assume you've seen Wizard Edward's message to Mage Curtis in Springfield," said the King to Wizard James. "I have." "What are your thoughts?" "Obviously, Edward knew that we'd read his message before sending it," said James. "Why do you say that?" asked the King. "Because Edward didn't even bother to seal the message. Moreover, there's no hidden text, nor is there any kind of Concealment spell cast on the parchment. Edward knew that we'd read the message. I suspect some of the words are for us." "Such as?" "Notice how he says that he has *"tentatively"* agreed to help us with the Salt Flats. Also, the suggestion that we should move some of our troops from the border, and re-establish friendly relations with Franconia."

"Yes. I noticed that," said the King. "So, what will you do?" asked James. "After I send Edward's message, I will send two of my own; the first, ordering the First Battalion back to Springfield. They should never have been moved to Westport in the first place. I've also prepared this message for King Henry of Franconia. I would like your opinion of it."

King Henry,

I recently made the acquaintance of Wizard Edward Francis of Franconia. He has informed us of the dangers posed to both our Kingdoms by these infernal dragons. Wizard Edward killed my Court Wizard, who was a dragon Changed One, and I am very grateful for his insight and assistance. I am moving my troops away from our cities along the border as a show of good faith. If you agree, I propose another exchange of Ambassadors. We should be together in this conflict with the dragons. Lastly, during his enlightening visit, Wizard Edward proposed a plan for stopping the spread of the Great Salt Flats in eastern Baize. This is a problem that has plagued us for decades, and I hope you will allow Wizard Edward to remain in Baize for a short time to oversee this vital project.

Donald, King of Baize

James read the message and considered the implications of it. Finally, he said, "I like it." "My only suggestion would be to strike through "King Henry" and write "My Friend." It would convey a more personal touch and would probably be more favorably considered." "An excellent suggestion, James." "Perhaps we should ask Wizard Edward's opinion of the message, Sire. After all, he does know King Henry and his whims." "An excellent suggestion. Please summon Edward so he can review the message."

Edward arrived a short time later. "You asked for me, Sire?" "Yes. I have just composed a message for King Henry and I would like your thoughts on it," said the King, handing the message scroll to Edward. Edward read it quickly and said, "Your Majesty, if I could add one sentence at the bottom of the message, I think it would help convince King Henry to allow me to remain in Baize for a time." "Certainly," said the King, handing Edward the pen. Edward mumbled something to himself as he considered what to write, then added:

If the Salt Flats expand further eastward, I fear that they will enter the Amber River, with adverse consequences for both our countries.

"I believe that if King Henry is made aware of the potential impact on Franconia, he'll be much more willing to allow me to assist you, sire." "An excellent suggestion," said the King. Edward nodded his thanks and left the room. Donald struck through 'King Henry' and wrote 'My Friend,' then rolled up the scroll and sealed it closed with green wax and his royal signet. He handed Wizard Edward's message and the other two scrolls to James. "Please have these three messages sent out at once." "Of course, sire. I'll go to the Hawk Tower immediately."

"James, there is one more thing," said the King. "Sire?" "Try to locate Mayor Slate, the former Mayor of Springfield. I find it curious that he hasn't been in court these last few days. Before Wizard Edward arrived, he was here every day, begging for a new appointment to some other, more prosperous town." "I shall send some men to search for him as soon as I've finished delivering the messages, Your Majesty." "Very good. You are dismissed," said the King.

Donovan and Rachel entered the Gatehouse arm-in-arm. Wizard Faith greeted them excitedly, "Well, let's see it!" Rachel showed her the ring, and Faith said, "Very nice. And a good fit, too. Now, Rachel, you dropped your shoe as you were running across the courtyard. I retrieved it for you. You really should keep up with it. It looks expensive." "It was," said Donovan. "The next time she wears them, I may have to use an Adhesive spell to keep them on her feet." Rachel blushed and said, "It really wasn't my fault. You're the one that caused all the commotion—both times!" Donovan could only shrug.

As they left the Gatehouse, Wizard Faith said, "By the way, Major Gerald from the Royal Expeditionary Force came by to see Wizard Noland. I think he wanted a word with you while he was here." "Where is he now?" asked Donovan. "I think he's still with Wizard Noland," said Faith.

Before heading to Wizard Noland's cottage, Rachel and Donovan went to Rachel's room in the Mentor's quarters and put her shoe away with the other one. As they were leaving, they ran into Leo, who was walking down the hall with several of Donovan's outfits in his arms. "Leo! What have you got there?" asked Donovan. "I understand you'll be moving back in here, so I took the liberty of bringing over some of your things," said Leo. Donovan laughed, "Thanks, Leo. News sure travels fast around here." "Well," said Leo, "I did see you moving around the Academy last night, then I saw Mentor Rachel retracing your steps this morning. When you came in together, I just figured..." "You're a lot sharper than some people give you credit for," said Donovan, "and you're right. I hope to be sleeping here from now on."

Leaving the Mentor's quarters, Donovan and Rachel headed over to the Headmaster's house. They knocked on the door, and Wizard Noland opened it and led them into the parlor where Major Gerald was seated. "Ah, there you are, Donovan. I understand congratulations are in order!" said Major Gerald. "Thank you, Major. It's good to see you again," said Donovan. "Sir, this is my fiancé, Sorceress Rachel Turner." "It's very nice to meet you, Sorceress Rachel," said Major Gerald. *I hope you can keep this young man out of trouble*, Major Gerald signed. Rachel beamed and replied in sign, *I will certainly try.* "Does everybody in the Royal Expeditionary Force know sign language?" asked Donovan.

"No, just me and the two Specialists. Corporal Knox is learning, though. *It's helpful to be able to communicate silently sometimes*, he signed. *I understand,* signed Donovan. Major Gerald smiled. "Is there any word about my father?" asked Donovan. "No, but I wouldn't worry. He was going to see King Donald to warn him about the dragons; then, he was planning to return to Springfield and lead the First Company back to Franconia. He should be back soon."

"I hope you didn't get into too much trouble after the Royal Ball," said Donovan. Major Gerald shook his head. "No, but I sure had some explaining to do. The King wanted to know how Corporal Sleet got his hands on a Concealment cloak, and I sure couldn't tell him the *real* reason." "So, how did you explain it?" "I told him that Corporal Sleet must have stolen the one he used from Specialist Lance," said Gerald, "as if anyone could ever steal somethin' from a Specialist." "Did he believe it? What did Minister Jasmine say?"

"I'm not sure the King totally believed it, but what could Minister Jasmine say? If she disclosed that she knew anything, she'd be admittin' her guilt," said Major Gerald. "I guess," said Donovan. "So, what brings you to the Academy?" "I was just tellin' Wizard Noland the problem we have with our cloaks." "What problem?" asked Rachel. "Well, the cloaks cover the men just fine, but when we're mounted, you can see the horses. It looks damn odd too."

"I never thought of that," said Donovan. "How did you sneak up on those Fire dragons?" "We circled around behind them at night," said Gerald. "How can we conceal the horses?" asked Donovan. "We were just discussing that," said Wizard Noland, "I suppose we could craft some sort of cover for the horses, but adding Concealment and Stamina spells could be complicated."

"What about horse blankets?" asked Donovan. "You mean the ones that go under the saddle? Their much too small," said Major Gerald. "No. *Blankets.* When we lived in Prarrieville, it got so cold in the winter that the farmers and ranchers used heavy quilted blankets to keep the horses warm and protected. We'd have to get one to use as a pattern, and use lighter material. I never saw anyone ride a horse with a blanket on, and the heavy winter blankets would be much too hot for the horses in the summer and fall. Once we had a pattern and the material, we could add the Concealment and Stamina spells." "Hmm, that might work, but as I recall, that kind of blanket doesn't cover the horse's neck and head," said Major Gerald.

"So we add an attachment to cover that," said Wizard Noland, "just like the armor the heavy cavalry use to protect their horses necks and heads. We can design something that connects with straps and buckles." "It might work," said Major Gerald. "Do you know a good tailor?"

Donovan looked sidelong at Rachel and said, "I might know someone we can ask." Major Gerald nodded and said, "That's why I came here, to see if your father could make some horse cloaks, since he's the man I bought the Specialist's cloaks from. The Specialist's cloaks were very expensive though, I think I paid five golds each for them. Concealment horse blankets will use a lot more material and probably cost ten or fifteen golds each. With fifty-one horses, the King will never go for that."

"We have an arrangement with Mr. Turner," said Wizard Noland. "He's making Concealment cloaks for all of the magicians in Franconia, and every new Sorcerer will receive one upon graduation. In order to keep the costs down, the Academy buys the cloth and adds the Concealment and Stamina spells, then the tailor fashions the cloaks. They only cost five silvers now. Horse blankets will be bigger, but we can probably get them for eight or nine silvers each."

Major Gerald did some quick math in his head and said, "That comes to about forty-one golds for fifty-one horse blankets. If we can negotiate the price to forty golds, I think I can swing that." "You'll need to talk to my father about that. I'm sure you can work something out," said Rachel. "When do you need them, and do you need me to help with the sign language?" Gerald looked over at Wizard Noland and said, "It would be a great help. My signing isn't great for negotiations, it's more for military communications, and we need them as soon as possible. We could be sent out any day."

Wizard Noland nodded and said, "All right, I'll extend the curfew for you two, but please be back by midnight. You both have classes tomorrow." Donovan, Rachel and Major Gerald left the Academy and hurried over to the Tailor shop. The purchase agreement was quick and easy. Brian showed Major Gerald several bolts of cloth for consideration. After selecting a lightweight cloth of reasonable price, Mr. Turner signed that he would prepare the blankets and send them to the Academy for concealment treatment. A horse blanket with that material normally cost about five silvers, but with the neck and head covering, it would run seven silvers. The entire order would be thirty-five golds, and seven silvers, but for the big order, Mr. Turner was willing to take thirty-five golds even. Major Gerald asked when they might be ready, since they were in a bit of a rush.

Come by on Midweek with a horse, and I will check the fit. Once I have the pattern, it should take no more than a week, Brian signed. *We have a deal,* signed Major Gerald. Major Gerald left the shop, considerably happier than he had been earlier in the day. With a few hours left in their extended curfew, Donovan invited Rachel and her parents to dinner at the King's Table Tavern. Rachel's parents declined the invitation, saying that the two of them should go alone to celebrate their engagement.

Wizard Noland sat at his desk. He should have sent this message days ago, but events were getting ahead of him. Besides, he wasn't exactly sure where Andrew was now. He assumed that the HMS VALOR was somewhere in the Eastern Ocean, on patrol. The Messenger Hawk would have to be sent to Sundock, since hawks couldn't find ships at sea. Finally, he wrote:

Battle Mage Andrew,

Sorceress Celeste learned something of great importance from Loren. Apparently both you and Donovan are descendants of Wizard Amanda, the magician who was responsible for healing many of the poisoned dragons at the end of the last conflict. Loren said that a Binding spell was placed on the members of the Dragon Council, that any progeny of Wizard Amanda must be located and protected during the current conflict. This is undoubtedly why the dragons have been unwilling to attack your ship. I do not know how many dragons are impacted by this Binding spell, or what use we can make of the information, but it appears that the dragons know which ship you are on, and will be reluctant to attack the HMS VALOR. I therefore recommend that you inform your superiors and <u>do not change ships</u>.

Noland

"Sir, is there any way to get a message to my father?" asked Donovan. Wizard Noland thought for a minute, then said, "Well, I suppose I could send a Messenger Hawk to Mage Curtis in Springfield. I'm not exactly sure where your father is right now, but Curtis should be able to get a message to him eventually." Donovan smiled and said, "Thank you. I just wanted him to know about my engagement." "I understand completely," said Noland. Reaching into his desk drawer, Noland extracted a small slip of parchment. "Here you go, sorry it's so small, but a Hawk can only carry so much weight, you understand."

"Yes, sir. Can I just write it out here?" "Certainly, then I will teach you a trick your father and I worked out a few years ago when sending messages." Donovan took the parchment and moved to the table in the parlor. Thinking quickly, he wrote:

Father,

How are you? How is Baize? I just wanted to let you know that I met someone (my Mentor, Rachel Turner) and we are engaged. We haven't set a date yet, and I will completely understand if you can't make it to the wedding. I just thought you should know.

Donovan

Donvan returned to Wizard Noland's study where the Headmaster was patiently waiting. "Here it is, sir." "Very good. Now, the most important thing to know when sending messages by Messenger Hawk is that the communication is not always secure. By that I mean that the hawk can be intercepted and the message never reach the intended recipient, or the message itself can be altered, often with disastrous consequences." "I never thought of that," said Donovan.

"I'm not surprised. Anyway, your father and I worked out a way to ensure that our messages to each other would be safe. Observe." Noland took the parchment, steepled his fingers and said, *"ODIOUS MAGNUS."* "I don't understand," said Donovan, "you just combined the Smell enhancement spell with the spell to Detect Magic." "Precisely! I also thought of the scent of oranges as I conjured the spell. Now, if anyone alters the message, in any way, the ink will give off the odor of oranges."

"Why oranges?" asked Donovan. "Because I *hate* oranges. As a child growing up in Eastport, oranges were too big a part of my diet. After eating oranges three times a day for fifteen years I hope to never see an orange again. Edward knew this and concocted a scent that I would immediately recognize. If you know a message has been altered with magic, you can use the Change spell to restore the message to its original form."

"That's genius!" exclaimed Donovan. "Indeed. Your father has always had a knack for combining spells in interesting ways to achieve unique results. Keep that in mind for the future. I'll send your message out today." "Thank you again, sir."

Chapter Twenty-Two:
DELIVERIES

Gek and Azure flew back to Acropo as soon as Gek returned from dropping (literally) Sorceress Anne into the sea near the Navy ships. Azure was becoming increasingly uncomfortable and grouchy as her due date approached, and she wanted to get back to her cavern where the rest of the Sea Dragon Clan was. As they entered the cavern complex, Azure said, "Hurry, Gek. It is time."

"So soon?" asked Gek. "I thought we had more time!" "So did I," replied Azure, grimacing. "Perhaps I have been pregnant for longer than I thought. I do not know. I have never been pregnant before." They rushed along the passageways until they came to the chamber that Teal had used as his home. Aqua was waiting there.

"Mother! It is time! What do I do?" asked Azure. "First, you calm down," said Aqua soothingly. "I know this is sudden and unexpected, but it should not be painful. It should also be over very quickly. Gek, please dig a shallow hole, about a foreleg deep in the floor, then gather some of that kelp in the corner and make a nest out of it in the hole. That is where the egg will rest until it hatches."

Gek moved quickly and used the Dig spell to create a circular hole in the floor; then, he lined it with the kelp that Aqua had obviously gathered in preparation for this moment. "Now, Azure, you need to squat over this nest and relax until the egg comes out. Do NOT push or squeeze the egg, or you could break it!"

Azure followed her mother's instructions and within the hour, a yellow/green dragon egg dropped from between her hind legs and landed softly in the nest of kelp. Azure sighed in relief as she moved off the nest. Aqua looked closely at the egg. "This is the most unique Sea Dragon egg I have ever seen," she said. "How so?" asked Gek. "For one thing, it is much larger than a normal Sea Dragon egg, and it is yellow and green. Sea Dragon eggs are usually blue or green. I guess it is because of her mating with a Great Dragon. The baby will be an interesting shade of gold and blue-green."

"Just as long as it is healthy," murmured Azure. "What do we do now?" "We need to keep the egg warm and the kelp moist until it hatches." "How long will that take?" asked Gek. "It normally takes one cycle of the moon for a Dragon egg to hatch, it may be a few days earlier, or a few days more. Because it is half Great Dragon and half Sea Dragon, I am not entirely sure. All I *do* know is that Azure must be here when it hatches."

"Why is that?" asked Azure groggily. "The baby will imprint and form an immediate bond to the first Dragon it sees. You do not want your child bonding with some other Dragon," explained Aqua. "Does that mean that I have to stay in this cave for a month?" "No, no. Anyone can lay on the nest and keep the egg warm, even Gek. You just need to be here when it hatches." Azure sighed with relief and Gek laughed.

"Just for that, you get the first turn," said Azure. "I am going out for a swim. If you are a good Dragon, I may bring you back some fish for dinner." "I am much better than a *good* Dragon," said Gek, "I am a *Great* Dragon." Aqua laughed and showed Gek the correct position for laying over the nest—just close enough to keep the egg warm, not so close that it might crack. Gek assumed the position and promptly fell asleep.

Aqua and Azure left quietly and proceeded down the passageway to the underwater entrance to the cavern complex. "How is the Clan doing?" asked Azure. "They are grieving," replied Aqua, "almost every family in the Clan had a loved one killed or injured in the battle. There is much anger at the humans, and some remorse for being dragged into the conflict in the first place." "Do you think the Truce will hold?" "It is hard to say," said Aqua, "the Sea Dragons that live in the Southern Ocean were not involved with the battle and will be harder to convince, and those to our north have always been more disagreeable than is seemly for a Sea Dragon."

Azure nodded her understanding and dove into the water, swimming down and then surfacing after she cleared the overhanging island shelf. Aqua appeared by her side a moment later and said, "Are you sure that you are up to this? Most new mothers just want to take a nap after giving birth." "I am sure," said Azure, as she frolicked among the waves. "It feels so good to have my natural body back again. But I still feel a little bloated." "That is natural," said Aqua, reassuringly, "you have been eating for two for the last several months, so you are bound to be heavier than normal. The weight will come off gradually as you become more active, but you will begin producing milk for the baby which will keep your weight higher than before for the next few months."

They swam in silence for a time, then crawled up on the beach to sun themselves. "So, tell me about Gek," said Aqua. Azure related how she met Gek and told Aqua the tales of their adventures together. She also mentioned that she enjoyed his company when they were in human form, almost more than when they were Dragons. "That is a dangerous thought," cautioned Aqua. "I know," said Azure, "but humans are able to touch one another in ways that Dragons cannot. I begin to understand why some of the Changed Ones prefer to remain in human form."

"That option is now foreclosed to you," said Aqua sternly. "You will soon have a Dragon baby, who will need a Dragon mother." "I know, but do not expect me to never transform again." "We should get back," said Aqua, changing the subject, "remember to grab a fish for Gek on our way *home*." Azure noted the emphasis on the word *home*.

The entourage left Baize just after midday on Firstday. There were twenty apprentice magicians, fifteen boys and five girls, along with ten surveyors, ten civil engineers and twenty-five wagons (with drivers). Most of the wagons were loaded down with provisions and supplies, two were dedicated to transporting the apprentice magicians, some of whom were too young to ride a horse all the way to Springfield, and a few wagons were empty and would be used for transporting goods and personnel to and from the construction site. Before departing, Wizard Edward addressed the assembled team of Baizians. "Ladies and Gentlemen, my name is Wizard Edward. King Donald has placed me and Mage Kathy here in charge of this project. Together, we will be constructing the most impressive and complex public works project in the history of the Kingdom of Baize."

Edward paused for his words to sink in, then he continued, "We will be traveling from here to the city of Springfield, stopping each evening at the rest stations along the road. We should reach the city in about two weeks. First, when we stop each evening, I want the wagons to form a circle around the watering hole. Stay in line so we can depart smoothly in the mornings, any individual horses will be tethered to the wagons on the inside of the circle. There will be a guard mounted each night of three four-glass shifts of five men each. The guard will consist of the engineers, surveyors, and wagon drivers. The apprentice magicians are too young for guard duty, but they will be receiving magical instruction from me, Wizard Timothy, and Mage Kathy each evening."

"I have noticed several casks of ale among the provisions," continued Edward, "the responsible consumption of alcohol is permitted. Drunkenness will be punished. Violence of any kind is unacceptable. I believe in second chances, but I do not give third chances. In case you're wondering, myself, Mage Kathy and Wizard Timothy will all be concealing ourselves through magic, and walking around the camp each night, checking the guards and watching for troublemakers." One of the wagon drivers began to grumble under his breath about not taking orders from a woman, even if she was a magician. Edward walked over to him and said, "Since you feel that way, you can remain here in Baize. I will find someone else to drive your wagon."

The driver attempted to apologize and take back his words, but Edward was having none of it. "Leave now while you can," said Edward, "or I will have Mage Kathy remove your right hand." The driver left quickly. "Can any of you engineers drive a wagon?" Edward asked loudly. A few hands went up. Edward selected the oldest of the volunteers and assigned him to the now driverless wagon. "Just tether your horse to the back of the wagon," said Edward. "Any more complaints? Then let's be off. The order of march is the engineers, followed by the wagons with their equipment, then the wagon with the apprentice magicians followed by the wagons with the provisions, then the surveyors followed by the wagons with their gear, and the empty wagons bringing up the rear."

The column moved out at a brisk pace. Fortunately, the first day would be the shortest before stopping, as the first rest station was just past the outskirts of Baize. Edward rode with Kathy and Timothy and gave them their instructions. "Kathy, I want you to work with the five female magicians, I will take the eight oldest, and Tim, you will work with the seven youngest male apprentices. Our first task will be to teach them the Dig spell. I want to practice it every night for the first five days of our journey. Make note of the most adept students." The two magicians nodded their understanding.

"I'm going to ride up front with the engineers for today, Kathy, I'd like you to ride with the apprentice magicians, and Timothy, you ride back with the surveyors today. We'll switch up each day," said Edward. "Where's Dirk?" whispered Kathy. "I think he's sleeping in one of the empty wagons," said Edward quietly, "his cloak isn't big enough to cover his horse." "Then where is his horse?" Kathy asked. "You're riding it," said Edward.

We need to get back to Sundock," said Commodore Matthews. "I need to send a Messenger Hawk to Admiral Cross and let him know about this 'truce' that Sorceress Anne arranged." "What do you think his response will be?" asked Mage Andrew. "The Admiral is a cautious man," said the Commodore, "but he's also beholden to the King. He may see this as an opportunity to strike while we have an advantage."

"Then I better get busy replicating more Seabows," said Andrew. "Only after all of the repairs are complete. I judge that we have at least a pause in the conflict right now. Let's get the ships in tip-top shape before we worry about more armament," said the Commodore. "Aye, Aye, Commodore. I'll get right on it," said Andrew. As Andrew left the Commodore's cabin, Anne was waiting in the passageway, "What did he say?" she asked. "Commodore Matthews said that we need to focus on repairing the damage to our ships first, then worry about replicating additional Seabows. We're also heading back to Sundock so he can send a Messenger Hawk to Admiral Cross, informing him of your agreement with the Sea dragons to see if he concurs," replied Andrew.

"Do you think he will?" "I'm not sure. I've only met the Admiral a couple of times, and once he nearly bit my head off when I told him about dragons masquerading as humans. Apparently, the King had not informed the Royal Army or Navy commanders. The Admiral was not pleased, especially when we found out that Wizard Lake's assistant was a Sea dragon Changed One. She got away before we could unmask her."

"Do you think she would have fought us?" asked Anne. "I doubt it," said Andrew, "she'd been with the Chief of Naval Wizardry Office for years, and didn't flee when the conflict with the dragons began. She may not have helped the dragons or us. I think she was either trying to remain neutral, or preferred to remain in human form and was worried about our reaction if she were discovered."

The two magicians returned to the weather deck and continued making repairs to the VALOR; there were railings to replace (one careless sailor had already fallen overboard); deck planks to repair and smooth (most sailors went barefoot while at sea and the splinters were causing injuries); sails to patch; and a myriad of spars and lines to repair or splice. The ships were limping along towards Sundock, but the prevailing wind out of the west, and their damaged sails were impeding their progress.

It took three days to repair most of the damage to the ships and finish healing all of the sailors with minor wounds. While morale had improved, it was obvious that none of the seamen were eager for another confrontation with the dragons. At midday on the fifth day, the port of Sundock came into view, and by nightfall all three ships were moored alongside the Navy piers. The crews were given a two-day shore leave, with only a skeleton crew remaining aboard each vessel. The Commodore immediately dispatched a Messenger Hawk to the Admiral. "It'll take at least two days to get a response," he said to Andrew. "The hawk should reach Grotton by tomorrow morning, then we just have to wait for an answer. I'm not going back out without orders." "Should we tell the other Squadrons and the Fleet Commander?" asked Andrew. "I would, if I knew how to get a message to them. Messenger Hawks can't find ships at sea. It's been tried. Sometimes they land on commercial ships, other times they're lost at sea. Those hawks take years to train, we can't waste them. I wish there was another way to communicate between Squadrons, or even between ships at sea and Naval Headquarters."

"I'll give it some thought, Sir," said Andrew. "Maybe I can come up with something." "You do that, and I'll promote you to Wizard myself," said Commodore Matthews. "I appreciate the thought, sir, but only the Wizards Academy Headmaster can give me that honor, and I'd have to pass the Wizard's Test first."

Ard plodded tiredly towards the rock quarry. It was becoming increasingly difficult for him to put one foot in front of the others. He had managed to fly from Southport to an area just north of Prarrieville before his strength gave out and he was forced to land in a wheat field and continue his journey on foot. Fortunately, the area he was in was sparsely populated, with only a few scattered farms and ranches on the open plains. He was certainly leaving a trail of destruction through the wheat field, but he just didn't care anymore.

Finally, he just couldn't take another step. His enormous bulk was simply too much weight to move. In desperation, he transformed into human form and continued his trek northeast towards the road to Colton and the quarry that was just north of the town. As he limped along the road, a farmer and his wife approached in an empty wagon. "You look about worn out," said the farmer, "would you like a ride?" "I would appreciate that very much," replied Ard. The farmer's wife stepped down from the buckboard and helped Ard into the wagon bed. Ard nodded his thanks, too exhausted to reply. "We're headed to Colton," said the farmer. "So am I," replied Ard, "and I am very grateful for the lift."

The farmer and his wife attempted to engage Ard in conversation, but he had already drifted off to sleep, despite the bumping of the wagon as it bounced along the dirt road. A few hours later, the wagon stopped in what passed for the Colton town square. The farmer roused Ard and let him know that they had arrived. "Do you have a place to stay tonight?" asked the woman. Not wishing to impose, Ard replied, "Yes. My grandson has a place in town. I will be fine. Thank you very much for the ride."

The farmer and his wife waved their goodbyes as they guided the wagon out of town, heading east. Ard resumed his trek north, now only a few miles from the quarry. Once he got there he could rest. Darkness fell and the night sky filled with stars, the three-quarter moon shined brightly, providing enough light to travel by. There were no other travelers on the road, just the weary, ancient dragon on his last trip.

"Wizard Noland, is it possible for a magician to change into a dragon?" asked Donovan. "It must be," said Noland, "otherwise the dragon Changed Ones would not be able to transform back into dragons." "Do we know how it's done?" "It's never occurred to me to explore the possibility," said Noland. "Why?" "Well, sir, it seems that they are constantly spying on us in human form. Maybe we should return the favor," said Donovan.

"That's an interesting suggestion. Who do you think will volunteer to try making that change for the first time? I mean, if it goes wrong and you can't speak or perform the gesture, you would be trapped in whatever dragon-shaped form you conjured." "Hmmm, that's a good point," said Donovan. "Maybe we could ask

Terry." "We could, but remember, he *started out* as a dragon, so he undoubtedly knows how to change back into one. We have no idea how many times dragons tried and failed before they learned how to change into humans," cautioned Wizard Noland.

"Still, I think it might be worth the risk," said Donovan thoughtfully. "I'm not sure Rachel would agree," said Noland sternly. "Can I at least talk to Terry about it?" "*Talk* only. No one is to attempt the Change without my expressed permission. Is that clear?" "Yes, sir. It's just that there would be so many advantages if we could master that Change. I mean, we could travel long distances quickly, scout out enemy positions from above, even infiltrate the dragon clans to learn their plans."

"I agree that there would certainly be advantages, but the risks are enormous. Talk to Terry. I will have Celeste speak with Loren, maybe between the two of them, we may learn something valuable."

Chapter Twenty-Three:
THE LONG AND WINDING ROAD

"My name is Wizard Edward. You may call me Wizard Edward or Sir," Edward said, addressing the eight oldest apprentice magicians in the group. "Now, by a show of hands, how many of you know how to conjure the Dig spell?" All eight magicians raised their hands. "Excellent! How many of you know how to form a protective shield?" Six of the eight students raised their hands. "And finally, how many of you know the Adhesive spell?" Four apprentices raised their hands. Edward smiled, "Before this project is over, you will all know how to cast all of these spells. In case you haven't heard yet, we are going to create a great salt lake in the flats just west of the city of Springfield. How many of you have heard of the Great Salt Flats?" All of the students raised their hands.

"Who can tell me why the Great Salt Flats have been expanding? No one? Very well, I'll explain it. Let's say that this area right here," said Edward pointing to the ground, "is the Great Salt Flats. It is composed of mostly sand, covered by a thin layer of salt." Edward used a

Wind spell to gather a clump of sand, then used a Change spell to turn the top layer of sand into salt. "So, we'll pretend that this is the Salt Flats. Here is what happens every time it rains." Edward sprinkled a good bit of water onto the mound of salt and sand. As the sand became saturated with water, the mound began to spread out as it was carried by the water. When Edward stopped adding water, the puddle of salty water and sand stopped spreading. Edward then used a Temperature spell to evaporate the water. The result was a much larger circle of salt-covered sand.

"You see how it expands?" The gathered students nodded their understanding. "Now, twenty years ago, the King of Baize sent a hundred magicians to try to keep the Salt Flats from expanding. What do you suppose they did?" "I know," shouted the oldest boy, "my father told me that they used Wind spells to blow the sand back." "Precisely," said Edward, "and were they successful?" "Not really," said the boy, "it worked for a little while, but the rain just pushed it right back after a few years." "Exactly!" said Edward. "The rain water pushed it back again. Does anyone know why the Salt Flats are expanding towards the Amber River?" The assembled students all shook their heads. "It's because water always flows downhill, and the terrain in the area slopes towards the river. What do you think is going to happen if the Salt Flats reach the river?"

The youngest of the eight students raised his hand, "It's going to kill the fish?" Edward nodded, "Yes. It's going to kill *all* of the fish from where the salt enters the river, all the way down to the sea." The students looked shocked by Edward's pronouncement. "So how are we going to stop it?" asked one. Edward smiled, "We are going to dig a giant hole in the ground, and put a wall around the edges to contain the rain water. First, we are going to create a trench along the edges using the Dig spell, then we'll scoop the sand and salt out of the middle and vanish it using the Remove spell." The students looked thoughtful.

"This is going to be a huge undertaking and will likely take almost a year to complete. While you're working on the hole, Mage Kathy and I will be giving you other magical instruction, so you won't just be digging holes. For the next few nights though, I want us to work on digging the deepest holes we can in the ground outside the camp grounds where we stop each night." "Why outside the camp?" asked one student. "Because I don't want to strike water," said Edward. He led the eight students out of the camp site and over to a patch of rocky ground. "Now, we'll start digging holes. I want each of you to dig as deep a hole as you can. Deeper is more important than wider. We should hit bedrock at about a hundred feet." "Bedrock?" asked the oldest boy.

"Yes," explained Edward, "you see, the earth consists of layers of soil. In the Salt Flats, the top layer is the salt and sand, beneath the sand is probably loose soil, like for farming, below that is harder, compacted dirt and rocks, at the bottom is solid rock, called bedrock. We will need to dig our hole all the way down to the bedrock, otherwise, the rainwater will seep into the ground and get under our walls. Once we get to bedrock, we will use Adhesive spells to glue all of the dirt, and rocks on the outside side of the trench together to make a wall that will contain the water."

"How big a hole are we going to dig?" asked another boy. "As I understand it, the Salt Flats are about fifty miles square. I plan to dig a U-shaped hole, fifty miles long, and twenty-five miles high on each side." "That's too big," said the youngest student, "we'll never make it." "Yes, we will," said Edward, forcefully. "There are apprentice magicians coming from all over Baize to help us. Nevertheless, it will be a lot of work. We will divide up into teams and work around the clock. The King is coming to check on our progress in a year and I want to be done by then."

"Now, what's your name?" "Tony, sir," said the oldest boy. "All right Tony, I want you to come over here and dig the deepest hole you can. It doesn't have to be very wide, just deep." Tony said the incantation, *'INTRENCHO,'* while making the 'Dig' gesture. A hole about twenty feet deep and five feet square appeared. "Very good," said Edward. "Only you need to murmur the incantation so no one else can hear and understand you. *I don't want any of the Engineers trying it*," whispered Edward. Tony smiled in understanding. "Now, to make the hole deeper, stretch your arm as low as you can as you recite the incantation. That will make the hole deeper. Try again in the same place." Reaching as low as he could, it took four tries to reach bedrock, about ninety feet down.

"Very good," said Edward. "Now, if you were to try to dig through the bedrock, it would take a lot more power, and you would get a shallower hole each time. Next," said Edward, beckoning the next student over. "Now, I want you to dig a hole next to Tony's and use the dirt from your hole to fill in his hole." Edward made each apprentice dig a hole down to bedrock, filling in the hole next to theirs. Once all eight students had completed the task, Edward used a Wind spell to fill in the last hole. "That's all for tonight. We'll work on this for the next four nights, then we'll work on our shields." "What will we use the shields for?" asked Tony. "The shields will keep the sides from collapsing and help us build the wall at the top of the trench."

When Edward was finished working with the apprentices, he met with Kathy and Timothy to discuss the abilities of the other young magicians. "So, Kathy, how are the girls doing?" "I expect most of them are going to be sore tomorrow from riding in the wagon all day and practicing magic," said Kathy. "Easily healed. I had not considered that. We may have to offer healing to some of the students, and maybe even to some of the adults in the morning. That may slow us down somewhat, but I think it'll be time well spent. Did they all know the Dig spell?"

"Yes, and the Shield spell too, but none of them knew the Adhesive spell." "I'm not surprised," said Edward, "The Adhesive spell is a Level Two spell at the Wizards Academy. It's not hard though. We have plenty of time for that instruction. Tim, you had the youngest magicians; how did it go?" "Only five of the seven apprentices knew the Dig spell, and none of them knew either the Shield or Adhesive spells," replied Timothy. "That's as expected," said Edward. "How old is the youngest?" "Only thirteen," said Timothy. Edward whistled. "We'll have to pay special attention to the youngest magicians. They will likely be homesick as well as afraid of falling short in their duties."

"For tonight, Timothy, I want you to take the first watch. Move around the camp both concealed and openly. I want the team to see you and also wonder where you might be. I will take the second watch in three glasses, then Kathy has the last watch. We wake everyone up at dawn, have a quick breakfast, heal anyone who requests it, then move out. The quicker we get on the road, the earlier we'll be able to stop each night. Questions?" "Where will you be?" "The three of us will sleep in the last empty wagon. That way, we can find each other in an emergency. Specialist Dirk will be patrolling around the camp as he sees fit, right Dirk?"

Specialist Dirk appeared beside the magicians. Timothy and Kathy jumped, while Edward looked amused. "Right, sir. Sorry Mage Kathy, Wizard Timothy, I didn't mean to startle you. I'll just be wandering around, as usual, on the lookout for trouble. I'll remain concealed." "Understood, Dirk. Kathy and Timothy, while you two are on patrol, use a Smell enhancement to see if you can detect any dragon Changed Ones in our crew. With all of the people we'll be using on this project I'm sure we're going to encounter one or two before we're done. Don't confront anyone, just let me know about them. They may be peaceful, neutral, or hostile. The last thing we need is an angry Stone dragon rampaging through the camp," cautioned Edward.

Dirk put his hood back on and proceeded out into the camp, while Timothy left on his first circuit, walking slowly and speaking to everyone he encountered. Kathy and Edward moved off to the wagon and climbed up into the bed. "I'm sorry there won't be much privacy until we reach Springfield," said Edward. Kathy gave him a kiss and said, "I understand. I anticipated as much." Edward wrapped his arms around her and asked, "How are you doing? I don't know how much riding you've done lately." "I'm fine," said Kathy. "In my job as Assistant Court Wizard I had to travel to outlying cities and towns regularly to check their accounts and inspect their treasuries. By the way, I really appreciated how you handled that disagreeable driver this morning."

"I have to admit, that was staged. I arranged that whole scene with Mr. Wood yesterday afternoon. He was never coming with us, he has a bad back. I just wanted to drive the point home with the other drivers, engineers and surveyors. They will all be taking orders from you soon, and I wanted them to know that I will brook no argument about it."

Kathy gave him another, longer kiss and said, "You really are special, you know?" Edward just shrugged and said, "I just want them all to know that I will tolerate no disrespect to you, or any of the other female magicians that we use in this project. Well, if you need any healing, don't be too proud to ask. I might even enjoy it," whispered Edward. "I'll keep that in mind," said Kathy.

A little past midnight Edward was shaken awake by Wizard Timothy. Edward quickly threw off his blanket and, being careful not to disturb Kathy, climbed down from the wagon. "Any problems?" "No. Everyone seems to think this is going to be a great adventure. It took a while to get the apprentices settled down. I suspect most of them have never slept outdoors before. Some of them are going to be tired and sore tomorrow." Timothy gingerly climbed up into the wagon and laid down, careful to keep well clear of Kathy's sleeping form. *He suspects,* thought Edward as he moved off into the camp. Edward made one lap of the camp, wandering between the sleeping forms, careful not to wake anyone. He greeted each of the five men on guard duty, asking their names and inquiring when they came on duty and when they would be able to get some sleep. After his first trip around the campsite, Edward cast a Concealment shield and moved near one of the glowing campfires to listen in on the conversations of the few men who were still awake.

"Ya think this time'll be different?" asked one grizzled engineer. "I hope so," said his companion, "I told 'em last time that the wind spell wouldn't work. Nobody listened to me. Those darn magicians blew sand and salt everywhere. We were coated from head to toe. The only relief we got was when it rained, which just spread the stuff back at us. At least the pay was good and the job lasted for a good long while." Edward withdrew a short distance, dropped his Concealment shield and walked into the firelight.

"I hear that you were on the crew that tried to contain the Salt Flats the last time." The elderly engineer nodded sadly and said, "Yes, sir Wizard. It seems like every decade or so, someone gets a new idea on how to stop the spread. I hope your plan works better than the last two." "Two?" said Edward, "I only heard about one attempt, when the magicians tried to use wind." "A'fore that, they tried to build walls around it, sir, but they didn't plant 'em deep enough and the water got under 'em. Then the walls fell down and the sand and salt just rolled over 'em."

"Well, at least my idea hasn't been tried yet," said Edward. "I tol' 'em last time that we should try digging a hole, but no one listened to me!" said the engineer. "Hopefully, we'll prove you were right this time," said Edward. "You really think those *children* can dig a big enough hole?" asked the engineer. "The Dig spell is one of the first spells we teach our students in Franconia. It's easy to conjure and requires very little power from the magician. With over a hundred apprentices, we should be able to dig a big enough hole in about six months; as long as it isn't too far down to bedrock," said Edward.

"You hit bedrock in the Salt Flats at about fifty feet," said the engineer. "Really?" asked Edward. "I was told it was closer to a hundred!" "Nah, that's why the sand spreads so quick. Because there's not a lot of soil under it to absorb the water."

"How do you know the bedrock is only fifty feet down?" asked Edward. "Before we pulled out the first time, I asked a Sorcerer to come with me to the center of the flats and dig a hole to find out how deep it was to bedrock. We determined it was about fifty feet. At least where we dug." "Who was this Sorcerer?" asked Edward. "He said his name was Louis."

For the next two weeks the convoy of wagons moved east toward Springfield. Every evening they would stop and the three experienced magicians would work with the apprentices, honing their abilities with the Dig, Shield and Adhesive spells. Edward was secretly pleased with the information that they might strike bedrock much sooner than they anticipated, which would mean that they might be done much, much sooner than expected. He wondered if Sorcerer Louis was the same man who would later become Court Wizard Louis, the dragon Changed One. If so, that would mean that this plot to undermine the Kingdom of Baize had been going on for decades, maybe even longer.

Admiral Cross re-read the message from Commodore Matthews.

Admiral Cross,

The Coral Islands are the home of the Sea dragons. We engaged them in a pitched battle, killing 19 Sea dragons, including their Chief, and injuring 33 more, but the HMS COMFORT was lost. The squadron had 79 killed and 64 wounded. Our magicians have healed all of our wounded. During the battle, Sorceress Anne of the COMFORT was swept overboard but managed to swim to the southernmost island, where she was captured by the Sea dragons who demanded that she heal their injured. She reluctantly agreed, but insisted on a Binding spell that required that none of the dragons she healed would ever attack humans again. They reluctantly agreed. This means that 52 Sea dragons are out of the fight. The dragons returned Sorceress Anne to the VALOR and she has informed me that the new Sea dragon Clan Chief has proposed a truce. If we do not attack them, they will not attack us. Standing by for your orders.

Commodore Horatio Matthews

A truce? What did that gain? If nothing else, it gained time to install these incredible new Seabows on all of his ships. "What do you think Wizard Lake?" "A temporary truce gives us time to refit and re-arm," said the Wizard. "It's going to take time to replicate crossbows for all of our sailors and Seabows for the ships. Commodore Matthews doesn't say it, but it seems like the Seabows worked remarkably well. It was a brilliant idea by Battle Mage Andrew to enlarge and modify his crossbows for use aboard ships." The Admiral chuckled. "Yes, that boy is really something."

"So, what are you going to tell Commodore Matthews?" "That I'm sending him back to the area around the Coral Islands to see if the dragons will actually honor this 'truce,' or if it's some kind of trick." "What if the truce is real?" asked Wizard Lake. "That decision is above my pay grade. Once we know for sure, we'll inform the King and ask him for instructions."

"So Terry, can you tell me how to change into a dragon?" asked Donovan. Terry hesitated, "Why do you want to know?" he asked. "I would think the answer is obvious. The hostile dragons have infiltrated many of our cities and institutions. It seems only fair that we return the favor." "I am not sure that I agree with your definition of 'fair,'" replied Terry. "If I tell you how to make the transformation, I would be betraying my Clan.

I agreed never to transform again, and not to injure humans, but I did not agree to this."

"Well, if I try the Change spell without your help and die as a result, wouldn't that be causing injury to a human?" Terry thought about it and said, "No. If you choose to take that risk, it is on you. Do not try to make me responsible for your actions." "I thought we were friends!" said Donovan. "I was your Mentor, and I agreed to answer any 'Dragon questions' you might have, but this is different." "How so?" "This is asking me to betray not only my Clan, but the entire Dragon Nation. I need to think about this." "Fine," said Donovan crossly, "Just think about who's side you're on."

Donovan stormed off across the central courtyard, toward the Headmaster's cottage. The door open as he reached the front porch. "Come in, Donovan," said Wizard Noland. Donovan entered and sat down in the parlor, "I don't think Terry is going to help us," he said. "So I heard. Did you really think it was going to be that easy?" asked Noland. "I thought that Terry was on our side! That he preferred living as a human and that he wanted to remain here at the Academy. I don't know if we can trust him anymore."

"Donovan, none of the dragon Changed Ones who submitted to the Binding spell agreed to assist us in our fight against the dragons. They simply agreed to remain neutral." "Still—" "Give Terry some time. He may reconsider his decision. He didn't say 'No,' he said 'I'll think about it.'" "I just don't understand," said Donovan. "The dragons consider him a traitor and will probably kill him if they catch him with his guard down; even his parents tried to *eat* him when he was younger. How can he stay loyal to a race that could do that?"

"Those are all things that he has to consider. From what Celeste has learned from talking with Loren, dragons have an intense sense of *honor*." "Honor?" "Yes. In their agreement at the end of the last war, dragons agreed not to eat humans." "So?" asked Donovan. "So that pledge has held for over two hundred years," said Wizard Noland. "But they killed dozens of Royal guardsmen!" "They didn't promise not to *kill* humans, just not to *eat* them." "That's just semantics," said Donovan. "Maybe, but we promised to give them cattle; we didn't promise not to poison them."

Donovan sat in thought for a moment. Finally, he said, "But Terry never promised not to tell anyone how to transform into a dragon." "I know, and I think he'll come around eventually." "What about Loren? Have we learned anything useful from her?" "Celeste is talking to her now. We should know shortly."

"Back for round two, dear?" asked Loren. "I didn't know we were sparring," replied Celeste. "Of course, you did, my dear, and you did incredibly well." Celeste blushed. "So, what do you want to know this time?" asked Loren.

"I'm curious why you stay in this room all of the time. I would expect you to want to go outside and get some fresh air occasionally. You know that you're not confined here." Loren hesitated, then said, "It would just be too embarrassing, dear. Walking around with everyone staring at me, the traitor with wooden hands," she said, holding up her prosthetic wooden hands. "Then keep your hands in your pockets," suggested Celeste.

"Why do you care?" asked Loren. "You were my favorite teacher," Celeste replied. "Despite everything, I don't want to see you suffer needlessly." "I am not sure that all of your classmates share your compassion," said Loren.

"What was it like to be a dragon? I mean, to be able to fly across the sky, see above the clouds, watch a sunrise from high above the earth. It must have been wonderous." Loren hesitated, looking for a trap in

Celeste's question, finally, she said, "Flying to a Dragon is not as wonderous as you suspect. It is like walking to a human, just something you learn in your childhood. As to the view, in the Snow Fields where I grew up, all I saw below me was white snow, speckled with grey stones, or the passing prey."

"I wish I could fly," said Celeste wistfully. "Then simply Change yourself and give it a try, you silly girl." "I'm sure that spell is much too complicated for me to master," replied Celeste softly. Loren huffed. "Then Wizard Mira failed utterly in teaching you the Change spell, and you should never have passed the Sorcerer's Test!" "But this is different!" shouted Celeste, "I know how to change a rock into a flower, but this would involve changing myself into something else. It just wouldn't work!"

"Of course, it would, you weak-minded simpleton! All you have to do is imagine yourself as a Dragon that can talk and perform the spell! Changing forms is easy if you have the courage of a Dragon!" Celeste recoiled in shock, "But I don't even know what a dragon looks like!" "Of course you do! You saw one when your carriage was attacked. Have you forgotten so soon?" asked Loren smugly.

"You're saying that all I have to do is remember what Azure looked like, think about having the ability to talk, then cast the Change spell, and I'll turn into a Sea dragon?" Celeste asked with more than a touch of disbelief in her voice. "That is exactly what—" Loren clamped her mouth shut, and the blood rushed from her face as she realized what she had just done.

"Thank you, Loren. That's all I wanted to know."

Minister Jasmine

Chapter Twenty-Four:
LIFE AND DEATH

Gek was not happy. While he was willing to help keep the egg warm and protected, he thought that Azure was taking advantage of him by asking him to mind the nest for much more than his fair share of the time. He was a Great Dragon, accustomed to the open country; the confining nature of the cavern was making him claustrophobic, and he was very tired of eating fish. Moreover, the cave was wet, cold, dark, and smelled funny. It had been almost three weeks now, and Gek had hardly seen the light of day.

Azure and Aqua came walking down the passageway, and Gek practically leaped off the nest. "Finally!" he said. "Where have you two been all day? I need a break!" "Calm down, grumpy," said Azure soothingly. "It is just after dawn. We took a quick trip to the mainland to get you something to eat besides fish." Azure dropped a wild boar carcass on the cavern floor next to Gek as she settled gently onto the nest, holding her Dragon egg.

Gek hungrily grabbed the boar and took it over to the corner of the cavern, where he consumed it with relish. "Thank you," he said, finishing the last of his breakfast, "what is happening out in the world?"

"Well," said Aqua, "most of the injured Dragons are now completely healed. Some of them are eager for revenge against the humans, while others have had their fill of fighting and are ready to see if the humans will keep their word about the truce this time."

"What does my father think?" asked Gek. "I think Cobalt is wishing that he was not the new Clan Chief. He prefers solitude, and the constant arguing and complaining is grinding on his nerves, but I think he fears even greater casualties if we attack again." "Why would that be?" asked Gek. "It is those new weapons with the long iron arrows. Now that the humans know how deadly they are to Dragons, he fears that the magic-users will construct even more of them for our next encounter." "He might be right," said Gek sadly. "The normal arrows killed my mother; these new weapons are an even greater threat to us."

"Have there been any attacks lately?" asked Gek. "No, not since you took Anne back to her ship. The humans have sailed back to their port in Sundock." "Hmm," said Gek. "Tell me again how we sank the human's ship." "According to Cobalt, Sky grabbed one of those poles sticking up from the deck, bit it in half, then flew as high as he could and dropped it back onto the ship. It went clean through the bottom and the hole it made let the water in."

"I wonder…" mused Gek. "What?" asked Azure. "Well, when I returned Anne to her ship, I used a Concealment spell to escape undetected. What if a Dragon picked up a heavy stone or a log, cast a Concealment spell, flew high above one of the human ships, and then dropped the stone on it? The humans would not be able to see us, especially if we were to attack at night." "That is brilliant!" said Azure excitedly. "We could sink their ships, and they would never see us coming!"

Azure got up and walked over to Gek, giving him a kiss on the cheek, "I knew there was a reason I liked you."

CRACK. The yellow-green egg suddenly had a large vertical crack down the side. "Azure! Hurry!" said Aqua. Azure moved quickly to the nest as Gek and Aqua retreated to the entrance of the cavern. Azure curled her body around the circular nest and waited. CRACK, CRACK, CRACK. Suddenly, the egg split open, and a golden Dragon with a Cyan-colored underbelly emerged. It was covered with a gelatinous slime. "Wash him off quickly," instructed Aqua. Azure gently washed the baby dragon clean. It blinked its eyes several times, then recognized Azure as its mother. The baby nestled under her wing and began suckling. "It is a girl!" proclaimed Azure proudly.

The caravan of engineers and apprentice magicians rode into Springfield just past noon and headed for the garrison. Edward had left the surveyors at the edge of the Salt Flats with orders to get to work laying out the edges of the reservoir. They had grumbled at first, but Edward would brook no argument. He wanted the first corner surveyed when he returned in a few days with the apprentice magicians. Edward instructed the surveyors to lay out a giant "U-shape" on the ground, as wide as the Salt Flats extended. The magicians would start excavating at the southeast corner, some teams working northward, the others digging to the west. Once the "U" shape trench was dug down to bedrock and the walls were built, the magicians would start excavating the inside of the "U" from south to north.

Edward promised that he would give the surveyors a break in Springfield once they had laid out enough of the outline for the apprentices to get started. After a break in Springfield, the surveyors would return and finish laying out the outline of the reservoir. Once the surveying was complete, they would be free to return to their families in Baize.

As they rode into the garrison, Mage Curtis came out of the Administration Office to greet them. "Welcome back, sir," he said. "This must be an enormous project you're going to start. Almost sixty young apprentice magicians have arrived already, and there are more coming in each day. It's a good thing this garrison was built to hold a regiment, or we might run out of room." "Hello, Curtis. It's good to be back. Allow me to introduce Mage Kathy, the Baizian magician who is going to help me supervise this project, and you're correct; it's going to be enormous."

Curtis shook hands with Kathy and said, "Welcome to Springfield, Kathy. I'm Curtis Martin, and I'm glad to meet you. Hello, Wizard Timothy, it's good to see you again." "Well met, Mage Curtis," said Timothy. "How are things here?" "Everyone is curious about the sudden influx of young magicians and your message about a project to restrict the expansion of the Salt Flats. Most of the members of the City Council don't believe it can be done. I told them that you must have a plan, or you wouldn't have agreed to try."

"I have a plan," confirmed Edward, "but it's going to take a lot of blood, sweat and tears. Where have you settled the apprentice magicians?" "They're all in the first-floor rooms around the compound. I moved the Royal Expeditionary Force soldiers up to the second-floor rooms so there would be some separation." "Good idea. Please find rooms for the twenty apprentices we brought with us and put the adult engineers up on the second floor as well. We need to get the wagons parked, no need to unload them, and the horses into the stable and cared for. The Franconians can help with the horses. Timothy, Kathy and I are going to meet with the City Council now. Once we're done with that, we'll return and let you know our plans. Is the Royal Expeditionary Force ready to depart?"

"We could leave tomorrow if we had to, but waiting one more day would be best," said Curtis. "Very well, you leave at dawn the day after tomorrow, and please ride my horse, Enduro, home. You can stable him in the Wizards Academy stables. As soon as you've departed, Kathy and I will be taking the engineers and apprentices back out to the edge of the Salt Flats to start our project. Has there been any sign of Baizian forces approaching?" "My map shows a Battalion of mixed mounted and foot soldiers headed this way from Westport. They should be here in three days," said Curtis. "Please continue to monitor them. It would be best if 1st Company were gone before they arrive," said Edward.

"Yes, sir," said Curtis. "By the way, a message arrived for you from your son." Curtis handed over the message scroll. "I hope everything's OK," said Edward, taking the scroll and briefly smelling it. Mage Curtis looked puzzled. "I'll explain later," said Edward. He quickly read the message and smiled, "It seems that Donovan has fallen in love with his Mentor, and they are engaged. He just wanted me to know. That boy never ceases to amaze me."

Edward, Timothy and Kathy rode to the City Hall, where they expected to find the City Council. Behind him, Edward could hear Curtis giving orders to the engineers and the apprentice magicians. When they reached the Council chambers, Edward was relieved to see all of the remaining Council members awaiting their arrival. "Good afternoon, Ladies and Gentlemen," said Edward. "This is Mage Kathy from Baize, and you all know Wizard Timothy. Please take your seats; we have much to discuss and only a little time."

Once the council was seated, Edward explained his plan for containing the Salt Flats and how he already had the Baizian surveyors working on outlining the boundaries of the reservoir they were planning to construct. The councilors were skeptical. "How are you going to dig a hole deep enough?" asked one. "By using magic," said Kathy. "And just what are you going to do with all the dirt you excavate?" asked another. "We'll vanish it with magic," replied Edward. The council members murmured amongst themselves for a while until Edward said, "This project has already been approved by the King and his Ministers, so there is really not much to discuss. His Majesty will visit Springfield in one year to check on our progress. I intend to be finished before he arrives."

"What do you need from us?" asked the Council Chairwoman, Kimberly. "We'll need provisions, food, water, grain for the horses, repairs for any equipment that breaks down, temporary bath houses, and many more things than I can probably imagine right now. I'll have engineers and apprentice magicians rotating through town on rest breaks, and they'll need supplies and entertainment. Keep in mind, there will be over a hundred young apprentice magicians working on this project, so plan some shops and activities that will be of interest to them. This town is going to be a hub of activity for the next year."

"And just who's going to pay for all this?" asked Kimberly. "The King has given us a budget of 200 golds every three months. That should be sufficient. Mage Kathy here and her team of accountants will be responsible for procuring supplies and paying vendors for their goods. A word of caution: this is a project for the crown. Any price gouging by unscrupulous merchants will result in their being barred from further work. I assure you, Mage Kathy has a very ordered mind and pays close attention to details. She is also authorized to employ Truth Serum when questioning vendors. If we find overcharging, *in the least,* the punishment will be severe," explained Edward.

"We'll be encouraging the creation of small businesses in order to promote competition and keep prices down. I know that in Baize, a few large trading houses control most of the products and services. That's going to change. While I'm new to Baize, Mage Kathy has spent the last several years monitoring the King's accounts and conducting audits of town treasuries. Do *not* give her cause for concern."

"The engineers and apprentice magicians will be leaving here in two days to begin the effort. The 1st Company of the Franconian Royal Expeditionary Force will be leaving in two days, but there is a battalion of Baizian soldiers returning from Westport who should be here in about three days. Wizard Timothy will meet with them when they arrive and explain our project to them."

"One last word of caution, while these apprentice magicians are young, they all have some practical use of their magical abilities; and Mage Kathy and I will be increasing their knowledge of magic and its uscs. I would not advise testing them. A ten-year-old who knows the Dig spell can drop an assailant into a twenty-foot hole with a wave of her hand."

Minister Jasmine collected the Messenger Hawk from the message tower. *So, a message from King Donald*, she thought. Jasmine first replicated the wax seal and setting the replica aside, removed the actual seal cleanly with a Remove spell. The message said:

~~King Henry~~, My friend,

I recently made the acquaintance of Wizard Edward Francis of Franconia. He has informed us of the dangers posed to both our Kingdoms by these infernal dragons. Wizard Edward killed my Court Wizard, who was a dragon Changed One, and I am very grateful for his insight and assistance. I am moving my troops away from our cities along the border as a show of good faith. If you agree, I propose another exchange of Ambassadors. We should be together in this conflict with the dragons. Lastly, during his enlightening visit, Wizard Edward proposed a plan for stopping the spread of the Great Salt Flats in eastern Baize. This is a problem that has plagued us for decades, and I hope you will allow Wizard Edward to remain in Baize for a short time to oversee this vital project. If the Salt Flats expand further eastward, I fear that they will enter the Amber River, with adverse consequences for both our countries.

Donald, King of Baize

This will never do, thought Jasmine. Thinking carefully, she cast a Change spell that reworded the message. Satisfied with her adjustments, she rolled up the parchment and affixed the wax seal she had replicated earlier. She hurried into the Throne Room, where King Henry was meeting with his advisors, including Wizard Noland. "Your Majesty, I have just received a message for you from King Donald of Baize." Jasmine handed over the seemingly sealed scroll. The King opened the scroll and quickly scanned the message, his face reddening in anger the further he read.

"Just who does Donald think he is to speak to me in this manner? I ought to order an immediate invasion of Baize in response to this insult!" raged the King. "Excuse me, Your Majesty, might I see the message?" asked Wizard Noland. The angry King practically threw the parchment at Wizard Noland. Noland made a careful examination of the seal, then oddly sniffed the parchment. He then read the message:

Henry,

I have captured Wizard Edward Francis of Franconia, who you so unwisely sent to invade my kingdom. He has confessed to your sending these infernal dragons against us. I am increasing my troops along the border in preparation for your imminent attack. If one more Franconian soldier or magician crosses the Amber River, it will be war!

Donald, King of Baize

Improbably, Wizard Noland smiled at the message. "You find something humorous in this insult, Wizard Noland?" demanded the King. "Yes, Sire, I do," said Noland. "Jasmine, why don't you tell us what the message really said?" Jasmine puffed up with self-righteous indignation, "HOW DARE YOU—" she began before Noland murmured, *NECESSITAS,* as he crossed the fingers of his left hand. "I would never read a message intended for the K— for the K—" stuttered Jasmine, fighting the Compulsion spell. "It's no use, you know," said Noland coldly. "I know you're a dragon Changed One, and you've been giving the King bad advice for several years now. I just couldn't prove it until now."

Jasmine raised her right hand and began the incantation, *"TER—"* as Wizard Noland said,

"MORPHIOUS," while clapping his hands together. Instantly, Minister Jasmine was transformed into a marble statue.

The King sat back, pale and shocked. "I hope you're right about this Wizard Noland," was all he could say. "Your Majesty, Wizard Edward, and I have suspected Minister Jasmine of being a Changed One for some time now, but we had no proof until she provided it just now." "What proof?" asked the confused King. "All she did was hand me a message from King Donald of Baize!"

"Your Majesty, could I impose on you to smell the message parchment?" "What?" "Just take a sniff of the parchment and tell me what you smell. Trust me, it won't hurt you." The King somewhat reluctantly took the message scroll from Wizard Noland and gave it a brief sniff, "It smells like oranges." "Exactly," said Wizard Noland. "You see, Sire, the crown is not the only organization in Franconia that uses Messenger Hawks; magicians use them too. We find it a convenient way to communicate across long distances. Unfortunately, in the past, we have found that messages can be intercepted and re-written, causing unintended consequences."

"So what was your solution?" asked the King. "Some time ago, Edward and I developed a spell that, when applied to messages, would cause the ink to give off the scent of oranges if the message was altered in any way; even adding a comma would trigger the spell." "But this message is from King Donald, not Wizard Edward," said the King. "Nevertheless, Edward wrote at least part of this message, or at least cast the spell over it to prevent alteration."

"Can you restore it to its original text?" "Of course, Your Majesty." Noland retrieved the scroll and quietly said *CODA, MORPHIOUS.* The words on the parchment rearranged themselves, back to the original message.

~~King Henry~~, My friend,

I recently made the acquaintance of Wizard Edward Francis of Franconia. He has informed us of the dangers posed to both our Kingdoms by these infernal dragons. Wizard Edward killed my Court Wizard, who was a dragon Changed One, and I am very grateful for his insight and assistance. I am moving my troops away from our cities along the border as a show of good faith. If you agree, I propose another exchange of Ambassadors. We should be together in this conflict with the dragons. Lastly, during his enlightening visit, Wizard Edward proposed a plan for stopping the spread of the Great Salt

Flats in eastern Baize. This is a problem that has plagued us for decades, and I hope you will allow Wizard Edward to remain in Baize for a short time to oversee this vital project. If the Salt Flats expand further eastward, I fear that they will enter the Amber River, with adverse consequences for both our countries.

Donald, King of Baize

"Here is the message that King Donald penned, Sire." The King read the message, very much happier with this version. After thinking about it for a minute, he handed the scroll around for the rest of his advisors to read. "So, King Donald's Court Wizard was a Changed One, too. Now, I don't feel quite so foolish. Noland, when did you suspect Minister Jasmine?" "After Edward's return, Your Majesty. When Edward and I swept the palace, looking for Changed Ones, Jasmine stayed in conference with you and avoided our search. Since then, I have listened to her speech carefully; she never used contractions, and she always wore a heavy vanilla scent. Her report of the demise of the Royal Expeditionary Force was also suspicious, but without concrete proof, I knew that it would be difficult to convince you of her guilt."

"Well, I'm convinced now. Who do you recommend I replace her with?" "Sire, Mistress Katelyn, Jasmine's assistant, has always been most diligent and attentive to her security duties. I can think of no one better." "Very well. I shall take your recommendation. Is there anything further we need to discuss?" "Yes, sire, Marshall Guzman and I have a few things to tell you in private and I need to perform a final adjustment to Jasmine's statue before you move it outside." "What adjustment is that?" asked the King. "I need to remove a thin slice of marble between the head and shoulders of the statue, Sire. Just in case some dragon Changed One has any ideas about restoring the Minister to life." The King understood immediately. "Of course, Wizard Noland. You may proceed." Using a Remove spell, Noland removed a thin slice of the statue's neck; then he used an Adhesive spell to re-attach the head of the statue to the body.

"If there's nothing further, the rest of you Ministers are dismissed. If Wizard Noland or Marshall Guzman informs me of anything that concerns you, I'll let you know later." The remaining Ministers and counselors filed out of the Throne Room. Once everyone else had departed, the King asked, "So what secrets are you two keeping from me?" "Sire," began Marshall Guzman, "when Major Gerald gave you his report of the expedition to Springfield, he left something out because he didn't want Minister Jasmine to learn of it. You see, during the trip, Wizard Edward and Mage Curtis discovered how to convert the Force's army-issued cloaks into Concealment cloaks. They made one for every member of the Royal Expeditionary Force. It was because of these cloaks that they were able to sneak up on the dragons from behind."

"Remarkable. But, why didn't you want me to know about this?" asked the King. "Because Minister Jasmine would have learned about them, Sire," said Noland. "We were trying to keep this knowledge from her. I should also add, that I've had Concealment cloaks made for every magician in Franconia and plan to issue them to each Academy student once they pass the Sorcerer's Test." "Why?" asked the King.

"Sire, as you know, a Sorcerer can only cast and hold one spell at a time. If he or she is using a Concealment spell, then they can't cast another spell without dropping their concealment. With one of these cloaks, they can remain hidden and still cast a spell, doubling their effectiveness. The same applies to Mages and even Wizards." "I see," said the King. "What's the downside?" "You witnessed it at the Royal Ball, Your Majesty. One of the Royal Expeditionary Force's soldiers was a dragon Changed One, and Major Gerald issued him a Concealment cloak, which almost cost me my life," replied Marshall Guzman.

"Hmm," said the King. "Yes, I see." "At one time, I was considering asking for your permission to equip the entire Royal Guard with Concealment cloaks, Sire. Think of the advantage of having an invisible Army! However, after the Ball, I think it best to restrict the cloaks to the Royal Expeditionary Force and the magicians. Unless you'd like to have some for your Personal Guard..." "No," said the King. "The risk is too great for my Personal Guard to have them; they could be bribed. You say the entire Royal Expeditionary Force has them? How much did that cost?"

"The cost of the cloaks for the men was free, Sire, since Wizard Edward and Mage Curtis made them out of their existing cloaks. We did have to invest thirty-five golds for Concealment blankets for their horses, though. The cloaks were too short to cover the mounts." "You're saying we have them already?" "Yes, Your Majesty, at least 2nd Company has the Concealment blankets for their mounts. We also have enough for 1st Company when they return from Springfield." "Let me get this straight: you're saying that for a mere thirty-five golds, I have an invisible Royal Expeditionary Force?"

"Gek, the baby wants you," said Azure tiredly. Gek groaned, "Again? Does she never sleep?" "She sleeps plenty. What she does too much of is drink Dragon milk!" "Come here, little one," said Gek. The baby Dragon cheerfully ran to Gek and began climbing up his back and then down his wings, using her father like a jungle gym. "She certainly has a lot of energy," said Azure. "What she *doesn't* have yet is a *name*. You two really have to decide soon, or she will think "little one" is her name, and that is a *terrible* name for a dragon."

"I know, you are right," said Azure. "OK, how about Liza, after your mother, Gek?" "No! I am sorry, but I do not want to be reminded of her every time I look at my child. Maybe Liz?" "I have been thinking. Maybe we should name her after a Dragon-friend, like Anne." "Absolutely not," said Aqua forcefully, "Anne is a human name, not fit for a Dragon." "What if we added part of your name?" said Gek to Azure, ignoring Aqua. "How about Annaliz?" "Close, but not quite right," said Azure. "How about Annalise?" "Anna for short," confirmed Gek. "I like it."

"Come to Grandma, Annalise," said Aqua, "and we will go meet the other Dragon babies in the Clan."

After leaving the City Council chambers, Edward and Kathy rode back to the garrison to confer with Mage Curtis and Captain Smith. Wizard Timothy went immediately to the Springfield Healing Clinic to see if anyone needed his assistance. Once they were seated at the conference table, Edward asked, "How have things been going in my absence?" "It's been pretty quiet, actually," said Captain Smith, "no real disturbances. People are going about their business, merchants are paying their taxes, the City Enforcers have all returned to their jobs, and the Healing Clinic has only been treating minor bumps and bruises lately."

"Corporal Knox," said Edward, "anything in the shadows that we should know about?" "No, sir. It's been strangely quiet." "How are the Baizian apprentices doing?" asked Edward. Mage Curtis said, "Well, sir, they're all pretty young, twelve to eighteen, I would guess; they're all wondering why they're here and what's in store for them." "How many apprentices are there so far?" "Eighty-five, including the twenty you brought yesterday and the five that came in this afternoon," said Curtis. "Do you have a roster of all of their names?" "No sir," said Curtis, slightly embarrassed. "It never occurred to me to make a list of all their names." "That's even better," said Edward reassuringly. "After dinner tonight, I want you to send them in, to this office, one at a time. Mage Kathy and I will start a roster of each apprentice, where they're from, and their approximate skill level. Round up some parchment and quills, please. While we question them we'll also be checking to see if any of them are dragon Changed Ones. I anticipate there being one or two, and I want to be prepared. Once we have identified and dealt with all of the Changed Ones, we'll send the apprentices off to bed."

"What's been their routine?" asked Kathy. "We wake them up at a glass past dawn and feed them breakfast once the soldiers are done eating; then I've been teaching them the Wind and Dig spells. We've also been working on Weather shields," said Curtis. "Excellent!" said Edward. "How are their skills?" "Some of the older ones might be able to pass the test for Level Three, but most are equivalent to our Level Ones or Twos," said Curtis. "That's OK," said Edward, "they're mostly going to be using the Dig, Shield and Adhesive spells for the next six months or so. In case you're wondering, we're going to dig a fifty-mile wide by twenty-five-mile high reservoir to contain the Great Salt Flats and keep the salt-infused sand from getting into the Amber River."

"Here's what we're going to do tomorrow. After breakfast, I want all of the apprentices formed up in the courtyard in ranks, sorted by age— oldest to youngest. Then we'll have the apprentices pair off into teams of six. Once we get the teams established, Kathy and I will give them some instruction on the most effective way to use the Dig spell. As soon as First Company leaves the day after tomorrow, the apprentices, the engineers and I will be headed back to the Salt Flats to get started. Any questions?"

After dinner that evening, Wizard Edward and Mage Kathy seated themselves behind the conference table, facing the door to the conference room. Edward said, "When the apprentices enter, I'm going to ask them all the same series of questions: What is your name? How old are you? Where did you come from, and is that your hometown? And, can you cast the Dig, Wind and Adhesive spells? Please note their names and answers. I will then hand them this piece of parchment and ask them to read it to me." The parchment said:

I'm an apprentice magician from the Kingdom of Baize, and I'll be working on a project for the next several months.

"I don't understand," said Kathy. "I'm trying to find any dragon Changed Ones," explained Edward. "If there are any amongst the apprentices, they'll say, 'I *am* an apprentice magician from the Kingdom of Baize, and I *will* be working on a project for the next several months,' rather than using the contractions on the parchment. If one of them does that, I will immediately cast a Tether spell around them, binding their arms to their sides, so they can't cast a spell or transform. Then we'll give them a choice between a Binding spell or death." Kathy blanched, "You would kill a child?" "No," said Edward, "but I will kill an enemy dragon without hesitation."

There were three Changed Ones among the apprentices; two Fire dragons who readily agreed to the Binding spell, and one Stone dragon Changed One who would not. Edward removed the Stone dragon's head without hesitation or remorse. He would explain 'Todd's disappearance to the other apprentices in the morning. "Are you all right, Kathy?" Edward asked. Kathy turned and embraced him. She was trembling. "I'm sorry," she said softly, "I've never seen you kill anyone before. I wasn't in the room when you killed Louis, and Marissa was dead when we found her." "But you saw me kill the Stone dragon in the courtyard," said Edward. "That was a dragon, this looked like a twelve-year old boy!" she sobbed.

"And that is exactly how he wanted to appear," said Edward, "young, helpless, and afraid. But for all we know he was a hundred years old, ruthless, and deadly. If we had not acted, he might have killed us both and then hunted down all of the apprentices, just for sport."

Chapter Twenty-Five:

DEATH AND LIFE

L oren died the morning after her last interview with Celeste. She finally left the confines of her room and went for a walk around the Academy. She entered the stables and somehow managed to provoke one of the big horses into kicking her in the head. While her death was quick, it was probably not painless.

"I guess she was distraught over my tricking her into telling me the way for a human to transform into a dragon," said Celeste sadly. "Maybe," replied Wizard Noland, "but it was undoubtedly more than just that. She has not had a very happy life these past few years. The death of her co-conspirator Stuart, the loss of her hands and her confinement all played a part in her despair. Do not blame yourself, Celeste."

"It's just that I'd hoped that she would find a way to adapt, maybe serve as an intermediary between us and the dragons; that she could bring us to a peaceful resolution of this conflict!" said Celeste. "I had the same hopes," said Wizard Noland, "but now, that task may fall on your shoulders." "Mine?" asked Celeste, shocked. "Yours," confirmed Noland. "You have been named a dragon-friend. I do not know of another human with that distinction. The dragons may be bound not to harm Donovan or Andrew, but that doesn't make them 'friends.' On the contrary, I suspect the dragons may hate those two more than any human alive."

Andrew read the message again. He just couldn't comprehend what Wizard Noland was saying. *He and Donovan* were descendants of Wizard Amanda, and any surviving members of the Dragon Council were bound by magic not to harm them. The dragons also knew that Andrew was assigned to the HMS VALOR. He was curious about how they figured *that* out, but it explained why the dragon attacks on Franconian ships always ceased when the VALOR appeared. The dragons didn't want to risk injuring Andrew. Suddenly, his magical prowess didn't seem as impressive as it did yesterday.

Andrew walked down the passageway to the Commodore's cabin, knocking softly; he didn't want to disturb the Commodore if he was busy. "COME!" said the Commodore. Andrew entered to find a very unhappy commander. "Come on in, Andrew, I was just about to send for you. I just received this message from the Admiral, and I'm none too happy about it," said

Commodore Matthews, handing over a piece of parchment. Andrew read:

Commodore Matthews,

After due consideration of your last message, I am ordering you to take your Squadron and return to the area around the Coral Islands. We need to ascertain whether this 'truce' with the dragons is real, or some sort of ruse to make us overconfident. Do not attack the dragons or provoke them in any way, just determine if they will keep their word. Return to Sundock in two weeks and inform me of the results of your patrol.

H.C. Cross, Commander, Royal Franconian Navy

"Can you believe that?" raged the Commodore. "He wants us to go back to those damn islands, just to see if we can trust the dragons!" Andrew hesitated, finally, he said, "Sir, I also received a message, this one from Wizard Noland at the Wizards Academy. It says, well, here, you can read it for yourself." Andrew handed over the parchment.

Battle Mage Andrew,

Sorceress Celeste learned something of great importance from Loren. Apparently both you and Donovan are descendants of Wizard Amanda, the magician who was responsible for healing many of the poisoned dragons at the end of the last conflict. Loren said that a Binding spell was placed on the members of the Dragon Council, that any progeny of Wizard Amanda must be located and protected during the current conflict. This is undoubtedly why the dragons have been unwilling to attack your ship. I do not know how many dragons are impacted by this Binding spell, or what use we can make of the information, but it appears that the dragons know which ship you are on, and will be reluctant to attack the VALOR. I therefore recommend that you inform your superiors and <u>do not change ships.</u>

Noland

"Well, that certainly explains a few things," said Commodore Matthews. "It also explains why during that last attack, that dragon tried to protect you. If the truce is a ruse, we can probably use this information to our advantage somehow." "I think it shows us something else, Commodore," said Andrew thoughtfully. "What might that be?" "That dragons keep their word. That last dragon died to keep the other from harming me. I think we'll be quite safe on this next patrol."

After breakfast the eighty-four apprentices assembled in the courtyard. It took them a few minutes to sort themselves by age, from oldest to youngest, but they eventually managed it. Once they were arranged in the order that Edward wished, he addressed the young magicians. "Ladies and Gentlemen, I'm Wizard Edward and this is Mage Kathy. We will be your supervisors and instructors for the next several months. In case you haven't heard yet, we will be creating a giant hole in the ground, at the bottom edge of the Great Salt Flats. This hole will prevent the Salt Flats from expanding as they have been for the last several decades."

"We will be leaving here after breakfast tomorrow morning and heading for our camp site near the Salt Flats. There is already a contingent of Baizian Surveyors there, laying out the boundaries of the hole we're going to dig. Now, this project is not going to be quick or easy. I expect it to take eight or nine months at least. The King thinks it's going to take over a year, and he is coming here next year to check on our progress. I hope to be finished before he arrives."

"I know that this isn't what any of you expected to be doing this summer. Frankly, it's not what I expected either. So, in a moment, I will divide you up into six-person teams. Once we begin our work, we'll work in shifts, all day and all night. We will not stop for rain, heat, snow or ice— the digging will continue. In addition to the Dig spell, you will all master shields and the Adhesive spell. As time permits, Mage Kathy and I will provide you with other magical instruction, and some of you should certainly be ready for your Sorcerer's test when we're done."

"Now, I want you to count off from one to fourteen, each of you gets a number, after you reach fourteen, start over at one, remember what number you are. Begin." The confused apprentices counted off as Edward instructed. When they were done, Edward said, "All right, I want you to make fourteen rows, the number ones in the first row, the twos in the second, you get the idea. If my math is right, there should be six of you in each row. This is your Team. You will eat together, work together and sleep in the same tent. The way I have mixed you up, there should be a fair distribution of older and younger magicians in each team."

"A word of caution for you older magicians; just because someone is younger or physically smaller than you, do not assume that you can bully them. We have the same problem at the Wizards Academy in Franconia, and every year, an older student ends up in the infirmary because they underestimated the magical abilities of another student. On that note, magical duels or fights of any kind are absolutely prohibited, and will be severely punished."

"I want you all to spend the rest of the day getting to know your teammates, eat lunch together, pack your belongings. I would advise getting to bed early tonight. Tomorrow is going to be a busy day. Any questions?" A boy on Team 6 raised his hand, "Yes?" asked Edward. "Where's Todd? He never came back to the room last night."

Edward sighed. He'd hoped to avoid this conversation, but there was no getting around it now. "I'm going to tell you something that is a secret. You are not to tell any non-magical people this. Do you all understand?" Eighty-four heads nodded. "You all know about the dragon attacks, right? Well, the secret is that dragons can do magic. There are many of the spells that you will learn that dragons can conjure; including the Change spell. Over the past several years, some dragons have changed themselves into humans. Most of them are not a threat, they just had unhappy lives as dragons and prefer to live as humans. Others are not so kind."

"Todd was a Stone dragon Changed One. When Mage Kathy and I interviewed him last night, we discovered that he was a dragon. He refused to submit to a Binding spell not to hurt humans, and never to transform back into a dragon, so I was forced to kill him." The assembled apprentices gasped. "Are there other dragons among us?" asked one girl, looking around at the other apprentices. "A few," confirmed Edward, "but they're not dangerous. They're under a Binding spell. If they ever try to hurt anyone, they'll die. Instantly."

"Who are they?" asked another boy. "That's not something I'm prepared to share with you at this time. For now, they're your teammates. Don't try to root them out, you'll probably be wrong and accuse someone of being a dragon who isn't. Mage Kathy and I know who they are. That's all you need to know."

"Now, I want you all to go off and introduce yourself to your teammates. Eat lunch together, then start packing. Mage Kathy and I will meet you here tomorrow after breakfast. Don't leave the compound today."

Edward and Kathy wandered back to their room in the barracks. It was stifling hot, even in the shade of the courtyard. Kathy absently fanned herself with the elaborate fan that she'd purchased from Prestige Arms. Edward gazed at the fan intently. "That's a very fine fan you have there. May I see it?" he asked. Kathy reluctantly handed over the fan. Edward examined it briefly, then depressed the decorative pearl button, activating the hidden blade. "So, how is James these days?" he asked. Kathy froze. She realized that she didn't want to lie to Edward, and the truth was probably better anyway.

"James was fine when I met him a few months ago," she said finally. Edward raised his eyebrows, asking for an explanation. "King Donald and Wizard Louis sent me on a mission into Franconia to investigate the reports of a dragon," said Kathy. "Rather than ride all the way to Farmdale, I traveled by ship from Baize to Westport, then was lucky enough to book passage on the HMS UNSINKABLE bound for Fairview. The UNSINKABLE was the ship that transported the Royal Expeditionary Force from Fairview back to Kingston after your fight with the dragon. The soldiers couldn't help but tell their stories to the crew of the UNSINKABLE. I was able to learn a great deal from them, including about those wonderful crossbows."

Edward waited for Kathy to continue. "When the ship docked in Southport, I was discovered by a Mage named Faith who was headed to Kingston." "You met

Faith?" asked Edward. "Yes," said Kathy, "she detected my spark all the way from the dock. Rather than try to hide, I simply waited for her in my cabin. We had a fairly pleasant chat before she insisted on placing a Binding spell on me because I was too old to enter the Wizards Academy." Edward looked shocked, "You mean that you can't use magic to harm another? That could be a problem."

"No," said Kathy, "I convinced Mage Faith that, as an attractive magician herself, she should understand that women like us are frequently accosted by aggressive suitors, and that, should I agree to her Binding spell, I would be defenseless against such an attack." "So, what did Faith do?" "She modified the Binding spell, so that I can't '*unjustly*' use magic to harm another," explained Kathy. "Hmm. Yes, I've always found Wizard Faith to be a reasonable magician." "*Wizard Faith?*" asked Kathy.

"Yes. She took and passed the Wizard's Test the day after she arrived in Kingston and was assigned as the Gatekeeper and Martial Arts instructor for the Wizards Academy," said Edward. "Yes, she told me that, but she didn't know what happened to the previous Gatekeeper, she just said that he was very old." Edward humphed, "Stuart was a dragon Changed One. He died shortly after I removed both of his hands. Apparently, he'd been using Healing spells and Serums to maintain himself.

With no hands to perform spells with, and no access to Serums, he died of old age in a few short days." Kathy gasped.

"So, why did you continue on to Fairview?" persisted Edward. "Because I needed more and better information," said Kathy. "All the sailors knew was second-hand stories, and you know how soldiers like to exaggerate. I needed to talk to an eyewitness, plus, I wanted to get my hands on a crossbow if I could." "So, you went to Prestige Arms," said Edward. "Yes, and you'll be glad to know that, even though he thought you were dead, James refused to sell me a crossbow for three years." Edward smiled, "James's word has always been good. So, what did you do?"

"I left him a one silver deposit for the first commercially available crossbow. I'll need to go back in three years to pick it up," said Kathy. "So, why did you buy the fan?" asked Edward. "I was trying to soften him up so he'd be more likely to sell me the crossbow, but it didn't work. Still, the fan is a fine piece of craftsmanship." "Yes. James had it for years, but because of the cost, he was never able to sell it. How much did you pay for it?" Edward asked. "A gold," said Kathy, "but it's been worth every copper."

"Yes, I can detect a faint trace of blood on the blade, who did you use it on?" "Admiral Vandall's secretary,

Charolette, probably on orders from Wizard Louis, tried to push me out of my bedroom window one evening. Fortunately, I was holding my fan in my hand. I was too startled to conjure a spell, but one push of that button and Charolette was dead on my floor," said Kathy. "What did you do then?" asked Edward. "I used a Remove spell to dispose of her body, and pretended that nothing ever happened."

"I take it that the threats to your life didn't stop," said Edward softly. "No, I was constantly finding my food or water was poisoned. Once I found a sand viper under my bed. I assume it was Louis's doing but was never able to prove anything. I was very glad when you made that snake drink his own Death Serum," said Kathy. "But why did you remove his head?" Edward grinned and said, "The last lesson that we teach students after they pass the Sorcerer's Test in Franconia, is to never assume that an enemy is dead unless his or her head is removed from their body. I have personally been assumed to be dead twice. I hope to never have to dig myself out of a grave again. It's not as easy as it sounds." Kathy shuddered.

"So, did you go to Farmdale?" asked Edward. "No. There was no need. There were plenty of people in Fairview who either fled from Farmdale and the dragon, or knew others who had. While I was in Fairview, I learned that the borders between Franconia and Baize had been closed. I immediately hopped on a ship bound for Westport. Unfortunately, once I got there, I couldn't get back across to this side of the border." "So, what did you do?" "I stood at the end of the pier and cast a Tether around a Baizian merchant ship that was leaving from our side of the port. After being dragged through the water for a few hundred yards, I released the Tether and swam to our side. Then I commandeered a Baizian Naval ship to take me back to Baize. The Captain was less than pleased."

"I bet. So, how did you come by the crossbow? I assume it was you?" asked Edward. Kathy grinned slyly. "I came across a drunken Franconian soldier who had just been tossed out of a tavern in Westport for being unable to pay his bill. I offered him two golds for his crossbow, one gold to settle his debt with the tavern owner, and one gold to pay the fine his Captain threatened him with if he lost his crossbow. He was so drunk, I could have probably just spelled him to sleep and taken it, but that didn't seem right." Edward just shook his head in amazement. He handed her back her fan and said, "Until we can get this Binding spell off you, how about you let me take care of any aggressive suitors for the time being. Other than myself, of course." Kathy smiled, "That sounds like an excellent plan."

"Gek, tomorrow we need to leave to attend the Dragon Council. The full moon is in two days," said Cobalt. "So soon?" "Yes. They say time flies when you have a newborn," chuckled Cobalt. "Who is coming with us?" "The Clan has formally elected me Chief, and Sky is the other member of the Clan who will serve on the council." "Is Azure coming?" "No. She needs to stay here with Anna. In a few days, Anna should be strong enough to swim out of the cavern. She needs to see the sun and become familiar with the island and the sea. It is not healthy for a baby Sea Dragon to remain in the caves for too long."

"Does Azure know?" asked Gek. "Yes, and I must admit, she is none too happy about being left behind, but Anna could not make the trip. They will be fine." Gek nodded and walked down to the cavern where Azure was resting. She sat up as he entered. "You heard?" she asked. "Yes. Do not worry. I will be back in just a couple of days." "What do you think the Council will do when they learn about our truce with the humans?"

"I doubt they will be very happy about it. Besides, there is always a chance that the humans will reject the truce and continue their attacks," said Azure. "I hope not," said Gek. "What? I thought you wanted to avenge your mother!" said Azure. "I do. But now that we have a baby, I am worried for her safety. Face it, Anne knows which island we live on, and where the entrance to the cavern system is. If the humans burn Acropo like they did Perfo, we could have real problems." "What about your idea of Concealment spells and rocks?" asked Azure. "That should still work," said Gek, "but the human magic-users have shields. It might not work as well as I thought it would. It should certainly surprise them once, but these humans are surprisingly adaptive."

Gek, Cobalt and Sky left for the quarry that evening. They made good time and stopped just east of the Crimson River. Dinner was fish from the river, of course. At least Gek preferred freshwater fish to fish from the sea. They took turns on watch the next day. Being so close to the river, there was always a chance that a human could wander by and discover them. The day passed slowly and as night fell, the dragons took flight, reaching the quarry well before moonrise.

When they arrived, they found Bliz and Frost, the two Snow Dragon members of the Dragon Council. Two Fire Dragons arrived next, Rose and Fern. Neither was the Dragon who had represented the Fire Dragons at the last Council meeting. The Stone Dragons arrived last (of course) Gek recognized Jasper, but the other

Stone Dragon was not Amber, the Stone Dragon who attended the last Dragon Council. Also missing was the Stone Dragon Queen whose name no one knew. The Dragons milled around, waiting for someone to take charge, finally, Cobalt said, "Are we all here?" The other Dragons all nodded, so Cobalt continued, "Very well, I declare this meeting of the Dragon Council open. Who would like to speak first?"

Rose, the Fire Dragon stepped forward, "I am Rose, the new Chief of the Fire Dragon Clan. I have come to demand to know what the other Dragon Clans are doing in this war! The Fire Dragons have suffered many casualties, including our Chief, and also my mate, since we last met. What have the rest of you been doing? The Fire Dragons will not fight this war alone!"

"Alone? The Sea Dragons have lost over *fifty* of our Clan. Do not talk to me of fighting the war alone! What have the Stone and Snow Dragons contributed to this effort?" Jasper raised himself up to his full height and said, "We too have lost several members of our Clan, and there are fewer of us left than any of you!" The three Dragon Clans all turned to look at the two smaller Snow Dragons. "We were waiting for orders that never came!" said Frost. Our Clan is even now poised at the edge of the Snow Fields awaiting our orders to attack!"

"So, you have done nothing!" raged Rose. The Dragon Clans all began arguing amongst themselves about who had suffered more and which Clans were shirking. There seemed no end in sight to this argument when Ard uncurled from his position near the quarry wall and roared, "ENOUGH!" The Dragons quieted, looking expectantly for some wise council from the ancient Dragon. "It is clear that Victor's plan has failed. The humans are not fighting each other! I do not know why this has not come to pass, but it is clear that we need a new plan."

"Whatever the new plan is, it may have to exclude the Sea Dragons. We have agreed to a temporary truce with the humans. If they do not attack us, we will not attack them." "Why would you ever agree to such a foolish truce?" asked Rose. "During our last battle with the humans, our Clan Chief, Teal, was killed, along with twenty others; many more were wounded. We captured a human magic-user and forced her to heal our wounded brothers, but she insisted on a Binding spell of her own. None of the thirty Sea Dragons she healed can kill a human. If they do, they will die."

"Then we fight on land," said Jasper. "We are not prepared to surrender just because the Sea Dragon Clan is weak!" "Nor are we!" shouted Rose. The Snow Dragons merely nodded their agreement. "Perhaps there is another way," said Ard quietly. "If we cannot get the humans to fight each other, maybe we can at least keep one side neutral." The assembled Dragons considered his words. "Which human kingdom is stronger?" asked Ard. "I believe it is the humans on the east side of the Amber River," said Gek, speaking for the first time.

"I concur," said Rose. "The humans on our side of the river are weak and scattered." "Very well," said Ard, "then we ignore the humans on this side of the river, and focus on those to the west. Cobalt, I suggest that you arrange for your temporary truce with the humans to be more permanent. If a Binding spell is required, make sure it is sufficiently vague so that we can exploit it later." Cobalt nodded his understanding.

"Bliz and Frost, we need the Snow Dragons to begin attacking the human cities on the west side of this river. Start with those towns closest to the Snow Fields. Rose, Jasper, you know what to do. Our goal is to either destroy the humans, or make them sue for peace on our terms. Does anyone else have anything to add?"

"I do," said Gek. "I have thought of a way to attack the humans without being seen." "Really," sneered Rose, "and what would a Great Dragon *child* know of war?" Gek rose to his full height, dwarfing the argumentative Fire Dragon. "I know that if you cast a Concealment spell you can drop trees, stones or other heavy objects on human ships, houses or formations of soldiers without being seen and attacked. You could also use it to get close before attacking with fire breath!"

Rose and the others considered Gek's words. Finally, Rose said, "I apologize, Great One. That is indeed an attack strategy worthy of a Great Dragon. It could be a great advantage. You are clearly wise beyond your years." "If there is nothing else, I suggest we all return to our Clans and prepare for the next phase of the conflict," said Ard.

Just then, Ig, the Great Dragon whose family lived on the eastern shore of Lake Ford in Baize arrived. "IG!" shouted Ard, "It is so good to see you! I thought you were lost!" "Well met, Ard. It has been many decades since I last saw you. I have come at the request of Lumen, a Stone Dragon Changed One I met while flying over the town of Lakeshore. I believe he said that, in his human form, he was the Court Wizard of the Kingdom of Baize. Lumen asked me to change into human form and search the town of Oceanside, looking for any other Dragon Changed Ones," said Ig.

"And what did you find?" asked Fern. "There are many Stone and Fire Dragon Changed Ones living in Oceanside, and also in the town of Lakeshore. In Baize, magic-users do not actively seek out those with the spark of magic, so it is easier for a Dragon Changed One to escape detection," replied Ig. "That is significant," said Gek. "In Franconia, the humans have magic-users in every city whose job it is to find those with the spark and send them to their wizard's school, whether they be willing or not."

"How could you know this?" asked Bliz. "Because I was captured by one while I was in human form in the city of Grotton. I was bound, paralyzed, and put in a coach taking me to the wizard school. If my mate, Azure, had not rescued me, I would be there right now," said Gek.

"This is an interesting development," said Ard. "Ig, do you know why the magic-users in Baize do not seek out others with the spark?" "I am not positive, but it could be because magic-users are esteemed in Baize. If someone believes they have the spark, they immediately come forward to be tested. It sounds like, in Franconia, some potential magic-users hide their spark for fear of being discovered," said Ig.

"This means that there may be many more Changed Ones in Baize than we hoped!" said Gek. "Maybe," said Ig. "However, not all of the Changed Ones will be willing to help us in this conflict." "It is much the same here," said Gek sadly. "Many of the Changed Ones that Azure and I found were happy with their lives as humans, and would not help us fight. Some even had human mates and children."

"We will need to search out any Changed Ones in Baize that will help us," said Cobalt. "That task must fall to the Fire and Stone Dragon Clans. I will have my Clan search for any Sea Dragon Changed Ones living along the coast of Baize. Our truce with the humans does not apply to those in Baize, and we have made that clear to the Franconians."

"That is good to know," said Rose. "For now, I suggest that the Snow Dragon Clan begin attacking the humans in Baize. It is past time for them to engage." The other Dragons nodded in agreement, and Bliz said, "Very well. We will attack soon."

"One last thing," said Ig. "Lumen informed me that a number of Dragons have moved to the western end of Baize, beyond the Great Desert. I know that some Dragons I knew flew off to explore that area, but none ever returned. It may be that there is a Dragon colony at the extreme western edge of Baize that none of us know about. Or it could be that there was no prey and all of the dragons that headed west perished in the desert. As a Dragon with two children, this was a task I am unwilling to undertake. Someone else will have to investigate this possibility. Where is Lumen, by the way? I expected to find him here."

"Lumen was discovered and killed by a human magic-user," said Jasper. "It is most unfortunate, since he was deep in the human's councils."

With nothing left to discuss, the dragons dispersed quickly, each wishing to be under cover before sunrise. Gek walked over to Ard and said, "Ard! You are still alive! It is so good to see you!" Ard smiled grimly, "Yes, Gek. I am alive for the moment, but it took all my strength just to get here and yelling at those idiot Stone and Snow Dragons has sapped my remaining strength. Where is Azure? I expected to see her here." "She is on Acropo with our daughter, Annalise," said Gek proudly.

"A daughter! How wonderful. Now I know that the Great Dragon line will not die out, especially since Ig is still alive and has a family of his own. Tell me, how did you discover that you could attack while under a Concealment spell?" Gek explained about Anne, and how they returned her to her ship, and how Sky sank a ship by dropping the mast onto it from a great height. "You have both done well," said Ard, "but it is time to say goodbye."

"Goodbye?" asked Gek. "I am fading fast, Gek. I guess three hundred years is the natural life span of a Great Dragon, and my time is almost up." Cobalt came forward and said, "Maybe I can help. I watched the human magician, Anne, closely as she healed many of my injured brothers. I think I can heal some of your afflictions."

"If you can do so, I would be grateful. I would really like to see my great-granddaughter," wheezed Ard. Cobalt moved to Ard's side and, placing his hands on Ard's side, said, *"SALVARE."* Instantly, Ard's moss-covered scales fell off and were replaced with bright shiny gold ones, Ard's labored breathing eased and his twisted and misshapen toes straightened, his talons lengthened and turned a glossy black.

"Cobalt! That is wonderful! I feel a hundred years younger! Thank You!" Ard turned to Cobalt only to find him prone on the ground, unconscious. "Cobalt!" shouted Gek. "He is all right," said Ard. "He just put too much power into healing me. I have seen this before, when human magic-users put too much of their power into a spell. He will be fine, but he may sleep for days, maybe even a week. This is not a spell that Dragons normally use, and I had many ailments to heal. I will stay with Cobalt, but you two must return to the Coral Islands and arrange the truce with the humans. We will be along once he wakes up." Gek and Sky reluctantly agreed and flew off toward the east, heading back to the Coral Islands.

Chapter Twenty-Six:
CHANGES

The Royal Expeditionary Force pulled out of Springfield just after dawn. It was a bittersweet parting, with several of the soldiers leaving behind girlfriends and lovers that they had become attached to during their stay in the city. Edward spoke to Curtis as they prepared to depart, "Take care of yourself on the way home. There are still angry dragons about. At least you should not have to worry about Baizian soldiers. Here, please deliver this message to Donovan for me."

Curtis took the message and placed it in his saddlebags. "How long will you remain here?" he asked. "I'm not entirely sure," said Edward, "at least until we get most of the reservoir built, or King Henry recalls me. Have you thought about what you would like your next assignment to be? I doubt that the King will let you remain with the Royal Expeditionary Force. Especially when he learns you can cast the Seeing spell."

"Actually, I had hoped to remain in Kingston; you see there is this girl…" Edward laughed, "I understand completely! Actually, I have my eye on a girl myself. I believe that the Kingston Regional Mage had not been replaced prior to our departure. That position may still be open." "I will certainly ask for it then. Well, goodbye, Edward. Good luck with the digging, and the courting," Curtis said with a wink. "Goodbye, Curtis, take care of my horse."

"Goodbye, Dirk. Try and stay out of trouble," said Edward. "Farewell, Sir Wizard. I'm sure we'll meet again." The 1st Company headed out of town, moving swiftly, back the way they came. Behind him, Edward could hear the sounds of the apprentice magicians loading up. The engineers were helping, but with eighty-four young apprentices and only ten engineers, it was taking longer than Edward had planned. When the last of the baggage was loaded Edward made an announcement. "If you need to use the privy, now is the time. We will not be stopping until we reach our campsite, about two glasses north of here." Several red-faced students quickly climbed down out of the wagons and ran for the barracks.

As they were preparing to depart, Wizard Timothy rode up. "Are you sure you don't want me to come with you?" "No, Timothy. Your place is here. Besides, Mage Kathy's staff will be returning in a couple of days to set up shop. The procurement office will be here in Springfield. I want to give the approaching Baizian battalion time to get settled in before we return and set up the office. While we're at the construction site, we'll figure out what kind of supplies and services we'll need, then we'll start posting notices to let the merchants know what sort of goods we'll be purchasing. I would appreciate it if you could gather up any late-arriving apprentices and find an empty barracks building where they can all stay together. I expect about twenty more. I'll be back next week to collect them and take them out to the construction site. By then I should have a better idea of what we're up against."

"Other than gather them up, is there anything else you'd like me to do?" asked Timothy. "You could smell them all and see if any of them are dragon Changed Ones. The same goes for the soldiers in the arriving battalion. I doubt we've seen the last dragon Changed One."

The HMS VALOR made its second lap around the Coral Islands with no excitement. The lookouts had spotted Sea dragons watching their ships sail up from Sundock, but so far there had been no attacks, not even an underwater bump. As night fell, the Commodore ordered his small fleet to move south, out of sight of the islands. Once anchored, he summoned Andrew and Anne to his cabin.

"So, it seems like the truce is holding," said the Commodore. "I'd like your thoughts on the matter." "Sir," said Andrew, "I'm not surprised that it's holding here, close to the islands. I don't know if the dragons here have been able to spread the word about the truce farther north, or to the dragons in the Low Sea. For that matter, I'm not even sure that their leader, Cobalt? Cobalt can speak for all of the Sea dragons. He may just be in charge of the ones that live on the islands. Maybe we should head farther north and see if we get a different reception."

"Can't," said the Commodore, "My orders are to be back in Sundock a little over a week from now, we don't have time to sail very far north and still be back in time." "I guess, we should just stay around here then," opined Anne. "We could move closer to the islands, but I'm not sure what else we can do. I wonder how the other Squadrons are faring?"

"I got no report," said Commodore Matthews, "and without any way to communicate between Squadrons, we won't know anything until they make port and inform command of what's happening in their patrol sectors. Well, get some sleep. We'll stay here tonight."

The morning dawned bright and clear, without a cloud in the sky. At just past eight bells in the morning, Andrew heard a lookout shout, "DRAGON HO!"

Andrew and Anne rushed up on deck and spotted an aqua-blue Sea dragon headed straight for the HMS VALOR.

"MAN YOUR BATTLE STATIONS! CREWS TO THE RAIL! PREPARE TO REPEL BOARDERS!" roared the Commodore. "HOLD YOUR FIRE!" screamed the dragon. The bewildered sailors looked to the Commodore and Andrew. "Let's hear what he has to say," suggested Andrew. "CLEAR THE AFT DECK! MAKE A HOLE!" ordered the Commodore. Sailors rushed to clear a space for the dragon who landed roughly on the deck. The dragon shook his head to clear it, then *rippled.* Before the astonished crew's eyes, the Sea dragon transformed into a naked woman.

"Celeste?" asked Anne. Celeste came forward and gave her sister a hug. "Yes, it's me. Please tell the men not to shoot, can I borrow your cloak?" "STAND DOWN!" shouted Andrew. The crewmen lowered their crossbows and slowly began returning to their duties, but they couldn't help staring at the nearly naked Sorceress that had just landed on their ship in dragon form.

The Commodore came forward cautiously, "Do you know this young woman?" "Commodore, this is my twin sister, Celeste," said Anne. "Your sister is a dragon?" "No, Commodore, but I've learned how to transform into one using the Change spell," Celeste replied. Andrew looked shocked. "You used the Change spell to transform into a dragon? Wasn't that extremely dangerous?"

"Not once Loren told me how to do it," replied Celeste. "Loren told you how to transform into a dragon? Why?" asked a confused Andrew. "She didn't mean to; I tricked it out of her by pretending to be too stupid to understand. The teacher in her just overcame her better judgement." "Incredible!" said Anne. "Well, Loren was so distraught that she managed to kill herself the next day. I felt horrible."

"Ahem," said Andrew, noticing the stares of the crew, "Commodore, I think we should take this discussion to your cabin." The Commodore shook himself like a wet dog and said, "Of course, you're right Andrew. This way Sorceress." They proceeded to the Commodore's cabin where a blanket was found for Celeste and they all sat down. "How did you find us?" asked Andrew. "Oh, it's easy from the air. I knew you were somewhere around the Coral Islands, so I just looked around. It probably would have been much harder to find you at night. Unless you had lights on the deck."

"Hmm, we'll have to change that. I'm sure you're right, a deck light on a dark ocean would be seen for miles," said the Commodore. "Anyway, I didn't want to surprise you by landing on your ship in the middle of the night. I might've been shot!" said Celeste. "True enough," said Anne.

"This is an incredible breakthrough!" said Andrew. "We can change ourselves into dragons!" "To what end?" asked the Commodore. "Well, sir, as dragons, we could send messages to other ships in the squadron, or even back to the Admiralty. Of course, the ships would have to be able to recognize friendly, messenger dragons from hostile ones." "That's true. So we won't be able to make use of this capability until all the Captains know that we have magicians that can transform into dragons. How will we tell the messenger dragons from enemies?"

"The messengers could all be Sea dragons! With the truce, the dragons shouldn't be able to trick us!" "Truce?" asked Celeste. "Yes," explained Anne, "after the last battle, I was swept overboard and ended up on the beach of the southernmost island. A dragon Changed One found me and thought I was you." "Azure?" "No, Gek," said Anne. "I met Azure later," Anne explained how she healed the injured Sea dragons, the truce she agreed to with Cobalt, and how the Admiral had sent the Squadron back out to see if the truce was real.

"How do you know Gek and Azure?" Andrew asked Celeste. Celeste blushed, "Gek was the boy I was transporting from Grotton to Kingston. He was captured by Mage Charles while he was in human form. Azure attacked the coach to rescue him, but the horses bolted at the sight of a dragon. Eventually, Azure used the Dig spell to stop the carriage but we ended up being catapulted end-over-end. Gek, who said his name was Jed, was badly injured and Azure did not know how to help him. After I healed him, they named me a dragon-friend and let me go.

"Then why did you get sent back to the Academy?" asked Anne. Celeste reddened, "Because I lied to Mage Charles about what happened. I told him it was bandits that attacked the coach. I didn't think he'd believe me if I said it was dragons."

"So, why are you here?" asked Andrew. "Mainly to see if it would work, finding a ship at sea, I mean. Also, Wizard Noland had a message for you Andrew. I'm so sorry, but your mother passed away recently. He would have gotten word to you sooner, but he only learned of her passing a few days ago and he didn't know how to get a message to you."

Rachel rolled over and said, "I have to get up now." "Why? We still have half a glass before Leo gets here," grumbled Donovan. "I know, but Wizard Noland wants to see me before breakfast this morning." "Why?" "I have no idea. Maybe he wants to order more Concealment cloaks." "He could have waited until *after* breakfast for that," said Donovan. "But he didn't. Now let me go, I have to get dressed!"

Rachel disengaged from their embrace and padded off to the shower. Donovan considered joining her, but decided that if he did that, she *would* be late for her meeting with Wizard Noland. As Rachel was hurriedly getting dressed, Donovan asked, "Do you believe in short engagements?" Rachel stopped lacing up her boot and said, "Why do you ask?" "Because Wizard Noland told me that I'm going to be taking the Sorcerer's Test soon; and after I pass, I'll be assigned to the 3rd Franconian Regiment in Fairview, and you'll be going to the Fairview Regional Mage's Office. I only know two people in Fairview. I'd rather get married here at the Academy so our friends and your parents can attend."

"What about your father?" asked Rachel. "I'm sure he'll try to make it, but if he can't I'm sure he'll understand. Besides, I have no idea how long he's going to be in Baize." "You make excellent points, and I shall give your proposal every consideration," said Rachel.

She gave him a kiss, then headed out the door. Donovan lay in bed for a minute, then decided that he might as well get up. He showered, made the bed, and headed over to the Level Three kitchen. Even though he was engaged to a Mentor, he still had to eat in his assigned dorm.

Donovan was just finishing his second cup of tea when Rachel entered carrying a piece of parchment. "What did Wizard Noland want?" asked Donovan. With trembling hands, Rachel raised the parchment and read formally:

"Level Three Donovan Francis, you are hereby officially notified that on Twoday morning you will begin the Sorcerer's Test. You will begin by casting a spell of your choosing that must last for three days. If, on Endday morning, your spell is still active, the rest of the test will commence.

Signed, Noland, Headmaster, Franconia Wizards Academy."

When they landed on Acropo, Sky informed the rest of the Sea Dragon Clan that the Dragon Council had decided that their truce with the humans should be extended (within reason), but that any agreement must be vague enough to resume hostilities if conditions warranted. There was some grumbling among the dragons who were not confined by Anne's Binding spell, but the majority of the Clan agreed that, if the humans would leave them alone, they saw no reason to continue the conflict.

When Gek broke the news to Azure she became angry. "They killed my father, and we are just supposed to let it go? What idiot proposed this plan, that Stone Dragon Queen?" "No. Ard, and I think the Stone Dragon Queen is dead; at least she was not at the Dragon Council," replied Gek. "Ard? How did he look?" "Like he was dying. It is OK, though. Cobalt healed him. Now he looks a hundred years younger!" "Where is he? I would like to give him a piece of my mind," said Azure angrily. "He is still with Cobalt in the quarry. After Cobalt healed him, he swooned and lost consciousness. Ard said he has seen it before; that Cobalt just put too much power into the healing spell. He said that Cobalt will sleep for several days before he wakes up. He sent Sky and me back because Ard says we need to formalize the truce before the next stage of the plan," said Gek.

"And just what is this *next stage* of the plan?" "The Snow, Fire and Stone Dragons are going to attack the humans on the west side of the river. The plan is to keep the humans on this side of the river from going to the aid of their fellow humans, to keep them neutral." "Humph, what else happened at the council?" "I told them about my idea of using a concealment spell to sneak up on humans in order to drop heavy objects on their ships, buildings, or soldiers. Rose, the new Fire Dragon Chief, said that I was 'wise beyond my years,'" said Gek with a smug smile. "You are only *five*, Gek. That is not a huge compliment,"

"We also met Ig, another Great Dragon who lives with his mate and two children on the shore of some lake in Baize. He said that there are many, many Changed Ones in Baize because there are no Regional Mages seeking out those with the spark. He also spoke about a possible Dragon colony in the extreme western area of Baize, beyond the Great Desert."

Just then, Sky entered the cave. "I am sorry to intrude, but I need a word. The Clan has decided to follow the recommendation of the Dragon Council and make a formal agreement with the humans. Since you two are known to them, we would ask you to go and negotiate the treaty. "US?" asked Azure. "Why us? Surely there are older, more experienced members of the Clan!" "There are," confirmed Sky, "but you are both known and trusted by at least some of the humans. We would have sent Cobalt, but he is not available. There is only you,"

"Fine," said Azure. "When should we leave?" "Tomorrow morning will be soon enough," said Sky. "I am sure Gek is fatigued after the long flight here." "We will be ready. Anne said that a white flag or cloth is the human sign for a truce or parlay. We will need one. Also, I will need some human clothes to wear. I am *not* going to negotiate a treaty while naked!" Sky laughed and said that he would see what he could come up with. As Gek was preparing to sleep, Azure asked him to go and make her a manta ray and seaweed salad for dinner.

The next morning as Gek and Azure prepared to depart, Azure hugged Annalise and said, "You be a good girl and stay with grandma. Mommy will be back in a few days." The baby dragon seemed to sense the parting and grabbed onto Azure's leg. "No, Anna, Mommy has to go out. You stay here." Eventually Aqua had to pry the baby dragon away from Azure as she cried. Gek and Azure hurried from the cave to get away from the sounds of their daughter's cries.

Once on the surface, they found Sky and several of the other adult Sea Dragons waiting. "Here is a white gown that washed up on the shore some years ago. It should serve as both a white flag and an outfit for you to wear. I cannot advise you on how to bargain with the humans since none of us were alive during the negotiations for the last treaty. Just do your best. Last time, we agreed not to *eat* the humans, but we did not agree not to *kill* them. You could agree not to *sink* their ships, but that does not mean that we could not attack them. Be cunning. One thing we cannot abide is a human outpost on one of our islands. Good luck."

Azure grasped the white gown in her claws and hoped it would fit her human form, she still felt bloated and uncomfortable. They flew south, scanning the ocean for the human ships. After about an hour, Gek spotted three ships, bobbing at anchor. "Which ship should we land on?" shouted Azure. "The VALOR! I want to get a look at this Andrew we are supposed to protect!" Azure nodded her agreement and they circled the ships until they identified the HMS VALOR.

"I will land first and transform, wait for my signal before you land!" Azure nodded. Gek flew low over the ship and landed on the aft part of the deck, away from the fearsome Seabows. He immediately changed into his human form and put on his tattered and bloody clothes.

"You really should get some new clothes," said a voice behind him. Gek turned and saw Celeste and Anne, standing side by side. "Anne?" he asked. "Yes?"

they both answered, grinning. Gek shook his head, sure that he was hallucinating. "It's all right Jed," said Celeste, "both Anne and I are on board. Is that Azure up there with the white flag?" "Yes," said Gek, "she is waiting for my signal that it is safe to land."

"It is perfectly safe," said Andrew, walking up to stand beside Celeste and Anne. "I am Mage Andrew." "I am Gek, and I promise that we will do no harm while we are here. We have come to negotiate a truce between the Sea Dragon Clan and those of you who dwell on the east side of the Amber River." "What about the Baizians?" asked Andrew. "You mean those humans on the other side of the river? That is a different Kingdom than yours, and a different agreement will be reached with them at the appropriate time," said Gek.

"Very well," said Commodore Matthews, stepping forward. "I am Commodore Matthews, commander of this ship. I promise that the men under my command will do you no harm during our negotiations." Gek waved his hand in the air and Azure nodded and began her descent to the ship. She landed on the aft deck as Gek had and began transforming when something went horribly wrong.

Instead of the instant transformation common with the Change spell, Azure transformed bit by bit. First, her wings disappeared, then her human legs replaced her dragon talons, then her arms, torso and head. Her tail vanished last. Azure screamed in pain and fell to the deck, blood and water running down her legs. Gek raced to her, frantic, "Azure, what is wrong?" "Hurts," gasped Azure, "hurts, hurts, hurts!" Then Anne, Celeste and Andrew were there, checking her injuries and offering words of comfort. "Let's get her below," said Anne, "Hurry!"

They carried Azure below, out of the blazing sun, to the Commodore's cabin, which was the biggest on the ship. Andrew swept the table clean of maps, quills and books with a gust of wind as the two Sorceresses assessed Azure's condition. Gek tried to edge his way into the cabin but there just wasn't enough room for five people in the confines of the cabin.

"Gek, Andrew, OUT!" said Celeste in a commanding voice that would brook no argument. The two men hastily left the cabin and Anne slammed and bolted the door behind them. They could hear Azure crying through the heavy oak door. A moment later Anne opened the door and said, "We need clean towels and hot water, immediately!" Andrew rushed forward to the laundry, Gek a step behind. Grabbing a handful of what passed for 'clean' towels on a ship, Andrew continued forward to the galley where he found a pot of water heating on the stove. He handed the towels to Gek and grabbed the pot of water, scalding his hands in the process.

They rushed back down the passageway and knocked on the door. Celeste opened the door just wide enough to take the pot and the towels, then slammed it shut again. Gek was beside himself, "What are they doing in there?! I have to help her!" "Calm yourself," said Andrew, projecting an aura of confidence and control. "Anne and Celeste are skilled healers. Azure is in good hands."

Azure's screams went on for almost a full glass, then suddenly stopped. Gek was overwhelmed, fearing the worst. Then the door opened and Anne emerged, wiping blood and fluids off her hands. She looked at Gek and smiled, "Congratulations! It's a boy!" Gek fainted.

Robert Jones

END OF BOOK III

Watch for Book IV, The Conflict of Interests

Coming soon.

Chapter One:
THE SORCERER'S TEST

Donovan grimaced as the fireball sped toward him. He had no idea whether it was a Seeming, a ball of flaming sawdust, or something else Wizard Noland, the hulking, dark-skinned Headmaster of the Franconian Wizards Academy, had conjured up to test him with. The Sorcerer's Test had really begun three days ago, on Twoday morning when Donovan had to cast a spell that would last for three days. Donovan had chosen the Tracer spell, the first spell that he'd learned when he arrived at the Wizards Academy a little over three years ago. On Endday morning, after Wizard Daniel had confirmed that Donovan's staff still had a Tracer spell on it, the test had begun in earnest.

The Sorcerer's Test had begun with a Military History exam, but it was unlike any test he had ever taken at the Academy. Wizard Daniel, a seasoned Battle Mage who had just recently passed the Wizards Test and been added to the Academy Faculty, was stocky, like a weight lifter, with dark hair. He walked with a limp from a battle injury that never quite healed right, but he had an easy smile and was a very good instructor.

He arrived at the Lecture Hall precisely at the appointed time and posed the following situation: An enemy force, consisting of a Brigade of Cavalry, supported by six Fire dragons, was advancing on Kingston. Using the forces known to be available in the city, plan the defense of the city. Include specific actions designed to protect the King and his five key Ministers. Donovan was given two hours to complete this task. Wizard Daniel turned the hourglass and limped out of the classroom.

Donovan started by making a list of the forces involved. On the enemy side, a Brigade of Cavalry was two Regiments; each regiment had four Squadrons, and each Squadron had three thirty-five-man companies, called Troops. So, a little over 900 horsemen, if he included the Brigade and Squadron staffs, plus six dragons. Donovan knew that Franconian Battalions normally acted independently. Deciding that, if he were the enemy commander, he would attack with six Battalions, each supported by a dragon, and keep two Battalions in reserve. Oddly, Wizard Daniel had not mentioned any enemy magicians. In Franconia, each Battalion was assigned a Sorcerer (who could only cast one spell at a time), and each Regiment a Battle Mage (who could cast two spells simultaneously). Suspecting a trick, Donovan listed two Mages and eight Sorcerers in his Enemy Forces list.

Under Friendly Forces, Donovan knew that there were normally two Franconian Regiments, the 1st and 2nd, stationed in Kingston. Each Regiment had three Battalions of Infantry and one Squadron of Cavalry. Then he remembered that King Henry had recently ordered the Cavalry Squadron from 2nd Regiment, along with their Sorcerer and the Regiment's Battle Mage to move to Prarrieville to guard against an invasion from Baize. That left seven Battalions, one Mage and seven Sorcerers. Wait—he should also include the Kingston Regional Mage and his Sorcerer, plus the Court Wizard to the list of Friendly Forces, as well as the King's Personal Guard, which had recently expanded to almost a hundred men (two companies). When he was finished, Donovan looked over his lists.

Enemy Forces	Friendly Forces
8 Sqdns Cavalry	5 Bns Infantry/1 Sqdn Cavalry/King's Personal Guard
2 Mages	2 Mages
8 Sorcerers	8 Sorcerers
6 Dragons	1 Wizard

The balance of forces didn't look too bad. Donovan knew that defenders usually enjoyed the advantage of prepared positions and knowing the terrain better than the attacking forces. It would be an even fight if it wasn't for those damn dragons!

Well, the rivers would help the defense. First they would need to drop the bridges over the Sapphire and Crimson Rivers; that should force the attackers to approach from the north, most likely down the roads from Fairview and Hayford. Trenches should slow down the horses, or he supposed Fire could be used to spook the enemy horses. With the Franconian infantry on the walls around the city, armed with crossbows, defending against the soldiers should be relatively easy.

Now for the dragons and the magicians. The magicians were evenly matched; in fact, Franconia had a Wizard that the enemy lacked. Unfortunately, it was unlikely that one Wizard could defeat six dragons. Donovan decided to set that problem aside for the moment while he considered the challenge of where to place the King and his Ministers for maximum protection. *The palace dungeon? Probably not. He couldn't stay in the palace; that would be the first place the enemy magicians or dragons would look for him. What about a shop in the city? No good. He needed a secure place, big enough for the King and five Ministers.*

Then the answer came to him. Not only where to secure the King and his Ministers but how to solve the rest of the problem as well. Just then, Wizard Daniel entered to turn the glass to start the time for the remaining hour of the test. As he did so, he grinned and said, "Oh, by the way, I think I forgot to mention that the attacking forces have magical support with them. If they are supported as our troops are, there would be two Mages and eight Sorcerers in the attacking force. Please include them in your calculations."

"I anticipated that, Sir, and I'm done," said Donovan. "So soon?" asked Wizard Daniel. "Well then, tell me how you've decided to defend Kingston." "Sir, this is too easy. On the surface, the forces look pretty evenly matched," said Donovan, showing him the list of forces he'd compiled. "I see, so how do we deal with the cavalry?" "Sir, trenches or fire could stop, scatter, or spook their horses. The enemy soldiers would not even reach the city walls."

"And the magicians and dragons?" asked Daniel. "At first glance, it looks like the magical forces are evenly matched," said Donovan. "But, when I considered where to put the King and his Ministers for maximum security against the dragons, the answer came to me." "And what did you decide?" "We secure them *here,* in the Wizards Academy, probably in the Mentor's quarters. We leave the Changed Ones, the Level Ones and Wizard Faith to guard the Academy and send the Level Twos, Level Threes and Mentors out to fight, along with the faculty. Even six dragons would have no chance against fifty of us."

Daniel smiled. "Exactly right, Donovan. Of all of the cities in Franconia, Kingston is the most secure. You forgot that there's one other element we might call upon: the rogue magicians in the city. I believe that there are actually several dozen that are too old to enter the Academy but have some practical use of their magical abilities, and we have a roster of all of those we have identified. Remember that if a similar situation ever arises."

"So I passed?" "You did, and it's because you used creative thinking. It might interest you to know that your classmate Laura spent both hours on this problem and never considered using any magical assistance from the Academy. She barely passed with a plan that would probably have seen most of our forces decimated and the King captured, injured, or fleeing for his life." "But she passed?" asked Donovan, concerned. "Barely. Which is why she was assigned to replace Sorceress Celeste in the Grotton Regional Mage's Office, rather than being placed with a military unit."

Wizard Daniel rose from his chair and said, "Your next examination is Serums. Please go across the hall and begin. Wizard Toffin is expecting you, but you're quite a bit early." Daniel patted Donovan on the shoulder as he left and said, "I'll see you later for your Enhancements test."

Donovan walked across the hall to the Serums laboratory, where he found Wizard Toffin, the portly Wizard with wild brown hair and a ridiculous orange waistcoat, dozing in his chair. Donovan cleared his throat as he approached, and Wizard Toffin sat up straighter and said, "Donovan! So soon? I didn't expect you for another glass yet! Well, everything about you happens sooner than we expect. Very well, your task this morning, as I'm sure you know, is to prepare a Love Serum, a Healing Serum for Mortal Wounds, and a Death Serum. You may prepare them in any order that you wish or simultaneously if you can. I'll explain how we'll test them once you're finished."

Donovan immediately set himself to the task of preparing the three Serums, knowing that they had to be perfect. Odorless, colorless and, with the exception of the Healing Serum, tasteless. It took almost three glasses of time before all three were ready. "All right, Sir, these are ready to be tested," said Donovan skeptically. Wizard Toffin picked up the Love and Death Serums and put them into secure pockets in his waistcoat, leaving the Healing Serum on the stand on the table.

"So, my boy, I'm going to run off to court with your Serums. I happen to know that there is one domestic felon who needs another dose of Love Serum and another prisoner awaiting his last meal who will receive a dose of your Death Serum. Once both have been administered, I will return and inform you of the results." "I guess it's fortunate that your brother is holding court today," said Donovan. "Please give him my regards." One of the judges in the Franconian Superior Court was Martin Toffin, Wizard Toffin's brother.

"You still think we schedule these tests randomly, don't you? My boy, you would have been tested last week if there were any court cases that would have required both Love and Death Serums." Donovan blushed in embarrassment. "How will you test the Healing Serum?" he asked.

Wizard Toffin smiled, "I watched you carefully as you prepared that one, and it is a Passing effort. You know, years ago, we made students test it on themselves. We enticed a sand viper to bite them, then had them swallow their Healing Serum immediately. Unfortunately, after we lost an otherwise promising Sorcerer during testing, we decided to eliminate that part of the test. Well, I must be off! I'll see you later this afternoon, hopefully with good news! Oh, your next test is Martial Arts; please saddle a mount and meet Wizard

Faith in the Forces Training Area. I'll let her know you'll be early!" With that, Wizard Toffin hustled out of the Lecture Hall and jogged (slowly) towards the Gatehouse, waving for Wizard Faith.

Donovan moved quickly to the stable and saddled Stam, his rather short, white Caspian horse, then headed over to the Forces Training Area. When he arrived, Wizard Faith was already there, mounted on an enormous Clydesdale. "You've got to be kidding me!" said Donovan. Wizard Faith smiled wickedly and said, "You never know who you'll be facing in combat or what they'll be riding. No spells, other than shields. First one knocked off their horse loses. Ready?"

Donovan wondered how in the world he was even going to be able to reach Wizard Faith with his staff when her mount was so much taller than his. He finally decided that he couldn't and that he would have to use his shield, but even that seemed like long odds. Then an idea came to him; previously, he'd always formed a round, pumpkin-sized invisible shield to deflect Faith's staff, *but who ever said the shield had to be round*? Instead, Donovan formed a long, thin, horizontal shield, about the width of his staff. As Wizard Faith charged in, he lowered his shield behind the Clydesdale's head and swept Faith off her horse while she was still ten feet away. Faith hit the ground hard, and Donovan reigned up quickly and dismounted to check on her.

"Are you alright?" "What was that?" asked Faith, groggily. Donovan smiled, "I formed my shield into a clothesline and dropped it behind your horse's head. Are you hurt?" "Only my pride," said Faith. "Who told you that you could make a shield in that shape?" "No one," replied Donovan. "Of course, no one ever told me that I couldn't either." Faith struggled to remount the towering horse, eventually giving up and leading him back to the stables. When she arrived, she said, "Sorry, Rachel. I tried to keep him here a few more weeks."

Donovan understood immediately, knowing that his Mentor and fiancé, Rachel Turner, was standing nearby, hidden under a Concealment shield. Mentors were not allowed to help their students in any way during testing and were only present in order to see what the students needed to improve on if they failed the test. "Donovan, Wizard Daniel should be waiting for you at the marina. Your Enhancements Test will be conducted on water."

Donovan nodded his understanding, and after returning Stam to the stable and handing him over to the stableboy, he walked briskly to the Academy boat dock, where Wizard Daniel was waiting. After Donovan climbed into the boat, Daniel cast off and said, "Now Donovan, we already know that your Seeking abilities are above and beyond what most magicians can accomplish." (Donovan had the rare ability to sense where someone was, just by thinking about them, without the need for an incantation or gesture.) "So, we'll begin with the Silence spell. Please cast the spell *on the boat*. The squeaking of the oarlocks annoys me."

Donovan said, *"SILENTIUM,"* while placing his left index finger to his lips, and the noise of the boat instantly muted. The power drain was more significant than Donovan anticipated, and he immediately reached for his water bottle. "You may release the spell," said Wizard Daniel. *"CODA,"* said Donovan, and the noise returned. "Next, I have cast a spell on something in this boat; please tell me what it is." Donovan looked around, then steepled his fingers and murmured, *"MAGNUS."* The boat's steel anchor began to glow with an eerie blue light. "Very good," said Daniel, "you may release the spell." Donovan released the spell and wondered what was next.

"Your last Level Three Enhancement spell is Healing of Mortal Wounds," said Daniel, "which is why we are on the river. I'm going to spear a fish and bring it aboard. Your task is to heal it and return it to the river. You must act quickly, or the fish will die. Do you understand?" Donovan nodded, and Daniel took a thin wooden rod from the pocket of his robes, enlarged it and sharpened the tip with magic. Then he scanned the river before thrusting the spear into the water, bringing up a large trout which he had speared cleanly through the body. The fish flopped around feebly as Donovan knelt down and placed his hands over the wound, palms down, and said, *"SALVARE."*

With the wound healed, the fish flopped around much more vigorously, and it took Donovan a minute to seize the slippery creature and return it to the water. "Nicely done," said Wizard Daniel. "Now, if you could please use a Wind spell and take us back to the dock, this part of your Sorcerer's Test is over."

Donovan easily executed the Wind spell and guided the small boat back to the dock. When they arrived, Wizard Daniel said, "Your next test is the Change spell. Wizard Mira is waiting for you in the Seemings and Changes Training Area. Good luck."

As Donovan entered the Seemings and Changes Training Area, he saw his former Mentor, Terry, a Fire dragon Changed One, standing beside Wizard Mira and immediately knew what lay before him. He stumbled briefly, then felt a soothing hand on his back and heard Rachel whisper, "You can do this."

Wizard Mira looked at Donovan with concern in her eyes. "Donovan, we know this Change can be performed; Sorceress Celeste successfully made the change some weeks ago, but you will be the first student ever to attempt this Change. Do you know what I want you to Change?" Donovan nodded solemnly, "Yes. You want me to change myself into a dragon." "Exactly right," said Mira. "Sorcerer Terry is here to help you. Terry?"

Terry said, "In order to make the Change, you must picture a dragon in your mind. I know that you have seen one before. That will be your model. Concentrate on that image and being able to retain the ability to speak. The transformation should happen immediately. To Change back, the spell is the same: think of returning to your true form and rear up on your hind legs. Clapping your hands together is not a natural motion for a dragon, but it can be done. Do you have any questions?"

"Will it hurt?" Terry smiled, "It should not; just make sure you picture an *uninjured* dragon in your mind. Do you understand what I am saying?" Donovan nodded. The only dragon he had seen before had been riddled with crossbow bolts, and Donovan had cut off its head to take it to the King. It would not do to remember that image. Steeling himself, Donovan said, "I am ready." Terry and Mira stepped back to give Donovan some space.

Donovan closed his eyes and concentrated on the image of a large, golden dragon, glittering in the sun; he said, *"MORPHIOUS,"* and clapped his hands. Donovan's body *rippled* and transformed into a fifty-foot-long golden dragon. Donovan shook his head to clear it. Everything looked *smaller*. Before stepping away from Terry and Mira, he said, "Rachel, where are you? I don't want to step on you." Rachel dropped her Concealment shield and moved to stand by Wizard Mira, beaming. "I told you; you could do it," she said.

Donovan raised each foot, shook his tail from side to side, then spread his wings. He desperately wanted to try flying, but Wizard Mira read his mind and said, "Please don't take off, Donovan. You would panic the other students and staff. Return to your human form now, please."

Somewhat reluctantly, Donovan pictured himself as a human, reared up and clapped his short, dragon-arms together and recited the incantation. He dropped to the ground, human but without a scrap of clothing on. The remnants of his clothes were scattered on the ground in pieces. "Oh, my," gasped Wizard Mira, averting her eyes. Terry laughed, "Sorry, I guess I should have mentioned that. You have to take off your human clothes before you transform." "Now you tell me," groused Donovan. "At least I wasn't wearing my expensive new clothes."

To cover his nakedness, Donovan cast a Seeming of clothes on himself and walked back to the Mentor's quarters to get dressed. Walking in a Seeming of clothes was *weird,* but none of the students that they passed seemed to notice. Once they reached the dormitory, Wizard Mira said, "Donovan, you obviously passed the Changes Test. Once you're dressed, Wizards Dylan and Noland will be waiting in the Forces Training Area to administer the last part of your Sorcerer's Test. Good Luck."

After dressing and stealing a quick kiss from Rachel, Donovan headed to the Forces Training Area. Both Wizards looked relieved to see him. "How did the Change go?" asked Wizard Noland. "It went fine, but Terry should have warned me to take off my clothes before transforming. The Change tore them asunder and left me naked when I Changed back into human form." Both Wizards laughed. "We'll have to remember that for future tests," said Wizard Dylan. "Oh my," said Wizard Noland, "That can only mean that when Celeste landed on the HMS VALOR and transformed back into human form…" "She probably fainted from embarrassment," said Dylan, struggling to contain his mirth.

Eventually, the two Wizards regained their composure and said, "Donovan, please Blast that boulder over there." Donovan Blasted the boulder to rubble. Next, Wizard Noland asked Donovan to Paralyze Wizard Dylan. This spell was also executed perfectly. Wizard Noland then asked Donovan to cast a

Compulsion spell on Wizard Dylan and force him to do something that he would not normally do.

Donovan thought for a moment, then said, *"NECESSITAS,"* while crossing the index and middle fingers of his left hand. Once he felt the power drain, he said to Dylan, "Wizard Dylan, please sing me a song." Dylan began, *"My bonnie lies over the ocean, my Bonnie lies over the sea..."* "Enough!" said Wizard Noland, "Pass!" Donovan released the spell, and Wizard Dylan grimaced and shook his finger at him.

"I have already observed your Replication spells, and they are excellent. There is no need to repeat them. There are only two spells that remain to be tested. I need you to cast a Binding spell on one of us. It should be of short duration." Donovan thought, then said, "Wizard Noland, never tell anyone that you have heard Wizard Dylan sing." Donovan drew his right index finger along the ground, and the spell settled on Wizard Noland. Wizard Dylan smiled and said, "Pass."

"Donovan, your last spell is the most lethal in a magicians' arsenal, and it is never to be used lightly or without cause. You know which spell I refer to?" Donovan nodded, "Yes, Sir. It is the Kill spell." Noland nodded somberly, and Donovan was shocked to see Wizard Mira leading Stam over to them from the stables. "Donovan, please kill your horse."

Donovan stood still, completely overwhelmed and shocked by Wizard Noland's order. He raised his hand but just couldn't do it. Stam had been with him too long and had been through too much with him. Even if it meant failing the Sorcerer's Test, Donovan resolved not to comply with the order.

"No, Sir. I'm sorry. I won't kill Stam just to prove that I can. There has to be another way." Surprisingly, Wizard Noland smiled, "Very good. I was hoping you would say that. If you had followed my orders blindly and killed without cause, you would have failed the test. Now, I assure you that this is just a Seeming of Stam, cast by Wizard Mira. If you look over there, you will see the real horse with Wizard Faith by the stables." Donovan looked over and saw Stam.

Wizard Noland then said, "Now, please demonstrate how you would use the Kill spell to dispatch this Seeming." Donovan raised his right hand and, with a quick slashing motion, said, *"TERMINA."* The Seeming vanished in a flash of light.

"The final element of the Sorcerers Test is to determine the strength of your shields. Are you prepared?" asked Wizard Dylan. Donovan took a quick sip from his water bottle, cast his shield and nodded. All hell broke loose.

It wasn't just Wizard Dylan throwing rocks, sand and nails at Donovan; Wizards Mira and Noland joined in as well. A maelstrom of debris struck his shield from all sides. Wizard Mira sent Seemings that looked like rocks at him. They passed right through his shield (because they weren't real). The Seemings didn't hurt, but they were certainly distracting. Finally, came the fireball. By now, Donovan was weary; his shield was battered, and his senses numb. Rather than wait for the fireball to reach him, he conjured a drenching gusher of water that fell from the sky and extinguished the fireball before it reached his shield.

The assembled Wizards all stopped their attacks in awe. "How in the world did he do that?" asked Wizard Mira. "He shouldn't be able to cast two spells at once!" "Donovan is just full of surprises," said Wizard Noland. "I think we've seen enough." Wizard Noland removed a scroll from his sleeve and read formally:

"Level Three Donovan Francis, pending verification of your Love and Death Serums by Wizard Toffin and the completion of your final task, you are hereby promoted to Sorcerer. You will receive your first assignment to the Armed Forces of Franconia in the coming weeks. Congratulations."

Rachel appeared by his side and wrapped him in an enthusiastic hug. "I guess we have a wedding to plan," she whispered.